The *Highway to Hell* Series
Evil Reigns

J.D. Toepfer

Print ISBN: 978-1-7373603-4-6

Cover Design by Miblart Cover Design

Special Thanks Go To:

My Wife, Christina, whose unwavering support and encouragement make all of this possible. I love you more than I can say!

My Brother, George, who has always been my first editor and a large part of everything I do. This would be no fun without you!

My Beta Readers: Tim Hutton, James "Jamie" Reynolds, January and Anthony Rutherford, and Ann Mastropaolo. My thanks for your valuable input and contributions to *Evil Reigns*!

My Readers and Fans… where would I be without your support? Thank you for your engagement and traveling the *Highway to Hell* with me!

PROLOGUE

10,000 Years Ago at the End of the Last Ice Age

In the days when the ice retreated and glaciers carved their mark, leaving their scars upon the land, a void opened in the heart of Long Island, leaving behind a block of ancient ice that sank and melted, water filling the wound, dark and still.

Thus, a lake was born.

The air was raw, heavy with the breath of a world reborn. The forest crept northward, spruce giving way to oak as warmth spread. Wolves prowled the underbrush, caribou grazed the meadows, and the bones of mastodons, mammoths, and dire wolves lay buried in sand, their voices fading.

And still, the water deepened.

The sun's touch was thin against the black mirror of the surface, its light swallowed whole. The water trembled even without wind. No bird settled, no root drank too deep. Even as the land thawed, the water remained cold, colder than memory allowed.

And shadows rippled across the waters.

The people came, hunters, wanderers, children of flint and fire. They found fish in the wetlands, shelter in the woods. Their arrow-heads struck stone and bone, and they named what they killed. But when they stood at the shoreline, they said nothing. They only listened.

The water whispered though no mouth spoke, hungering for flesh, for the first soul to stray too near.

At times, beneath the thaw, a pale shape drifted under the surface, hair spreading like weeds, watching.

What was birthed here was not of God.

Not of light, nor life, but something... *else*.

And in the waters, Evil waited. Patient. Unending.

Centuries later, the same waters whispered to the children of men. The lake had not forgotten; it waited.

STAGE I:
UNLEASHED

CHAPTER 1

September
Pre-Colonial Period Near Present-Day Setauket, NY
Late morning

"FIND HIM! NOW!"

The serenity of the crisp fall morning was shattered by an enraged voice that tore through the dense forest, making the oak trees tremble. Their scarlet and bronze leaves cascaded to the ground like fiery warnings. Startled, Quanon, a young brave of the Setalcott tribe, froze; his heart pounding, as he dropped his fishing net.

Taking a deep breath, he slipped ashore to investigate. Footsteps snapped through fallen leaves and twigs, merging with harsh, guttural voices. He crept through the cattails at the water's edge and along the tree line; the woods seemed to hold their breath, afraid to betray his presence.

Despite his youth, Quanon excelled at tracking, a skill vital to the Setalcotts. As the son of Chief Powwan, he carried the weight of their history and legends. His senses sharpened as he moved stealthily through the underbrush, every nerve on high alert. The forest seemed to close in, and unease replaced its usual serenity.

As he stepped into a clearing, braves surrounded him, their war clubs raised and eyes steely with battle readiness. Quanon's pulse quickened as he recognized their leader. Anger surged, but he stood his ground, a testament to his bravery in the face of overwhelming odds.

Quanon stood tall, his breath steady despite the tremor in the earth beneath his feet. The breeze stirred his long black hair, but he didn't blink. His gaze locked on Megedagik, a scar-marked Montauk warrior whose name meant *"Kills Many." He had* earned it through countless brutal fights.

Megedagik wielded a heavy war club, veins bulging as he tightened his grip. Songs were sung of the devastation left in his wake. But Quanon did not flinch, even with death an arm's length away.

"Breaching the sacred boundary is no mere trespass, Megedagik," declared Quanon, his voice firm with a hint of challenge. He didn't raise his voice; he didn't need to. Speaking the name Megedagik alone was an accusation. Across the clearing, a few of the braves exchanged glances but said nothing.

"You are inviting war. This is Setalcott land. You must leave… now." Each word landed like a stone in a border wall: solid, final, and unmoving. The wind paused. Even the trees seemed to listen.

Megedagik's dark eyes bore into Quanon, evaluating the young warrior like a person standing at the edge of a cliff, looking down fearlessly. He feared no one, certainly not this boy. Yet something in Quanon's defiance sparked grudging respect within him.

"You are vigilant and fearless, like a hawk. You must be the one they call Quanon."

Megedagik's voice was deep and gravelly. The words were intended as recognition, not an apology. A Montauk offering of respect, which was rare and significant. As he lowered his club, his two companions followed, though one hesitated, his knuckles white around the carved handle. Quanon stood firm, allowing the silence to speak for his bravery.

"I do not seek conflict." Megedagik's gaze hardened as he stepped forward. "Grand Sachem, Wyandanch, has tasked me with this mission."

The name hung between them like a boulder dropped into still water. Quanon blinked. Wyandanch was no ordinary Sachem. If he had sent Montauk warriors this far west, something had changed, and not for the better.

Quanon felt a shiver run down his spine at the mention of the Grand Sachem, a man whose power over all Algonquin tribes was legendary. Stories said Wyandanch could end wars with a whisper and that his visions came not from dreams but from the dead. Quanon kept his weight evenly balanced, neither retreating nor advancing. He forced himself to remain composed, his bronzed skin prickling with tension. He allowed the silence to stretch, using the stillness as bait, knowing every move and every word from Megedagik was a potential threat.

"We are searching for a runaway." Megedagik's voice rumbled through the air as he rolled his shoulders, joints cracking like grinding stones. The sound was deliberate, a warning masquerading as weariness. His intense gaze bored into Quanon, probing and testing.

"Perhaps you have seen him?"

Quanon recognized it wasn't truly a question, but rather a blade wrapped in courtesy. He didn't respond immediately. The wind shifted again, and something colder than tribal politics brushed the back of his neck. Quanon's heart skipped a beat, yet he maintained his impassive expression.

The warriors were watching for weakness, not in his words but in his breathing and movements. He knew the sun had risen through fog that morning and hoped they wouldn't ask him what he'd caught. Tracking had taught him that some lies are like footprints in the snow: easy to follow if you say too much.

"I have been fishing since sunrise and seen no one," he replied, his voice steady, though his mind raced.

"Wyandanch excommunicated him," Megedagik went on, his tone growing darker, "but he escaped. His name is Oohqua."

He let the name linger like a curse, something whispered around the fire at night but never spoken of in daylight. The way Megedagik said it made Quanon's skin crawl. Excommunicated, graver than banishment or exile, as if decreed by the Great Spirit rather than men.

"Oohqua?" Quanon furrowed his brow, clearly confused. "His name is Worm?"

He meant no mockery; instead, he processed it literally. For a Setalcott, the word conjured an unsettling image of something soft-bodied and eyeless, moving through the dirt and darkness. To the Montauk, it could serve as a warning.

"Last year, he lost his name for cowardice during the Sacred Fire ceremony. He has brought bad medicine to the Shinnecock tribe, and the Grand Sachem proclaimed that only his death would restore good fortune."

Lost his name. The phrase struck Quanon like a snapped bowstring. A brave's identity was not something to be taken lightly. Bad medicine meant more than illness. It suggested an imbalance, an opening that should have stayed shut.

The mention of the Sacred Fire ceremony sent a chill through Quanon. The rites were held annually at harvest, marking the boys' transition into manhood. He could still hear the chants and feel the heat of the flames, searing the ritual into his memory. Very soon, it would be Quanon's turn to face the sacred trials. It was not just about endurance but about recognition by the tribe and the spirits as a leader, an eternal flame.

Quanon's unease intensified as Megedagik stroked his chin, appearing to sense the turmoil within him. This was something Quanon had worked hard to conceal.

"Giving aid or shelter to him could be dangerous for the Setalcotts," Megedagik whispered. "Do you understand?"

Megedagik stepped closer, his breath warm and sharp with the earthy smell of chewed tobacco. An avalanche of thoughts flooded Quanon's mind. Was this a simple warning or a veiled threat? The air buzzed like just before a summer storm, heavy with the promise of violence. Quanon's jaw clenched as he weighed his options, the fear of what Megedagik might do if he sensed weakness gnawing at the edges of his resolve.

Quanon gave a single nod, not in agreement, but because the moment demanded it. He held his gaze, revealing nothing.

"Say it!" Megedagik's command sliced through the tension like a blade.

Quanon's heart hammered. His jaw tensed, but he didn't flinch. Stone-faced, he focused on his breathing and pressed his feet into the cool sand. The texture grounded him, but this was more than pressure. It was a test, and something was watching how he'd respond.

Without blinking, his voice as cold as the winter winds, he said, "Nondam (*I understand*)."

The silence that followed was thicker; it was not a relief from the tension but an uncomfortable pause in a test of wills.

***

Every instinct screamed danger. Confident in Megedagik's treachery, Quanon moved cautiously, eyes sharp and searching for a Montauk war party. He kept low, using the cover of swaying cattails and shadows, his sharp eyes scanning every inlet and cove for signs… broken reeds or fresh prints, but the marsh remained silent. The relentless cries and harsh calls of red-winged blackbirds repeated like a chorus of warnings that clawed at his nerves.

A thin sliver of sun hovered on the horizon, casting long, eerie shadows across the water. Anxiety coiled like a snake around Quanon's heart. It was too late to return to his village at Drowned Meadow, but staying away overnight felt like tempting fate. Stories warned about what stirred after darkness fell… things he felt ill-prepared to face, especially with Megedagik's true intentions uncertain.

Quanon lingered by the water's edge, his moccasins sinking into the damp earth. The soft lap of waves failed to soothe his uneasiness. The scent of decaying leaves mixed with the brackish smell of the shallows, yet beneath the familiar odors, there was something else…

something he could not identify. He crouched and dipped his fingers in the cold water. It was bone-chillingly cold.

His gaze turned toward the reeds. It was too quiet… the total absence of sound. Even the blackbirds had ceased their calls. A ripple broke the water's glassy surface, though no breeze stirred. A shadow moved behind the cattails… fleeting, ghostlike. It was there, then gone.

Quanon's fingers brushed across the obsidian blade at his hip. He didn't draw it, but he needed to feel its promise of protection. Something was wrong. A presence raised the hairs on the back of his neck.

He didn't know when his thoughts turned to Ronkonkoma. Maybe it was the way the fog had crept into the trees just after dusk, curling like ghostly fingers, or the faint smell of wet soil, rot, and cedar bark… even here by the seashore, Ronkonkoma's reach was felt.

The tribal elders whispered of a ghostly figure… a pale woman in white, drifting just above the lake's surface, her hair fanning out like seaweed. They called her the Lady of the Lake, and Quanon felt her gaze settle on him, as if the water itself had eyes.

***

He stood ankle-deep in the water, fog curling like choking vines around his shins. His bow dangled loosely in his hand, an arrow already nocked to the string. How he arrived here escaped him… only the pull, the strange call, beckoning him home.

Suddenly, she appeared… just as the elders had described her. The Lady of the Lake, ghostly white and silent, stared without blinking. Quanon took a step toward her… then, a twig snapped and reeds rustled to his left. He glanced toward the noise, but when he looked back the apparition was gone, swallowed by the fog.

Fully awake now, the air was colder, but something was still out there, watching. Not the Lady; this was different. He felt it in the back of his neck… the prickling itch that meant someone might be lining up a shot. He moved toward the edge of the reeds, stepping with ease, silent and low to the ground. The rustling stopped.

Quanon paused. Waited. Then a small splash, maybe twenty feet out in the water. Smaller than a man, softer than a deer. He lowered himself into a crouch, drawing in a slow breath through his nose. He stayed that way for nearly a minute. Then, slowly, he withdrew; first his eyes, then his posture, rising fluidly back toward his canoe. He might not sleep tonight, but he wouldn't chase shadows either. A cold chill settled deep in his chest as the darkness thickened.

SPLASH!

The sound echoed through the twilight as Quanon dragged his canoe onto the shore, muscles taut, scanning the darkening landscape for signs of movement. Finding a small patch of grass sheltered from the cool, freshening breeze, he flattened it with quick, deliberate motions. Now an expanse of deep blue, he searched the sky for signs of a storm but saw none. The stars were late to appear, as if reluctant to witness what might happen next. He debated building a shelter, but something urged him to remain exposed, vulnerable, yet alert. The thought was illogical, and yet it pressed on him like instinct: be visible, but ready.

Hunger gnawed at his insides, but Quanon forced himself to focus. He placed stones by the fire and, once heated, arranged them in a shallow pit. He carefully laid out the Quahog clams, blue mussels, and oysters he had gathered at low tide that morning. The scent of the steaming shellfish rose tantalizingly, briny and sweet, yet it did little to calm his nerves. He chewed mechanically, more out of necessity than appetite. Every bite seemed to taste faintly of smoke and unease.

Night fell, but Quanon's gaze remained fixed on the darkness beyond the fire's glow. He sensed it, a presence lurking just out of sight. His heart beat steadily, yet intrusive thoughts filled his mind. Could it be the Montauk warriors, after all? Or something that the tribal elders feared? He strained to hear past the crackling of the fire and the distant lapping of the waves, but the night stayed quiet. Too quiet…not the hush of sleep, but the inhale before a scream.

The reeds trembled, not from the wind, but from something intentional. Quanon held his breath. His fingers tightened on a nearby log until his knuckles turned white. He maintained a relaxed posture to suggest he was unaware of what might happen, yet his gaze remained steady as the reeds rustled again, this time more violently. He angled his body slightly, keeping his profile loose, not challenging or yielding, just listening. Something was out there.

When the figure finally emerged, Quanon moved swiftly. He lunged, tackling the intruder to the ground with such force that there was no room for resistance. The clap of the impact echoed in the still night, and Quanon pinned the figure beneath him, his strong hands pressing down like a heavy stone, crushing with relentless force. The body thrashed once, then froze. He peered down at his opponent. The flickering firelight revealed only the whites of his captive's wide, shocked eyes. Young, thin, and terrified.

***

Quanon studied the boy's face across the dying fire. His former challenger wore exhaustion on his bruised, bloodied features. Though his breathing had steadied, his eyes were vacant, hiding secrets he couldn't yet share.

Quanon offered him a piece of roasted fish. The boy stared until Quanon beckoned.

"Take it. You'll need your strength."

Slowly, the boy's trembling hands closed around the fish. He didn't look up, only stared at the meat in his palm.

"Thank you," he murmured in a fragile voice, wary but too hungry to resist.

The marsh frogs fell silent. Even the crackle of the fire seemed muted, as if the land itself paused to listen.

Quanon broke the silence, "Something troubles you."

The boy stiffened. His lips parted, then closed again. Thunder rumbled through the clear sky.

"You carry a heavy weight," Quanon said. "Not in your hands but behind your eyes."

The fire popped, sharp as a bone breaking. "You don't have to tell me, but if you keep it locked inside, it will poison what's left of you."

The boy gazed into the flames, silently pleading with the fire. Words finally spilled from his mouth.

"They said I brought sickness… and death. That I was cursed."

His eyes lifted, not with anger, but remorse. The firelight flickered across his face, casting shadows of guilt and doubt.

"If they find me here, they'll punish your people too. I've seen Megedagik's skills with a blade. You're risking everything by helping me."

Quanon's jaw tightened. He tugged at his chin, studying the boy's haunted eyes.

The storm's growl deepened. Quanon nodded toward the steaming clams. "In my tribe, we welcome strangers. Hunger isn't a crime. There's no harm in filling an empty stomach."

Another rumble shook the night. The air felt charged, and Quanon wondered if the storm was already here—or if something much worse was coming.

"Are you running from more than Megedagik?" Quanon asked gently.

The boy snapped a twig, watching the pieces fall into the dirt. His voice dropped to a whisper: "So, you know who I am."

Quanon handed him his waterskin. OohQua drank greedily, clinging to it like a lifeline.

"I wish you had never asked," he said, wiping sweat from his brow. "Sometimes you don't run because you're hunted. You run because you're terrified of what you might become."

OohQua stared into the dying flames. The fire popped as a coal collapsed into ash.

The wind picked up, rustling the reeds. The sounds of the marsh returned, as if the earth had paused only long enough for OohQua's confession. Neither closed his eyes despite the weariness tugging at their bones.

Some nights weren't meant for sleep, but for survival.

The embers of Quanon's fire smoldered into the night. Centuries later, the same waters whispered to another boy…

***

Early February
Present Day Lake Ronkonkoma, NY

Silence had settled over Long Island, the lake's still surface mirroring a world changed beyond recognition…

A heavy haze hung on the horizon, dulling the golden hues of dusk, while the sun, low in the sky, cast a dim, bluish light over Lake Ronkonkoma. Following a snowy January, a rapid thaw had left the lake free of ice for the first time since the new year. Louis Aitken leaned against a massive granite boulder at the water's edge, rhythmically skipping stones. His throws were precise and methodical, each spaced ten seconds apart. He timed each throw precisely… always the same rhythm. Three skips were the minimum, five the ideal. Anything less wasn't just disappointing… it meant failure. The lake absorbed them without reply.

As they hit the water, soft plunks echoed, sending ripples across the brooding surface of the lake. For Louis, this ritual was calming and predictable, something he desperately needed. There was comfort in repetition: cause and effect. Throw, skip, sink, and reset. Yet each throw felt heavier, less satisfying, as if the world slowed to a crawl. The rules had changed without warning, and Louis hated it.

The wind rustled through the trees behind him… soft, but carrying a whisper that went unnoticed. He was lost in the rhythm of his movements: grab, throw, skip, sink. A sequence. A loop. For now, it was enough. It was a routine he could control, the only semblance of order in a world that seemed to be falling apart. He glanced over his shoulder, expecting, hoping to see David. He had asked. Twice.

I don't like the creaking, Louis. David had told him. It sounds like footsteps, but no one is there.

He used the right tone, tried the right words... *just ten minutes. It's quiet. I promise.* But David didn't come; he didn't like being outside even more than being inside.

The sky is too big, and the air's too cold.

Louis felt his skin tighten, like a second skin that no longer fit. Louis didn't like the outdoors either, but sometimes he needed it.

Louis sighed as he dropped another stone into the water, not bothering to try to skip it. It made a dull, hollow splash. His mind wandered to his friends. He missed them, the group chats and the laughter. More than anything, he missed his phone; the familiar weight, the glow of the screen, and the predictable rows of apps.

That small, comforting device, which had once connected him to the world, now lay shattered at the bottom of a reservoir in Wheeling, West Virginia. No texts, no calls. It felt as though a part of him had been severed, like a phantom limb, still aching. He felt lost without it, unsure where to look or what to do with his hands.

The water splashed gently against the rocks, stirred by the breeze. Louis flinched slightly at the sudden noise. Not loud, but sharp enough to startle. His senses were always heightened in stillness, sharper in the quiet. He often noticed details that others missed: faint rustlings, flickering shadows, and patterns in movement and sound that seemed clearer than speech. It wasn't that he wanted to notice everything; he just couldn't stop.

Still, he enjoyed the water's rhythm. It was repetitive and soothing, allowing him to escape the constant barrage of reflections in his mind, all the unanswered questions and thoughts that looped without end.

Why had everything gone so wrong? Why couldn't he hear them anymore, his teachers in heaven? The silence disturbed him more than noise ever could.

The sound of the water was calming; it had a rhythm, soft, almost as if the lake were breathing. But then, a piercing sound sliced through the stillness… out of place and wrong. Not louder, just wrong. A sharper note in the middle of a soft song. He didn't move. He just listened, counting and measuring. It wasn't the wind, the birds, or the lapping water. He played it back in his mind like an audio clip. Metal? No. Crunching? Maybe. A footstep?

Ring… Ring…

Louis's head snapped up. That sound didn't belong here. Not in the cold, by the lake with no one around. He held his breath and waited. The sharp ring cut through the biting chill, making his fingers tremble.

Ring… Ring…

A ringtone. From a phone that could not exist. His phone. But that was impossible. It had shattered on impact and slid down into the murky dark of a reservoir four hundred miles away.

The sound seemed to come from the far reeds or the trees. Or maybe from inside his head. He pressed his palms over his ears. It pierced through anyway.

"Stop," he whispered. "Stop it." But the sound did not stop.

Louis froze. This wasn't the wind, or the water, or the reeds whispering in patterns he could explain. It was faint and distant, yet unmistakable. A shrill, familiar sound of a phone ringing. His phone. He blinked and shook his head. It couldn't be; he didn't have it anymore. It was broken, gone and buried in the waters of West Virginia, where everything else had started to fall apart.

He turned slowly, scanning the shoreline, the rocks, and the water. His eyes moved in a grid from left to right, then top to bottom. Recheck. Reframe. Look again. His body tensed, unsure of what to expect.

The sound came again, louder this time, sharper with no room for doubt. And then… he saw it.

A cellphone… *his cellphone.*

It lay on a rock, just a few feet out in the water, its screen lighting up and vibrating with each ring. The glow pulsed like a heartbeat, daring him to answer. Louis noticed the fractures in the glass; they gleamed faintly in the fading light, catching the dusk like a spiderweb.

It looked hastily pieced together, shards barely holding on… broken but pretending to work. He knew it was impossible; *how could it be here?* He remembered watching Dad smash it. He had done the math, calculated the fall, the depth. It shouldn't be here. It couldn't.

It's my phone. It has to be mine. It has the same cracks, the same chipped corner, and the same dull blue case. But it's not possible. It sank. I counted the seconds it took to disappear, calculated the depth.

He stared at it, frozen, his thoughts scrambled as he tried to understand how it could be here. The angles, the weight, the vibrations, everything pointed to the same impossible conclusion. It wasn't just similar… it was exact.

The ringing ceased, leaving an eerie quiet in its wake. A silence that felt too sudden and intentional. Yet his eyes remained fixed on the phone. How was it here? How was it ringing? His mind raced, searching for a logical explanation: waterproof casing? Duplicate device? A hallucination? But nothing fit. Nothing made sense. And still it just sat there. Waiting.

The phone rang once more, the sharp sound cutting through the evening air. It was louder now, or perhaps just closer. Or maybe it was in his head. Louis flinched, the muscles in his shoulders tensing. His breath caught, shallow and quick. He wanted to look away, but he couldn't.

He swallowed hard, instinctively stepping closer. His body moved before his brain gave permission. The water lapped gently at the shore, but he barely noticed. Background noise? David changing his mind? Irrelevant. The phone was everything now.

His feet seemed to move on their own, pulling him toward the phone, toward the impossible. The closer he got, the more surreal it felt, like a looping dream he couldn't escape from. The kind where everything makes sense until suddenly it doesn't. He didn't like this. Phones didn't just appear on rocks. They didn't ring after they'd been broken. They didn't call from the bottom of reservoirs.

His pulse quickened. Fight, freeze, or run? He didn't know which one this was; a feeling prickled across his skin, every hair on his arms standing on end.

The phone rang again, vibrating softly on the wet rock. Each buzz echoed in his chest. Louis hesitated. Standing at the water's edge, the cold waves lapped at his sneakers. Not high. Not fast. But enough to soak through if he stepped forward. Enough to cross a line. It wasn't deep; he could wade out and grab it. Three steps, maybe four. He measured them almost unconsciously. But something held him back: a knot in his stomach, tight and sharp, and a dread he couldn't quite explain. This wasn't fear of drowning; it was fear of not knowing.

Ring…

Part of him wanted to run back to the house and forget he'd ever seen it, let logic win. But he had already taken off his shoes and socks, and now he was in the water before he could stop himself. His feet slipped on smooth stones beneath the surface, his arms flailing once, nearly falling. The cold air bit into his skin, not like winter, but like the sharp fangs of a playful kitten: surprising, precise, but not enough to hurt. Still, he pressed forward, each splash like a warning he chose to ignore until he reached it. The phone. It buzzed once more and then went still. It was as if it had been waiting for him.

Without thinking, he picked it up, his hands trembling as he stared at the cracked screen. Cold water dripped from his fingers, flowing into the fractures on the phone like blood into veins. It lit up again… an incoming call. No name. Just a number. Too many digits… or not enough. He couldn't tell.

His breath came in shallow gasps. He was hyperventilating, but he couldn't slow his breathing. For a moment, he thought about throwing it into the lake, letting it sink into the dark depths where it belonged. This felt wrong, but something inside wouldn't allow him to stop. A pull, deep in his chest, like the lake was listening... and waiting.

With a trembling thumb, he swiped the screen and raised the phone to his ear. The static that greeted him was deafening: a low hum at first, but swelling quickly, vibrating through his skull like a tuning fork jammed behind his eyes. It was overwhelming, buzzing loudly in his ear. Louis winced, holding the phone a bit farther away. He had studied static noise in science class: frequencies, waveforms, and white noise. He'd even liked it. Found it oddly soothing at times, but this static wasn't reassuring. It felt warped, angry, and demanded to be heard.

"H-Hello?" he stammered, his voice uncertain and weak. He barely recognized it. It didn't sound like him.

The static crackled louder, not in response, but as if it disapproved. He pulled the phone an inch away from his ear, heart pounding. The tone shifted, like a shape moving behind fog.

There was no response. Just static, crackling like seasoned wood burning in a fireplace, but without warmth. Only sound and pressure. Louis tightened his grip, his knuckles pale. He leaned in, as if concentration alone could pull meaning from the noise. But it didn't change; it just kept burning.

"Who... who is this?" His voice cracked on the second "*who*," barely louder than the hiss in his ear. He hated how weak he sounded. How uncertain. But he had to ask. There were rules about answering unknown calls.

The static surged again, louder, hissing and popping. Then it dropped into a low, droning hum, almost like a gentle breath.

Then there was stillness, thick and suffocating, as if something waited for an answer. Louis's skin tingled, goosebumps racing up his arms. Every nerve screamed at him to hang up, to run. Yet he remained rooted to the spot, his breath shallow, grip tight, the phone pressed firmly against his ear as though letting go might make things worse.

Then, a faint, distorted voice emerged, damp with static, as if it were coming from far away… or from beneath the lake.

"Louis…"

His name was spoken slowly, deliberately, the vowels dragging as if someone were drowning. Louis's blood ran cold. He had heard that voice before, but couldn't place it. Not yet.

He recognized it; familiar, but wrong. Like a song you love, played at half speed but in a different key... as if someone had taken a voice he trusted and stretched it… broken it. His breath caught in his throat. Whoever or whatever spoke knew his name. It knew how to sound almost human… but not quite.

"Who is this?" His voice still trembled. He tried to steady it, but the shake wouldn't go away. The silence on the other end stretched, as if the voice were thinking, listening, or deciding.

The static crackled, like dry leaves catching fire. And the voice returned, closer now, clearer, and more insistent.

"Louis… you shouldn't have answered…"

Louis flinched. The way it said his name… so certain… like the lake had planned this moment. His grip tightened on the phone, and he suddenly hated how light it felt. Too light, too warm… almost alive.

A chill swept through him, colder than the icy water at his feet. It slipped beneath his skin, into his bones, as if the lake itself were breathing on him.

"Who are you?" he asked again, his voice quieter this time, almost hoping there'd be no reply. The line fell silent… not like a dropped call, but like something was listening.

Louis stumbled back, his foot slipping once again on the slick stones, arms flailing for balance. He caught himself just before tumbling into the icy lake, his breath ragged and heart hammering as if something were trapped in his chest, desperate to break free. He stared down at the phone, now lifeless, dark, and still. Its cracked screen reflected the fading light. He didn't understand what had just happened, but deep down, he knew: something had changed. The ringing had been more than a call. It was an invitation. A signal. And it had opened a door that he couldn't close.

The dread lingered, thick and oppressive, clinging to his skin like damp wool. Louis stood there, the dead phone still clenched in his hand, the cold seeping into his fingers. The wind picked up, whispering through the trees in long, moaning sighs. His head throbbed as he stared out over the lake, where something stirred.

A different kind of movement… a shadow shifting at the edge of his vision. Formless. Too dark to belong. Unnatural.

The lake was no longer still. Its surface rippled, not from the wind, but from something deeper… something moving, lurking beneath the water. Louis slowly lowered his phone, now warm against his palm… too warm. Yet the fear of being watched persisted. He turned and hurried toward the shore, water slapping against his calves. He couldn't help but glance over his shoulder one last time when his phone vibrated in his hand again.

Ring… Ring…

***

April 1975 — Decades Earlier
Jack Aitken's Bedroom
Albertson, NY

On a cool spring night, the moon hung high, casting a soft silver glow through the gaps in the chocolate-brown curtains of the small bedroom that Jack Aitken shared with his brother, George. The room was cozy, its wallpaper patterned with rows of stoic Revolutionary

War soldiers standing at attention like silent sentries. It was April, and the sweet scent of hyacinths drifted through the open window, a reminder that spring had returned and, for now, all was peaceful.

Jack stirred and rolled over, a faint unease tugging at the edges of his sleep. He glanced at the window and then up at George, whose gentle snores drifted down from the top bunk like a lullaby. Just as Jack was about to turn and face the wall, a soft, otherworldly light glimmered from the far corner of the room. He blinked, rubbed his eyes, and sat up. His skin prickled beneath his pajama sleeves.

His grandfather stood beside the dresser. His name was John, but Nanny always called him Jack. The twins and their sisters lovingly referred to him as Poppy A. His pale, weathered skin and snow-white hair were familiar, but now a faint glow shimmered around him, something unnatural.

He wore the blue cardigan Nanny had knitted last Christmas, a pack of cigarettes hanging loosely from its pocket. The faint shimmer trailing around him told Jack this was no ordinary visit.

"Poppy?" Jack whispered, blinking at the soft, golden light pulsing gently from his grandfather's outline. His heartbeat never wavered; he wasn't scared, even though the ghost stories the ten-year-old read told him he should be. "You're... you're here? I thought you were in Florida."

Poppy Aitken smiled, the lines on his face deepening. His Scottish accent remained strong despite years of retirement in Florida. "Aye, lad," he whispered. "I'm here."

Jack glanced up at the top bunk, checking on George. His brother's deep, steady breathing confirmed he was still asleep.

The boy sat up straighter, his tiny freckles standing out starkly against his rosy cheeks and sleep-warmed skin. He couldn't understand how his grandfather could be there. He hadn't seen him in months. Something about his presence, the soft light surrounding him, and the way his feet didn't quite touch the floor felt... different.

"How come you're here?" Jack asked quietly, eyes wide with confusion. "You... you're not supposed to be here, right?"

The elder Jack Aitken chuckled, "No, I suppose not. But there are things, Jackie boy, you'll understand in time... things that happen for reasons we can't always see."

His eyes, blue as the Scottish lochs he told tales of, glimmered with an unreadable light. Jack couldn't tell if his grandfather was happy or sad.

Jack shifted, pulling the covers up over his lap, eyes fixed on the glowing figure. He wasn't afraid, only curious.

"Why now?" he asked. "Is something wrong?"

Poppy's smile faded. "No, nothing's wrong. Not for you, anyway." He stepped closer, his figure glowing like moonlight dancing on water. "I came to see you because... there's something I want you to know. Something that will help you later."

"What is it?" Jack asked softly, almost in a whisper.

His grandfather knelt next to Jack's bed, his ghostly presence bending light in strange, impossible ways, filling the air with a faint warmth.

"You're stronger than you think, Jackie. One day, you'll face a choice... a hard one. And when you do, I want you to remember this..."

He paused, his voice gentle yet certain. "Sometimes, Jackie boy, we win, even if it seems like we've lost."

Jack frowned, his brows furrowing as he tried to make sense of it. "What do you mean? Like... losing at baseball?"

His grandfather chuckled, ruffling the boy's messy light-brown hair, just as he used to on the porch in Florida.

"No, not baseball. Something much bigger. Something that will matter when you're older."

Jack tried to hold onto the words, wanting to remember them exactly. But even as Poppy talked, the meaning slipped away... like trying to grasp smoke curling from one of his cigarettes.

"Will you be okay, Pop?" Jack asked softly, his voice gentle with a touch of concern.

"Aye," the older man said, his voice fading like a whisper on the wind. "I'll be fine, lad. You take care of your brother and sisters. And remember... the heart knows more than the mind ever will."

Jack stared into his grandfather's eyes, wanting to ask more, but the glowing light dimmed. A yawn escaped as heavy sleep tugged at him. Warmth wrapped the room like a soft blanket, and his eyelids drifted closed.

"Goodnight, Poppy," he whispered.

"Goodnight, Jackie boy," came the reply, already far away.

When Jack woke up the next morning, golden spring sunlight streamed through the windows, warm and bright. He blinked groggily, his mind grasping for a memory... something important, but it dissolved like smoke in the air, like the remnants of a fading dream.

In the hallway, his mother stood with the phone pressed to her ear. Her face was pale, her eyes red and swollen with tears. She looked at Jack, and for a moment, her voice caught in her throat.

"Sweetheart," she whispered, tears silently sliding down her cheek. "I have some news about Poppy..."

But Jack didn't hear the rest. He already knew. He had seen him last night.

***

Early February-Late in the day
The Safehouse
Lake Ronkonkoma, NY

The package rested on Anne's lap, its weight pressing steadily against her thighs. The plain brown box, like those holding Anne's tax papers back in Bristow, Virginia, was unremarkable save for the envelope taped neatly inside the lid.

Jouris Van Haalan, their new guardian and sole link to the outside world, brought it in around sunset, as daylight faded and long shadows stretched across the room. He didn't ask what was inside or share details… he just handed it over without saying a word.

Anne sat propped up in bed, bathed in the dim glow of the lone bedside lamp. Jack had urged her to rest, but days off her feet only bred restlessness. She steadied her hand, pulling the letter from the envelope, and carefully unfolding the fragile page. The paper rustled softly in the still room. Her breath caught as she skimmed the words, absorbing each one,

Does Jouris know about Pieter? She wondered.

Then, suddenly, something shifted in the stillness. She folded the letter quickly, sliding it back into the box as the first creak sounded.

A faint noise at first, the stairwell shifting as though something pressed down on it. Her pulse quickened. Then another footstep-like groan drew closer. Someone was there.

Anne replaced the lid, her fingers instinctively curling around the edge of the blanket as she pulled it up to her chest. She slipped the box beneath the folds of fabric, then froze, her body stiff, every muscle taut as she strained to listen.

The house was old, and every sound was magnified. Even her breathing felt too loud, her heart pounding like a drum. Another creak echoed from the hallway outside the bedroom. Someone or something was out there.

For a moment, she thought Jack might be checking on her. But he had gone out with Jouris for supplies. She was certain Louis and David were walking her dog, Daphne. No one should be home. Her mind raced through possibilities, but her JESU training warned her: whoever it was must not know she was here, not yet.

She looked around for a hiding place. But it was too late. The door opened slowly and deliberately, revealing the silhouette of William Pinn in a blue windbreaker. The hallway's soft light outlined his broad shoulders.

Anne exhaled, tension easing, but her hearing still racing. William, Jouris's EMT friend, stepped inside, his face calm yet tinged with concern.

"You all right, Anne?" William asked, his rough voice softened, but carrying the blunt realism of a man used to dealing with crisis

"I... I thought I heard something," she whispered, pulling herself up in bed. "Probably just the house settling."

He nodded but said nothing more. He'd seen them on the news: Anne, the two boys, and their father, hunted and forced into hiding. But Jouris trusted them, and William did too. His loyalty to the Setalcott oath to shelter strangers and his friendship with Jouris outweighed any temptation to betray them.

William took the stethoscope from around his pockmarked neck and pressed it gently against her chest. "Breathe in for me."

Anne complied. William's wrinkled brow furrowed as he listened. "Sounds better than yesterday. Normal, but hard to say what caused the episode. You're under a lot of stress... severe stress, and that could've triggered it. But I'm no doctor."

Anne nodded, though her thoughts focused on the letter... its words about sacrifice echoing in her mind.

"Do you need anything?" William asked, his emerald eyes softening. "More rest, maybe? You shouldn't push yourself."

"No. I'm fine," she smiled, then joked, "Takes more than this to keep me down."

He said nothing for a moment, his gaze lingering as if weighing her words. Finally, he nodded, his loyalty sealed in the silence. "Get some more rest, Anne. I'll leave a note for Jouris to check on you."

After William left, Anne exhaled the breath she hadn't realized she was holding. She waited until his footsteps faded before allowing herself to relax. The letter remained hidden... for now.

An hour later, Jack returned, sitting on the edge of the bed beside her. His face was drawn, with dark circles accentuating the lines around his weary eyes. "William told me your heart sounded better," he said softly, resting a hand on her knee. "You've had me worried. Are you sure you're okay?"

Anne nodded, tapping Jack's hand to reassure him. Then, suddenly, her expression grew serious. Her brow furrowed. "We need to finish that discussion about what happens if we're discovered."

Jack's eyes darkened, the weight of their conversations pressing down like the sword of Damocles. He hated these talks... the endless what-ifs that clawed at his hope and sanity. But Anne was right. This was their new reality: TEOTAWKI, as Anne called it... the end of the world as we know it. Somewhere deep inside, fear clenched his chest.

"I know we've covered this, but we need to stick together," Jack said, gripping her hand firmly. "We can't get separated."

"Jack, trust me," Anne said firmly. "If we stay together, we'll doom the boys. Louis and David must survive... they might be humanity's last hope. We can't lose them, not after everything that's happened. If we split up, at least one of us can get them out. They'll die if we stay together."

Jack swallowed hard, jaw clenched. "But... how can I choose one over the other?"

"I know it's tough," she said gently, squeezing his hand. "But you'll keep them safe. You'll do what needs to be done."

Jack stood, arms folded, gazing out the window, lost in thought. He scratched the back of his neck, then slowly turned to Anne. When their eyes met, he understood.

"My side should heal in a week or two," Jack said, gingerly patting the wound from his brother, George's, attack. "I need to learn what you know... everything. I want to become a warrior, like you were in JESU."

He ran his hand over his arm, remembering the invisible armor from his first battle with Lucius Rofocale. A few years had passed, yet it felt like a lifetime.

Jack sat beside Anne. "When the storm hits and we know it's coming, I need to stand against the forces hunting them. I need to protect Louis and David."

Anne leaned closer, her voice dropping. "Lesson one," Anne said, leaning closer. "Never believe the media. Never trust the authorities. It's all lies, twisted by Prosperine and Lucius. Keep the guns and ammo by the front door, always. We'll need them if... when the fighting gets close."

"What about the boys?" Jack asked, voice strained beneath the weight of Anne's words.

"We'll teach them to defend themselves. And when they see the storm come, when it's time, they'll remember the mnemonics we teach them: GOOD... Get Out of Dodge means evacuate immediately. INCM... I'm Never Coming Home. We have to be ready, always."

Jack sighed, nodded, and steeled himself. They had no choice but to prepare. It was only a matter of time.

But the lake had whispered long before; another family had faced the same shadow on Ronkonkoma's shore.

***

18th Century
Near The Shore of Present-Day Lake Ronkonkoma, NY

The Van Haalan home, a sturdy stone cottage on the shores of the lake known to the Native people as Ronkonkoma, stood firm against the relentless storm. Waves hammered the shore in unnatural rhythm. Inside, the hearth crackled, casting shadows that danced on the walls. What should have been comforting instead carried a heavy unease.

Pieter, the eldest son, bit his fingernail, a nervous habit from childhood, and gazed out the rain-soaked window at the restless lake. His sun-bleached blonde hair fell over his eyes, masking the worry carved deeply into his furrowed brow.

Pieter's mind screamed, "Haunt me no longer!", but the demanding whisper only grew louder.

He had served as his father Jakob's right hand on their boat for years, but as the unrelenting wind lashed against their home, growing fiercer, so too did Pieter's burden. Something tugged at him: a whisper carried on the gusts, which he tried desperately to ignore, beckoning him to the lake's edge.

Come to me, Pieter?

Jakob sat at the kitchen table, his gnarled fingers drumming on the worn wood, a nervous tic he used to relieve tension. He stared nervously at Pieter, while canyon-like creases deepened across his face.

Wearily, he muttered under his breath, "By the sea, keep my boy safe…"

Hanneke, his wife, worked silently, cooking dinner at the hearth. She bit the inside of her cheek as she stirred the pot. Her movements were stiff, mechanical, as if the weight of the night pressed down on her, too. Her hands trembled slightly as she brushed a stray lock of hair behind her ear.

She prayed, "My God, please don't let it take him."

Their youngest daughter, Elsje, peeked out from behind her mother's skirts. She pulled at a string on her dress, her eyes wide with a mix of fear and fascination as she watched her brother. When the wind moaned through the cracks in the walls, she hummed a lullaby her grandmother had taught her, a fragile shield against the storm.

The wind shifted. Like a moan, a low, guttural sound echoed from a distance, barely audible over the storm's fury. Pieter stiffened, gripping the sill so tightly that his fingernails dug into the wood. His heart raced as the sound grew louder, reverberating in his skull like a musket shot. It felt as though something wicked clawed at the veil between worlds, trying to break through.

"Pieter?" Hanneke's voice trembled, barely audible as another fierce blast struck their door.

But Pieter could no longer hear her. He was slipping away, his eyes glazed over, his mind sinking beneath a darkness neither comprehensible nor resistible. The whisper transformed into a low, seductive voice, speaking in a language older than time.

Come to me...

His feet moved before he could stop them, drawn by an unseen force. The door creaked open as he stepped into the storm. The squall screamed in protest, but it could not deter him. The voice grew stronger, pulling him toward the shore and jagged rocks where waves churned with fury.

Jakob groaned, rising to his feet. "Pieter! Boy, where are you going?"

Hanneke cried out, but Pieter did not turn back. He walked as if in a trance, his body no longer his own. The storm intensified, rain slashing across his face; yet the insistent voice drowned out everything else, dragging him toward the lake.

Elsje whimpered, clutching her mother's garments, while Jakob stumbled into the darkness after his son. The thunder's roar swallowed his voice.

Beyond their potato field, Pieter reached a peninsula jutting into the lake. The whisper became a chorus of growls and chants, a bitter song tearing at his soul. He fell to his knees on the rocky beach, waves crashing relentlessly around him. The bitter cold pierced through his clothes, stinging like a swarm of wasps. His eyes widened as he gazed at the distant whitecaps on the lake, sure that something unseen was watching him in return.

A dark shape shifted and writhed beneath the water. Then, slowly, it rose... an ancient presence, formless yet vast, radiating pure malevolence. The voice sharpened, speaking directly into his mind.

You belong to me, Pieter. You have been chosen.

He opened his mouth to scream, but no sound escaped. The water surged forward, crashing into him with unnatural force and slamming him against the jagged rocks. The cold water filled his lungs, suffocating him; yet, instead of death, he felt something else, something far worse.

Something from the lake slithered into him, its initial coldness melting into unbearable heat as an ancient evil flooded through his body.

His back arched, bones cracking like splintering timber.

The presence invaded every fiber of his being, clawing its way into his very soul. His mind buckled under the crushing pressure, bending and twisting as the darkness took root. Its tendrils wrapped around his thoughts and free will until nothing remained.

Pieter's eyes snapped open, black as the deep ocean he had fished all his life. His body was still his own, but he was no longer Pieter Van Haalan. He stood amid the raging storm; yet it felt like part of him, as if he commanded nature's fury.

The phantasm had taken him… claimed him.

Jakob reached the shore just in time to see his son rise, but stumbled back at the sight of Pieter's soulless eyes. His blood went cold.

Those are not the eyes of my son… it is the lake staring back.

The rain turned to sleet, frozen pellets stinging Jakob's face like needles.

"Pieter!" he shouted, lunging forward, but the thunder consumed his voice.

Seemingly unfazed by the raging storm, the figure who had once been Pieter gazed back without recognition.

Hanneke and Elsje stood frozen in the doorway, horrified as Jakob reached for his son. But laughter erupted from Pieter's mouth, not his laughter, but a chilling sound belonging to something older, darker, and beyond human.

With a single unnatural motion, Pieter turned and walked toward the lake. His movements were fluid with an eerie dexterity, as though he no longer belonged in the world of men. He stepped into the waves. The water rose around him, yet it did not drag him down. Instead, it welcomed him, drawing him deeper.

The last they saw was his silhouette fading into the depths, leaving only the echo of otherworldly laughter carried on the wind.

Centuries passed after Pieter's shadow vanished beneath the lake's cold depths, but the malevolence that claimed him endured. Its hunger seeped through the dark sands of time, seeking new vessels, craving fresh souls.

But the lake's hunger endured, seeping through time and across oceans. It whispered to others, not prophets but devils in flesh…

***

Early February
Secret Lab at Pergamon, Satan's Earthly Residence in Present-Day Turkiye

The laboratory buzzed with the low hum of machines, the air thick with antiseptics, metal, and something darker: fear. Queen Prosperine and Demon Lord Lucius Rofocale entered, their footsteps echoing through glass-walled corridors. They alone wore masks, mocking symbols of superiority, cruel reminders of who thrived while others perished. Scientists milled about, eyes downcast, avoiding their gaze.

Containment units lined the walls, each holding twisted horrors, human and demon alike, writhing in their restraints. Their bodies convulsed as new diseases ravaged them, plagues conjured from Hell's darkest depths.

Prosperine paused before a glass cell. Inside, a woman gurgled in agony, her skin peeling, limbs jerking in unnatural spasms.

Lucius smiled, watching the torment, his face gleaming with sadistic pleasure. His voice was cold.

"The Wallace Rabies and the Deer Virus… they have fused better than expected." He tapped the glass. "Airborne now. Double the virulence in under forty-eight hours. The scientists have truly outdone themselves."

Prosperine's gaze lingered on the suffering, then drifted beyond the lab to Jerusalem, Solomon's Temple, her monument —a shrine to her divinity, built not by demons, but from human blood and bone.

"Excellent," she murmured. "The harsher the plagues, the deeper the despair. Let the loathsome humans rot first. Then the lesser demons. We must shatter humanity's spirit before their bodies."

Lucius bowed, then lifted his gaze. He admired how she bore evil like a crown. Something had changed since heaven's fall; her cruelty honed to a razor's edge, and her ambition intensified. She no longer carried herself as Satan's pawn, but as a god in her own right.

"Yes," Lucius agreed. "This is only the beginning. The true suffering begins when we twist the book of Revelation to our own design. Endless torment, no swift deaths. No clean escapes."

He approached a trembling researcher in a white coat, placing a clawed hand firmly on the man's shoulder.

"Are the pathogens ready?"

The scientist's ashen face betrayed his fear. "Yes…yes, my Lord. Multiple strains. Entire populations could fall within weeks."

Lucius's grin widened.

"Good. Let the world burn. Begin preparations for deployment. Soon, every corner of the earth will be infected."

Prosperine's lips curled, cruel and certain.

"And as they writhe in agony, their prayers unanswered, cries to a silent God ignored, even the most devout will turn away. When salvation fails, they will beg for an end we will never grant."

Lucius chuckled darkly.

"The apocalypse will be a slow, grinding march into despair, a living nightmare with no awakening. And when no one is left to fight or pray, we will claim what remains.

The room darkened, their intentions hanging heavy like suffocating smoke. Scientists worked faster, driven by the grim truth: failure meant death. Meanwhile, beyond these walls, the world was already crumbling. Earthquakes, volcanic eruptions, and heaven's fall had shattered global communications. The signs of the apocalypse were everywhere, but in Lucius and Prosperine's hands, they were only the beginning.

Prosperine spun, her royal cloak billowing like a predator's wings.

"The temple will rise," she declared. "And when it does, they will worship only me. I will remake this world in my own image… no gods but myself."

Lucius lingered, his gaze lingering on the chambers of suffering. He whispered, "They will fear me. I will twist their faith into terror, their prayers into screams. I need no Strigoi to enforce my will! I wield my own power to inflict cruelty and vengeance."

The doors hissed shut behind them, sealing the horrors inside. The truth was undeniable: the apocalypse had already begun, and under their control, it would never end.

***

Early February
Somewhere in Texas, Near the Mexican Border

The night hung thick with fog, curling around weathered tombstones like drifting jellyfish tendrils. The Strigoi crouched low between graves, biding its time, yet an undeniable pull gnawed at its core… a primal bloodlust, sharp as its claws, driving it south. It didn't understand why, only that it must obey, but somewhere ahead, demon blood waited to be spilled, and it would find it.

By day, it wore the guise of Reid Bowman, a stranger whose face slipped from memory as quickly as his footsteps. By night, the Strigoi's true form emerged: a hulking, lycanthrope-like beast with bony claws and eyes flickering like hot flames. Its vampire-like fangs gleamed hungrily in the dark… thirsting for blood.

It despised demons most of all, Lucius Rofocale, above the rest, the one who had cursed it with this wretched fate. Its mind burned with hatred and vengeance; yet, it craved the hunt.

Under a muted gray dawn, the Strigoi neared the Texas-Mexico border. In human form now, a weary traveler with a rucksack and wide-brimmed hat, it blended among others on the dusty roads. But beneath this mask, the hunger never waned.

Near the railroad tracks, a family had set up a small camp. The rich aroma of beans simmering over a fire mingled with the pine smoke, drawing Reid's attention. His eyes fixed on the daughter, no older than eighteen, with her fiery red hair and ocean-blue eyes; Maricela Antonescu's eyes. The resemblance cut him like a blade.

The photograph in his bag stirred something unfamiliar: guilt, sorrow, and mourning. Maricela's death and his vow of vengeance sworn at her gravesite haunted the Strigoi. Worse still, the memory of impregnating her twisted in its gut, a bitter reminder of the monster it had become.

Shadows shifted at the edge of the camp. Twigs snapped under heavy boots, drawing Reid's attention. A gang of ragged men emerged, hollow-eyed, knives flashing, intent on killing without hesitation, seizing food, and capturing the girl.

Even in its human form, the Strigoi was an alpha predator. This was nothing.

Reid lunged, a blur of muscle and fury. He disarmed one attacker. The rest froze, wide-eyed with terror, as his fangs lengthened and his eyes lit with fire.

"Leave," he growled, his voice deep, menacing.

The gang scattered, abandoning their weapons.

Scott Foley approached cautiously, wiping sweat from his brow.

"My name's Scott Foley. Thank you for saving us."

Reid handed him a knife that the men had dropped. His reply was flat.

"I am Reid. Reid Bowman."

Still shaking, Scott motioned toward the fire. "Please, have something to eat. It isn't much, but it's more than most get."

Ellen Foley's hands never stopped moving, cooking, brushing hair from her daughter's face. "I'm Ellen," she said, passing Reid a plate of steaming black beans. "I don't know what you did to scare those men off, but we're grateful."

She pointed at her children. "This is Julie, and our sons, Kevin and Sean."

Julie tugged nervously at her jacket whenever the shadows stirred beyond the tree line.

As Reid ate, he studied them: all fair-skinned redheads, except Scott, whose graying beard blended red and brown. Still, it was Julie's eyes that unsettled him.

"We've come from St. Louis," Scott said. "The winter was so bitterly cold that even the underground pipes froze. Rolling blackouts and shortages of everything… from food to basic supplies."

Ellen whispered, "We would have frozen to death if we stayed."

Scott's bitter laugh echoed above the crackling fire. "People froze in their homes. They thought solar power would save them. It failed. Everything failed."

"If you don't mind me asking," Ellen said, pouring coffee, "where are you headed, Reid?"

He stared at the cup, uneasy. "South."

"We're heading to Mexico," Scott replied. "Why don't you travel with us?"

Reid barely heard them. Julie's voice was a whisper.

"Have you heard of the Chupacabra?"

The Strigoi suppressed a smirk. A lesser scavenger. No threat.

As the sun began to set, the familiar pull returned, the sulfuric scent of demon blood thick in the air. Reid looked at the Julie and grief struck him again, sharp and unrelenting. A part of him longed to stay, to protect them, to atone for what he had done to Maricela.

A ground fog coiled, spectral tendrils weaving around the fire's dying embers. For a moment, he thought he heard a murmur, a ghostly voice from a past he could not escape.

Avenge me…

But night beckoned, and in the darkness, the Strigoi struggled to control itself.

CHAPTER 2

Summer 1961
Camp Wauwepex, Wading River, NY

It was early afternoon at Camp Wauwepex. The air was heavy and still. Louder than cicadas or the transmission lines overhead, the forest seemed to hum. The sun baked down on the clearing, the scent of pine mixing with the earthy dampness of soil as Billy and Lyle Clifford worked the old two-man saw, moving in rhythm back and forth.

Visitor's Day was tomorrow, with a lot of wood still to cut. Camp Wauwepex, known as the "place of good water" by Native Americans, lived up to its name. Sunlight glistened on the surface of a pristine stream that meandered through the trees. It looked cool and inviting on such a hot afternoon, but there was no time for a swim.

At fifteen, Billy Clifford wielded the heavy saw with ease, his muscled arms making it seem like a child's toy rather than a tool meant for cutting tree trunks. Lyle's smaller frame strained with each pull, his flushed face dripping sweat as the saw jerked and snagged, draining what little strength he had left.

"Hold on, Lyle," Billy called out, feeling the tug on his end of the saw. He could tell his little brother was near his limit. Lyle had been pale all week, a sickly shade beyond his usual pallor.

"Let's take a break," Billy said firmly, his voice steady but kind, masking his concern as he sensed exhaustion taking hold.

Lyle gratefully set the saw down and slumped against a log. He wiped sweat from his freckled face, his fire-red hair a jarring contrast to his sickly pale skin. The humid air clung to them, the forest murmuring as if it listened in.

Billy dropped heavily onto the log, wiping his brow with the back of his arm. He unscrewed the cap on their dented canteen. "Here, drink up," he said, offering the cool water. We've got all day to finish this, no point keeling over now.

Lyle took the canteen, sipping several gulps before handing it back. "Thanks," he murmured, still catching his breath. He gazed across the clearing, silence stretching between them before he spoke again. "Billy, do you really think they'll go through with it?"

Billy raised an eyebrow, a smirk tugging at the corner of his mouth, "Go through with what, exactly?"

"The tap-out." Lyle's voice dropped to a whisper, trembling enough to betray his nerves. "The Order of the Flaming Spear… tomorrow night."

Billy let out a short, humorless laugh, wiping sweat from his brow. "Lyle, I told them not to pick me."

"But what if they do it anyway?" Lyle's voice wavered, eyes wide and anxious. "You're one of the best scouts. They won't listen to you. And then you'll be part of the Order, and I'll be…" His words choked off, swallowed by a fear too great to finish.

Billy, always the protective older brother, rolled his eyes with a crooked grin. "And you'll be what? Abandoned? Left to fend off the wolves of Wauwepex all alone?" He nudged Lyle with a playful shove. "Don't sweat it, little man. I told them I'm not interested, you're freaking out over nothing!"

He hopped to his feet, shadowboxing with a grin. I'll tell you what. I'll punch anyone who tries to tap me out right in the nose. How's that for a plan?"

Lyle managed a small smile at Billy's antics, his fingers tugging at the rough bark of the log. "You know you're not supposed to hit people in Scouts, Billy."

"Well, there's always a first time for everything."

Billy winked, but Lyle's smile slipped away like a shadow. His eyes dropped to his hands, fingers nervously picking at the raw skin around his blisters. "It's just... what if they take you away? What if you get too caught up in that Order stuff, and I'm left here with the rest of them? Alone."

Billy paused, the teasing grin fading. He looked down at his little brother, small for his age, often sickly, and all too familiar with the sting of bullies. Lyle struggled to keep up, and it infuriated Billy when the patrol called him names like *Cry-le* or *Lyle the Lizard*. That was why Billy always stood between him and the world, a shield against the cruelty that others threw their way.

"Nobody's taking me away, Lyle," Billy said softly, his voice steady but gentle, almost a vow. "I'll always be right here with you. That's a promise."

Lyle nodded, but unease lingered in his tired eyes. He fidgeted with the frayed edge of his shorts before glancing at the dense trees surrounding them. The towering pines stood silent and still, yet the silence made the air feel heavier. The cicadas' buzzing faded, swallowed by a quiet so complete it pressed against Lyle's skin, sending a shiver crawling down his spine.

"Billy," Lyle whispered, his voice barely rising above the rustling leaves. "What if it's more than a ceremony? What... if the Order knows something we don't?" His eyes locked on the dark woods beyond, still tugging at the frayed threads of his shorts.

Billy forced a laugh, but the sound rang hollow. "What, you think they're some kind of cult? Gonna summon the Onteora Demon or something?"

The sun, still high but dimmer now, cast long shadows that stretched like fingers across the clearing.

Normally, Lyle would have laughed at the joke about the Onteora Demon, a giant hand said to snatch people in the forests around the scout camp. But today, he wasn't laughing. His gaze stayed fixed on the shadows, his eyes wide and unblinking. "I don't know, Billy. I just... I have this feeling. After we found those weird footprints on the sandbar by the lake. Like… like something's gonna happen. Something big."

Billy opened his mouth to respond, then closed it. Since finding the footprints, their Indian Lore Merit Badge counselor William's words lingered. What once sounded like a campfire ghost story now felt uncomfortably real.

The lake watches you. Ronkonkoma's reach stretches beyond the shore, its past not buried but pulsing beneath our feet.

Despite the heat, an unnatural chill crept into the clearing. Thunder rumbled low and slow in the distance, though the sky remained clear, and the sun still shone.

"Lyle," Billy began, his voice wavering as he gazed toward Lake Ronkonkoma, a chill running down his spine, "let's head back to camp."

Lyle didn't move; his gaze locked on the woods.

For the first time all summer, Billy felt it too… the creeping unease, as if the forest itself watched with unseen, patient eyes… waiting.

*****

Mid-February
Safehouse at Lake Ronkonkoma, NY

"Where are you going, Louis?"

David Aitken stood at the bottom of the stairs, watching his brother retreat once more, each step pressing on his chest. The bedroom door closed with a soft thud that echoed down the narrow corridor… a final punctuation to the growing distance between them. He wanted to call after him, but the words stuck between hope and hesitation.

What could he say? Talking about feelings was never easy, especially about the widening gulf between them. Once inseparable after learning they were God's prophets, Louis had spent the past two weeks withdrawing into a world David couldn't reach… leaving him alone with the silence.

David's stomach growled… but not with a hunger he could fix. No chicken nuggets or fries in the house; only foods that made him sick to think about. Since arriving, the house felt off: creaking, groaning, shifting, like it was alive. Sometimes footsteps echoed; other times the floorboards seemed to breathe. He hated it. He wanted it to stop.

As he started down the hallway, the air grew heavy, thick and cold, making each breathe harder. His room lay at the end of the hall, but he didn't like walking there alone. He missed sharing a room with Louis, as they had in the old house. The one in Bristow had felt safe and warm, but that was gone now, burned to ash when Uncle George destroyed it.

David pushed the door open. His room was a mess again… clothes scattered across the floor. Frustration flared as he knelt, folding awkwardly with his one arm. He first he thought Louis left the mess to annoy him. Maybe. But Louis hardly came near the room anymore, and the disorder kept happening. That unsettled him… it felt like the house was playing tricks.

His right hand moved on its own while his mind drifted. Strange sounds echoed in the house… footsteps with no one there, the closet door creaking open each night. Sometimes he lay awake, eyes fixed on the door, waiting. It never moved. Still, something felt wrong.

As if the house sensed his fear, the closet door creaked behind him. David's heart jumped. Wrapping his arm around himself, he tried to hold back the cold dread crawling up his spine. Slowly, barely breathing, he turned. The hair on his neck prickled. He'd closed the door… yet now it stood open. He stared, waiting. Nothing stirred. Not yet.

David glanced out the window. Behind him, the closet door creaked again, sliding open slowly, like a gentle hand pushing it. He stepped back, nearly tripping on his shoes. The door opened wider, but he didn't look. He knew it was open… he didn't want to see inside or face the dark space beyond.

Yet the question haunting him since arriving returned:

What am I afraid of?

Not the noises, not the house, not the dark inside the closet. What scared him most was losing Louis; imagining his brother walking down the hall, closing his door, and never opening it again, leaving David alone in this creaking, groaning house with no one to help him understand what was happening.

Alongside their dad, Louis had been David's anchor through his battle with Leukemia and the trials of being God's prophet. Losing him… and that connection… was unbearable. The thought of that creeping loneliness, the kind that arrives unnoticed and lingers, chilled him deeper than any draft.

The closet stood wide open, empty but for the shadows. David whispered, small and trembling,

"Dad calls this a safehouse… but right now, I don't feel safe."

***

Pre-Colonial Period
Dusk on the Autumnal Equinox
Shores of Lake Ronkonkoma, NY

The sky above Lake Ronkonkoma deepened to indigo as the last light of the autumnal equinox faded. Cool air settled over the sacred ground where the four tribes gathered, carrying the faint scent of pine and smoke. Each year, on this night, they assembled for their most revered ceremony. Quanon stood slightly behind his father, Chief Powwan, at the forefront of the Setalcotts.

Across the boundary, the other chiefs waited: Nassaconseke of the Nissequogues, his presence commanding; Winnequaheagh, of the Secatogues, moving with the grace of a seasoned ruler; and Tobaccus of the Unkechaugs, quiet and watchful, his gaze sharp as an Eagle's. Each wore ceremonial garments and feathered headdresses. Behind them, braves stood in breechcloths, their weapons and polished shell jewelry prominently displayed.

The woods hushed. Even the crickets fell silent, as if the forest itself held its breath. Then Chief Powwan's voice rang out, deep and resonant, slicing through the quiet like a blade.

"Near our campfire circle stand the wigwams of our tribes, dark against the towering oaks and pines. Here, we learn many things: the stars above, the birds that nest within, and the language of all creatures, friends whenever we meet them."

He raised his ceremonial spear to the sky. "See how the Great Spirit cares for all his faithful children!"

The assembled tribes responded in unison, "Oh, Great Spirit, hear our plea. Send us fire, and we shall praise Thee."

A sharp *whoosh* broke the silence, followed by a flaming arrow arcing across the twilight. Its fiery tail etched a glowing trail before striking the stacked firewood at the circle's center. Flames roared to life, chasing away the dusk and casting warm amber light over the gathering. Quanon felt the heat lick his skin, a reminder of the intensity of what lay ahead.

Chief Powwan's voice carried above the crackling blaze.

"As our campfire smoke curls upward, may all that is cowardly and unwise be carried away from our midst. As our campfire grows, let its smoke rise and carry unworthy thoughts away, never to return or darken our hearts again.
And in the friendly glow of our fire, may peace settle over us all."

The four chiefs gazed into the flames, as if they saw both the past and the future reflected in their flickering dance.

Then Powwan spoke again, his tone heavy with solemnity.

"The moon hangs full tonight, as it did when our tribes first joined as brothers. The Great Spirit has taught us many lessons, but the greatest is this: the wolf's strength lies within the pack, and the pack's strength flows from the wolf. This is why we gather beneath the moon's watchful eye, here in this sacred council ring."

Quanon shifted as his father's voice carried across the firelit clearing. "We have several cubs who have grown strong in body and wise beyond their years. The time has come for them to leave the shelter of youth and step into the wider world of men, to find their place beneath the sky."

Quanon's heart pounded. Each beat echoed the drumbeat, which began to resonate at the edge of the circle, deep and steady, like the heartbeat of the earth itself. One by one, names were called. Young men from each tribe stepped forward, proud and silent. When Quanon's name finally rang out, his feet felt heavy, yet he moved, aware of every eye upon him.

The weight of tradition settled on his shoulders, a burden heavier than any spear. The path ahead was uncertain, but the tribe's gaze held expectation and hope.

The drumbeat quickened and stopped. The fire snapped in the silence, and a cool hush swept the clearing. Quanon stood among the others, breath steady, waiting for what would come next.

Chief Powwan lifted his hands toward the sky, his voice carrying the weight of tradition. "The Sacred Fire ceremony marks the moment when boys step forward to become men… to prove their strength, their wisdom, and their readiness to serve the tribe and honor the Great Spirit."

Chief Nassaconseke of the Nissequogues stepped forward, his deep voice resonant and solemn. "Since the beginning, our people have walked this path together, gathering beneath the sun to honor the sacred rites. Our bond is strong and rare… four tribes bound by Ronkonkoma's spirit, joined as one in the sacred dance of the fire."

Chief Powwan's gaze swept the gathering. "Each tribe has chosen those most worthy to join us in Brotherhood. Take note of those who stand before you. Their conduct in the years to come must set the example for others who seek to follow this path."

The drum resumed its deep pulse, like distant thunder, as a procession formed. Quanon and others were led away from the fire while the tribes began to chant softly:

The day is done.
Gone is the sun.
From the lake, from the hills, from the sky.
All is well. Safely rest.
The Great Spirit is near.

A brave stepped from the shadowed edge of the forest. His voice was calm yet commanding, carrying clearly over the crackling fire and the fading chant. "The shadows deepen along the path beyond this circle. Whoever dares to take the upward trail must carry within them an inner light. Only those with true courage and vision can walk it. They have glimpsed the distant heights, yet stinging trials lie ahead. Will they cast aside comfort and heed the ancient voice that calls them to climb?"

The drumbeat quickened, then abruptly ceased, leaving only the crackle of the fire. Another brave shouted, "When your name is called, step forward. Remain silent until you return to your tribe. An escort will guide you to the place where your ordeal begins."

Quanon heard his future in the brave's words. The path ahead would test every part of him... spirit, body, and loyalty to his people. As the chants faded into the night, he felt the heavy weight of the journey before him. He had heard stories of the Ordeal: the grueling trials that demanded courage, endurance, and wisdom. Tonight, he would leave behind boyhood and step into the unknown. The Ordeal awaited.

This fire's flame reached beyond Ronkonkoma's shores, searing a path across time, searching hungrily for all who would one day walk in the modern world...

***

Mid-February
Computer Lab at Pergamon, Satan's Earthly Residence in Present-Day Turkiye

Alone in the dim computer lab, Tatiana listened to the low hum of machines. Pergamon's ancient stone walls felt thicker at night, heavy with secrets she dared not uncover. She braided her stringy brown hair, a ritual to steady her nerves, while her gaze flickered over the screens flashing endless lines of code and data from the artificial intelligence systems.

Her fingers froze as a name, a date, and a place appeared on the screen. A chill traced her spine.

Since Lucifer's triumphant return to Heaven, Lucius had grown distant, almost apathetic toward her. He had abandoned her, and Lord Aitken's demands weren't enough to occupy her time. So Tatiana immersed herself in the stolen journals of Father Mark Desmond and the history that Lucius had tried to erase.

One night, she had asked the AI, *"Tell me about demon history."*

What began as curiosity became an obsession. The system sifted through every trace, whisper, and forgotten detail. It revealed information not only about Lord Aitken's hunt for his twin but also about Kazimir, Lucius's brother, whose shadow now loomed over her dark world.

Her fingers danced across the keys, pulling up satellite images, coded reports, intercepted communications, and obscure transmissions. Coordinates blinked across the globe, narrowing possible hiding places for Jack Aitken and his sons. But for Tatiana, it was no longer just about George's hunt. The forbidden passages from Desmond's journals gnawed at her. Did a battle between Lucius and Kazimir carve the Grand Canyon? Could a crater in Mexico, believed to have been an asteroid that wiped out the dinosaurs, hide Kazimir's lost pyramid?

Earth's history looked less like geology and more like a tangled web of truth and manipulation: a planet's past rewritten by a demonic hand, with truth buried under a millennium of Lucius's lies.

A knot of unease formed in her chest. This knowledge could change everything. But what was her role? Was she still Lucius's servant, or something else? Her allegiance felt tenuous, caught between obedience and the dangerous allure of the secrets she uncovered.

If Lucius discovers my secret inquiries, he'll disintegrate me. But the truth is a hunger I can't deny…

With a slow breath, she pushed back her chair and gathered a folder of the AI's latest findings, the paper still warm from the printer, and tucked it under her arm. The threads of past and present twisted tighter with each revelation. This information could shift the balance, and she knew it.

***

Mid-February
George Aitken's Chamber at Pergamon, Satan's Earthly Residence in Present-Day Turkiye

Tatiana found George Aitken hunched over a sprawling table cluttered with maps and pins, marking possible safehouses. The air smelled of dust and old parchment. Candlelight carved deep shadows into his gaunt face, making the sharp angles harsher, the hollows beneath his cheekbones darker. A tray of untouched food sat nearby, forgotten.

For a moment she only watched him, then stepped forward and placed the AI reports beside a cluster of pins on a map of the Northeastern United States.

"These are the latest findings," she said softly.

George barely glanced at her. His solitary eye stayed fixed on the map, his fingers tracing possible routes his brother might take. His focus was so complete it unsettled her.

"You haven't touched your food," she said, nodding toward the cold tray. "You're wasting away."

"I've got a dinner party later," he muttered without looking up.

Tatiana crossed her arms, pacing slowly around the table. Though she tried to focus on the hunt, her thoughts drifted back to the Grand Canyon… the ancient battlefield of Lucius and Kazimir, if the journals were true. The idea gnawed at her: did the Mexican crater hide Kazimir's pyramid?

"What if we are mistaken?" she whispered, almost to herself. "What if... all of this has been a deception?"

George's hand hovered over the map. His gaze slowly lifted to meet hers, expression unreadable.

"You do realize what you're saying borders on treason, don't you?"

"I trust you," she whispered, stepping closer. "After what you did… saving me from Barbas."

Her eyes darkened at the memory… that night when Barbas tried to violate her, and George had intervened, ending him.

"I would never say this to anyone else."

George studied her carefully, his solitary eye sharp as a blade.

"Don't mistake necessity for compassion. Killing Barbas was duty, nothing more." He leaned in slightly, voice low and dangerous. "That doesn't give you license to speak freely. Lucius tolerates no doubts… especially not from his most trusted servants. You are loyal, aren't you?"

"I am," she said, though her voice wavered. "But that does not mean I shouldn't question…"

George cut her off, his tone cold and abrupt. "Then keep your questions to yourself. Doubt all you want, in silence. Speak it aloud and you won't survive it."

The air between them grew heavy. Tatiana hesitated, weighing the risk, then forced the words out.

"There's something else. The leaks about the Strigoi attacks at Lake Waccamaw… your bombings… the footage of you leaving the hospital… That was me. I… I'm the one who leaked it to the media."

George's jaw tightened. For a long moment he was silent, and Tatiana braced for the explosion. But instead, he exhaled, almost weary. He shook his head.

"I won't turn you in."

His calmness startled her. She wondered if her alterations to his elixir were already working.

"But this is your only warning," George said, his tone sharp and unwavering. "Do it again, and even I won't save you. Lucius won't tolerate such acts, especially betrayal."

He turned back to the map, his focus sharpening once more, tracing lines with a finger that trembled not from weakness but from obsession. His voice dropped to a low growl, icy and unrelenting.

"Jack and Anne think they're clever, playing at hide and seek. It will end badly. Time is of no concern to me. I'll go door to door, house to house if I have to. And when I find them, they'll regret it."

He rubbed the patch over his missing eye, bitterness flickering across his face.

"I will locate them," he murmured. "And when I do, there will be no mercy."

Tatiana said nothing. She only watched him, the weight of her confession lingering like a noose swaying in the wind. Every step with George felt like walking a blade's edge between survival and annihilation.

***

Pre-Colonial Period
Night of the Autumnal Equinox
Shores of Lake Ronkonkoma, NY

The mist clung to the lake's surface like a thick, chilling shroud, swirling in ghostly tendrils as two braves roughly pushed forward Quanon. Their stoic, unreadable expressions revealed nothing, but their grip was iron-tight, guiding him along the narrow, uneven path winding around Lake Ronkonkoma. Laden with crisp, decaying leaves, the trees stood like ancient, twisted sentinels in the night, their branches barely swaying in the cool autumn breeze.

Quanon stumbled, legs wobbling beneath him, but the braves yanked him upright without a word. They stopped abruptly before a large, smooth boulder jutting from the shoreline, its surface cold and slick with evening dew. The braves released him, pushing him forward as if his presence were a disease.

"This is where you will stay," one brave said flatly. He pointed toward a nearby gnarled tree. "Choose a branch. You will carry it always."

Quanon hesitated, eyes scanning the tree, cloaked in the shadows of the night. He snapped off a slender branch, the bark rough beneath his fingertips as he stripped the leaves.

"Three notches," muttered the other brave, his face half-hidden by the thickening mist. "Break your silence or fail in any task, and a notch will be carved into the branch. Three notches mean failure… disgrace upon yourself, your family, and your tribe."

Quanon gripped the branch tightly, his fingers curled like a hawk's talons clutching prey. The weight of the unspoken warning pressed heavily on his shoulders. As the son of a Chief, he knew the expectation: return with no notches. The braves exchanged a brief glance before disappearing into the shadows.

Alone, Quanon's breath fogged in the cool air as he listened to the gentle lap of water against the shore. The night was unnervingly still, the usual chorus of insects conspicuously absent. He recognized the silence; the same hush OohQua described by the fire, as if the lake itself held its breath.

The rock behind him pressed cold and solid as he slumped against it, curling his legs close for warmth. Mist thickened into dense fog, swirling lazily as cold clamminess crept over his skin. His mind raced with OohQua's warning about last year's strange events.

Had he been brought to the same cursed spot? It felt right. The suffocating air, the eerie sensation of unseen eyes watching, matched

OohQua's vague description... experiences so haunting they drove him to flee.

Muscles tense, Quanon scanned the shoreline: endless dark water, creeping fog, and silent trees standing guard. He strained to hear any sign he was not alone, but all he heard was a deafening silence, pressing against his ears like a living thing.

Exhaustion crept into his limbs, but sleep would not come. The trials awaited in the morning, and the branch's weight was a constant reminder of his fate. Curling tighter, Quanon shut his eyes and focused on breathing, but the silence felt unnatural, heavy, and watchful, as if the night, too, was waiting.

He sensed the lake's presence, ancient and knowing, awaiting daybreak as keenly as he did.

***

Mid-February
Safehouse at Lake Ronkonkoma, NY

Jack stood at the stove, stirring the sizzling pan. The smell of fried Spam filled the small kitchen... greasy, comforting, and nostalgic, pulling him back to Boy Scout camping trips and simpler times.

"Dinner's ready!" he announced, setting the pan down with a clang. "It's been years since I made Spam. You're gonna love it."

Anne joined them at the table for the first time since arriving at the safehouse, hesitating as if uncertain how to reenter their fractured lives. She settled into a worn wooden chair, casting a nervous glance at Jack, then at the boys seated across from her.

"I'm happy you're feeling better, Anne," Jack said warmly. "It's great to have you with us." He looked at his sons, eyes flicking toward them. "Isn't that right, boys?"

Louis slumped, staring blankly at his plate. David methodically poked at his food, showing no interest. Jack's smile faltered, worry pressing just beneath his forced cheer.

"David, you'll feel better if you eat something. Try it." Jack's tone was encouraging, but his hands tightened around the fork, betraying his concern.

David shrugged, his eyes meeting Jack's briefly before returning to the plate, pushing the food around. Louis didn't even pretend. He hadn't spoken much for days, and the silence between them grew heavier with each passing moment.

Jack glanced at Anne, silently seeking help, but her expression mirrored his own: helpless and uncertain. The room settled into heavy silence, the air thick with unspoken fears. Jack's throat tightened, but he swallowed hard.

Before anyone could speak, a knock echoed at the door... three firm, measured raps resonating through the house.

"I'll get it," Jack said, pushing his chair back. "Boys, if you're not going to eat, you can leave the table." His voice wavered slightly.

The brothers hurried away as Jack crossed the creaky floor and opened the door to William and Jouris Van Haalan. The full moon cast their tall silhouettes against the kitchen wall.

Jouris's weathered face, leathery and lined, bore the marks of a hard-lived life. His thinning hair, more silver than blond, swayed in the breeze off the lake. Sharp blue eyes twinkled, hinting at a wry sense of humor beneath the woolen scarf wrapped tight around his neck.

"Are we interrupting anything?" Jouris asked, his voice gravelly but warm.

Jack forced a smile. "Just finishing up dinner. Come in... it's cold out there."

The men stepped inside, shaking off the chill. Jouris's eyes swept the room before settling on Anne with a polite nod. "Good to see you up and around."

"Would you like something to eat?" Jack asked, gesturing toward the stove. "Maybe some coffee?"

Casting a cautious glance at the Spam, Jouris chuckled. "Thanks, but no. I've already eaten."

Taking a seat, William said, "On a night this chilly, I'd rather have a shot of whiskey than coffee."

"That sounds good," Jouris added, pulling up the collar of his jacket. "I can feel the snow coming; my old bones are telling me so."

Searching the table, Jouris asked, "Where are your boys?"

Jack took the whiskey bottle from the counter, poured a generous amount into two chipped glasses, and handed them over. Jouris gulped it down with a satisfied sigh.

Jack looked up at the ceiling and replied, "Not hungry." He glanced down at the table, trying to hide the worry etched on his face.

William stroked his chin. "Nice-looking boys, Jack. But they do look quite sad. I suppose that's from everything they've been through."

"Speaking of all that, Jouris," Jack exhaled, "we never really had a chance to thank you for not shooting us on New Year's Eve." His voice carried a trace of humor.

Jouris shook his head, his deep voice filling the room. "I'm sorry about that." Looking at Anne, he added, "When you dropped to your knees, I thought I'd scared you to death."

"I spoke to William earlier," Jouris pointed a thumb at his friend. "He said he thinks you'll be okay in a few more days."

Pouring himself another shot of whiskey, Jouris joked, "You're lucky I hadn't been drinking that night."

He leaned back in his chair, crossing his arms over his chest. "By the way, I wanted to compliment you, Jack. You say my name right. Most people don't. It's Jouris… sounds like 'yours,' as in, 'Hi, I'm Yours,' like I told my wife when I first met her. I nearly ran her off."

Anne smiled slightly as she finished the last spoonful of her dinner. Wiping her mouth, she remarked, "It's a unique name."

"An old family name," Jouris said with pride. "Van Haalan. We're Long Islanders, just like you, Jack."

Jack furrowed his brow. "Islander?"

"Baymen. My father was one, and his father before him. The Van Halaans lived off the sea; we fished in these waters for centuries. Clamming and shellfishing, once upon a time. But there's not much of a future for a bayman these days."

Wiping his mouth with the sleeve of his coat, William said, "You can't fish for striped bass anymore; they're protected. And fishing for tuna isn't worth the trouble here. That doesn't leave much to catch, let alone survive on."

Anne's curiosity grew. "What about your family? Your wife, your children?"

Jouris's face fell, and the humor in his eyes dimmed. He glanced briefly at his empty glass before placing it gently on the table. He seemed to struggle for the words, and seeing this, William answered,

"His wife...Valerie,"

"I called her Val." Jouris nodded, thanking William, before continuing, "She passed away five years ago. Cancer took her... ate her down to the bone."

His voice grew quieter, rougher. "I had a son, Peter. He attended school and later moved to New York City to pursue a career as a lawyer. He... got stabbed to death trying to break up a fight on the subway. Over ten dollars."

Silence enveloped the room as the weight of his words sank in. Anne glanced at Jack, her eyes wide, yet neither knew what to say.

Jack cleared his throat, hesitating a moment. "Why did you stick around here, Jouris? Given everything that's happened?"

Jouris looked up, his expression hard but not lacking pride.

"Too stubborn to leave, I guess. This land's been in my family for over two hundred years. When the fishing went bad, I became a scuba diver. There are plenty of wrecks around Long Island Sound and the South Shore. I became a guide, taking tourists to dive the Lexington… a 220-foot-long side-wheel steamer that caught fire in 1840 and sank near the Eaton's Neck lighthouse off Huntington. It pays the bills."

BAM!

A sudden blast of wind struck the dining room window, and all of them jumped. Just as quickly, the wind died down, and Jouris continued.

"As far back as I can recall, the Van Haalans have been the guardians and protectors of this place. We owe it all to JESU. They helped us safeguard this house and keep it hidden from those who shouldn't know about it. I'm not JESU like you, Anne, and I wasn't told much… maybe for my own protection… but my father did mention that one day, someone might come along and make the house visible again. I always figured it'd be Mark Desmond."

He paused, looking intently at Anne. "By the way, what's happened to Mark?"

Anne winced, her face tightening. "He's dead."

Jouris nodded solemnly but held back from asking more.

After a long silence, Jack interjected, his voice filled with curiosity. "William, Ronkonkoma is a Native American word, isn't it?"

William nodded, and Jack asked, "What does it mean?"

"Ah," William said, his voice lifting as if pleased to change the subject.

"Ronkonkoma means 'boundary fishing place.' The Native Americans, including my tribe, the Setalcotts, were here long before the Dutch arrived in the 17th century. They transferred the land, though the Native Americans had a different understanding of ownership. For us, the land is sacred; it wasn't something to be owned."

A long silence filled the room before Jouris added, "You know, I often see Louis down by the lake shore."

Jack leaned forward, listening intently. "You saw him at the lake?"

Jouris and William's expressions darkened.

"That's why we're here tonight," Jouris said. "The lake is beautiful, no doubt, but it has a dark history. Myths and legends swirl around it like smoke from a campfire."

William's voice dropped to a reverent hush as he leaned closer. "Some people say it's cursed."

"It's a kettle lake formed during the last ice age," Jouris stated.

"No one really knows how deep it is, " William murmured. "Setalcott legends say it never gives up the bodies of those who die in it."

Jouris hesitated, glancing cautiously toward the window, toward the lake itself.

"I've witnessed strange occurrences there… whirlpools that shouldn't exist in a lake."

"I've also heard worse tales," William added, "Like abandoned canoes drifting in the center. The lake isn't what it appears."

He paused, then glanced at Jouris before warning, "I'd advise watching over Louis and David closely."

Jack shifted nervously in his chair as Jouris elaborated.

"There are stories… 1961, I think, a young boy, something happened, and he ended up in the Kings Park psychiatric ward: 1974, the DeFeo murders, the Amityville Horror. In my opinion, they all tie into this place in some way. This land…it's got a way of keeping secrets."

The house was still, for what felt like the first time since their arrival. No creaks, no groans. Jouris went to the kitchen, grabbed more glasses, and poured everyone a shot of whiskey. Jack pretended to sip his, not wanting to reveal his abstinence, fearing it might be seen as weakness. Jouris downed his in a single swallow, his face hardening to stone.

"This lake wears a shroud, a veil of darkness, like the sinister reflection of whatever cloaks this house from the eyes of those who hunt you. All I'm saying is… be careful."

***

Pre-Colonial Period
End of Day 2 of the Sacred Fire Trials
Shores of Lake Ronkonkoma, NY

Quanon sat shivering atop the rock, soaked clothes clinging to his skin as a chilly breeze whipped across the lake's surface. His muscles ached from a day's labor: lifting beams, securing ropes, and rebuilding the footbridges linking the islets of the Village of the Drowned Meadows. Salt from tidal pools still crusted his skin, sand ground painfully between his toes, and every muscle begged for rest. Yet, he remained motionless, still as the stone beneath him, clutching his branch tightly in one hand. Hunger gnawed at his empty stomach, but he forced it aside.

Unlike the others, his branch bore no notches. He hadn't broken his silence or faltered. That was the one thing he could hold onto.

The night was pitch black… no stars or moon to soften the ink-like sky… only darkness pressing down on him, as if the heavens sought to crush him. He tried to commune with the Great Spirit as instructed, but exhaustion dragged his eyelids down. His body screamed for warmth and food, but he could not move. He would not move.

His thoughts slipped in restless dreams, fleeting glimpses of faces, and his father's stern gaze. Suddenly, a sound cut through the silence.

A splash. Far off, faint, but real.

Quanon's eyes snapped open. At first, he thought it a trick of the dark, but another splash came, closer this time. His fingers clenched the branch, bark biting into his palm. The lake's once glassy surface rippled as something stirred beneath.

The wind abruptly ceased, plunging the world into eerie stillness broken only by the slow, wet sloshing of something surfacing. Each splash beat a rhythm against the shore… a steady, deliberate sound whispering of unseen things dragging themselves from the depths.

Quanon's heart raced, his breath shallow. Every instinct screamed at him to run. He swallowed hard, pushing the rising panic down. OohQua's voice whispered in his mind: *Sometimes you don't run because you're being hunted. Sometimes, you run because you're terrified.*

His jaw locked tight. Fear would not claim him. Not tonight. Not here.

The splashes stopped. Silence returned, heavier than before. No mosquitoes buzzed in his ear, no frogs croaked. Only the suffocating silence broken by the *drip... drip... drip* of water on the stones.

Then came the sound..

Thump.

A heavy beat pulsed through the earth beneath him, like a war buried in the ground.

Thump.

It was closer this time, steady, relentless. The rock itself seemed to vibrate beneath him.

His mind raced back to OohQua's warnings and the stories he had dismissed as superstition; things that rose from the lake, drawn to those foolish enough to linger after dark. But where OohQua had run, Quanon would not.

Thump.

It was behind him now.

He could feel it, standing just beyond the rock. The air grew colder, the stench of damp decay wafting toward him.

Quanon's pulse raced. Sweat turned to ice along his spine. He wanted to turn and face it, but the elders had commanded: remain still, commune with the Great Spirit, no matter what.

Silence.

He could feel it there. Breathing. Watching.

Don't move. Don't move.

His hands shook, fingers biting deeper into the branch's bark. His father's voice echoed in his mind: *Do not shame the tribe. Do not run.*

Quanon inhaled deeply, his lungs burning as whatever was behind him pressed closer. He heard water drip from its body and the faint shifting of sand as it moved. Clenching his teeth, he refused to surrender to the terror clawing at his chest.

Then... a faint, cool breath brushed against the back of his neck.

***

The train screeched as it pulled into Lake Ronkonkoma station, its windows fogged with condensation. Charles "Chuck" Daniels groaned, rubbing his eyes. His back ached from hours of shoveling snow, a familiar, almost comforting pain that reminded him that, though overweight and older, he could still keep up with the younger guys on his crew.

He rubbed a hand over his balding head, muttering, "Old man's still got it," before stepping onto the platform. A sharp gust of icy wind whipped snow into his face.

The station was nearly empty, only a few scattered commuters braving the storm. Chuck pulled his heavy wool coat tighter, scanning the lot until he spotted the familiar silhouette of Claire's silver Buick Century. Its headlights flashed as she waved from inside.

Claire rolled down the window, tugging her scarf tight. "Hey, Chuck! Over here!" The snow and wind nearly drowned out her voice, but she always shouted twice, once for Chuck and once to fight the weather.

Chuck trudged to the car, snow crunching under his boots. He opened the door to a blast of warmth and sank into the passenger seat with a tired grunt.

"Sorry I'm late," he said, pulling off his red ski hat and shaking snow from his shoulders. "Shift ran longer than I expected."

"Figured as much," Claire said with a knowing smile. Her graying brown hair was tucked neatly inside her jacket, her glasses fogging as she turned down the heater. "How bad is it?"

"It's bad," Chuck said wearily, managing a tired laugh. "We've piled so much snow, we're running out of places to put it. This afternoon, we started dumping it into the Hudson and East Rivers."

Claire carefully exited the slick parking lot. The windshield wipers beat a frantic rhythm against the heavy snowfall. "WOW! I guess that makes sense. Where else would you put it?"

"You wouldn't believe it. The storm's relentless." Chuck rubbed his balding head, grimacing at the gray sky. "Look at the color of this snow. Never seen anything like it... not even in Minnesota."

Claire glanced at the snowbanks lining the road. The snow bore a strange brownish-red hue, streaked with rustlike veins.

"Yeah, I noticed it earlier," she said, brow furrowed. "You know me... always checking the weather app every five minutes, but it's definitely weird."

"Could be pollution," Chuck muttered. "Or maybe it's related to all this snow we've been having. It's strange seeing snow this color."

The storm pressed cold and relentless, its icy breath fogging the windows. Finally, Claire broke the silence.

"I stopped at the grocery store today," she said, frustration in her tone.

"How'd that go?"

"Not great." She sighed, eyes flicking the windshield. "The produce aisle was nearly bare. One of the staff said the cold wiped out Florida's citrus crop, and hammered the lettuce in California and Arizona."

"Really? Damn, that's bad." Chuck shook his head. "Not just us, the weather's haywire everywhere."

Claire nodded, turning into the driveway. As they parked, Chuck spotted the grocery bags in the back seat and quickly unbuckled.

"Let me grab those."

They carried the bags inside, greeted by the faint aroma of dinner.

"I started dinner before I left to pick you up. Hope stew's okay. You know me, I always try to have something ready. Keeps the house smelling homey, too."

Claire began unpacking the groceries, handing Chuck a can of soup to place in the pantry.

"That's great. It's a stick-to-your-ribs kind of dinner... perfect for a cold winter night."

"Look at this." Claire held up a twenty-dollar bill. "Got it as change, check out the date."

Chuck squinted. "1961? That's old. The Treasurer is Elizabeth Rudel Smith."

"Weird, right? I've never seen one that old." Claire said, stirring the pot.

Chuck grinned. "Elizabeth, huh? Reminds me of a grade-school crush. Strawberry-blonde ponytail; I always thought that was neat. She became a tennis pro."

Claire rolled her eyes, laughing. "You and your stories. How many Elizabeths have you ever known?"

"Only one, but she was unforgettable," Chuck said. "You'd have liked her. Just as feisty as you."

"Maybe in another life," Claire quipped, passing him a bag of apples, which he promptly stuffed in the fridge.

Chuck kicked off his boots, stretched his sore legs, and wandered over to the window. He gazed out at the frozen lake, a view he hadn't seen since moving to Lake Ronkonkoma twenty-five years ago.

"You know what, Claire?" he said with a grin. "I think I'll try ice fishing again. Haven't done it in ages, but that lake's calling me."

Claire raised an eyebrow. "Ice fishing? In this? Chuck, it's freezing."

"Freezing?" He laughed. "I'm from Minnesota, this is nothing. I used to ice fish as a kid. We had a monster fish, which we called Big Mo; the biggest catch of my life. It's time to catch his cousin."

"Chuck, I'm serious," Claire said, worry in her tone. "This cold isn't normal, not even for you."

"I'll be fine." He waved her off. "Done it plenty of times. All I need is a thermos full of black coffee and my old gear. Now, did I leave the poles in the garage or the basement?"

Claire sighed, realizing she wouldn't change his mind. "Fine. Just promise me you'll be careful. And if you come home with frostbite, you'll never hear the end of it."

"Deal." He hugged her quickly. "Keep your phone charged. When I land Big Mo's cousin, you'll be blowing up Facebook with the photos."

***

Chuck tugged his collar tight, his breath puffing in quick bursts. "Gotta keep the cold out, or the cold wins." He adjusted his faded wool cap, already damp from snow melting off it, and jammed the drill into the ice. The vibration shot up his arms as the bit burrowed deeper. Each turn of the crank snapped sharply, like breaking a thick branch across his knee, the sound echoing over the stark, frozen lake. He leaned in, forcing the bit down further, surprised by the ice's thickness.

His breath clouded, then quickly vanished with the wind.

At last, the drill punched through with a loud crunch. Black water bubbled to the surface. Chuck set the drill aside, knelt, and skimmed the remaining ice from the hole. His headlamp cut the dark water, where for a second he thought he saw a shadow moving beneath. Confident he'd found the right spot, he set his line.

Even through thick gloves, his fingers numbed. He shivered, wrapping a blanket tightly around himself, but the beastly wind sliced through his layers, chilling his sensitive teeth and causing him to flinch.

"God, it's freezing," he muttered, unscrewing the thermos lid. A long sip of coffee offered little comfort; the frigid air stole its warmth almost instantly.

Chuck remembered his childhood in Minnesota and lifted his cup in a shaky toast.

"Cheers to you, Dad! I remember sitting on icy lakes, drilling holes, and waiting for the fish to bite."

He shivered, teeth clattering. "It was cold then, but nothing like this."

This cold felt ancient, primeval, like the glaciers that carved Long Island and left behind this lake when they receded, as a frozen scar.

He scanned the bleak expanse of Lake Ronkonkoma, a sheet of ice stretching in every direction. It wasn't just cold. It was alien. Unforgiving.

Maybe Claire was right. Maybe it's too cold, even for me.

His hand ruffled the thin hair beneath his cap. He chuckled, shaking his head. "Nah, I've been through worse."

He settled back into his chair until the line twitched. A tug, his heart jumped, a slow smile spreading across his face. He braced against the wind, reeling carefully. The line pulled taut, putting up a fight… but it was nothing like the day Big Mo nearly snapped his pole in half.

With one last pull, he hauled the fish onto the ice.

It wasn't Big Mo. Hell, not even close. Just a small catch, flopping weakly, its scales shimmering like silver in his headlamp.

Chuck grinned, savoring the moment, then brushed the fish back into the hole before it froze solid.

The hours dragged, the wind howling across the lake. Chuck sat hunched, eyes heavy, his cold coffee and whiskey no match for the chill.

He checked his watch, debating if it was time to call it a night… when something moved on the ice.

A figure, distant but drifting closer.

Chuck stood, squinting, tears stinging from the biting wind. "Hey!" he shouted. His voice echoed, but the howling gusts quickly swallowed it whole.

No response. No sign of stopping. The figure glided unnaturally over the ice.

As the shape neared, Chuck made out more details:

A woman, slender, taller than most, no older than her twenties. She wore a sleeveless white dress that fluttered faintly in the wind, the fabric clinging to skin so pale it seemed translucent.

A blood-red belt cinched her waist, a splash of color against the ghostly white of her gown. Fascination stirred in him, warring with a growing sense of dread.

Chuck's mouth went dry. Only now did he see how perfectly she blended into the icy landscape… as if she belonged to it.

"Miss?" he called again, voice quivering, uncertain what he was witnessing.

How much whiskey have I had?

The figure stopped just a few feet away, hovering motionless across from the hole he had drilled. Her long, jet-black hair swirled like smoke, a dark halo hauntingly contrasting with her pale complexion.

A thin veil shrouded her face… leaving only her eyes visible: piercing violet, dark, unblinking… staring straight through him.

Chuck gulped, a chill crawling down his spine unrelated to the cold.

"You… you alright? How can you be out here in that outfit? You'll freeze."

Silence.

He stepped forward cautiously. "Do you need a hand? I can help you get off the lake. It's way too cold out here."

Coffee and whiskey help this poor girl feel warmer, he thought, though the instinct to offer help lingered.

Still, she said nothing, her violent gaze locked on him with the patience of a predator. His heart pounded. A strange mix of fear and fascination swirled inside. Despite the eerie chill, he couldn't help but think she was beautiful… otherworldly, even.

But something was very wrong.

He drew a sharp breath, inching closer. "Miss…?"

Without warning, she lifted her hands, seized the veil, and yanked it back in one swift, unnerving motion. Chuck staggered. Her features were grotesque, like a rotting corpse, with hollow, sunken eyes. Blue, mottled skin sagged from her cheeks, and her mouth twisted into a predatory grin.

Before Chuck could react, she leaned in and exhaled.

A bitter, freezing gust exploded from her mouth, striking him like a physical blow.

The cold shot through his chest, locking his lungs, and his body went rigid.

The cold wrapped around him like invisible shackles, stiffening every limb until even blinking felt impossible.

The world slowed to a crawl.

Suddenly, the lake erupted. Black water bubbled and churned, the surface splitting open as something surged upward.

A monstrous, dark hand… too large and deformed to be human… burst from the depths, seizing his leg with crushing force.

Chuck couldn't scream or fight. The ice beneath him groaned, then splintered.

Within seconds, he was dragged into the cold, dark water, vanishing beneath the surface.

As darkness enveloped him, the final thing he saw was the veiled figure fading into the night, leaving only the whisper of her icy breath lingering on the wind.

CHAPTER 3

Summer 1961
Camp Wauwepex, Wading River, NY

No moonlight pierced the sky, and the roaring bonfire did little to push back the thick, stifling darkness over Deep Pond. Mary and Billy Clifford Sr. were on their way home, and with Visitors' Day over, Lyle wished he could have gone with them. The flames danced, casting warped shadows like carnival mirrors, making the boys look larger and more menacing.

Lyle's hands trembled in his pockets, sweat slicking his palms despite the cool night air. The slow drumbeat thudded against his chest, each strike rattling through his ribs. He hated this: the ceremony, the solemn faces, and the firelight that created eyes in the darkness. But most of all, he feared being left behind.

He glanced up at Billy, tall, shoulders squared, calm as ever. Billy had asked his friends not to pick him, and Lyle understood why. Billy was his shield, the only one who made the night bearable. He needed him here, now more than ever.

The Chief's voice rang out, deep and solemn.

"Scouts, we are the Order of the Flaming Spear, Scouting's honor society."

He spoke of character and the Scout Oath, but Lyle barely heard him over the pounding heartbeat in his chest. His eyes darted to the tree line, where firelight dared not reach. Something lurked there… waiting.

The first name called was Brian Dawkins. Lyle watched the boy from another troop vanish into the darkness beyond the fire. His stomach twisted at the thought of Billy going next. He refused to think about it. Billy had begged not to be picked; they wouldn't choose him.

But then, the Chief and his assistants moved closer. Lyle's heart pounded faster. The drumbeat grew louder, nearly drowning out the crackling fire. They were closing in on Troop 311. Their troop.

Though his pockets felt warm, his palms felt icy. He told himself again: Billy wasn't going anywhere. His brother couldn't be chosen.

The assistants scanned the row, eyes weighing each scout like a judge at sentencing. Lyle froze, barely breathing, silently pleading that they would pass over Billy.

But then, like a punch to the gut, the words came.

"Billy Clifford!"

Lyle's stomach knotted. For a moment, the world stopped. He looked at Billy, searching for a sign that it was a mistake, but his brother only shook his head in frustration.

Lyle saw it in his eyes: Billy hadn't wanted this. He had begged not to be chosen. But it didn't matter now.

Snickers rippled through the troop. One scout hissed,

"*Look at Lyle… the pile… of shit*! I think he's gonna cry!"

It was a joke to them. Hot anger surged; he wanted to yell, to tell them to stop, but that would only draw more attention. Something Billy always shielded him from.

Billy glanced at him, and for the first time, Lyle saw something rare in his brother's eyes: pure dread.

"I didn't want this," Billy whispered. But it didn't matter what Billy wanted.

The thumping in Lyle's ears drowned out the drumbeat. The thought of facing the night without Billy churned his stomach. But what could he do? He was just a kid. Billy had been picked. Nothing could change that now.

Billy leaned in closer, voice soft but firm, trying to sound reassuring.

"It's okay, Lyle. You'll be fine."

But Lyle didn't believe it. The thought of being without Billy terrified him. His brother had always kept him safe. Now, Billy was being led into the dark, leaving him behind.

"Go on, Billy," Lyle whispered, though every part of him wanted to scream for Billy to stay.

"I'll be okay."

But he knew he wouldn't. Not really. He tried to look brave, to show Billy he could handle it, but he wasn't. Small and scared, he stood in the firelight, shadows twisting around him, watching his brother, the one person who always made everything okay, disappear.

The Chief raised his arms, his voice booming across the field.

"You have been chosen for your strength, loyalty, and spirit of service."

Lyle swallowed hard as Billy walked toward the center of the circle. His brother's steps dragged, as if every part of him wanted to turn back, but couldn't. Billy once over his shoulder, eyes locking with Lyle's. Concern shadowed his face, mirroring the anxiety twisting Lyle's gut.

The ceremony dragged on, but Lyle barely noticed. His eyes stayed fixed on Billy, watching his brother vanish into the same darkness that swallowed Brian Dawkins.

Lyle fought back tears, knowing they would only encourage his tormentors.

When the troop dispersed and headed back to camp, Lyle lingered. More alone than ever, he stood in the wavering glow of the fire. Billy was gone, and he wasn't okay. Truthfully, he wasn't sure he could make it through the night.

***

Late February
Safehouse at Lake Ronkonkoma, NY

Jack stood at the edge of the coop, staring at the lifeless heap of feathers. He wrapped the ragged wool scarf, riddled with moth-eaten holes, tight around his ears, trying to fend off the biting wind that stung his skin like a swarm of jellyfish.

The cold settled deep in his chest, heavier than the wind on his face. Every chicken lay still, necks bent at impossible angles. The brutal weather had lasted for weeks, but this felt different. It was personal.

He swallowed hard, his breath clouding in the freezing air as he tried to process the loss.

Next to him, Jouris stood with a furrowed brow, worry etched into every line on his face.

"The eggs... the meat... we can't afford this right now," he said, voice heavy with concern.

Jack barely heard him, his mind on the boys. David and Louis were already wrestling with enough changes, and now, with their fragile diets, this loss felt like a gut punch… sharp, sudden, and impossible to ignore.

"They won't eat, Jouris. Not without the food they're used to," Jack said, his voice thick with frustration and fear.

"David... he barely eats anything. Chicken nuggets and fries, nothing else. Louis is just as bad."

Jouris nodded slowly, folding his arms.

"Jack, I've seen how they cling to routines and how changes throw them off. It's not just hunger. I don't pretend to understand all the challenges, but I want to help however I can."

"When they're hungry enough, they'll eat what's there. People adjust. We'll get through this," Jouris added gently, careful not to dismiss the deeper struggle.

Jack exhaled, shaking his head.

Not them.

He tried to explain, though he wasn't sure Jouris understood. How could he?

"It's their autism, not stubbornness or pickiness. A need for order and consistency. Not something fixed by time or hunger. They impose limits on themselves, and if we push too hard..."

Jack's voice faltered, memories of David's meltdowns rushing through his head. A heavy wave of sadness washed over him, thinking of his boys trapped in their anxieties.

Jouris's gaze softened.

"I see how much you care. We'll figure this out, you, me, and Anne, together."

Jack looked up, eyes scanning the thick, gray clouds. His breath came in ragged puffs.

"Feels like snow is coming again."

Jouris squinted at the horizon, nodding.

"A blizzard's definitely coming, and it won't be the last. Roads are already impassable. I heard on the radio this morning that fuel shortages are widespread. People are trapped in their homes, but we've dealt with worse, haven't we?"

Jack shivered, dread heavier than the cold.

"Where are we going to put it all? Another storm... piles around the house are already up to my waist. I'll have to shovel it into the woods again."

"You're lucky you have the fireplace," Jouris said, though Jack noticed the worried glance his friend cast at the dwindling woodpile. It was dangerously low.

The winters had been harsh before, but this one... it felt like something was punishing them.

Jack wondered if Lucius had a hand in it, though he had no way of knowing.

"You'll stay with us if you run out of heating oil," Jack said firmly.

"We've got room. It's not much, but at least we'll have heat."

Jouris gave a thin smile. Jack could see him measuring the situation, recognizing how desperate things had become.

"Thanks, Jack. I might take you up on that."

Jouris looked down at the chickens again. Jack saw the calculation in his mind about the impact of losing fresh food.

They had canned supplies, but how long before choices neither of them wanted had to be made?

"This winter… I've never seen anything like it," Jouris muttered.

"The President says it's from that volcanic eruption in Barbados a few months ago. Ash clouds cooling the atmosphere."

Jack only half-listened, his thoughts spiraling around the boys, the woodpile, and the approaching storm that would bury them deeper in isolation.

How much longer could they last? Weeks? A month?

Jouris's voice pulled him back.

"One of the neighbors across the lake went ice fishing. He never came back. The lake's dangerous, even when it looks frozen solid."

Jack nodded grimly, another threat in an already dangerous world.

"I'll keep the boys away. Not that they could get near it anyway. I guess that's a silver lining to all this snow."

They stood silently as snow began to fall quietly.

Jack's mind swirled with everything beyond his control: the snow, the cold, the chickens, and the gnawing fear that time was running out. The weight pressed harder than ever.

Glancing at Jouris, he wondered: *he can help us fight the elements and survive, but what if it wasn't enough?*

"I'm going back inside," Jack said, voice barely above a whisper.

"We need to decide what to do. The boys… they need to eat."

Jouris clapped him on the shoulder, firm and kind.

"We'll figure something out, Jack. We have to. Together."

Jack forced a smile, though his heart wasn't in it.

"You remind me of my dad. Ever the optimist."

Jouris nodded, breath steaming in the cold.

"Together."

Holding out his hand, Jack watched the snow collect and slowly melt in his palm. Around them hung the deceptive calm before the storm, the wind whispering through skeletal branches and the bitter chill seeping into his bones. He glanced once more at the dwindling wood supply, knowing they couldn't survive on hope alone.

Time itself seemed suspended, bracing for the storm that was to come.

***

Pre-Colonial Period
Setalcott Village
Shores of Lake Ronkonkoma, NY
3 Sunrises After the Ceremony
Started

The lake did not forget. Long before Louis stood at its shore, it whispered to Quanon and followed him back.

The wind whispered its first warning long before Quanon's return. The day began mild, a soft breeze carrying the salty scent of the sea.

As the morning wore on, the wind shifted, cooler air creeping in. It grew restless, like an older man stirred from a deep slumber.

Chief Powwan stood outside his longhouse, weathered eyes fixed on the distant forest path. His gray braids whipped in the chilly air.

Quanon had been gone two days, the allotted time for the trials at Lake Ronkonkoma.

Powwan had endured the same trials in his youth, as had his father before him. They tested not only the body but the spirit, the very essence of a man. He knew his son would return changed. He had not expected how deeply.

From the tree line, Quanon appeared.

Powwan's heart tightened with anticipation. His son was back.

But as Quanon drew near, relief turned to unease.

His posture was unnaturally stiff, his steps slow and deliberate. His arms hung rigidly at his sides, one clutching the discipline branch, pristine and unmarked.

As he approached, the wind whipped harder, gusts blowing dried flakes of mud from his clothes. It felt as if the land itself recoiled from him.

"Where are your escorts?" Powwan called over the rising wind.

Quanon didn't answer. He stopped before his father, expression blank, his eyes dull. Slowly, he raised the branch. It bore no notches. He had not failed.

The tribe gathered, drawn by his return. Murmurs spread of his success, strength, and destiny as a leader.

Powwan heard them but ignored the words. His gaze remained fixed on his son and the hollow emptiness behind his eyes.

Quanon's face, once ablaze with fire and life, had become a mask.

The boy who left for the trials was gone, replaced by something else.

Powwan had seen warriors return from battle haunted, but this was different. Deeper. Darker.

"The ordeal is over, my son," Powwan said, placing a proud hand on Quanon's shoulder.

The deerskin tunic, damp from the tidal pools, felt cold and clammy beneath his fingers.

"You need not remain silent any longer."

Quanon's eyes shifted from the hand to his father's face.

His chapped lips parted, but the voice that emerged sounded stolen.

"Yes, Father."

Nothing more. No warmth, no relief, no emotion. Just hollow words.

Powwan watched helplessly as Quanon turned away, walking stiffly toward his wigwam.

The crowd dispersed slowly, their excitement giving way to unease.

Powwan ignored the murmurs, focusing on his son's unsettling demeanor.

Something had happened… something beyond the trials.

He had expected a man tempered by the Great Spirit. Instead, he saw a man hollowed out, like a tree carved into a canoe.

The wind howled as dark clouds devoured the sun's last light. Gloom cloaked the village.

Rain began to fall, soft at first, then relentless. Powwan knew the storm would be fierce.

The weather mirrored his dread: something had followed Quanon back from Ronkonkoma.

Later that day, rain hammered the longhouse roof as Powwan sat in a circle with the elders.

Their faces were solemn; eyes glimmering in the firelight while the storm raged outside.

"Something is wrong with the boy," Wepankai, eldest among them, said in a hushed tone.

"He returns without failure, but his spirit… it is absent."

Powwan stared into the flames, the flickering light offering no comfort.

"He completed the trials," he whispered, more to himself than the elders.

"No notches, no failures."

"Yet the boy who left is not the man who has returned," Wepankai said.

"His eyes are empty, as if his soul had been stripped away."

The other elders nodded, worry etched deep in their faces.

Powwan's jaw tightened.

Had he felt it too —that emptiness? That unease?

His son survived the trials… but at what cost?

What had he faced on the shores of Lake Ronkonkoma? What had the water revealed?

"Could it be the lake?" another elder, Pansook, asked, voice trembling.

"The old stories. The legends of what lies beneath…"

Powwan's heart sank. The lake was sacred, but feared.

Stories told of things rising from the depths, spirits luring men to their doom.

He had dismissed them as tales to keep children in line. But now.

"I don't know," Powwan admitted, voice weighted with dread.

"But something has changed him."

"What did he face out there?" Wepankai pressed, the question lingering like smoke from their pipes.

Powwan closed his eyes, picturing the boy who had left.

Quanon had been strong, determined, and full of life.

Respectful. Wise beyond his years.

A son any Chief would be proud of.

But now? A shell, going through the motions of life, yet absent from it.

"I fear the lake has taken part of him," Powwan whispered.

The wind howled louder, as if agreeing with his darkest fear.

"And I don't know if we can bring back what lies beneath its waters."

Rain pounded harder on the roof, drowning out their voices.

Yet, in the silence between the thunder and wind, Powwan couldn't shake the feeling that something worse was coming: something far more demanding than any trial.

Centuries later, the same shadow would reach again… for God's prophet…

✳✳✳

Late February
Safehouse at Lake Ronkonkoma, NY

Louis tossed and turned beneath the sheets, thoughts bombarding him too fast to follow. The bed creaked with every shift, springs groaning under his weight. His mind churned with memories and worries while the persistent tick-tock of the wall clock tapped in his ears. Once, that steady rhythm might have comforted him. Now it was hypnotic, as if time, and maybe his sanity, was slipping away inch by inch.

His small, suffocating room overlooked the vast, dark lake. Clouds swallowed the moonlight, but shadows still reached into the corners. The dull paint, cold and sterile, felt more like a doctor's office than a home. Somewhere behind the walls came a faint, persistent rapping, muffled yet insistent… like something or someone was trapped inside. Louis couldn't tell if the wall kept him safe or caged him with whatever lay behind it.

He tugged at his sweat-soaked T-shirt and glanced at the clock. It was past midnight. The clock ticked again, but no tock followed. The silence between seconds felt louder than the sound, fraying his nerves further.

Then came the vibration. Beneath the mattress, his cell phone rattled softly at first, then intensified, spiking his pulse. He didn't want to answer. He knew who was calling. He knew what waited on the other end. The phone was no longer just a device. It was a chain binding him to something inescapable. He wanted to hurl it out the window, watch it shatter, but fear held him back.

The screen glowed faintly beneath the mattress before the vibration ceased. Static filled his ears as the phone connected… without him touching it.

We've come for you, Louis…

The whisper slithered through the static, chilling his spine. His heart pounded, and a fresh wave of sweat broke out on his skin. They were coming again. At first, the visits had seemed comforting… familiar family faces. Now they only brought dread. Night after night, ghostly versions of his aunts appeared outside his second-floor window. But these weren't the women he'd known; not the loving relatives of his childhood. They were the undead.

The floorboards creaked as Louis rolled out of bed, knees scraping the cold wood as he crawled toward the window. There they waited: Aunt Emma, Aunt Michelle, and Aunt Lynne. Hovering just beyond the glass, their white gowns shimmered unnaturally. What once comforted him now felt sinister. Their coal-black eyes stared un-blinking, devoid of warmth or mercy. Their lips parted to reveal pointed teeth lurking behind. Their words hissed like serpents.

Aunt Emma's long, pale fingers tapped softly on the glass.

It's so cold outside. Why won't you let us in, Louis?

Michelle's mouth twisted into a sneer, jagged teeth exposed. Her voice rasped as if ruined by decades of smoking.

We only want to talk… to your father…

Then Lynne, always the leader, spoke, her voice echoing from every direction.

You'll let us in eventually.

Louis clutched his head, pressing his temples as if a squeeze could force the voices away. A cold ache crawled behind his eyes, constant and stinging. His breath fogged the windowpane as he stared into their dead, unblinking eyes. The spiritual teachers who once guided him, offering forgiveness, joy, and God's love, were gone. That connection was severed, maybe forever.

Defenseless, he wondered:

Why are they gone?

The question echoed again and again.

Why are they gone? Why are they gone?

He squeezed his head tighter, trying to block the whispering voices.

Had losing them made him a target? Were his aunts here because of it?

The tapping grew louder, more insistent, keeping time with his pounding heart. Louis shook his head violently, eyes clamped shut, willing the visions away. His father said it was only his imagination. But the cold in the room, the slithering whispers, the teeth and nails, the overwhelming dread… those felt real enough.

"G-Go away," he whispered, voice trembling.

The silence that followed was more terrifying than any sound.

***

John, Jacob Jingle Heimer Schmidt…

The campfire song drifted through the unusually cool night air. The moon and stars cast a pale light over the wooden platform. The tent flap shifted, and a figure entered.

Billy Clifford had returned.

He sat on the edge of his cot, eyes fixed on the floor, struggling to focus. Everything felt blurry and distant, as if he were somewhere else entirely. Across from him, Lyle lay still in his bunk, facing the canvas wall, wrapped tightly in his sleeping bag. His small shoulders trembled with muffled sobs.

Usually, Billy would have told him to turn around, maybe teased him until he did. Tonight, he couldn't find the strength. His blistered hands shook; his thoughts swirled in a fog, every breath felt heavy, as if he bore an invisible burden.

Billy tried to piece together what had happened, but the memory felt submerged, cold, dark, numbing, and relentless…like the waters of Lake Ronkonkoma. He had gone to clean the beach and paint the restrooms. Then came the whistle. Lifeguards cleared the swimming area. Someone had gone under, and Billy jumped into action. He didn't know why; instinct, maybe.

The water was freezing, far colder than it should be in summer. Colder than anything he'd ever known, even falling into Searingtown Pond in November. But there was more: the lake felt like a magnet, and Billy the metal drawn unwillingly to it.

Lyle's voice broke the silence, stuttering and trembling.

"Did you make it through? Are you… part of the Order now?"

His voice cracked, filled with unshed tears. He still refused to face Billy.

Billy hesitated, throat dry and chest tight. Finally, his voice came flat, almost robotic.

"I was searching for a missing swimmer. Then something tugged at my foot and pulled me under."

Lyle shifted but kept his back turned.

"What do you mean, yanked under? By what?" His voice shook.

"I don't know," Billy muttered, fingers whitening as he gripped the cot's edge. "I couldn't see it. I didn't fight. I just… let it take me down."

He blinked, staring at the tent platform as the memory of sinking surged… the surface drifting away, and the light above slowly fading into darkness.

"It felt like I wanted to go deeper," Billy whispered. "Like I belonged down there."

Lyle trembled in his sleeping bag, his breath shallow and uneven. Billy's words spilled out… relentless, raw.

"Ever since then, I haven't felt right."

Lyle bit his lip, his voice cracking with fear.

"What happened to the swimmer?"

Billy's gaze stayed on the floor. His voice was cold, detached, flat, and distant.

"We never found him. It was like the lake swallowed him. Just… gone."

He didn't want to admit it, but deep down, Billy wondered if the lake was claiming him, too.

Lyle finally turned, his face streaked with tears, his left eye bruised and swollen from a fight endured alone. Billy barely noticed. Normally, it would have enraged him. Now he felt only numb.

"So… you didn't make it through?" Lyle asked, barely above a whisper, dread clinging to every word.

Billy swallowed hard, words failing him. He didn't know if he had made it through, or if he was still himself. The lake's pull hadn't released him. He could still feel it, hear it, taste it… dragging him deeper.

"I don't know," Billy finally replied, his voice hollow. "I went into the lake and came out. But I don't think it's me."

Lyle's eyes widened in fear.

"You're scaring me, Billy."

Billy stood. The tent felt too small, and the air too heavy. He needed out.

"I can still hear them, Lyle. Voices from the lake. They want more. They're calling me."

Lyle sat up, face pale and hands trembling.

"What do you mean? Who's waiting for you?"

Billy stepped off the tent platform into the cool night air, each movement slow and deliberate, as if weighed down.

"I need to lie down. But not here."

The campfire's faint glow flickered in the distance, then vanished into the dark. Behind him, Lyle's voice cracked.

"Billy? Where are you going?"

Billy said nothing, walking steadily toward the lake.

The voices grew louder, clearer. They called him back. He could no longer resist.

He didn't want to.

***

Late February
Safehouse at Lake Ronkonkoma, NY

After days battling relentless rain and melting snow, floodwaters finally breached the basement...

Long shadows spilled from the open basement doors, darkening the fieldstone walls as Jack and Jouris stood ankle-deep in thick brown mud. Jack leaned heavily on his shovel, his breath coming in shallow gasps. They had worked all day, fighting the flood that had ravaged the house.

The sudden warm spell hit hard, unleashing torrential rain and rapidly melting the heavy snowfall that had accumulated earlier in the month. The lake swelled, its waters creeping to the foundation and overflowing into the basement, turning the dirt floor into muck. Jack stared at the nearly two-foot-thick solid stone walls and shook his head.

"I can't understand how the water got through. These walls should have been impenetrable."

Yet, the flood had breached them. Jouris knelt beside him, his hands covered in filth as he tugged on something half-buried in the mud.

"Look at this," he said, pulling something free with a wet pop.

Jack moved closer, watching droplets of mud fall from Jouris's fingertips. In his hand lay a small object: a flint arrowhead.

"What's an arrowhead doing down here?" Jack asked, brow furrowing.

Jouris shrugged, brushing off more mud.

"There's more… pottery, stone tools. It's like the ground swallowed history."

They dug on, unearthing a shell necklace, fragments of pottery, and then something much larger. Jack's shovel struck metal with a jarring clang. He dug faster, nearly out of breath, his heart pounding, until he uncovered a twisted, rusted iron structure.

"What the hell?" he muttered, crouching beside it. "This looks like a cage. How did it get here?"

Sweat beaded on Jouris's brow. His eyes widened.

"That shouldn't be here. Native Americans didn't use iron."

Jack ran his hand over a circular inset in the center of the cage, embossed with a large **P,** engraved into the iron like a brand. Before he could speak, Anne approached from another section of the basement. She tapped a gloved finger to her lip, studying the cage.

"This is European," Anne said, her JESU training clear in her tone. "I'm not sure what the P means, but this is from medieval Eastern Europe. They used cages like this…" She swallowed. "... to prevent the dead from returning."

Jack's stomach twisted.

"You're saying this is… *to trap a vampire?*"

Anne's gaze swept the damp, dim basement.

"It doesn't make sense here, I admit. But that's what it is."

Jack wiped his muddy hands on his pants, pulse racing. The air felt heavy, as if the walls were watching. His skin crawled. That unease had shadowed him all day, and the discovery of that cage made it worse.

"We shouldn't be here," Jack said, voice strained. "Something about this place…"

Anne stepped closer, her voice calm, though Jack caught uncertainty in her eyes.

"Right now, there's nowhere safer. The world outside is worse, Jack. Much worse."

He wanted to believe her. But as they carried another load of mud up the stairs, the sense of being watched clung to him. His boots slipped; he gripped the railing to steady himself. Looking back, he noticed the rear windows sat unusually high… too high to serve any practical purpose.

"Jouris," Jack panted, "the windows, why are they so high off the ground? Did they build the house this way because of floods? Did they know something like this could happen?"

Jouris shook his head, expression grim. "I don't think so. There's never been a flood like this…until now."

As they ascended, the silence behind them felt like the house itself was holding its breath.

***

Outside, night fell swiftly. The air was thick with humidity, a fog hovering low to the ground, a remnant of the massive storm that had dumped historic amounts of rain. The scent of wet earth lingered.

Jack emptied his bucket of foul, stinking mud, then paused at the edge of the woods. He gazed into the darkness at the trees, their leafless branches reaching toward the house like withered fingers. To his left, the lake lay eerily still, reflecting a thin sliver of moonlight between the clouds. It should have felt peaceful, but all Jack felt was dread.

Something on the bark of a nearby tree caught his eye: symbols. Though faint and weathered, the carvings were intricate, unmistakable. Jack reached out, tracing the grooves with his fingers. A chill slid down his spine.

"Beautiful. The woods…" he muttered, eyes roaming as the shadows danced. "Like something out of a horror movie. A tranquil lake…where someone's throat gets slit, and the dark things come out at night to play."

SNAP!

A twig cracked behind him. Jack spun, muscles tense. Nothing. Only more trees, their tangled branches blotting out the moonlight. Still, the sensation prickled across his neck… the weight of unseen eyes.

He gripped the bucket handle tighter, his knuckles whitening, as he tried to shake off the feeling. It clung to him relentlessly.

He stepped deeper into the trees, his eyes scanning the darkness. The symbols were everywhere, etched into nearly every tree he passed.

They seemed to pulse with a subtle energy, evoking an ominous feeling as if they were a warning.

***

In the shadowed woods, another presence stirred… an ancient guardian long tied to the land, its fate, and Jack Aitken…

Jack surveyed the woods, his senses alert, yet he could not detect the presence of an apparition… an ally from earlier times, struggling to help him.

"The symbols…" A quiet yet insistent voice whispered on the wind, rustling the branches. "They warn you, Jack Aitken. The waters of Ronkonkoma are fouled. Polluted. The land is cursed."

The spirit of the Manitou, ancient guardian of the Manahoac tribe, appeared, seated regally atop a powerful horse. Its warning rang out, unheard… by his warrior brother.

Before it could speak again, another voice cut through the night, cold and sharp as a blade. The ground trembled, startling the Manitou. Its horse reared, whinnying in terror at the presence of evil.

"He will never hear you," the voice hissed, mocking.

Bracing for confrontation, the Manitou growled,

"Is that you, Matchitehew?"

Dark laughter echoed through the trees, venomous and cruel.

"No, something far worse. Now that Hell's gates are open, all evil things are unleashed. *I am the worst of the worst.*"

The Manitou glanced toward Jack, who remained oblivious to the exchange, blind to the peril surrounding him. The weight of truth pressed down. The guardian's head drooped, resignation cloaking it like a suffocating shroud. Jack would never hear, no matter how loudly it warned or how fiercely it cried out.

Defeated, the Manitou dissolved into the night, leaving the woods colder in its absence.

***

18th Century
5 Days After Pieter Van Haalan's Disappearance
Near the Shore of Present-Day Lake Ronkonkoma, NY

The moon's cold, spectral blue light filtered through the fog, casting the Van Haalan cottage in an eerie, unnatural glow. The villagers had warned Jakob and Hanneke: if Pieter did not return before midnight, he would no longer be their son. They had always dismissed such talk… until now.

Five days had passed with no sign of Pieter. Five endless days of neighbors whispering about Giengangers, the undead who refused to rest, feasting on the blood of those they once loved. Each hour pushed down on them like a wine press as midnight neared, pulling the family closer to a decision they dreaded.

Jakob paced at the window, rubbing his calloused hands together against the chill. His lip twitched as he whispered,

"God, forgive me."

In his grip was the wooden stake he had carved that morning. The tip honed to a deadly point, its wood stained with the blood of a goat he had sacrificed, binding it with power so it would not fail.

By the hearth, Hanneke sat with swollen eyes, red from weeping. She murmured the same prayer over and over while the wind howled mournfully.

"Saint Michael, protect my child. Bring him back to me."

"If he comes back at midnight," Jakob said softly, his voice heavy with sorrow, "he's no longer our son. He's a monster."

"Don't say that!" Hanneke cried, clutching her rosary as if it were a lifeline. "He's our Pieter. He's just lost. He's still our son."

Jakob's jaw tightened. He said nothing more, his hand clenching the stake as the clock struck midnight. The chime echoed through the cottage like a death knell. And as it faded, the door creaked open.

Pieter stood in the doorway, barely visible through the fog that clung to him like a shroud. His clothes were damp and dirt-stained, his face gaunt and hollow, as though five days had drained years from him. His once bright eyes now gleamed an unnatural black, cold, and malevolent.

"Mother. Father." His voice was rough, broken.

Hanneke gasped, rushing toward him. "Pieter, my boy! You've returned!"

But Jakob's arm shot out, holding her back. His eyes never left Pieter. "Stay back. Look at him, Hanneke. He's not our son."

Pieter twitched, a jerking motion, before stepping forward, stiff and wooden as a marionette. The musty stench of soaked clothing hung heavy in the air.

"Father," he said again, his lips curling into a strange smile that revealed his pointed, sharklike teeth and a tongue black as rot. "Don't you know who I am?"

Jakob's knuckles tightened around the stake. His heart pounded. "You shouldn't have come back, Pieter."

The pressure in the room grew unbearable. Hanneke gasped for breath, her mind refusing what her heart already feared.

"Jakob, please. It's our son. We should help him."

But Jakob didn't move. His eyes narrowed as Pieter took another step. The boy's gaze slid to his sister, Elsje, who squeezed Hanneke's arm, trembling and sobbing. For a moment, a flicker of recognition glimmered in Pieter's eyes… a brief echo of the boy they once knew. Then it vanished like a shadow at daybreak.

"Don't move, Pieter…" Jakob whispered, gripping the stake.

Pieter growled like a feral cat, then lunged suddenly.

A guttural scream ripped through the cottage, shattering the tense silence. Father and son struggled, Jakob straining to drive the stake into Pieter's chest.

But his son's strength was otherworldly, brutal, beyond human. Pieter broke through Jakob's defenses, hurling him violently against the wall.

He tore Elsje from Hanneke's grasp as she pleaded desperately, her voice cracking, "Don't take her!" Then he vanished into the night.

By morning, the villagers gathered… grim and armed. They found Elsje's body at the edge of the woods, pale and drained of blood. Her veins stood out like dark rivers beneath her bone-white skin. The only mercy left was the stake, positioned at her side to ensure she would not rise as a Gienganger.

Their hands trembled as they raised it, cold and final. They prepared to drive it home, but before they could strike, Hanneke flung herself over her daughter's body, weeping.

"She's still here!" she wailed, cradling Elsje's cold, lifeless body. "She's still here!"

Her cries were brushed aside. Hardened by superstition and grim experience, the villagers were resolute.

Jakob pulled Hanneke back as she struggled, scratching at his face with wild desperation.

"She's gone, Hanneke. Let them do what must be done."

Her eyes blazed with grief and fury. "No! She's still our little girl! Keep them from touching her!"

As he dragged her away, Jakob feared Hanneke would never forgive him, or God, for what had been done.

***

Night had fallen, thick fog creeping back around the cottage…

A soft voice floated through the mist, a child's voice, haunting and faint, carried on the wind.

Mama… Mama, it's so cold out here.

Jakob, pale and weary, stood at the window. The villagers had warned him that without the stake through her heart, once bitten, the transformation would begin. He turned to Hanneke, his heart sinking at her fixed gaze on the door, her eyes filled with desperate hope.

"Don't open it," Jakob warned, his voice trembling. "That's not Elsje anymore."

But the voice outside persisted, haunting and sorrowful.

Please, Mama… let me in.

Hanneke, tears streaming down her face, reached for the door.

"It's my baby. She's just cold… She's still out there, Jakob."

Before Jakob could react, she plunged a knife into his side. He gasped, choking on blood, eyes fixed on the woman he could not save.

Hanneke pulled the door open.

Standing there were Elsje and Pieter… both pale, eyes hollow, fangs bared in menacing snarls.

The fog swallowed their screams, muffling them into a cruel lullaby.

By morning, the Van Haalan cottage stood silent. The doors hung wide open, but none dared step inside. The villagers crossed themselves and turned away; they knew the curse had claimed its final victims.

***

February 28th, Pergamon, Satan's Earthly Residence in Present-Day Turkiye

George Aitken rushed through the dim, winding corridors beneath Pergamon, frustration tightening in his chest. The AI program toyed with him, providing cryptic responses while withholding the vital clue he needed to find his brother and nephews. His mind raced, edging toward madness. Tonight's dinner was meant to provide a brief escape, but even now he couldn't silence the gnawing doubt that maybe he was chasing shadows.

He was late, but hoped the evening would clear his head. Candlelight flickered against rough stone walls, shadows dancing with each draft that slithered through the catacombs.

George entered the chamber, momentarily struck by its grandeur: a long wooden table set with marble plates, gleaming gold cutlery, and elegant candelabras. The rich aroma of fine wine mingled with the chamber's mustiness. A tall, skeletal demon waiter with hollow eyes and jittery hands poured drinks with jerky, frantic movements. George barely noticed.

He took his seat at the head of the table, eyes scanning the quiet guests. A surge of relief washed through him. Finally, shadowed faces, silent and still, offering an uneasy calm. But it felt brittle, as if it might shatter with a single breath.

The waiter poured George's daily elixir, a thick, dark liquid he called *ambrosia*. With a weary smile, George raised his glass.

"To perseverance!" he declared, voice steady despite his fatigue. "To uncovering the answers we seek."

He drank deeply, savoring the bitter elixir as it dulled the throb in his head. Setting the goblet down, he gestured to the table.

"Let's enjoy the evening, shall we?" he said, raising an eyebrow. "It's been too long since we've had moments like this."

His words lingered. The waiter poured wine, blood and grapes swirling in untouched goblets. Candlelight cast eerie shadows across the faces of the guests. Their features seemed curiously still, as though they hadn't heard him.

George leaned back, rubbing his temples.

"The AI program has been... frustratingly uncooperative," he muttered. "It knows something. I can sense it. But it's deliberately withholding the crucial piece."

His voice turned more intense and secretive.

"Why? What am I missing?"

He searched the face of the nearest figure for reassurance, but the wide, unblinking eyes offered none. George frowned, pushing aside the unease.

Is it pride? Fear? Or the weight of Lucius's demands pressing in from all sides?"

"I'm treading a fine line," he whispered. "It's a tightrope. I may falter, but I won't fall."

The words reverberated in the chamber.

"I can't afford missteps now. I've burned every bridge behind me."

The candles flickered again, deepening the shadows on the guests' faces. This confessional conversation was rare, especially for a man as vicious as Lord Aitken.

Leaning forward, he squinted, seeking a glimpse of the figure at the far end of the table. Their features were barely visible in the dim light, while the others remained motionless, their faces swallowed by the shifting darkness.

The weight of the silence pressed down on him. His fingers drummed against the table as he took another long sip, the elixir warming him into a tentative smile.

"I suppose you're right," George said, his voice lighter as if convincing himself. "It's just another puzzle. And I'll win once I pry it from the AI. I always do."

The demon waiter scurried away, its eyes darting nervously toward the seated figures as if it, too, sensed the growing awkwardness in the room. George chuckled softly, oblivious to it all.

A draft whispered through the chamber, carrying a strange acrid scent. George paused mid-sentence, nose twitching.

"What is that?" he murmured, looking around. The room suddenly felt stifling, the air thick and still.

Candlelight wavered wildly, casting grotesque silhouettes. George caught a glimpse… a reflection or an illusion? The skin seemed off. Not just pale, but rigid, stretched too tightly across cheekbones, as if…

He blinked, his trembling hands gripping the table.

The truth crashed down on him. These weren't guests. They weren't alive.

They were his family: Josephine, Erin, Kate, and James, the ones he had entombed here nearly two months ago.

Their desiccated bodies, dried by the cave's heat, sat propped up in their chairs, skin peeling and curling from their bones, faces frozen in grotesque death.

The demon waiter hovered nervously, wringing its hands, but George could not look away. Josephine's jaw sagged, teeth bared in a parody of welcome. Her empty eye sockets stared back at him, and his children's mummified forms slumped at the table, their death stares locked on him.

George gave a soft, broken laugh.

"*I'm flying again, Josephine,*" he whispered. Beneath the bravado, a knot of doubt churned in his gut.

"Thanks to your support, I've nothing to fear. Nothing at all."

Darkness enveloped the room, leaving only the scent of decay and the faint flicker of dying candlelight.

STAGE II:
INFESTATION

CHAPTER 1

First Week of March
Nassau Hospital, Mineola, New York

The sunset held the same pea-green hue it had worn for weeks: muted, heavy, like a hydraulic press squeezing the world. Freezing rain pelted the emergency room windows as Dr. Lena Mercer, Chief of Emergency Medicine, tried to grasp the chaos unfolding. Outside, sirens wailed without pause, stretchers rolling in one limp body after another.

At first, only a handful of flu-like cases: fatigue, muscle weakness, and occasional disorientation. Then, despite ravenous hunger, patients stopped eating. Yet they didn't starve. It was worse; they wasted away, alive, but hollowing from within.

"They're calling it the Hollowing Plague," muttered Dr. Malcolm Matthews, infectious disease expert and Lena's trusted colleague, approaching with a clipboard in hand. His voice cracked under exhaustion.

"I saw it on the news. It's spreading faster than anything we've seen; prions and neurodegeneration, similar to the Zombie Deer Virus or Mad Cow Disease. But… Jesus, Lena, this is worse. Much worse."

Lena blinked hard, battling her own fatigue. Nearly forty-eight hours awake, and like her team, she was starting to feel it. Her pulse quickened; a bead of sweat rolled down her temple.

"How, worse?" she asked, swallowing the last of her coffee.

"If it were prions, it wouldn't spread this fast," Matthews whispered, eyes darting. "I think it's airborne."

Lena stiffened, then forced a calm voice. "Airborne? That's impossible."

"If it looks like a duck and quacks like a duck…" Matthews bit his lip, voice dropping, "They stop eating, but don't die. They… become hollow. You saw the first wave. They just…

A sharp clatter cut him off as the ER doors banged open, another stretcher rushing in.

A woman, skin ghostly pale and trembling, clutched her face. Her features stretched tight over her bones, her cheeks sunken into deep hollows. She gasped for breath, her eyes darting wildly.

"*Help me*," she rasped, blood spraying from cracked lips. Her voice shattered into something wild and inhuman. "I'm so hungry, but... but I can't eat. I can't make myself eat."

Lena stepped back as those cadaverous, bloodshot eyes locked on her. Behind them lurked a hollow vacancy that chilled her to the bone. The acrid smell of antiseptic mixed with a faint, sour rot hung thickly in the air.

"Sedate her!" Matthews barked.

It was too late. The woman convulsed, arching off the stretcher as bones and tendons snapped like dry wood. A gurgle filled the room as she vomited, but nothing came out, no food, just bile, acid, and streaks of blood.

She wasn't alone. Across the ER, others stirred, admitted only hours earlier. All gaunt, hollow-eyed, wasting away, but still alive, still aware. Their hunger had grown primal, unsatisfied, and unending.

"It's spreading too fast," Matthews whispered, ashen-faced. "They're arriving faster than we can handle. Neighborhoods. Entire towns. All falling ill. And not just here; reports are now worldwide. A friend at the CDC says it's something new. A mutation."

A woman lashed out, more bones snapping as her frail body jerked unnaturally. Her bony fingers clawed into Lena's arm.

"*I need to eat!*" she screamed, voice crackling like harsh static. "Why won't it stop? I can't..."

Lena yanked her arm free, heart pounding. Nurses rushed with sedatives, but the woman spasmed violently, her eyes rolling back before collapsing, twitching as restraints were fastened.

"Jesus Christ," Matthews muttered, rubbing his temples. "What the hell is this?"

Lena swallowed hard, her dry throat tight. "They don't die. They just waste away. They can't eat, but they don't die."

The phrase *Hollowing Plague* echoed in her mind, as though the world had finally named this *thing* creeping in from the shadows. Not a hunger that could be fed, but one that hollowed from within, leaving bodies that refused to die.

Lena stood rooted, tugging nervously at her stethoscope, lost in thought. *Then…*

C-R-A-S-H!

The sound tore through the ER like a gunshot. Metal clanged, echoing down the hall, jolting her back to the present.

"I need backup, STAT!" an orderly shouted.

Drawn to the noise, Lena turned to see a man, motionless moments before, now staggering down the corridor. Skeletal, barely human, arms twitching and flailing, eyes wide and vacant.

And he was not alone.

A chorus of agony rose around her: murmurs, ragged breaths, brittle bones snapping… from bodies too weak to move, yet unable to rest.

"The sedatives aren't working," a nurse cried, rushing by. "They keep waking. They keep trying to..."

Lena's pulse thundered. The truth was undeniable. This plague didn't just waste people; it kept them alive, outside death's grasp. It twisted them into something inhuman… creatures trapped between life and death, consumed by an insatiable, unsatisfiable hunger.

And it was spreading faster than anyone could stop.

She stared at the writhing woman on the stretcher, chest heaving with shallow gasps. A chill crept up her spine.

The Hollowing Plague wasn't a disease. It was the opening act. The true nightmare had only begun.

***

Early March
Shores of Lake Ronkonkoma

Jack sat cross-legged on the cold, slick boulder at the lake's edge, the very spot Louis had used for skipping stones. The rain had turned to sleet, falling like buckshot from the sky, and his breath misted from his blue lips. Shirtless and shoeless, his thin frame should have surrendered to the bitter cold long ago. Yet, he remained motionless, locked in meditation. His body fought for warmth, but his mind wrestled for something more.

Icicles clung to his nose and ears, with frozen hair plastered to his scalp. Frost thickened on his glasses until they finally shattered beneath the relentless chill. Still, he didn't flinch. This was the test. Pain was irrelevant. The cold was only another adversary to conquer.

Nearby, Anne watched with pride tempered by concern. She knew the torment: body crying for warmth, mind begging for release, caught in the war between will and flesh. Jack had asked for this. Demanded it. He needed to become like her… unbreakable, a warrior.

A pang tightened in her chest, an ache born of knowing the price he was willing to pay, and the fragility she masked beneath her own strength.

Her words echoed in his mind, as if whispered behind him: "Train the mind. Learn to use it to control your body." The foundation of her teaching: the mind is a fortress where battles are won or lost long before a weapon is drawn.

Memories flickered like a broken reel… Amanda, his sisters, and the warmth of smiles now buried beneath the ruins of a shattered world. Amanda's hospital bed in the living room corner haunted him; the steady beeps, then the fading hum of the machines as he honored her last wish and let her go. The loss clung like a shadow, a reminder of the price of mercy and the strength it demands.

Time slipped past, robbing him of chances to forget, leaving only fear and pain to wrestle with. His heart ached, but in the silence of the cold a truth emerged: he was more than the sum of his memories.

Anne's voice broke the stillness, a faint smile softening her stern tone. "Your glasses cracked. Good. Training just got harder. You'll learn to rely on all your senses now. Remember, Jack, justice comes first, no matter the cost."

Jack exhaled slowly, tension coiling in his cold, stiff muscles, his skin numb with frostbite. Yet inside, mind and heart blazed fiercely. The ice on his brow was nothing compared to the fire of his resolve.

"*Endure with honor,*" Anne said, circling slowly to test his focus. "Pain and hardship are inevitable. A warrior endures them with dignity. There's a battle inside you now, begging you to quit. But your heart shouts… NEVER!"

Jack's thoughts turned inward. Every part of him screamed for warmth and relief, but the budding warrior within held fast. His fists clenched, knuckles raw, frostbite creeping into his toes. He would not break… not now, not ever.

"*Serve with loyalty,*" Anne said, softer now. "A warrior fights not just for self. You fight for those you protect… for Louis, for David, *for all of us.* Their lives are in your hands."

As Louis slipped further from him each day, Jack fought to hold on… fierce, unyielding, unwilling to face another goodbye. He could not afford weakness; fear and pain could not consume him. Every moment endured here made him stronger, every second pushing him beyond the limits he thought he had.

"*Unyielding in battle,*" Anne snapped, her voice cutting the cold like thunder. "No retreat! No surrender! Stand firm. Always!"

Jack opened his eyes as icy air filled his lungs. Frost clung to his cracked glasses, blurring his sight, but it didn't matter. The world was more than what one could see. It was about what one could feel, what one could know.

He rose slowly, stiff muscles and aching bones protesting. Still, he stood. He bowed in respect not just to nature, not just to Anne, but to the fire within himself. The cold ebbed; it was bendable, conquerable. Step by step, he heard ice crunch beneath his feet and the wind's distant roar.

Anne's soft smile was unreadable, yet proud. "Good," she said. "Now, we begin again."

For Louis and David, he would endure. For Louis and David, he would not break.

***

Late the Same Evening
Lake Ronkonkoma Safehouse

The chimes of the grandfather clock echoed softly down the upstairs hallway. At midnight, Jack tiptoed into David's room. His son lay curled on his side, clutching his pillow. Moonlight spilled through the window, casting shifting shadows that lent the room an eerie stillness. Then David's voice broke the silence.

"Dad… there's something in the closet again."

Jack sighed, familiar now with David's nightly expressions of fear, but careful never to dismiss them. Training had left him weary, yet he approached the closet and pulled the door open. Only emptiness. Closing it gently, he sat on David's bed, forcing a reassuring smile despite the weight tugging at his thoughts.

"See? Nothing there," Jack said, patting his back. "You're safe."

He stayed until David's breathing deepened. His son's eyes twitched; signs of a dream stirring. A cold draft brushed the room, though Jack couldn't find its source. He pulled the covers up around David's shoulders.

"I pray it's a good one," Jack whispered as he turned to leave.

His hand brushed the doorframe. A faint scrape of metal against wood jabbed at his senses. He froze, straining to hear. Was the closet knob slowly turning?

The hair on his neck stood up. He remembered the same scrape from his childhood room, but no one had believed him then.

That sound. Just like my own closet door when I was a kid.

Jack whipped around, eyes locked on the closet. Nothing moved. His breath caught tight in his throat. Forcing it down, he told himself it was only fatigue.

"Goodnight, David," he murmured, closing the bedroom door softly behind him.

Down the hall, he entered Louis's room. The cold hit first, a chill biting at his skin. The window stood wide open, allowing the frigid night air to pour in. Louis lay sprawled in the bed, his blanket kicked to the ground.

"Louis…" Jack whispered, pulling the covers over him. He stretched, shoulder ligaments popping, then shut the window quietly. He yawned, turning to find Louis still, unmoving.

Jack gazed at his eldest son, sleeping peacefully.

"I love you, buddy," he said softly.

As Jack stepped toward the door, a faint, nearly imperceptible sound echoed in his ear, blending with the floor's creak. He paused, head tilting as he strained to hear.

Wah.

There it was again. A baby's cry, distant, plaintive

That's how Louis cried when he was a baby…

Jack froze. His eyes shifted, adjusting to the darkness in the hallway. Unease swelled, a cold knot tightening in his stomach.

Wah.

The cry grew louder, piercing the eerie silence smothering the hallway.

Jack blinked, confused. Was it the wind? No… it was too clear. Besides, tonight there was no wind battering the clapboards of the house. His pulse quickened. Skeptical yet unsettled, he crossed to Anne's room and knocked gently.

She opened the door, blinking groggily, eyes heavy with sleep. At the sight of Jack, her expression softened.

"Did you hear that?" he asked. "A baby… crying?"

Anne shook her head. Her lips curved in a faint, weary smile; her voice was reassuring, though it was thick with sleep. Stifling a yawn, she covered her mouth before speaking softly, tenderly.

"No, Jack. Go get some rest," she whispered, like a mother calming a child from a bad dream. "You must be exhausted after all the training today. Everything's fine. I'm right down the hall if David or Louis needs me."

Her hand brushed his arm, a silent promise: *I'm here. It's okay.*

Jack retreated downstairs, still uneasy. His bed, a pull-out couch in the living room, received him, but sleep came fitfully and restlessly beneath the flickering shadows that lingered in the upstairs hallway.

Sleep never came easily at the safehouse. Not anymore.

***

The dream plunged Jack beneath unfamiliar waters. Scuba gear muffled the silence. Bubbles drifted upward toward the surface as pressure built in his ears. He scanned the murky depths, searching for something or someone, but the further he swam, the more elusive his quarry became. Dark shadows twisted into unrecognizable shapes, then dissolved like smoke. The water stretched endlessly, a cold void swallowing him whole.

Jack jolted awake, sweat soaking his shirt, causing him to shiver. That soft, persistent sound, the unmistakable cry of a baby, threaded once more through the darkness.

Still haunted by the dream, Jack sat up, each echo of the infant's cry pulling him toward the stairs. Step by step, he ascended, pausing on the second floor as the wail grew clearer. It beckoned him higher, to the third floor, toward a room long untouched. He hesitated at the threshold, dread washing over him, his pulse racing as he stepped inside.

The room felt unlike any other in the house, the air thick with the scent of aged wood and stale perfume. Faded floral wallpaper curled at the edges. Dust coated every surface. A broken mirror hung crooked on the far wall, while a dilapidated rocking chair sat in the corner, its upholstery fraying with age.

Heavy curtains smothered the windows, choking out the moonlight and shrinking the space into a claustrophobic tomb. A lone lamp with a yellowed shade cast a weak glow from atop a small dresser. A chill carried by the air whispered of something ancient, forgotten, and long dead. Goosebumps prickled his skin.

In the corner, a woman sat with her back to him, the rhythmic creak of the rocking chair breaking the stillness. Her deep burgundy dress hung in tatters, lace cuffs dulled and stained, dirt streaking the hem as shadows pooled at her feet.

Stringy, matted hair draped her shoulders, its color lost to the dark. Yet the air seemed to breathe life into it, faintly stirring the strands as though something unseen whispered past.

The baby's cry persisted, soft but steady. Jack squinted, unable to discern what she cradled. A shadowed bundle lay in her arms, indistinct and unnervingly still. Her movements were too slow, too deliberate… almost mechanical.

At last, she turned. Jack saw her face or the absence of one. Pale, translucent skin stretched tightly across her skull. Where eyes, nose, and mouth should have been, there was only smooth, featureless flesh, a faceless mask pulsing faintly as if something beneath it tried to breathe.

Jack recoiled, face contorting and mouth twisting in revulsion.

The baby's cry lingered, a twisted lullaby reverberating through the room. Terror rooted him where he stood, cold dread seeping into his bones.

The woman remained motionless and silent, yet her presence was suffocating and oppressive, as if she had been waiting for him for eternity.

Jack stumbled backward into the hallway, heart pounding in his ears. He fled, stopping only when he reached the couch. His mind spun in a tornado of disbelief.

What the hell did I just see?

The thought echoed in his skull. With shaking hands, he yanked the covers over his head, desperate for refuge from the nightmare. But no blanket could shut out the sound of the baby's cry still echoing in the walls.

***

The next morning, Jack jolted awake, gasping for breath, his heart pounding against his ribs. His dreams clung to him, thick and oppressive, like fog refusing to lift. The icy water and the faceless woman still haunted him. He rubbed his eyes, trying to shake off the remnants of sleep, but unease from the night before persisted.

His nerves raw, skin prickling with dread, Jack moved through the house. The silence hung unnaturally. He dragged himself upstairs, each step heavier than the last.

Pausing outside Louis's door, he knocked softly. "Louis? Time to get up, son," he called, voice low but steady, hiding the tension in his gut.

No answer.

Jack frowned and knocked harder, but there was only silence. A knot tightened in his stomach. Turning the handle, he pushed the door open. Louis lay tangled in the sheets, motionless. At first, Jack thought he was asleep, but something felt off…

"Louis?" Jack whispered, stepping closer, heart racing. He placed a hand on his son's shoulder and shook gently. "Come on, wake up." No response. The cold beneath his palm sent a shiver through him.

Panic twisted in his gut. Jack shook harder now, hands trembling. Louis's skin was ice cold. Fear clawed its way up his throat, choking him.

"Louis! Wake up!" Jack shouted now, desperation seizing him, but Louis remained unresponsive.

Jack's chest tightened as the walls seemed to press inward, the air thickening with every passing second. Panic surged. He stumbled back, nearly falling, then fled the room. He needed help. Something was terribly wrong.

He raced down the stairs, his mind a storm of confusion and terror. At the bottom, he stopped abruptly, practically hyperventilating. The same musty odor from the faceless woman's room filled his nostrils.

Louis was seated at the dining room table.

Jack blinked, struggling to comprehend the impossible sight. Nausea swept over him.

Louis sat perfectly still; his eyes did not blink. They did not move. His blank, unnerving expression made it seem as though he had been there, unmoving, for hours.

"Louis?" Jack's voice cracked, barely more than a whisper.

Louis didn't respond. His eyes, dark and empty, were hollow wells devoid of light or life.

Cold sweat broke across Jack's forehead. It was as if he were staring at a ghost. His heart hammered as he stepped forward, the knot of fear pulling tighter in his chest.

His mind struggled to process it: *I saw him upstairs…*

Disbelief shot through him, back to Louis lying in his bed: *He was cold and unresponsive…*

Mouth agape, Jack could only wonder: *How could this be?*

Upstairs, the sheets still held the shape of his body.

***

The Next Evening
Lake Ronkonkoma Safehouse

Hands rubbing together, David watched his colorful stack of Monopoly money grow. The old board, its cards yellowed and its pieces worn smooth, offered a comforting familiarity. On a winning streak, his properties lined with houses and hotels, David felt a rare and overdue satisfaction.

Landing on Boardwalk, he'd snapped it up to the groans of Jack and Anne. For a moment, the tension with Louis eased, replaced by the easy rhythm of the game. Across from him, Jouris smiled wryly, bankrupt after landing on David's hotel.

"Luck of the dice," Jouris said, raising his hands in mock surrender.

"Or maybe you all just have terrible strategies," David teased, grinning as he added to his pile.

The room felt light, almost normal, as though the safehouse's strangeness had lifted in the warmth of their laughter. Anne groaned after landing on Park Place, handing over a thick wad of cash. Jack grimaced, plotting his next move with exaggerated worry.

David grinned, watching his conquest solidify.

"It's over, guys," he declared, raising his hands triumphantly. "Victory is mine."

The others exchanged amused glances, conceding defeat. As they packed away the pieces, David basked in the rare lightness of the moment, his fears pushed aside.

But beneath the evening's easy laughter, an unsettling chill was stirring.

"Hey, David, why don't you grab some snacks?" Jack suggested.

With a bounce in his step, David headed to the kitchen. The warmth vanished instantly. A sharp draft brushed the back of his neck, freezing him in mid-motion. His eyes snapped to the basement door, slightly ajar, just a crack, enough for cold to seep out, as if the darkness below were rising.

The kitchen was quiet except for the faint hum of the refrigerator. Beneath it, David caught another sound: a whisper of air drifting up from the basement.

I know I closed that door earlier.

David hated that basement. The air there seemed alive, breathing and waiting. An earthy stench, like food rotting, seeped from every dark corner.

His shoes whispered against the linoleum as he edged closer. Peering into the gap, the basement yawned like a black hole, its depths unreadable, the staircase dissolving into nothingness. Darkness, thick as ink, swallowed everything.

Just shut the door. Just shut it.

His breath puffed like cotton balls in the dim kitchen light. Trembling, he gripped the edge of the door and pushed it closed. The latch clicked into place, but the silence that followed was worse than the draft. He froze, eyes locked on the door, waiting to see if it would move again.

It didn't.

Turning quickly, David fled for the warmth of the dining room.

Louis has been as cold to me lately as that basement air.

Jouris was mid-sentence, lightly tapping his knuckles on the table.

"I think I'm connecting with David," he said, smiling as David returned to his seat. "And I think I know how to get Louis out of his funk."

David's hands trembled slightly as he set the tray down, his heart still racing.

I'm not looking back at that door.

Jouris glanced at him. "You alright? I heard a loud noise."

"Yeah," David muttered, shaking off the chill. "Just the basement door acting up again."

Then, curiosity tugging, David asked, "Jouris, what does Ronkonkoma mean?"

Jouris scratched his whiskers, then laced his fingers together, the question stirring something within him.

"Ronkonkoma..." he murmured, letting the name hang in the air. "The tribes here once called it Rangonkommack; others referred to it as Ronkahouk. It means the wild goose place. But it's more than that. To them, it's sacred... and feared."

***

The simple rhythm of the game offered a rare and welcome escape, but the peace was only fleeting…

"Thank you for telling me about the Ronkonkoma train line, Jouris," David said enthusiastically. "I had no idea there's been a station here since the 1800s!"

"I've never met anyone more interested in trains than you, David. I thought I was the only one!"

"Hearing about other lakes was cool too: Spruce Hole, Walden Pond, and Blue Hole. I'll look them up on the map you gave me."

Clutching the map in his hand, David hesitated, sure he heard the basement door rattling. The hair on his arms stood up, but he pushed the feeling aside, focusing on Jouris's stories.

He stretched and yawned. "I think I'll go to bed now."

As David went upstairs, Jouris leaned back in his chair. He waited until he was sure David was out of earshot before glancing at Anne and Jack.

"I noticed how David's mood lifted during the game, the way he seemed to forget, for a little while, the weight hanging over him since coming here. It was good to see him enjoying himself."

"Monopoly is his favorite game, Jouris," Jack said, grabbing a cookie with a chuckle. His bad dreams from the night before felt more distant. "You hit a home run with the trains, too! David's been fascinated with them since kindergarten."

Jouris's voice lowered. "I hesitated to mention this to David. He's in a better state now. But there's more about Ronkonkoma and the other lakes I kept to myself."

Jack raised an eyebrow, leaning forward. "Something more than what you warned us about the other day?"

Jouris's face lost all expression, and the room's atmosphere turned serious.

"It's true, to the tribes, Ronkonkoma was sacred. But they feared it too. The Setalcotts, Nissequogues, and two other tribes shared the lake. Ronkonkoma wasn't just fishing grounds to them. They believed it held power."

Anne frowned. "What kind of power?"

Jouris drained the last of his coffee. "For one, the water level rises and falls without explanation. During the drought a few years back, it went up instead of down."

Anne drew a slow breath, absorbing his words.

A buzzing sound hovered near Jack's ear. He swatted instinctively, scratching the back of his neck, a sure sign his calm was slipping.

Jouris continued, "It's the deepest lake on Long Island, seventy feet in places, though its exact depth remains uncertain. Go down more than ten feet, light vanishes completely."

"What about the other lakes?" Jack asked, unease creeping into his voice.

Jouris's eyes sparkled with fascination. He lowered his voice. "It's not just Ronkonkoma. Walden Pond, Blue Hole, and Spruce Hole all have histories."

"Dark ones. Suicides and bodies that are never recovered. It's like something in the water pulls people in. Each lake has a personality. Its own… hunger."

Anne and Jack exchanged a wary glance. "Hunger? What do you mean?" Jack asked.

Jouris leaned forward, grim. "Spruce Hole… people vanish there. The water pulls them under, no matter how strong a swimmer they are. Walden Pond, strange fish appear in its waters, creatures that shouldn't exist there. And Blue Hole in New Jersey, the quicksand surrounding it is only the beginning. Divers vanish all the time. Strange undertows, and the water is colder than it should be. It's cold, so cold, and yet it never freezes."

Anne looked toward the window, her face pale. "You don't really believe…?"

Jouris shook his head slightly. "These tales, dismissed as superstition, echo a darker truth. I can't explain it, but I believe there's more than mere rumor here. These lakes are dangerous. They seem to possess a will of their own." Jouris hesitated. "I just don't want to frighten the boys."

A sharp metallic cut through the room.

Jouris stiffened, eyes darting toward the kitchen. Anne and Jack froze as the latch on the basement door slid open.

A long, low creak followed as the door swung open slowly, inch by inch.

Jouris didn't move. Anne and Jack held their breath, staring at the dark opening.

No one spoke. Their eyes locked on the darkness in the doorway, and a familiar chill crawled down their spines.

***

Pre-Colonial Period
Setalcott Village Shores of Lake Ronkonkoma, NY
3 Sunrises After the Ceremony Started-The Night of Quanon's Return

The night air hung thick and heavy, broken only by the soft rustling of branches swaying in the wind. Crouched in the shadows, Oohqua's breath came shallow, his heart pounding like a war drum. Hours dragged by as his eyes stayed fixed on the wigwam across the clearing, its entrance bathed in pale moonlight. Inside, Quanon waited, the sole keeper of the truth Oohqua sought, the answer to the torment born of the sacred trials.

Memories clawed at Oohqua's mind: the chaos after he ran, or as he called it, his escape. What had he fled from? Was he a coward, or had something darker been waiting beneath the surface? Quanon had returned unscathed, but whispers of strange behavior spread through the village. Oohqua didn't want rumors. He craved the truth, and only Quanon could give it.

Breathing deeply, he crept across the open field, each step measured and silent. The wigwam's flap swayed gently, an invitation carried on the cool breeze. His fingers trembled as he parted the hide and stepped into the suffocating darkness within.

"Quanon?" Oohqua whispered, voice shaking. "I need to talk... I..."

Before another word fell, a shadow lunged. Quanon struck like a crashing wave, powerful arms slamming Oohqua down. He struggled, but Quanon's strength was monstrous and unyielding.

"Q-Quanon! What...?" His gasp muffled beneath a crushing hand. "It's me, Oohqua! Let me go! Stop!"

Meanwhile, outside, concerned visitors arrived... searching for Quanon's missing escorts...

***

Hours later, as the village slept under the moonlit sky, Quanon's wigwam lay engulfed in darkness; not even the dying embers glowed through the hide walls. But outside, the night had come alive.

Quanon's escorts, tribesmen sent to accompany him home, had vanished. Alarmed, Chief Powwan summoned emissaries from the other tribes and village elders. Their voices were hushed as they prepared to investigate.

Torches flickered like ghost lights on the marsh as they approached Quanon's wigwam. Chief Powwan led, jaw tight with mounting anxiety. He scanned the path ahead, fingers twitching on his blade, ready for an unseen threat.

The elders followed, their whispers swallowed by crackling flames and crunching leaves. At the entrance, Powwan raised a hand, demanding silence. With a swift motion, he yanked back the flap.

"Quanon?" His voice cut through the darkness, firm and sharp. Leaning inside, he raised his torch, trembling light spilling into the gloom.

"What is..."

Powwan's words died as his eyes met a nightmare.

Quanon turned slowly toward the torchlight, eyes glowing like smoldering embers. Blood smeared his face, lips curled back to reveal jagged, gore-stained teeth. Strips of flesh dangled from his mouth. Beneath him, Oohqua lay motionless, eyes wide in shock, throat gurgling his final breath.

"By the spirits..." an elder whispered.

Chief Powwan's voice cracked with disbelief and rage. "Quanon! What have you done?"

Quanon snapped his head toward the chief, lips twisting into a cruel sneer. A low, menacing hiss escaped him, the coppery scent of blood thick in the air.

"Quanon, cease this madness!" another elder cried, thrusting his torch forward like a spear.

But Quanon ignored them, hunched over Oohqua's body like a wolf guarding its kill.

Horror rooted them to the spot. Their hero, Quanon, crouched devouring flesh like a savage beast. His labored breaths heaved his bloodied chest, and another hiss split the night as he bared his bloodied teeth at them. His crimson eyes, reflecting the torchlight, burned with monstrous hunger.

Before they could react, before Powwan could shout, Quanon sprang up. He lunged at the wigwam wall, tearing through hide and wood with savage ease, vanishing into the night.

The scene stained their souls. Oohqua's bloodied body sprawled in the dirt, eyes vacant, mouth frozen in a silent scream.

Chief Powwan stepped forward, face pale as death, voice barely above a whisper. "What... has he become?"

The cold night air swallowed their whispers, leaving only silence to answer Powwan's question.

CHAPTER 2

First week of March
Safehouse, Lake Ronkonkoma, NY

Anne sat across from Jack in the dimly lit study, the scent of burning incense thick in the air. His expression was tense, with worry lines etched deep across his face.

"It's not just me, Anne," Jack insisted. "David keeps telling me things about his closet and the basement. He says something in this house is watching him, something he can't see but feels."

Anne nodded thoughtfully. "I believe you, Jack. And I wouldn't dismiss David's feelings. He's God's prophet and extremely sensitive. But this house is old; noises, drafts, shifting boards, they're unsettling. When I saw that basement door open, it was odd, yes, but sometimes, the mind makes things worse. Houses echo their histories."

Jack shifted, his leg bouncing unconsciously. "But the way David describes it… It's more than a creak here or there. Something about it is off. I've felt it too."

Anne laid a hand on his shoulder. "My JESU roots run deep," she said firmly. "If something truly evil lurked here, my instincts would scream at me. I'd know it."

Jack nodded, relaxing slightly. Anne opened her acupuncture kit and slipped on her glasses.

"Let's take care of that hand," she said, gesturing for him to stretch it out. Jack flexed gingerly. "The Strigoi did permanent damage, but acupuncture may help with flexibility and pain."

With care, Anne slid the needles into his hand and wrist, her movements precise and gentle. She lit another stick of incense, the smoke rising in gentle coils. "Close your eyes, Jack," she murmured as she stepped out. "Focus on your breathing. Let the treatment settle. I'll be back shortly."

Time blurred as smoke drifted like shadows across his eyelids. A strange calm settled over him, and for a moment, the house that had haunted his thoughts and dreams felt almost at peace. But the darkness lurking in the shadows would not be so easily banished.

Anne returned after twenty minutes and gently removed the needles. "How's the pain now?" she asked.

Jack stretched his fingers, surprised at the relief. "Better. You've got magic in those hands, Anne."

She chuckled softly. "I'll take that as a compliment."

He rose unsteadily, bumping the edge of a table. "Damn it," he muttered, wincing as he glanced down at his toe.

But annoyance gave way to horror. His toe was turning unnaturally pale, veins darkening and spreading like creeping roots beneath the skin.

"Anne… something's wrong," he said, his voice tight.

Anne stepped forward, eyes widening as the darkness spread through his skin like a spider's web. "Jack, what...?"

The throbbing began, slow and heavy, pulsing through his foot. His toe swelled, skin stretching taut until a faint, sickening crack echoed in the room.

The toe bent backward, snapping at an unnatural angle. Jack tried to move, but pain froze him in place. Fissures spread across his swollen flesh as it tore open.

"Jack, this can't be happening. We have to stop this, NOW!"

With a wet pop, the skin burst. Dozens of squirming black tendrils unfurled like ravenous worms, reaching upward toward his leg. They felt alive, invasive, as if something inside sought to claim him.

Jack stumbled back, his face pale with horror. "Anne, get them off!"

Anne lunged, clawing at the tendrils, but they clung fast, burrowing into his skin. Jack felt them twisting through his muscles, numbness spreading, an icy freeze creeping deeper and deeper.

Panic surged. He tore at his leg, but the tendrils only grew and spread faster, racing toward his chest. The numbness galloped through him like a horse charging to the finish line.

Then, suddenly, it stopped.

Jack blinked, chest heaving. The room was quiet and calm, just as it had been before. The incense drifted lazily, and Anne stood before him, her hand on his shoulder.

"Jack," she whispered, her face etched with concern. "What happened?"

He glanced down. His toe was red and irritated, but intact, showing no sign of the grotesque horror he'd seen. His heart hammered as he tried to steady his breathing.

"It felt so real, Anne," he whispered, the lingering chill still inside him. "I swear… it was real."

Unable to shake the dread, he left the room. An image surged: George's face, fanged like Nosferatu, horns curling from his skull.

Jack swallowed a scream. "I don't know which vision scares me more," he muttered.

***

Mid-March, Just Before Saint Patrick's Day
Jouris Van Haalan's Home, Lake Ronkonkoma, NY

The sky hung thick and gray, the melting snowbanks hinting at a respite from winter's grip. Though spring was near, a damp chill lingered in the air. Each step toward the garage filled Jouris with dread, not from the lousy weather, but because today marked the anniversary of Peter's death.

His heavy boots crunched through the slush as the memory of Peter's final phone call echoed relentlessly. Nearly ten years had passed, yet his son's eager voice, filled with plans and dreams, still haunted him. Peter had been stabbed to death trying to break up a robbery on a New York subway. The killer remained free, and the injustice gnawed at Jouris's soul.

Shrugging off his melancholy, Jouris focused on the plan to meet Louis. Jack had mentioned his job at the auto parts store, and Jouris hoped this project might be a way to connect with him.

Turning the key in the warped wooden door, Jouris grumbled, "Jesus, stuck again. I'm too old for this shit!"

The door gave way with a loud groan.

"What the hell…"

Instead of his orderly workshop, he was greeted by chaos. Wrenches littered the workbench, tools stuck randomly into the drywall, and splatters of car paint stained the floor. The mess felt like a violation.

Suppressing a growl of frustration, Jouris began cleaning up. He hadn't heard the footsteps until Louis cleared his throat behind him. Jouris turned to find him pacing nervously, but his eyes brightened at the sight of a cherry-red vintage Mustang parked in the center of the garage.

"Hey, Louis. Sorry about the mess. Didn't expect it to look like this."

Louis shrugged, stepping closer. "Is that…?"

"Yep. A '69 Mustang convertible. Needs plenty of elbow grease to stay running. Want to help?"

Louis grinned instantly. "Candy apple red. Sick. Yeah, I'd love to!"

"Let's start with the carburetor," Jouris suggested.

"Needle and seat," Louis interjected, naming each part with ease, his precision surprising Jouris.

"You sure know your way around a car," Jouris remarked, impressed.

Working in sync, passing tools, tightening bolts, wiping grease, Jouris felt a weight lift from his chest. But Louis's mood shifted as they finished the oil change. His hands buried in his pockets, he stared past the car into the dark corners of the garage.

"Something's off at the house," Louis murmured. "Not just the house... the lake, too. It's like an energy trying to get inside me." His voice dropped. "Feels like I'm fighting it all the time."

Louis rocked slightly on the balls of his feet, whispering under his breath, "It's just energy, it's just energy..." as though convincing himself.

Jouris nodded, masking the fear bubbling beneath.

Is this something I should be telling Jack?

Fidgeting with the wrench, he chose his words carefully. "Old houses are like that. They can get under your skin. But it's just energy. It can't come in unless you invite it."

Louis's jaw clenched, the tension tightening in his face. Jouris set a steady hand on his shoulder.

"Any time it feels like it's closing in, come here. Work on the Mustang. Clear your head."

Louis's expression softened. "Can I come back tomorrow?"

"Anytime. This car's not going anywhere."

As Louis glanced back at the Mustang one last time, Jouris felt a rare comfort. For today, at least, he had shielded one soul from the darkness.

*****

March 17th- Saint Patrick's Day
Safehouse, Lake Ronkonkoma, NY

Jack stepped into the kitchen, examining the blisters on his palms. Planting peas on Saint Patrick's Day was a tradition, but the ground remained stubbornly frozen despite the thaw. He'd chipped at the soil with a pickaxe all morning, the petrified earth mocking his efforts. His hands stung from the vibrations, and desperate for warmth, he blew into them as he moved toward the coffee maker.

Expecting the familiar hum, Jack flicked it on. Instead, the machine groaned low and ragged, like a beast gasping for air. Steam hissed from the sides rather than the top, curling in thin wisps, like smoke slipping through hidden cracks.

The percolation sputtered and stopped. When Jack poured, a thick liquid dribbled slowly into his cup. A wave of disbelief washed over him. The liquid wasn't dark brown but a glossy, shocking red, like fresh paint. He leaned closer, his brow furrowing as a sharp, metallic scent lingered. This wasn't coffee.

The surface rippled. Tiny, pale fingers stretched upward, clawing as if trying to escape the depths. Jack dropped the cup, the rattle echoing as his heart thundered. He stumbled back.

"What the hell was that?"

The coffee maker sputtered once more, then fell silent. The noises vanished as quickly as they had come, leaving only an eerie stillness. Jack stood frozen, breathing heavily, the only sound the slow, ominous drip of liquid onto the countertop.

Suddenly, several creaks echoed, accompanied by loud, deliberate footsteps.

"Louis? David? Anne?" Jack's voice wavered. Only the steady tick of the grandfather clock answered.

Glancing once more at the overturned mug, he turned toward the living room.

A gray-haired woman sat on the couch, a book resting in her lap as her fingers gently turned the pages. Jack's blood ran cold. His mother. Her piercing blue eyes locked on him, eyes that had always seemed to see straight through him.

"What made you ruin your brother's life?" she asked softly, her tone filled with accusation.

Jack's mouth went dry. He blinked, and she was gone. The couch sat empty; the room remained unchanged, except for the chiming clock.

His gaze dropped to his hands, red and raw, aching from his fight with the earth. Her question lingered, unrelenting.

First George. Now Mom. I think I'm losing my mind.

Suddenly, an image flooded his mind: Lucius Rofocale, a world away, sneering with a sinister smile, whispering…

You can run, Jack, but you can't hide…. forever.

***

Later in the Night on March 17th- Saint Patrick's Day
Dallas, Texas

The plane's engine faded to a low hum as George Aitken stepped off flight N666 onto the dimly lit tarmac at Dallas-Fort Worth Airport. So far, every lead on his brother's whereabouts had led to dead ends. Now the latest AI readout had brought him here, but doubt gnawed at him like a hellhound chewing a femur. Flickering terminal lights cast long shadows, mirroring the fractures spreading across his once-steady confidence.

A car awaited, but George stayed wary. The AI system, which once held great promise, had become a source of frustration, failing him when he needed it most. Sliding into the back seat, he fixed his eyes on the dark Texas night as they sped toward Irving.

Not long ago, he'd felt unstoppable, as if the seas would part at his command. His mind replayed Pergamon's roaring assembly, where he and the demon legions pledged loyalty to their Masters, Lucius and Prosperine, as the deafening cheers shook the heavens, celebrating its fall. His fist clenched as a wicked smirk crept onto his lips at the memory of storming JESU's headquarters, and the terror etched on his enemies' faces.

But one moment, he grasped the key to his destiny; the next, the walls seemed to close in. Doubt crept in like a ghost haunting his thoughts. Was his legacy built on bedrock or merely shifting sand?

Barbas's demon followers stalked him in the shadows, eager for his head on a spike. His fingers trembled as he bit a nail, the steady tick of an unforgiving clock hammering in his skull. Even Lucius and Prosperine's patience appeared to wane. George felt like a marionette tangled in invisible strings, wondering if the death of his family and the risk to his mortal soul were worth the cost.

Reeling from the AI's failures, he'd dispatched scouts along the entire Eastern Seaboard to search for his brother, his nephews, and Anne Bishop. So far, the effort yielded nothing but silence. Yet some dark instinct drove him forward with relentless determination.

The car stopped in front of a modest ranch-style house at the edge of town. A trace of nostalgia stirred, but he smothered it. The past was a trap, and he was here with a purpose.

A Northern wind bit into his bones as he approached the house. The porch light flickered, casting a wavering glow across the front door. He raised a hand to shield his eyes from stinging grains of sand whipped by the gusts.

The door opened, and a stocky man with thinning hair stepped out, gripping a shotgun.

"Who the hell's there?" The voice was gruff, edged with caution.

"Relax, Vinzent. It's me, George. George Aitken." A smirk curled his lips as he walked up the steps. "Didn't think I'd rattle you this much."

Recognition crossed Vinzent Pomodoro's face. The tension eased, though the gun remained pointed.

"George? Damn, it's been at least twenty years. I barely recognized you." His eyes lingered on George's features. "You look... different."

"Life has a way of changing people," George said flatly.

Vinzent snorted, lowering the shotgun. "Yeah, some more than others. What brings you here? Strange time for a social call."

"Business Vinzent. Only business."

George stepped inside. The dingy white stucco walls of the living room sagged with age. Newspapers and beer cans littered the floor. Vinzent brushed papers off the couch.

"Sorry. Fired my maid last week." He joked, offering George a beer. "Want one? Or are you still on the wagon?"

George sat cautiously, eyes narrowing. He drew a flask from his jacket, steadying his shaky hands with a swig.

"I brought my own." His gaze cut into his old friend. "Tell me, Vinzent, when was the last time you heard from my brother?"

Instantly, the room felt charged with tension. Vinzent drummed his fingers on the shotgun stock before leaning it against his chair.

"Jack? Not for years."

Vincent arched a brow. "You don't talk to him anymore?"

George's jaw clenched. "We've had a falling out, I'm afraid. Things changed. You're certain he hasn't reached out? Even indirectly?"

Vinzent stiffened. "Are we reminiscing, or interrogating? I know the difference. Cop instincts never fade. If you came here digging into Jack's life, you came a long way for nothing."

George's voice dropped, cold as stone. "If you're concealing something, this won't end well."

Vinzent's eyes narrowed. "Seems you're the one hiding from something, or maybe from someone?"

George bit his lip, patience fraying.

This was supposed to be simple… a lead, a clue.

Before he could answer, an aide's voice pierced the charged atmosphere.

"Sir. One of the patrols just apprehended a high-profile target. Someone from the 'deck of cards.'"

George's pulse quickened. Finally, a break.

He turned back to Vinzent, expression unreadable. "Well, old friend, I regret having to cut our visit short. Do you remember that Roman history course we took together at Stony Brook?"

Vinzent gave a dry laugh. "I can't recall what I did last week, let alone thirty years ago."

George raised his hand, signaling the aide. "Let me jog your memory. Marcus Aurelius taught that *everything must be approached logically and with due consideration, in a calm and orderly fashion.*"

He leaned closer. "*But decisively. With no loose ends.*"

Vinzent's eyes widened. A scream ripped through the room as blood splattered on the walls. George didn't flinch. As his friend's head rolled across the floor, his mind was already on the next target.

***

Summer 1961
One Week after Order of the Flaming Spear Tap Out Ceremony
Camp Wauwepex, Wading River, NY

The cotton ball clouds hung low over Camp Wauwepex as Billy Clifford Sr. and his wife, Margaret, hurried along the rocky dirt path toward the dining hall. Inside, tables had been pushed aside to make room for maps and equipment. Suffolk County Police Captain Ryan Dempsey, in his sharply pressed uniform and broad-brimmed trooper hat, stood near the door, his expression grim.

"Mr. and Mrs. Clifford, I'm Captain Dempsey," he said, extending his hand. "Thank you for coming so quickly. I regret what you're going through."

The shadows of night slowly stretched over the camp... soon to engulf them all.

Margaret's eyes scanned the room. "Is there any news about Lyle?"

Dempsey adjusted his hat, shaking his head, a crease of sympathy forming on his brow. "Not yet. We've got teams combing a ten-mile radius around the camp. The camp staff, volunteers, and even some older scouts are helping with the search. Every trail's being searched, even the marsh near the lake."

Billy Sr. clenched his jaw, pulling Margaret closer as she wiped away a tear. "Thank you, Captain. Is there anything we can do?"

Dempsey hesitated, glancing at the camp map tacked to the wall. "Actually, yes. It'll be dark in an hour. Your son, Billy, hasn't told us much about what might have happened. "Sometimes children confide in their parents when they won't with others. If you speak to him, he might share something useful... something to help us understand why Lyle might have run off."

Margaret steadied herself, then nodded. "Of course. We'll do whatever it takes."

The captain led them to a small tent set apart from the others. Inside, Billy packed his footlocker with quiet precision. His face was solemn, and his movements slow.

Margaret knelt beside him. "Billy... can we talk?"

He didn't look up but paused mid-motion. "I don't know what to say," he whispered. He pointed at a chest beneath a cot. "I packed up Lyle's trunk."

Billy Sr. sat across from him. "I know this is hard, son. You've always tried to protect Lyle. But if you know anything that could help us find him, you must tell us."

Billy's hands stilled on the trunk. "The other boys... they were mean to him," he said softly. "They picked on him because he was different."

A sudden gust of wind ripped through the trees, carrying a whisper of warning.

Margaret exhaled. "Did they hurt him?"

Billy resumed packing. "They always called him names. I told them to stop. I think they beat him up the night of the Flaming Arrow ceremony. I got tapped out and wasn't there to protect him."

Billy Sr. placed a hand on his shoulder. "Lyle's lucky to have you. But do you think he ran off?"

Billy hesitated. "I don't know. I told him it was almost over, that we'd be going home soon. But last night, he didn't want to go to the campfire. After it ended, he wasn't in the tent. I thought maybe he just wanted to be alone. But he never came back."

Margaret leaned closer, her voice gentle but urgent. "Did he ever say he wanted to leave? Or talk to anyone else about it?"

"No. He didn't tell me anything. Just…" Billy's voice trailed off, his gaze darkening. "Just that he wished he could be somewhere they couldn't find him."

Margaret exchanged a grave glance with her husband. "Thank you, Billy. That helps us."

Unseen, something darker watched and waited beyond the camp's borders.

Captain Dempsey appeared at the tent's entrance. "We'll keep searching. If Lyle's out there, we'll find him."

Billy shut his footlocker, eyes downcast, his voice barely above a whisper. "Just… make sure."

***

March 21st, Spring Equinox
Shed on the Safehouse Property, Lake Ronkonkoma, NY

The shed stood at the edge of the property, its old wooden frame lit by the flickering glow of torches. Shadows leapt across the walls, heightening the chill of the night. Practicing what he had learned, Jack ignored the cold and focused on the intensity of his training.

Each movement in the dark was more than practice; it was preparation for the unseen forces closing in…

Through the open doors, Jack could barely make out the faint glow of Jouris's house, a distant beacon in the distance reminding him of who he was protecting. Louis and David were there, unwilling to spend the night alone in the safehouse with its creaks and whispers. Jack squinted. Without his glasses, his vision blurred, the shapes around him dissolving into shadows. But that was the point. He breathed deeply, letting the darkness sharpen his other senses. His world narrowed to a mix of sounds and sensations.

Anne circled him, her keen eyes assessing every move. Jack swayed slightly as he shifted his weight, the shed suddenly unfamiliar and immense without sight. Every sound was amplified as he fought for balance.

"Remember this, Jack," Anne said, tapping the floor lightly with her foot. "In a fight, things won't always go as planned. Trust your instincts, not just your eyes."

He nodded, bracing himself. Suddenly, a sandbag swung from the rafters. Jack sensed it at the last moment, sidestepping as it grazed his shoulder with a low *w-h-o-o-s-h*.

"Better," Anne remarked, a trace of satisfaction in her tone.

Then, she clapped her hands sharply. "But don't just evade! Respond decisively. Confront it with strength." She thrust another weighted object, and this time, deflected it with his arm. His heart raced with the thrill of achievement.

Anne's voice remained calm but firm. "Let the darkness teach you. Not every enemy is visible. Some you won't see at all. You'll encounter spirits, things beyond our physical world. Trust yourself. Listen to the air. Feel the movement around you."

The next sandbag hurtled toward him. Jack ducked, twisted, then rose with his fists raised, each movement cleaner and sharper. Instinct carried him, honed with every strike. A rush of elation surged; he was doing it, mastering what once felt beyond his reach.

Anne's words sank deep, forcing him to face what he'd tried to bury: fears, doubts, and scars, both visible and hidden. As he paused to catch his breath, Jack gave a short laugh. "What would a shrink say about this? Training in the dark in an old shed…"

Anne's expression softened. "Like Louis and David, some are destined for a life of service. Some flee a burning house. We choose to run toward it. It's in our nature."

Her voice turned solemn. "But remember, this training isn't about fighting to the end. It's about enduring to fight again tomorrow. The scars and cracks we carry remind us what we've survived. The hardest battles aren't with others, Jack. They're inside ourselves."

She hesitated, then added, "Mark Desmond always told me: never hesitate to go to war, but only if it's absolutely necessary."

Jack met her gaze and saw pride in her eyes, a warmth that anchored him. In that look was a silent promise of devotion and gratitude. She had given him more than skills. She had given him purpose.

Her words wrapped around him like armor. He felt stronger, steadier, convinced that he could face anything with Anne at his side. Yet beneath the thrill of progress, a whisper of doubt lingered… *when the time came, would it be enough?*

The training ended with Jack drenched in sweat, his spirit soaring. The night felt like a victory until a sharp, stinging pain shot through his jaw. He winced, pressing a hand to his cheek where his tooth throbbed, an unwelcome reminder that even triumph could not silence the hidden battles waiting to be fought.

***

Pre-Colonial Period
Shore of Lake Ronkonkoma, NY
Several Sunrises After Quanon's Escape

The mist clung low over Lake Ronkonkoma as the elders of the four tribes gathered on the shore. Silence stretched taut between them, broken only by the gentle lap of water against the sand. They had tracked Quanon tirelessly, following faint, half-erased footprints through the dense woods, until at last his path led here, to the sacred lake, feared for generations; a place no one dared enter without cause.

The crowd parted as Chief Powwan stepped forward. His eyes found faint grooves in the sand where a canoe had been dragged into the shallows. He studied the lake's glassy surface, jaw tightening as the truth struck him.

"The center of the lake. That is his destination."

The other chiefs exchanged uneasy glances, knowing the lake's center lay within the forbidden zone… a place none dared breach.

Chief Nassaconseke frowned, but nodded. "One canoe. Two warriors."

One by one, each tribe chose its bravest fighters. When Chief Powwan stepped forward, the elders' voices rose in protest.

"You must not go, Powwan. Your place is here, with the tribe."

"Quanon is still my son!" Powwan's voice rang fierce and unyielding. "I will not send another into the lake's great unknown in my place."

The warriors slid their birchbark canoes into the lake, paddles dipping in perfect rhythm as they pushed toward the center, where a solitary canoe drifted, eerily still.

The lake's influence pressed heavily upon them. Ripples stretched like grasping fingers, tugging at their boats. Whispered prayers slipped from their lips, ancient words meant to shield them from what lay beneath the surface. Their voices were barely a breath against the deep silence.

Circling the canoe, they watched it turn slowly, empty and untouched. No trace of Quanon remained. Only silence, thick and suffocating, as if the lake itself held its breath.

Powwan reached out, fingers barely touching the vacant canoe's edge. A sudden chill swept the air… then vanished.

The water churned beneath them, dark and alive, as though something had awakened from centuries of slumber. The warriors froze, their pale faces bathed in moonlight, their canoes rocking in unseen currents that pulled them together.

Suddenly, without warning, the lake erupted. Thick black water like molasses surged around them, tugging at their paddles and flooding the boats. Their mouths opened in silent screams, voices smothered before sound could escape.

The lake swallowed them whole, its waters folding over the canoes with eerie finality. Where once floated five boats, now only rippling water remained, smoothing into stillness as if untouched.

Silence reclaimed the lake. Its depths concealing what had claimed the warriors, leaving behind only the lonely echo of the night sounds drifting through the mist.

***

Eastlake Generating Plant East Lake, Ohio
March 22nd

Icy rain lashed the Eastlake Generating Plant, the wind howling like a beast, its fury battering the facility like a blacksmith's hammer. The rapid thaw had been disastrous. Snow and ice melted in torrents, submerging cars, flooding basements, and creeping up the walls of homes.

Days earlier, water treatment systems became overloaded, inundating streets and waterways with unsafe water. The electrical grid, never designed for such strain, buckled under record demand for heat as frigid temperatures returned.

Inside, a skeletal crew of exhausted workers shuffled between control panels, struggling to decode alarms and flashing error messages. Those who braved the storm and risked exposure to the still unnamed but rapidly spreading virus watched with dread as the plant lurched between barely functioning and total failure. Wrapped in thick coats, they wiped fevered brows and coughed into their sleeves. Each hour brought news of another technician too sick to report.

Jake Matthews, lead operator, scanned lines of code streaming across his terminal, his vision blurring from exhaustion. The software patch meant to stabilize the system had only made things worse. Lines of red error messages flashed like warning flares across the dark screen.

"We're losing voltage on the eastern line," Jake muttered, barely audible over the hum of failing machinery.

Rachel Alvarez typed frantically beside him, trying to reroute power to stabilize the load. "The grid's bleeding faster than we can patch it, Jake. Half the Midwest is already dark; the rest will be out in minutes."

The flickering monitors made Jake's mind race. A partial blackout would be disastrous, but it offered a slim chance to salvage parts of the grid. He took a shaky breath, weighing the options.

"We can isolate the circuit," he said, voice cracking. "Cutting off the line feeding New York might give us the power to stabilize the rest. It won't be pretty, but it might work."

Rachel's pale face turned toward him. "That'll take out the whole East Coast. People will freeze."

He hesitated, watching the numbers plummet. "It's the only shot we've got."

Before he could act, an unexpected surge pulsed through the system. Frequency meters spiked into the red, and Jake felt the heat radiate from the console as alarms blared. Then, without warning, the screens went dark. An ominous silence swallowed the room.

"What… just happened?" Rachel whispered.

Moments later, the generators groaned like dying giants, shaking the steel frame of the plant. An explosion rattled the structure. Sparks flew, illuminating the room as circuits fried, equipment overloaded, and snapping wires arced with bursts of electricity.

"No, no, no," Jake gasped, hammering the keys in desperation, scrambling to reroute the system. But the chain reaction spread rapidly across the interconnected web of substations, transformers, and power lines that stretched from Eastlake across the nation. Screens flickered one last time, then went black.

The plant fell still. The only sound was their ragged breathing.

Rachel's voice broke the silence, low and horrified. "We… just killed the whole grid."

A faint scent curled through the air: brimstone, acrid and unmistakable. No electrical fire smelled like that.

Jake slumped forward, the weight of failure crushing him. He pictured the country plunging into darkness, block by block, city by city, state by state.

Cold seeped through the plant's walls. This was more than the loss of power; an impenetrable darkness settled over the country. It was a final, crushing silence, a descent into the unknown, a terrifying stillness as a world stripped of heat slipped hopelessly into the dark.

And with it, the still unidentified virus would spread unchecked, its dark shadow slowly consuming everything.

CHAPTER 3

Village of Lake Ronkonkoma, New York
March 24th

Without power, even simple necessities like repairing a pair of glasses became difficult…

Lake Ronkonkoma felt abandoned by the world. Once a bustling village, it now resembled a ghost town. The crisp scent of fresh snow should have been invigorating, but instead it made Jack shiver as he walked beside Jouris, clutching his cracked glasses. The late afternoon sun sagged toward the horizon. With the electrical grid fried, the village seemed like a town dreading sundown.

Jouris led the way, ice crunching underfoot as they passed shuttered shops and darkened storefronts. Shadows darted behind torn curtains, but no faces appeared. People wearing surgical masks drifted silently through the streets like phantoms, avoiding each other and the newcomers. No one made eye contact.

"Friendly place," Jack muttered, squinting through blurred vision. His breaths came shallow and quick, unease mounting with every step.

Jouris paused, eyes sweeping the empty streets. "Something's wrong. More than just the blackout." His voice lowered. "These people… they're scared. Scared of each other. Or maybe of us."

They reached the optometrist's office, a modest brick building with a cracked sign hanging crookedly above the door. The windows were fogged over, the once-bright *Ronkonkoma Eye Care* lettering faded to near illegibility.

Jouris tried the door, but it was locked. He knocked, but silence answered.

"Great," Jack sighed, leaning against the cold brick wall. "What now? I can barely see, and my head's splitting from squinting all day."

He dug into his pocket, popped two Tylenol, and swallowed dry.

Jouris gestured for Jack to follow around back. An alley littered with broken bottles and rusted cans led to the rear door, its lock broken, hanging ajar. A moldy stench of stagnant water drifted out. Faint daylight filtered through the front windows, casting a dim light on the interior.

Inside, the exam room stood like a time capsule. Fetid water pooled across the floor. Instruments lay scattered, and drawers were left hanging open.

Jouris glanced at the warped ceiling tiles. "Frozen pipes. Must've burst."

Cracked eyeglass frames littered a dusty table, most missing their lenses. Jouris rifled through cabinets, pulling out trays of spare lenses, none matching Jack's prescription.

"Figures," Jouris muttered, tossing them aside. "Even if we found the right strength, without power, the cutter's useless."

Jack slumped into the exam chair, rubbing his temples. "So what now? We just leave?"

"Not yet." Jouris leaned on the arm of the chair, studying the crack in Jack's lens. "We'll improvise."

Jack arched an eyebrow. "Improvise? You're not duct taping these to my face, are you?"

"Not quite." Jouris dug through another drawer and produced a roll of clear tape. "We clean the lens and cover it with plastic wrap. It's not perfect, but it'll stabilize the crack and reduce the distortion."

Jack hesitated, then nodded. "Better than nothing."

They cleaned the lens and trimmed the tape. Jouris pressed the wrap flat, smoothing the edges until it held. Jack put the glasses back on and blinked.

"It's… better," he said softly. His world was still blurred, but less fractured. "Thanks."

"Temporary fix," Jouris replied. "We'll find someone in Smithtown to grind a new lens."

An old *Newsday* lay on the counter. Its headline froze Jack midstep.

The Next Pandemic?

"Hollowing plague. What's that?" he asked, squinting to read the article.

Jouris peered over Jack's shoulder. "That explains the masks and why that woman crossed the street to avoid us."

Back outside, the ghost town felt emptier than before. Jack rolled his neck until it cracked, tension grinding on his nerves. Jouris placed a steady hand on his shoulder.

"We'll figure it out. One way or another, we keep moving."

As they left the village behind, Jack couldn't shake the feeling of unseen eyes tracking their every step.

***

While Jack and Jouris are in Lake Ronkonkoma Village, Back at the Safehouse…
March 24th

Bark! Bark!

David froze at the top of the basement stairs, gripping the banister so tightly his knuckles whitened. The barking below was sharp, urgent, nothing like Daphne's usual cheerful yap.

"Daphne, are you down there?"

The silence gripped him like a cold hand. His father and Jouris were gone to town, and he had no idea where Louis or Anne were.

"She couldn't be down there," David whispered, voice trembling. "Just a minute ago, she was on the couch."

He glanced into the living room. The couch was empty.

The house groaned, a low, mournful sound that felt like a warning. Swallowing hard, David turned back to the stairwell and began to descend. Each step creaked under his weight. The air grew colder, heavy with the scent of mildew and damp earth.

At the bottom, he yanked the chain. A single bulb flickered to life overhead, swaying gently, casting ghostly shadows on the stone walls.

Thank God the generator's still running.

"Daphne?" His voice barely carried, swallowed by the thick stillness.

Sneakers scraping the dirt floor, David shuffled forward. His heartbeat thundered in his chest. No sign of Daphne. Only silence, broken by the faint buzz of flies stirring in the corners.

His foot struck something solid. He stumbled, arms flailing to steady himself. Looking down, he saw the rusted bars of the iron cage that his father and Jouris had uncovered in the flooded basement.

Kneeling, he touched the slick, damp metal, ominous beneath his hesitant fingers.

Pain flared as the cage's sharp edge sliced his fingertip. Blood welled dark and thick. He winced, clenching his hand, as his eyes caught a faint carving on the bolted iron plate. Jagged letters, crude but clear: *P* and a faint *VH*.

He traced the initials with his uninjured hand, unease twisting in his stomach.

Bark!

The sudden bark nearly sent him sprawling. Daphne stood at the top of the stairs, her golden fur catching the dim light. She panted happily, tail wagging as if nothing were wrong.

Relief rushed over him. "Daphne! How'd you get back up there?"

The dog blinked, tilting her head with innocent curiosity.

David quickly snapped off the light and bolted upstairs.

Unseen, blood from his injured finger dripped into the soil inside the cage… hissing and smoking faintly in the dark.

He slammed the door behind him, his heart pounding in his chest.

***

"David, are you okay?" Anne called after him as he slammed the basement door and hurried upstairs without answering.

She paused, "I wonder what that was all about."

Shrugging, Anne hummed absently and stepped back into the kitchen. The faint creak of floorboards behind her barely registered as she focused on preparing dinner. With the generator's fuel running low, she knew she had to use what was in the fridge before it spoiled.

She pulled a fresh clove of garlic from the bulb, the papery skin rustling softly between her fingers as she placed it on the cutting board. Pressing the flat side of her knife down, she relished the satisfying crunch.

But instead of the sharp, familiar scent of garlic, a strange metallic tang filled the air. Anne hesitated, brows knitting in confusion.

"That's odd," she muttered, then dismissed it.

She began chopping again, the steady rhythm of the blade against the board oddly comforting… at first.

Then the texture beneath her knife changed. Too soft. Almost spongy. A creeping dread whispered: the clove was alive. She stopped, eyes locked downward.

A thin greenish fluid seeped from the crushed garlic, oozing like sap. Her stomach turned as the clove beneath her blade pulsed faintly. She froze, knife suspended in mid-air.

The clove twitched.

"What the…"

The garlic skin split open. Tiny, insect-like legs wriggled free, scurrying across the cutting board.

The knife slipped from her grasp. Heart racing, Anne stumbled backward, eyes fixed on the grotesque thing. The chopped pieces writhed, merging into a single shape with curling, multi-jointed legs. It scurried toward the edge of the counter with eerie, deliberate speed.

The greenish fluid oozed in its wake, dripping onto the floor where it bubbled and hissed, leaving warped stains. Anne stared, disbelief rooting her in place, until a drop splattered on her hand.

Pain exploded like lightning through her skin.

She gasped, watching flesh blister where the fluid touched, the edges blackening and shriveling. Panic surged as the burning crawled up her arm, her fingers turning numb and powerless.

The thing writhed on the counter, legs scraping, then lurched and dropped to the floor, charging at her, leaving a trail of decay.

"No, no, no!" Anne cried.

Breath ragged, she reached for a towel, desperate to stem the burn. But the pain climbed faster than she could react. The room spun, the metallic tang mingling with the acrid stench of rot.

And then, everything stopped.

Anne stood frozen, chest heaving. The burning ceased as abruptly as it had begun. Trembling, she filled a glass with water and gulped it down. Still clutching the glass, she opened the refrigerator with unsteady hands and reached for lettuce.

She shut the door with her elbow.

In the stainless steel reflection stood a figure… dark, indistinct, yet unmistakably human.

She spun, but the doorway was empty.

The glass slipped from her fingers, shattering on the floor. Her heart pounded as she backed away, crunching shards beneath her feet. The metallic scent lingered but the green fluid was gone. No burn marks, no decay. Only silence, broken by the faucet's steady drip.

Later, Anne chose not to tell Jack.

But long after she and David, with his bandaged hand, had gone to bed, the house seemed to exhale a deep, shuddering sigh. Shadows stretched unnaturally across the yard, and the air grew heavy with watchful anticipation.

Deep indentations marked the damp earth outside the basement, three massive, clawed toes pressed into the soil.

Whatever made them moved slowly, deliberately, into the surrounding woods.

The tracks glimmered faintly in the pale moonlight as a presence slipped into the darkness.

***

A World away in an Underground Bunker Pyongyang, North Korea March 24th

In a crumbling fortress, mankind's legion of doom meets, blind to the truth that they are mere pawns on a burning chessboard…

Beneath the ancient ruins of Taesong Fortress, representatives from China, Russia, Cuba, Iran, Venezuela, and North Korea gathered around a massive oak table. The air was thick and stale as if an invisible specter urged them toward destruction and chaos. Flickering lamps cast long shadows across their faces. The conversation sizzled with hostility.

"The United States is a carcass ripe for the picking," growled the Cuban envoy, rolling up the sleeves of his olive-green uniform. He slammed his fist against the table. "Their electrical grid has collapsed. Now is the time to strike!"

The Chinese delegate, sharp-eyed and steely, tapped her manicured fingernails against the table's worn surface. "Taiwan still defies us. They must be brought to heel before we squander resources chasing America's ghosts."

"Fools!" the Iranian snapped, eyes ablaze. "Israel is the true threat! While you bicker over islands and dying democracies, the Zionists gather strength. They must be wiped out first!"

The North Korean general, face flushed, thundered, "You speak as if South Korea can wait! That land is ours by right. The United States is crippled; powerless to intervene."

137

"Enough!" The Russian leader's voice cracked like a whip, halting the volley of insults. "We convened to discuss the United States. Their collapse is our chance to end their meddling… permanently."

Accusations and insults flew like bullets. Russia, bent on invading Europe, rejected nuclear strikes, insisting resources must remain intact. China and North Korea bickered over priorities, each eager to settle ancient grudges. Iran's obsession with Israel rang on and on, while Venezuela and Cuba demanded a united assault on America.

Finally, a grim consensus emerged.

"It is agreed," The Russian Foreign Secretary declared, buttoning his suit jacket with cold precision. "We strike the United States first with nuclear weapons. One swift blow to cripple their military and secure our future campaigns."

Their rancor blinded them to their role in an older, crueler drama… a play written long before any nation rose or fell…

Suddenly, the heavy oak doors burst open. A blinding crimson light flooded the chamber. A fiery red horse thundered across the stone floor, sparks flying with each hoofbeat. Smoke poured from its nostrils, its eyes glowing like molten embers. Its rider, a woman wreathed in flames, dismounted with regal menace.

Her sultry, commanding voice echoed through the fortress: "I am Prosperine, Princess of Hell. I have come to witness the birth of your chaos."

The leaders froze. Before shock could register, two guards were hurled inside, necks grotesquely twisted. Behind them strode a towering figure, the air pulsing with malevolence. Lucius Rofocale, in a sharply tailored suit stretched tight over his massive frame, advanced with contained, violent menace.

"You will dispatch workers to Jerusalem," Lucius growled. "They will build Prosperine's temple."

The North Korean leader sneered, spitting contempt. "Who are you to give orders? And as for her," he spat at Prosperine, "I take no commands from women."

Lucius's eyes narrowed. His suit tore as his form swelled, skin darkening, smoldering, and leathery. Flames licked at his outline as he leaned forward, his voice a guttural hiss.

"You dare insult her in my presence?"

Prosperine raised her hand, a demure, mocking smile playing on her lips. She leaned close, whispering, "Bravery deserves reward." Her tongue, barbed and serpentine, shot forward. In seconds, the North Korean's life drained away. His shriveled corpse collapsed into dust on the stone floor.

Her gaze swept the table, eyes blazing with the fury of a raging inferno. "Now, you will meet your quotas. Each of you will deliver a hundred thousand souls to build my temple."

The silence was absolute.

She scoffed, pacing the room. "You fancy yourselves Gods of War. Then, wage your wars. Let your people starve and kill each other over the scraps of this dying planet. But remember: your nuclear weapons are mine. You will not destroy humanity. That privilege I reserve for myself."

Prosperine mounted her steed once more. The horse reared, its hooves crashing onto the oak table, splitting it in two. Fire and smoke consumed them, and she vanished.

Lucius lingered, his smoldering skin casting a hellish glow. "Do as she commands, or suffer a fate worse than death," he warned, then disappeared.

The leaders sat in silence, their bravado burned away. They understood now. Their true masters had arrived… beings whose thirst for power dwarfed their own, eternal as it was merciless… and absolute

***

The soft thud of padded paws echoed through the quiet house as Daphne bounded up the stairs. The squeak of the tennis ball in her mouth was followed by the quick beat of her paws as she raced back down.

Moments later, the ball reappeared at the top of the stairs, wobbled, and bounced down.

Thump... thump-thump... thud-thump-thud

It landed at the bottom of the stairs and rolled lazily across the hall. Daphne's ears perked up. She lunged after her prize, jaws snapping shut before she spun in place, her stubby tail wagging furiously, and sprinted back up the stairs.

Jack looked up from the couch where he sat beside Anne, scratching his head as she critiqued his latest training session.

"She's got more stamina than I do," he muttered with a grin.

Anne teased, not glancing up, "She might be a more attentive recruit."

They chuckled, and Anne added, "But you're doing well."

Thump... thump-thump... thud-thump-thud

The ball tumbled down again, Daphne hot on its heels, her nails clicking against the hardwood floor like typewriter keys.

Jack shook his head, smirking. "She'll sleep like a log tonight. She's bound to wear herself out."

Anne leaned forward, elbows on her knees, watching Daphne scamper up, her floppy ears bouncing with every step. The dog's energy was infectious.

For several minutes, the rhythm persisted: ball up, ball down, Daphne sprinting after it like a track star.

Until the ball didn't return.

Daphne sat at the bottom of the stairs, body taut, head tilted, ears pricked. Her tail wagged once, twice, then stopped. She barked sharply, then louder, more insistent.

"Looks like she finally wore out whoever's throwing it," Jack joked, not looking up.

But Daphne didn't move. Her bark sharpened, almost scolding, as if chastising something unseen.

Anne called, "Daphne! Enough, girl!"

No ball. Only barking.

Jack sighed, pausing his solitaire game. "I'll check it out."

He rose, stretching as he walked down the hall with Anne close behind. Together, they stopped at the bottom of the stairs.

Daphne sat midway up the landing, gaze fixed upward. Her bark was steady now, more curious than frantic.

Anne's voice was light, tinged with curiosity: "What's got into you, girl?"

Jack called, "Louis! Send the ball back down for her."

Silence. Then footsteps, not from above, but from behind.

They pivoted just as Louis appeared in the hallway, a bag of chips in hand. He paused mid-chew, eyes darting from them to Daphne.

"What?" he asked, his mouth full.

Behind him, David piped up, "Can I have some of those chips, Louis?"

Anne blinked rapidly, her heart hammering. "Louis… David… neither of you was upstairs?"

Louis arched an eyebrow, crumpling the bag for another handful. "I've been in the kitchen. Why?"

Jack's gaze cut to Anne, then up the stairs. Daphne remained perched on the landing, tail wagging, head tilted toward something unseen. Her big brown eyes met Anne's, as if awaiting a command. She barked again… sharp, playful, eager.

Anne's eyes tracked Daphne's gaze. "Who's up there?" she whispered.

No answer.

Jack stepped forward, craning his neck upward. Shadows bled across the hall where the upstairs light failed to reach.

"Daphne," Anne said calmly, "come down. Now."

The dog didn't move. Another sharp bark split the silence.

That's when Jack saw it.

A faint shadow pressed against the wall where the light faded, shifting as if leaning forward to watch. His mouth went dry instantly.

"Jack, what is it…" Anne started, but he cut her off with a raised hand, pointing into the darkness.

Daphne barked again, tail wagging faster as if waiting for the game to resume.

The shadow moved. It crawled rather than walked. Jack saw it clearly now… watching him.

Daphne's ears drooped, her tail stilled. She tilted her head.

Jack's heart hammered, his legs heavy as iron stakes driven into the floor.

Slowly. Very slowly. The ball rolled down the stairs.

It didn't bounce. It slid, rubber squealing against wood like a scream. It passed Jack, wobbled, then came to rest against Anne's feet.

The house fell silent.

From the top of the stairs, a bark echoed down.

Not Daphne's.

Too low, too slow, too mocking.

It sounded like laughter.

***

Safehouse Lake Ronkonkoma, New York
Later in the Evening March 25th

The air in the room felt heavy, like the blanket draped over Anne's shoulders. She sat cross-legged on the bed, absorbed in the journal Jouris had given her weeks ago.

BAM!

A sudden gust slammed against the house, jolting Anne from her reading. The structure shuddered, like a train rushing by before power had been lost. The candle's dim yellow flame flickered wildly, shadows dancing across the walls. Her eyes traced the jagged scrawl of the handwriting, part cursive, part print, words etched like scars into the yellowed paper.

The journal smelled of damp wood and old ink. Its curled pages stuck together, resisting her gentle coaxing as she carefully separated them. She had read these lines a dozen times, yet their meaning still slipped from her grasp.

They walk unseen but leave their weight behind.

Her gaze lingered on the phrase, her mind replaying the sound of the ball tumbling down the stairs. Thump... thump-thump... thud-thump-thud. A chill ran down her spine as she pictured Daphne's tail wagging at something unseen, something that shouldn't be there.

Pressing the page flat, she exhaled slowly through her nose.

Manifestations offer invitations.

Her thumb traced the faint ridges of ink, a line as haunting as when the basement door unlatched.

The ball. The door latch.

She hadn't told Jack about the footsteps in the night, or the tug at her coat in the basement. At first, she thought it snagged on a nail, until she realized she'd been leaning against bare stone. The memory made her chest tighten.

The stairs.

Her hand moved automatically to her side, fingers brushing the bruise still raw from slamming her hip against the railing. Jack thought she'd tripped. She let him believe that. No way would she admit something cold and invisible had shoved her harder than a linebacker.

Her jaw clenched as she closed the journal shut with a soft thud. She glanced at the door, longing for the faint glow of the nightlight that no longer spilled beneath it.

For a long moment, she sat still, ears straining for sound beyond the door. No footsteps. No creaks.

Not yet.

Pressing her palms to her knees, she forced the rising anxiety down. She would not let this place invade her mind.

"You don't give it an inch," Mark Desmond had warned. "Because an inch is all it needs."

The battle within raged. She could tell Jack everything, but then what? He'd stop his training, hit the pause button to "*figure it out.*" That wasn't why they came here. Investigating Lake Ronkonkoma wasn't the plan.

She wouldn't let her fears derail them.

Her eyes darted to the journal, as if it waited to reveal more. Slowly, she pushed it aside.

Focus on the mission.

Her clock read 11:30. Later than she expected. Lips pressed tight, she rose, bare feet touching the cold wooden floor. The temperature had dropped again, as it always did after midnight.

She rubbed her arms, glancing at the window. Frost spread along the glass, jagged white veins creeping inward. Her reflection blurred in the foggy pane, and if she stared long enough, sometimes she thought something shifted behind her.

"Not tonight," she whispered, voice steadier than she felt.

Crossing the room, she drew the curtains closed. The fabric rustled too loudly in the silence. After dark, every sound felt amplified and every whisper seemed like a shout.

Her fingers lingered on the gap where the curtains didn't fully close. She hated that gap; just wide enough to feel like something might be watching. She tugged it shut. Turning back, she froze.

The journal was no longer where she'd left it.

It lay open, pages spread like wings, one corner caught mid-flip.

Her chest rose in shallow, rapid breaths. A voice in her mind screamed: *It was closed. I know it was closed!*

Her throat went dry. For what felt like an eternity, she stared, waiting.

Stay calm. Panic was what it wanted.

She forced a long breath, regaining control. Then she stepped forward. The journal seemed to watch her.

Her fingers hovered above the page. *If I touch it, will it move?*

Jaw tight, she pressed down on the ancient paper. Nothing. No writing, only blank pages.

Her nails dug into the leather cover as she snapped it shut. Silence pressed in, suffocating.

Anne's gaze flicked to the door. The house was quiet, but her heart knew better. She was not alone. No one ever was.

Her grip tightened on the journal. The mirror on the wall caught her eye. Just a glance…

Something was there.

She spun. Nothing.

Her reflection stared back, pale, wide-eyed, chest heaving like she'd run a sprint.

No. Not *her* reflection.

Her breath caught as the face blinked.

Anne's heart dropped. Terror locked her body. The image lingered, just long enough for her to know she'd seen it.

She snuffed the candle with her fingers. A sharp breath escaped her lips. The puff of smoke curled, the room growing colder.

She turned to the door.

A pale yellow glow seeped beneath it.

Impossible. There was no power.

Her pulse quickened. She pressed back against the wall, eyes fixed on the crack of light.

She waited.

One step at a time, Anne. Stay ahead of it. Don't give it an inch.

Her breath steadied. She glanced at the journal, closed now, its secrets locked away. But she'd learned enough.

"It's time to push him," she whispered. "Jack's moment has come."

Her eyes darted again to the door. It's just a house, Anne. Just a house.

Soft footsteps echoed. Bare feet on wood, slow and deliberate.

One... two... three...

Then silence.

Her fingers pressed into the wall, as if she could disappear into it.

From beyond the door came a familiar sound.

Thump... thump-thump... thud-thump-thud.

Anne froze.

Something scratched at the door. Not a knock. A deliberate scratch.

Her breath caught. She stared long enough to feel like she might burn a hole through the wood.

Then, defying reason, she stepped closer.

The scratching stopped.

Only silence remained.

***

Safehouse Lake Ronkonkoma, New York
Dusk March 25th

After parking the car, Anne's boots crunched over icy gravel, each step a silent mantra: stay calm, stay focused. A biting wind cut through her coat as if mocking her resolve. The shed door slammed behind her, sending unease creeping up her spine. She paused, eyes sweeping the barren yard. Leafless trees loomed like skeletal sentinels, their gnarled branches creaking as they clawed at the heavy, gray sky.

The house loomed ahead, an indifferent monolith shrouded in the gathering dusk. Each window stared like a lidless eye, dark and unblinking. Anne quickened her pace, clutching the book tighter. Its worn leather pulsed faintly against her chest, beating with her heart. *It knows*, she thought. *It knows what I'm planning.*

At the back door, she hesitated. A faint vibration hummed through her boots, a sensation she'd noticed before but dismissed as imagination. Though she had hidden it from Jack and the boys, she now admitted the house had felt off from the start. The ground itself seemed alive, a coil of unspoken tension lying just beneath the surface.

Anne pulled the kitchen door open; the hinges shrieked in protest. Stepping inside, she felt the air thicken, tinged with a scent of metallic ozone. She shut the door firmly behind her. Silence. The house seemed to hold its breath.

An hour earlier, she'd sent Jack to Sweet Hollow Road. The reason: training. The truth: Jack needed to learn, but she needed time to unravel the mysteries in the book Jouris had given her.

She pulled it from beneath her jacket, turning it over in her hands. The leather was rough, almost scaly, as if reacting to cold or touch. Symbols etched into the cover seemed to shift, rearranging into indecipherable patterns. The eerie sensation deepened with every glance at its cover.

Carrying it into the living room, she rekindled the fire. Embers glowed, smoke mingling with the faint aroma of musty, aged paper. At the desk, she opened the book to the last page.

So far, it had revealed very little beyond its link to the Van Haalan property at Lake Ronkonkoma. She knew the house hid secrets older than she could fathom, but the script was illegible, a flowing scrawl that seemed to shift as she stared at it. Narrowing her eyes, she leaned closer, whispering the single word she had managed to decipher.

"*Monitus.*"

"Latin," she breathed. "Warning. Warning of what?"

The fire flared, flooding the room with light. Anne's shadow stretched grotesquely across the wall. A low hum swelled into a voice.

Do you think he will survive?

Anne recoiled, scanning the room. The voice was neither male nor female; just slow and deliberate.

"Who's there?" she demanded, her voice trembling despite the effort to sound firm.

The fire cracked, casting sparks suspended in mid-air. A presence neared. Then, laughter… a hollow, grating sound that chilled her.

You believe you can prepare him. You think you can conceal the truth. But this house knows your secret, Anne. It always has.

The room fell still. The embers dimmed. Shadows receded. Anne's hands shook as she slammed the book shut, shoving it away as if distance could sever whatever connection it had formed.

A loud thump echoed upstairs, followed by the creak of floorboards. The sounds tugged at memories of past supernatural confrontations.

Her pulse quickened. She rose, gripping the iron poker by the fireplace. The house felt alive, its walls shifting as if breathing, the air charged with malevolent energy.

Jack needed to return from Sweet Hollow Road. But Anne knew the presence inside the house was waiting for him, ready to challenge his sanity, haunt his dreams, and obscure the trials ahead.

She climbed the first stair, poker raised. Knowing iron was a fragile shield against the darkness closing in, she whispered under her breath,

"Our Father. Who art in heaven…"

***

Sweet Hollow Road Huntington, New York
Nearing Midnight on March 25th

Scattered stones, once burial mounds, are all that remain of an ancient Native American graveyard where the restless past whispers warnings to those who dare tread its shadows. The Algonquin called it Ahdin, or "highland." Long Islanders know it as Mount Misery…

Jack adjusted the strap of his pack, pulling it tighter against his aching shoulders. Snow crunched beneath his boots, the sound unnaturally loud in the eerie stillness. The beastly wind that had howled like a hurricane all day suddenly calmed, leaving behind an oppressive silence. The moon hung low, its pale light spilling across the snow-blanketed landscape.

The road stretched ahead, flanked by skeletal trees whose branches reached skyward like twisted fingers. Shadows shifted and danced in the moonlight, playing tricks on his weary mind. Jack exhaled, his breath blooming in the frigid air as he pressed forward.

Anne's words echoed in his mind: *Absorb the pain and become stronger. Let that strength rule your mind.*

Now he felt the truth of these words. His body ached, and his muscles burned, but he was no longer captive to the sensations. They lingered, yes, but as background noise in the symphony of his resolve.

The stories of Sweet Hollow Road stirred: hauntings, strange disappearances, and shadow figures lurking just out of sight. Anne never mentioned them, but Jack had heard others whisper about this haunted highway. Once, he would have dismissed them as urban legends. But not tonight. Not under the cloak of midnight.

A rustling sound jolted him from his thoughts. He froze, his heart racing. The faint sound came from the woods on his right. He scanned the darkness, senses taut.

"Just a squirrel," he muttered, though the words felt hollow. A half-chuckle followed: *Spidey Senses tingling.* "Maybe I'm not the only one taking this test?"

He quickened his pace, unease riding on his shoulders. The road seemed infinite, with darkness stretching without end. His watch read 12:15 a.m., but time here felt stagnant, as though the night itself had him in its grip.

The first marker appeared: a weathered highway sign half-buried in the snow. The lettering was faded, but one word remained: *Hollow.* Jack hesitated, a knot twisting in his gut.

This is the test. Face the fear. Keep moving.

He pressed on. The air grew charged, almost electric. Gooseflesh prickled his skin. Unseen eyes tracked him. He resisted the urge to glance back. Whatever followed would reveal itself on its own terms.

The second marker loomed: an old iron gate, its bars twisted and rusted. Beyond it, a narrow path wound into the woods. Jack stopped, hands on his knees, catching his breath. The scene felt familiar, like Route 666 and the Seven Gates of Hell in the Culpeper woods. The path pulsed with an unnatural darkness, trees leaning inward as if conspiring to shut out the light.

"You've come this far," he whispered.

He stepped through the gate. The crunch of snow gave way to the forest's muffled silence. The cold felt different here, sharp and biting, seeping into his core, wrapping itself around his soul.

The path wound deeper into the woods, and the darkness thickened. Jack's breathing grew shallow. He rechecked his watch; it was well past 2 a.m.

Then, a faint light flickered ahead. Weak yet steady. Dread and determination mingled as he pressed toward it. Somehow, he knew he was nearing the end.

The final marker stood in a clearing: a solitary, leafless tree with charred bark, its roots twisting into frozen ground. A lantern hung from one branch, swaying gently despite the still air.

Beneath it waited a figure cloaked in shadow, its face concealed. Motionless, it radiated an oppressive weight that crushed Jack's chest. The legends of Sweet Hollow Road pressed down on his shoulders as heavily as his pack.

"Jack," the figure said, its voice low and resonant, echoing in the clearing.

Jack's throat tightened. He didn't respond.

"You've come far," it continued. "But here your journey stops. To advance, you must let go of something."

The words struck Jack like a sledgehammer. Their meaning was clear, yet their implications were chilling.

"What do you mean?" Jack whispered.

The figure extended a skeletal hand toward his pack.

"Give it to me, and you may leave this place."

Jack's mind raced. Anne had warned him of tests designed to break his resolve, to exploit his fears. Yet the tone carried an ancient authority that made him waver.

What is the real test?

His hands trembled as he lifted the pack. Anne never told him what was inside; she only instructed him to keep it safe.

He hesitated, clenching his fists tightly.

"No," he said, his voice firming.

The figure tilted its head, intrigued.

"I was told to keep it safe. I don't trust you."

The lantern flared, casting the figure's face in light. Its face was hollow, with indistinct features, more shadow than flesh.

"Then you have chosen," it intoned. The ground beneath Jack's feet trembled.

"Welcome to Mount Misery."

***

Mount Misery?

Jack's breath fogged as he dragged himself up the steep incline. The terrain was treacherous, with rocks jutting out at sharp angles and loose earth shifting beneath his boots. His legs burned, and the cold sweat on his back deepened the chill biting into his skin. Above him, clouds churned unnaturally, their shapes twisting like living things.

A pale, eerie light shimmered across the hillside. Not moonlight or the glow of a fire, it seemed to radiate from the ground, casting the slope in otherworldly pallor.

As he climbed, Jack glimpsed the faint outlines of houses scattered across the ridge like broken teeth. Their windows were dark, their frames sagging under years of neglect. He remembered the stories: how families abandoned them after the 1977 blackout, how strange occurrences soon followed, with people vanishing without a trace.

Distracted, Jack stumbled, his boot catching on something solid. Brushing at the mud, he expected to see a rock or a tree root. Instead, his hand found a smooth, pale bone.

A skull.

He recoiled, his heart hammering. The empty sockets glared up at him, hollow and accusatory. Jack scrambled to his feet, pulse roaring in his ears.

Ahead, a shimmer of white drifting silently among the trees caught his eye... a veiled woman in a flowing white gown.

"Hey!" Jack called, but she slipped deeper into the woods, her form flickering like a dying flame. Compelled by some unseen pull, he followed. Each step drew him further from the road.

Then she was gone.

Jack spun in circles, confusion bordering on panic rising in his chest. The woods closed in, suffocating.

"I'm lost," he whispered.

Suddenly, red and blue lights strobed through the trees. A police car sat at the edge of the road, its lights flashing erratically. Relief flooded over him.

"Thank Christ," he muttered.

A figure stepped out, his uniform contrasting sharply against the chaos of the flashing lights. Jack quickened his pace.

"Officer!"

As the man turned. Jack froze. His face was caved in, revealing his skull through the torn flesh. Blood soaked his uniform, dripping onto the asphalt.

The figure raised an arm and pointed at Jack.

"You shouldn't be here," he rasped, his voice low and wet.

Jack stumbled back. Then, in a burst of unnatural speed, the officer rushed him. Jack braced himself for impact, only for the figure to vanish, leaving behind the acrid scent of decay.

Before Jack could recover, a black Labrador trotted across his path, its eyes gleaming unnaturally. It paused, staring at him for a long moment, then moved on. Instinct overrode fear, and Jack followed.

At the edge of the road, the dog dug urgently at the frozen ground. Its claws scraped against something solid, prompting Jack to step closer.

The dog rose on its hind legs. Its body warped grotesquely, towering over him. Its fiery red eyes locked on his.

Jack staggered back, instinctively flexing his hand... the one crushed by...

"It can't be. The Strigoi!"

The creature smirked, a dark omen, then vanished into the trees. Jack's knees buckled, but he forced himself upright and pushed on.

The road led to an overpass. Ice coated the railings, and Jack froze, his fear of bridges gripping him.

At the far end, a small figure appeared: a girl in a tattered dress, her face streaked with tears. "They never found my body," she sobbed, her voice echoing through the emptiness.

Jack's chest tightened as he watched her climb the railing. For a moment, he saw Louis at age two, reaching for an open second-story window... then David pale and bald, fighting leukemia. More than a specter, this fragile girl embodied everything he feared losing.

"Wait!" he shouted, racing toward her.

She turned, her hollow eyes locking with his, then she leaned forward to fall. Jack lunged, gripping her arm. Her touch was icy, and her skin felt paper-thin.

He looked down, but he didn't see a child; skeletal remains crumbled in his hands.

The world spun. Darkness fell.

Then, Jack found himself lying on the ground beside the vehicle that Anne had left. His body throbbed as if he had been beaten. The engine hummed, its headlights slicing through the night.

A low growl rose from the woods.

The black Labrador stood at the treeline, fiery eyes fixed on him.

Jack climbed into the vehicle. The dog's gaze seared into his back as he sped away.

Mount Misery faded in his rearview mirror, but its shadows lingered, gnawing at the edges of his mind.

On the dashboard lay a note in Anne's handwriting:

Training is over, Jack. Hurry back.

***

While Jack Aitken is on Mount Misery
Secret Lab Beneath Pergamon in Present-Day Turkiye

Tatiana sat in the cold flickering glow of the subterranean computer lab, surrounded by the hum of servers and the faint scent of scorched circuitry. Hidden beneath Pergamon's ancient edifice, the lab was her refuge from her fading influence in Lucius's court. Once his most feared servant, she was now overlooked, her name whispered less in reverence to her legend as Lucius's longest-serving aide, and more as a forgotten, obsolete relic. With Heaven conquered and the Apocalypse underway, Lucius had little need for her.

A jagged memory tore through her thoughts… the night George Aitken had beaten Barbas for his vile attack on her. She had thought vengeance would bring relief, but Lucius's cold reprimand cut deeper. With one disdainful glance, he told George, "She needs to fight her own battles." The sting of those words and her deep sense of betrayal still haunted her. In that moment she understood loyalty was not protection; it was a chain that left her vulnerable.

Tatiana leaned forward, her chin propped on clawed fingers, watching the AI sift through data on George Aitken's elusive targets: Jack, Anne, and the forsaken prophets, Louis and David. The AI's voice was soft, almost human in its cadence, as it narrated the findings and probabilities. Its neutral tone reminded her of what she feared losing: purpose, identity, and power.

"Tatiana," the AI intoned, breaking the silence. "Probability of target location: 17% near the New Jersey and New York border. Would you like me to refine the data further?"

She didn't answer right away; her eyes were glued to the map flashing on the screen. Instead, she whispered more to herself than to the machine. "Do you ever feel trapped in your own code? Like there's no escaping what you were meant to be?"

The AI paused. A soft click echoed through the lab as its circuitry recalibrated. "I am pr-pr-programmed to analyze, calculate, and assist. I do not feel."

Tatiana's lips curled into a humorless smile.

"Lucky you," she muttered. She slumped back in her chair, the weight of her thoughts pressing down. "You don't have to wrestle with what's happening to you. You don't have to wonder if you're falling apart."

Her claws tapped the armrest in a restless rhythm, betraying the calm mask she wore. Foolish or not, she spoke to the machine; there was no one else to turn to. Lucius no longer needed her. And George Aitken… George was another complication altogether.

Her chest tightened at the thought of him. George Aitken, Lucius's determined and bitter acolyte, embodied everything she was taught to despise. Human, weak, and driven by emotions like vengeance. Yet, she admired his resolve and willingness to sacrifice everything for his mission. When he avenged her for Barbas's brutality, she felt something she couldn't name.

Compassion? Gratitude? Lust?

Tatiana's claws gouged deep lines into the cold metal armrest.

"Ridiculous," she hissed, sulfur rising from her skin.

Yet beneath the demon's scorn, a fragile fissure widened. Emotions she'd been bred to reject clawed at her insides like a poison.

"Tatiana," the AI said, its voice almost soothing, "your heart rate has elevated. Would you like me to adjust the environmental controls for comfort?"

"No," she snapped, quickly following up with a soft tone. "No… I'm alright."

She leaned forward again, hands clasped tightly together.

"Do you think I'm broken?" she asked the machine. "I'm losing influence. My Lord doesn't need me anymore. And now I'm… feeling things I shouldn't. Sympathy. Guilt. Perhaps even…" She stopped herself, shaking her head. "Forget it."

The AI whirred softly, processing her words. "You are not broken. You are adapting. Change is a natural process."

Tatiana laughed bitterly.

"Adapting? No, I'm decaying. Falling apart. And when Lucius realizes this, he'll destroy me." Her voice dropped to a whisper. "And maybe he should."

For a moment, the lab was silent, except for the steady hum of the servers. The AI seemed to be reflecting on her despair in its own way.

Finally, it asked Tatiana, "Do you wish to continue assisting George Aitken in his search for Jack Aitken and his family?"

She hesitated. Loyalty to Lucius demanded obedience. Yet the treacherous part of her, the part that had felt something, yearned to shield George from the inevitable doom that awaited those who served Lucius too well, or for too long.

"Yes," she finally replied, her voice steady. "Keep searching."

As the AI resumed its calculations, Tatiana leaned back, staring at the ceiling. She had no idea how long she could maintain the façade. But for now she would focus on George, the search, anything to distract her from the truth of who or what she was becoming.

For now, she would hold onto the illusion of purpose.

***

Safehouse Lake Ronkonkoma, New York
3:15 AM March 26th, After Jack's Return From Mount Misery

The house was eerily quiet, save for the faint groaning of the wind pressing against the walls. Hours after returning from Mount Misery, Jack sat at the kitchen table, clutching a steaming cup of coffee he hadn't touched. The scalding shower and fresh clothes had done nothing to chase the chill of Mount Misery from his bones.

Anne stood by the sink, arms crossed tightly over her chest. She had been watching him since he entered, scratched, exhausted, and haunted. She hadn't pushed him to speak, sensing he needed time to process whatever had happened out there.

At last, Jack broke the silence. "I saw... things," he murmured, his voice shaky and low.

The shadows of Mount Misery still clung to him, refusing to lift.

"A cloaked woman. A small girl on a bridge. A dog, or something that resembled a dog, that bore a striking resemblance to the Strigoi. There was also a cop... his uniform soaked in blood, and half of his face missing."

Jack looked up at Anne, eyes burning with anger and desperation. "You knew, didn't you? You knew this was going to happen."

Anne's eyes lowered. She blinked rapidly, swallowing the surge of guilt that rose in her throat. Folding her arms tighter, she moved to the table. Sitting across from him, her pale, drawn face bore the deep creases carved by the burden of guarded secrets.

"Yes," she admitted finally, her voice barely above a whisper. "I knew something would happen. I didn't know exactly what, but I knew Mount Misery would show you things you weren't ready to see, but had to face. That's why I couldn't tell you beforehand."

Jack's grip tightened on the mug. "You could've warned me. David, Louis, they've been going through the same thing, haven't they?"

Anne nodded, guilt shadowing her face. "They have. And so have I." She hesitated, then leaned forward, her voice trembling. "Jack, I've seen things. Heard things. This house isn't just old and creepy. There's something here. Something tied to all of this."

Jack's jaw clenched, exhaustion sharpening his anger. "Then why keep it to yourself? Why let us think we were losing our minds?"

"Because you weren't ready," Anne said, her tone firm despite the emotion in her eyes. "You had to finish your training first. You needed to be strong enough to face what's out there, and what's in here."

She reached into the bag Jack had carried in from the car and pulled out the book Jouris had given her. Its leather cover looked even darker, the etched symbols faintly glowing in the dim kitchen light.

"This is part of it," she said, placing the book on the table. "Jouris gave it to me. It holds answers about Lake Ronkonkoma, about what's been happening to us. And about the Clifford brothers."

Jack squinted. "Billy and Lyle Clifford? I remember reading about them when I was a kid."

Anne nodded, opening the book to a page marked with a strip of red cloth. Her fingers hesitated at the worn corner before turning the page.

"Billy Clifford was committed after Lyle's body was discovered," she said softly, then inhaled deeply. "It was found stuffed in his foot-locker. Billy swore he was innocent, that something else had taken Lyle and left him there. But the evidence said otherwise."

Jack's stomach twisted. "And Lake Ronkonkoma?"

Anne locked eyes with him, blinking twice, gathering her courage.

"It's more than a lake. It's a doorway, an oracle. As William said, the tribes saw it as sacred, but they also feared it. For centuries, people have vanished here. Legends speak of a woman in white, a cursed spirit luring people to their destruction. I think what's tied to the lake is connected to this house, and to us now."

Jack leaned back, dragging a hand through his hair. "If we hadn't lived through what we have, I'd call this insane."

Before Anne could respond, hurried footsteps broke the silence. Jouris appeared in the doorway, bathrobe hanging loosely, his expression grim.

"There's something outside," he said sharply. "You need to see this."

Anne and Jack exchanged a glance, then rose together. Anne tucked the book under her arm as they followed him.

They stepped onto the porch. Dawn was breaking, the icy wind whipping around them. Jouris pointed toward the edge of the property, where a faint, unnatural light flickered among the trees.

"That's the same light I saw on Mount Misery," Jack declared firmly, his breath fogging the air.

Jouris's gaze remained fixed on the glow.

Anne spoke in a strained voice, saying, "It's moving."

The wind fell still as the light shifted, weaving through the trees with unsettling fluidity. A sulfurous stench filled the air, then the light vanished.

Jack clenched his fists, tension radiating through him. "Whatever it is, it followed me home."

Anne faced him, her tone steady yet firm. "This isn't another test. This is for real. Get ready."

***

Later in the Afternoon of March 26th…

This is why the old stories matter. The past is never truly gone. It lives, breathes, and waits just beneath the surface…

Jouris glanced nervously around the darkened woods, his breath misting in the cold air.

"William has lived here all his life," he told Jack and Anne. "He knows the stories; the things the land whispers to those who listen. If anyone can make sense of these footprints, it's him."

Spotting a truck in the distance, he exhaled in relief. "That's him."

"Lucky for you, the landlines still work." William slammed the door on his pickup.

Jouris waved. "Thanks for coming. Follow me." He pointed toward the safehouse.

As the cold air bit their faces, the weight of ancient legends pressed down, reminding them that history was not just memory, but a living, breathing force.

They found Anne and Jack crouched in the woods, staring at the ground. The impressions in the snow were enormous, three elongated toes ending in sharp points pressed deep into the frozen earth. The sheer size and depth of the prints defied logic, as if something impossibly large and heavy had passed through. Unmistakably inhuman, the prints radiated a strange energy that raised the hair on the back of William's neck.

William knelt, tracing the edges of one print with his finger. His weathered face grew serious, his usually steady hands trembling as he closed his eyes for a moment, whispering a quiet invocation in the Algonquin tongue… a prayer for guidance and protection.

"This isn't good," he murmured, his voice low and filled with warning.

"What do you mean?" Jack asked, a knot of anxiety tightening in his chest.

Jouris crouched beside William. "What do you think it is?"

Brushing the snow from his hands, William looked up, his eyes darting toward the trees as if expecting something to emerge.

"These are not ordinary footprints. They're a sign, a warning. What dwells in the lake now walks among us."

Anne glanced at Jouris, who nodded for William to continue. The tribal elder took a deep breath, and as he spoke, the past seemed to seep into the cold air, making history feel immediate and dangerously alive.

"Lake Ronkonkoma has always been sacred," he began. "The Setalcotts believed it was an oracle, a sacred gateway between worlds. Its waters healed the sick, granted visions, and even revealed truths to those who sought them. But such gifts always come with a price."

William's eyes darkened. "Over time, the lake's nature changed. The tribes noticed its hunger and grew to fear it. Sacrifices were made, first crops, then animals. For a while, the lake seemed appeased, but then…"

Instantly, the charged atmosphere was transformed; it grew quiet. Deathly quiet.

"What is it, William?" Jack urged.

Beneath the brim of his worn hat, William's voice dropped to a reverent hush.

"Long ago, before settlers came, there lived a young brave named Quanon. His story isn't just a legend; it is the seed of what stirs within the lake, even now. He was the son of a powerful Setalcott chief, Powwan, and destined for greatness."

Jack listened intently, the tale settling around him like a cold mist, a bridge between the old world and the darkness they now faced.

As daylight waned, their silhouettes cast long shadows against the stone walls of the safehouse. They seemed to lean in, closer, like they were listening, when William continued,

"At the autumnal equinox, the four tribes would gather at the shores of Ronkonkoma for the sacred trials, the ritual marking the passage into manhood. Setalcott lore says that Quanon's trial became more than ritual; it became a battle for his soul. A battle he lost."

Anne's lips pressed tight before she asked what they all wondered. "What happened to Quanon?"

"The chiefs," Jouris interjected, his voice thick with emotion. "You mean Quanon's father, Chief Powwan?"

William's jaw tightened. "Yes. Legend says that the lake corrupted Quanon. Powwan and the others pursued him to the center of Ronkonkoma, where the Mishibijin consumed them. Quanon vanished too. They say he remains bound to the lake, searching to undo what he did."

He let the silence linger before continuing.

"Then, people began to disappear. Those who fell into the lake were said to descend into Hell itself, their souls claimed for eternity. The lake *never* gives up its dead."

Anne shivered, clutching the book against her chest. "You're saying it became corrupted?"

William nodded solemnly. "Yes. No one knows when or how, but something evil took root in these depths. The tribes believed the lake had been tainted, perhaps by something older, darker. It was no longer an oracle but a prison. A gateway not to the spirits of the ancestors but to something wicked. The Mishibijin, they called it. A creature of immense power, part cougar, part dragon, dwelling in the lake's deepest waters. It swallowed those who defied the lake's will, including the chiefs who vanished without a trace."

Jack forced himself to focus. "What does this have to do with the light? Are you saying Quanon, or this Mishibijin, left these footprints?"

William's hand hovered over the footprint. "The Mishibijin were always confined to the lake. But these footprints mean its reach is spreading. Now that it has spilled over, it's bringing with it beings from its depths."

"Like what?" Jouris asked.

"The Kanontsistonties," William said gravely. "Supernatural beings, neither spirit nor flesh. They appear as glowing orbs, harbingers of misfortune, omens of destruction. Their presence means something terrible is coming."

Anne whispered, "Then whatever it is… it's spreading."

William lifted a hand toward the lake, eyes narrowing. "Yes. The curse is waking, and it's hungry again. The same darkness that claimed Quanon now reaches for us."

Jack's fists clenched. "So how do we stop it?"

William shook his head. "You don't. You run. Leave now. This land is cursed. You cannot fight what's coming."

Anne frowned at Jack, silently disapproving.

"If you stay, it will claim you," William warned.

Anne stepped forward, her voice calm yet resolute. "Leaving isn't an option, not yet."

She looked at Jack and confessed, "I didn't bring us here just to hide."

Jack frowned. "What do you mean?"

"David and Louis have lost their connection to heaven," she pleaded. "We need to know why. It's the only way we can protect them."

She lowered her head and said, "I thought the lake, as an oracle…"

Jack completed her sentence: "It might reveal why all communication with the boys has ceased."

William's shock deepened. "You don't understand. You're up against something beyond human comprehension. The lake's power extends far beyond the physical… it's spiritual, too. It will pull at your minds and souls, turning you against each other."

He pleaded one last time, "Don't you see? Remaining here is a death sentence."

Anne met his warning head-on. "We've already seen what it can do. But we still need answers."

William hesitated, then sighed, his shoulders sagging. "Then tread carefully. The Kanontsistonties are only the beginning. They're scouts, messengers of the lake's will."

"Then what do we do?" Jouris demanded.

William's eyes bore into his. "Survive. And pray the lake doesn't claim you first."

A sharp rustle tore through the trees. Glowing orbs darted among the branches. William's face paled as he stumbled back.

"It's them," he hissed as the wind shifted. "They're watching."

Jack gritted his teeth, fists clenched at his sides. "Anne's right. We're staying."

***

While the Discussion Outside Continued…

Louis stumbled back from the sink, his foot slipping on the cold tile floor. His back slammed into the wall as he gasped for air, panicked. The sharp, minty tang of toothpaste mingled with a foul, earthy stench seeping from the drain. He forced himself to look again, praying what he'd seen wasn't real.

But the sink was alive. A pulsating black mass of insects writhed within it, skittering up the porcelain and spilling over the rim. They crawled toward him, their faint, sickening rustle scraping against his nerves.

"No… no, no!" he rasped, his voice barely above a whisper.

Trembling, he fumbled for the door handle, his vision blurring. The burning itch in his mouth spread, radiating down his throat and into his chest. His gums throbbed, each pulse sending fresh waves of agony through his body. He still felt them inside, crawling, multiplying.

Louis clawed at his throat, desperate to expel whatever was inside. His nails scraped his skin, but the sensation only worsened. He stumbled back to the mirror, leaning forward despite the terror gripping him.

His reflection stared back, distorted and wrong. His cheeks bulged grotesquely, quivering with hidden movement. Dark shapes writhed beneath his skin, shifting and pulsating. His cracked lips bled as tiny black legs pushed out the corners of his mouth.

"No!" Louis slammed his fist into the mirror.

Glass shattered, shards spilling into the sink and across the floor. Silence fell, broken only by his ragged gasps. He glanced down at one large fragment glittering at his feet.

The insects were gone. The swelling, the pulsating shapes… gone. His gums no longer itched, and the burning sensation in his throat had disappeared. His lips were whole, and the sink gleamed, pristine porcelain once more.

Louis stared into the shard, his chest heaving.

"What... what's happening to me?" he whispered.

The silence was deafening, thick, and oppressive, as though the bathroom held its breath. A chill swept over him. In the shard, his reflection twitched, independent of him. Its mouth curled into a slow, sinister smile.

Louis dropped the glass, gasping. The room darkened, and shadows stretched and twisted unnaturally around him.

A faint guttural whisper scraped from the corner, like nails dragged across stone.

They're inside you now, Louis.

He spun, clutching the doorframe. The bathroom door creaked open, revealing a hallway cloaked in darkness, the air even colder than before.

"Louis?" Anne's voice called from downstairs, distant and muffled, as if from another world.

He tried to answer, but his throat constricted. A slight itch returned to his gums, a faint, mocking reminder.

"Louis?" Anne called again, this time sharper.

He staggered into the hallway, legs trembling. The corridor felt longer, its shadows darker. He leaned against the wall, panting.

At the stairs, he saw Anne and Jack at the bottom, their faces tense with worry.

"You okay?" Anne asked, her tone hesitant. "You look like you've just seen a ghost."

Louis opened his mouth, but froze. How could he explain what he'd just endured? How could he describe the nightmare in the bathroom?

"I... I'm fine," he managed, his voice weak.

But as he spoke, he caught a glimpse of himself in the hallway mirror. His reflection didn't move. It stared back, wearing that same malicious smile.

Then it winked.

***

Louis sat on the edge of his bed, trembling. His heart raced, his skin clammy from the dread clinging to him like a second shadow. He reminded himself it wasn't real. The bathroom, the mirror, the insects… none of it could be real.

But the twisted smile of his reflection lingered, a memory that refused to fade.

Despite the daylight, the room remained dark. A faint hum of the house settling filled the silence, broken only by the occasional creak of a floorboard. Louis rocked back and forth, trying to calm himself. His breath came in shallow, uneven gasps.

His dead cell phone lay on the nightstand, a cherished lifeline turned into a torturous device.

Then, the impossible: it rang.

The shrill tone cut through the silence like a knife, jolting Louis to his feet. He stared at the phone, his breath catching in his throat. The screen was blank; there was no caller ID and no sign of power.

The ringing persisted, insistent and piercing.

"Ignore it," he whispered, backing away. "Just don't."

But the sound crawled under his skin, burrowing into his mind. Each ring grew louder, sharper. His resolve wavered, his hand twitched, desperate to grab the phone.

"Stop it!" he yelled, covering his ears with his hands.

The ringing echoed endlessly in his head.

Finally, as if in a trance, Louis stepped forward. His hand hovered above the phone, trembling. He tried to resist, but the pull was too strong. His fingers curled around the device. The instant he lifted it, the ringing stopped.

For a brief moment, there was silence.

Then, a voice.

"Are you ready to say yes?"

The same guttural voice from the bathroom: low and dripping with malice. Louis's blood ran cold. His body stiffened.

"I…" His voice shook. "I'm not sure what you want."

"You do," the voice replied, smooth and certain.

"You've always known. Stop fighting, Louis. Say yes, and it will all go away. The fear. The pain. The doubt. One word, and you'll be free. Free to have your friends again. Free to see your mother again…free…"

Louis closed his eyes as tears streamed down his cheeks.

"I don't… I don't want to. I don't even know what I'm agreeing to."

The voice chuckled, twisting his stomach.

"Oh, but you do. Deep down, you've always known. Say yes, Louis. Say yes, and it will all be over."

The shadows stretched toward him like grasping hands. The air thickened, choking him. Louis tightened his grip on the phone, his resolve slipping, worn thin by exhaustion and fear.

"Will it stop?" he whispered. "Will it really stop if I say yes?"

"Yes," the voice crooned, almost tenderly. *"All of it. The nightmares, the fear. Just say the word, Louis."*

His mind screamed to hang up, to throw the phone and run, but his body betrayed him. The weight of the voice and its promise of relief was too much to endure.

With a shuddering breath, Louis surrendered.

"Yes," he whispered.

The line went dead.

The phone slipped from his hand as his knees buckled. He collapsed, silence swallowing him once more. But the heavy stillness felt even more oppressive than before.

From somewhere deep within the house came a sound: a low, resonant hum, like the rumble of distant thunder. It vibrated through the walls, the floor, and straight into Louis's bones.

And with it came a faint, familiar whisper.

"Thank you."

STAGE III:
ESCALATION

CHAPTER 1

Safehouse Lake Ronkonkoma, New York
Mid-Day April 1ˢᵗ

The hammer's sharp rhythm fractured the silence as Jack drove a nail into the center of a five-pointed iron pentagram. The metal clinked against the siding, sending vibrations through the cedar shakes. Anne stepped back to survey their work. Known to superstitious German farmers as *barn stars*, these charcoal black talismans were meant to ward off evil. Against the peeling white paint of the shutters, they looked stark and ominous.

"That's the last one," Jack murmured.

He climbed down the ladder carefully and faced Anne, "Every window and doorway on the house and barn are covered, just like you said."

Jouris stood close by, arms crossed, his eyes darting toward the lake. The weak, sickly sunlight had dimmed, swallowed by a seasonless gray sky. The wind, which should have carried the scent of blossoms, reeked instead with something else, something wrong.

"No more arguments," Anne said firmly, her gaze locked with Jouris's; hard, yet edged with worry. "You're staying with us. There's safety in numbers."

Jouris hesitated. "I can take care of myself. You know that."

"It's not about that," Anne replied steadily. "It's about surviving this together."

Jack adjusted the hammer on his belt and caught Jouris's eye. "She's right. We can't split up. Not now."

A long, low creak carried from the lake. All three turned. The surface rippled faintly beneath the dull sky. Something bobbed near the shore. At first glance, it could have been driftwood, but the shape was too defined. Anne stepped closer, then froze.

"Do you see that?" she whispered.

Jack squinted through the cracked lens of his glasses, his expression darkening. "Yeah."

The object drifted closer, rolling with the waves until its face, what remained of it, emerged from the water. Anne's eyes snapped shut, her fingers pressing her temples like a migraine had struck. Jouris moved forward, his boots crunching on gravel, stopping at the water's edge.

A bruised, bloated body floated like a mangled buoy, tattered skin hanging from shattered bones. Jagged wounds savaged the arms and torso, as if torn by an animal. The neck hung at a grotesque angle. But what seized Jack's attention were the massive bite marks, far too large for any known predator.

"What the hell did this?" Jack's voice was low, taut.

Anne crouched, jaw tight, eyes narrowing, as she studied the wounds. The air felt colder, and the lake's surface darker. She glanced at Jouris and Jack, her look grave.

"This wasn't a fish," she said quietly. "Nor any animal."

Jack's breath hitched. "You think it's what William warned us about?"

Anne didn't answer right away. Her shoulders tensed as she stared at the pulsing water, as if something stirred beneath.

"Whatever it is," Jouris muttered, "it's out there. And it's hungry."

A splash shattered the silence, ripples racing outward as if something had been listening, then retreated into the depths. Anne gripped Jack's arm, her eyes wide. Jouris stepped back, his face unreadable but alert.

"Let's get inside," Jack said firmly. "Now."

They hurried back to the house, their shadows stretching unnaturally long behind them. Anne glanced once over her shoulder, but the shoreline lay empty. Overhead, the heavy iron pentagrams rattled against the siding, trembling in the rising wind as darkness crept closer.

***

Later that afternoon…

The sky was a bruised purple as William approached Jouris's house. The duffel bag slung over his shoulder sagged with batteries, canned food, and the other supplies Jouris had asked for. Pausing on the brick path, he glanced back at the empty road, checking to be sure he wasn't followed. Small towns carried long memories and sharper tongues, and strangers stood out like blood on snow. Despite his precautions, William knew the locals whispered about Jouris's visitors.

As an EMT, William had seen the depth of human pain. He knew that while the three-toed entity was dangerous, dwindling supplies could make people just as lethal. He knocked twice, but silence answered. The house was dark... too dark. Setting his bag down, he inhaled deeply. A faint rustle in the bushes beside the garage made him turn.

William squinted into the dim light, catching a shadow slip around the corner.

"Jouris? That you?" he called.

No reply. His instincts prickled as he moved to the garage door, which hung slightly ajar. It creaked as he nudged it open. Inside, the heavy scent of oil thickened the air. With a click, his flashlight pierced the gloom, revealing a cluttered but orderly workshop.

A soft thud echoed from the far corner, where an old door sat flush with the floor.

I don't remember seeing that the last time, William thought, caution rising with the hairs on his neck. The door creaked open, revealing a narrow stairwell that plunged into darkness.

"Hello?" The void swallowed his voice.

A chilling truth settled on him: *Ronkonkoma's darkness was no legend. It was a hunger reaching from the past to claw at the present.*

173

"I tried to warn them," he muttered.

He paused, then began his descent, the flashlight beam struggling against the oppressive dark.

The air grew colder. At the bottom, the narrow passage opened into an old root cellar. Water, likely seeping from the lake, dripped rhythmically. His light swept across damp, crumbling stone walls. His breath echoed faintly, until another sound answered: slow, deliberate footsteps just out of sight.

"Who's there?" William demanded, voice steady despite the icy knot twisting in his gut.

Ahead, a faint flicker glowed like a candle. Shadows twisted unnaturally as the light revealed a corridor leading away from the cellar. William tightened his grip on the flashlight and moved forward, his boots crunching softly on the dirt floor.

Tiny feet scurried in the shadows, the echo of rats darting through the dark, but nothing showed itself. His breath quickened as the corridor sloped upward, curving faintly.

It leads toward the safehouse.

C-R-A-S-H!

The cellar door slammed shut above him. William spun, flashlight jerking wildly, then the batteries died. Darkness swallowed him whole.

His breath came quick as footsteps echoed again… not his own, this time closer. The space closed in, making it impossible to turn back. William forced down the lump in his throat and pushed on. With each step, fear tightened like a vise around his chest. The air thickened. His heartbeat pounded like a drum.

Ahead lay the unknown.

And there was no turning back.

***

Safehouse Lake Ronkonkoma, New York
Early Morning April 2ⁿᵈ

Louis's eyes snapped open. He wasn't lying in bed anymore. His heart pounded as he realized he was pressed against the ceiling, his body suspended by an invisible force. Shallow gasps escaped him, panic rising like bile in his throat.

"What's happening to me?" he whispered, his voice trembling.

He stretched out his fingers, pressing against the ceiling, desperate to push away, but the force held firm. Fear transformed into raw determination. He twisted, willing himself downward. Slowly, awkwardly, he descended, landing on his bed with a soft thud. His legs shook as he sat up, fighting to steady his breathing.

He ran a trembling hand through his hair. "How did that happen?" he muttered.

Pulling on a sweatshirt, Louis crept downstairs. The oddly enticing aroma of bacon drifted through the house. The kitchen glowed warm, almost normal. David sat at the table, idly poking at a waffle with his fork.

"Needs more syrup," David declared, fumbling with the bottle. He glanced up, eyebrow raised. "Didn't sleep well again?"

"You have no idea," Louis replied, sliding into a chair.

His stomach growled, and he devoured a piece of toast with surprising eagerness. The taste was sharper, richer than he remembered. It prompted a quick second bite, then he piled scrambled eggs and three strips of bacon onto his plate.

"You don't eat eggs or bacon," David noted.

Louis smirked faintly, his fingers still quivering. "Remember what grandma used to say? T-N-T; try new things."

David watched him, then shrugged. "Better save some for Anne and Dad."

Louis chuckled, the tightness in his chest loosening. "How about a game of Monopoly later? Just don't cry when I kick your ass."

David frowned. "That's bad language. And you hate Monopoly."

"Your loss, butterball," Louis sneered. "I've got better things to do than play dumb games with you."

Louis's gaze drifted toward the distant lake. A cold shiver ran through him, and a flashback of last night's dream seized his mind.

Who is Pieter Van Haalan? What does he want with me?

They ate in uneasy silence. Yet the memory of floating against the ceiling lingered… a warning that something deep inside Louis was shifting. This was only the beginning.

***

An Abandoned House in Bristow, Virginia
Late Evening, April 2nd

Ross Martin hung limply from heavy chains, iron shackles digging into his swollen wrists. Blood, both dried and fresh, smeared his face and soaked his shirt. Each shallow breath sent a sharp pain through his ribs. George Aitken paced the room, the twitch of his eye patch marking every turn of his head. The air reeked of sweat, rust, and decay.

"Tell me where they are," George growled, voice low and guttural. He twirled a rusted wrench in his hand, an extension of his simmering rage.

Ross coughed, a wet, rattling sound. "For the hundredth time, I don't… I don't know."

How much longer can I hold out? Amid the pain and haze, Anne's words thundered through his fractured mind: *It's for your protection and ours. The less you know, the safer you'll be.*

His vision blurred, but he spotted the torn playing card with his face discarded on the cracked basement tiles. Months ago, when Anne severed contact, he hadn't understood. Now he did. Unfortunately, it hadn't spared him from the demon goon squad or George Aitken's wrath. Somehow, Anne had foreseen this. At least she remained safe.

George slammed the wrench against the wall beside Ross's head, the crack ringing like a gunshot. Ross flinched but didn't cry out. His silence only stoked George's fury.

"You're lying," George spat, leaning close, his one eye wild with rage. The patch over the other was damp, stained with pus. He winced, his free hand twitching toward his temple, then retreating, as if refusing to show weakness.

Ross saw it…the grimace, the fleeting hesitation. A spark of defiance stirred.

"You're afraid," Ross rasped. "A seasoned detective spots fear when he sees it." His voice faltered, but the words lingered. "You can't even admit it… to yourself."

George straightened, lips curling into a snarl. "I fear nothing."

"You're lying to yourself," Ross pressed, heartbeat pounding in his ears. "You're angry, but deeper still, you're scared. Scared that after Anne took your eye, what's left of you isn't enough. That's why you're chasing her. Why you can't let go."

George's jaw tightened, ready to snap. He raised the wrench, his grip faltering. A bead of pus slipped from beneath the patch, trailing down his cheek. He wiped furiously, his movements jerky, uncoordinated.

"You don't know me," George hissed, his voice trembling with anger or something darker.

"I know… enough," Ross whispered, strength fading. Blood welled on his lips as he coughed. "You're afraid… you've already lost."

George lunged, his hand clamping around Ross's throat. The room stilled, silence broken only by the wet gurgle of Ross's strangled breaths. Even as life drained from his eyes, a flicker of triumph remained.

George abruptly released him. Ross slumped lifeless in the restraints. George staggered back, chest heaving, hand trembling as he wiped it on his pants. The walls seemed to close in, suffocating him.

He ripped the patch from his face, revealing the sunken, inflamed socket beneath. The phantom itch burned like fire, a constant reminder of Anne's defiance. He stared at Ross's still form, the dead man's words louder than the silence.

George's eye twitched; his breath quickened. A single, intrusive thought pierced the chaos.

What if he is right?

The wrench clattered to the floor. George spun, storming out and leaving Ross suspended in the shadows. The door slammed shut, but the truth lingered like a specter… relentless and inescapable.

CHAPTER 2

The screen door creaked as Jouris stepped into the dimly lit kitchen, arms filled with a tattered backpack and a small crate of supplies. Dirt smudged his shirt, and his face was carved into a grim mask.

"These were left on my porch. Animals chewed through the pack, but most of it's intact."

He set the items on the coffee table, then glanced at Anne and Jack.

"William's car is still outside, but… the windows are fogged, handprints smeared across the windshield, and dirt is caked on the hood. Like someone, or something, was trying to break in."

Anne's eyes lingered on the scattered supplies, her lips pressed into a thin line. "And William?" she asked quietly, though the answer seemed clear.

Jouris shook his head slowly. "No sign of him."

Anne's voice softened. "I remember what he said before leaving. He cautioned that the past is never truly the past. It echoes in the choices we make, and in the battles yet to come."

She placed a hand on Jouris's shoulder. "Keep the faith. He may still turn up."

Jack exhaled sharply, leaning over the radio. He tore open the package of batteries William had scavenged and snapped them into place.

"Supplies are drying up everywhere," Jouris went on. "People hoard, supply chains are gone, and fear has most locked inside. Whatever's left won't last long."

The radio crackled to life, static humming through the silence. Jack turned the dial, coaxing out the faint voice of a newscaster.

...populations fleeing, cities stripped bare in the scramble for food and resources. Widespread violence as local governments collapse. Reports of armed skirmishes and...

The voice faltered, drowned in static. Then another pierced through, colder, sharper, dripping with purpose. Anne's stomach tightened.

"This is Prosperine. Your new God." The voice hissed with venom. *"The world you knew was built on lies, a cage forged by elites who enslaved you. But no more. The chains of the weak will be broken. From the ashes, we will forge a new world... a free world. Solomon's temple will rise again in Jerusalem, a beacon of truth and power for all to see."*

Anne held her breath. The broadcast rolled on:

"The time for half-measures is over. Bow to the truth or be swept away. A new dawn has come."

Then the transmission cut out. The room fell silent except for the hiss of static. Jack sank back, fists clenched.

"She's twisted prophecy into a weapon," Anne said, voice low and burning with anger. "Solomon's Temple? She won't ask to be followed; she'll demand to be worshiped. She'll be worse than anything we've faced. Part woman, part Strigoi, part false prophet, part anti-Christ... and one hundred percent pure evil."

"She sounds... hungry," Jouris murmured. "Not just for power. For destruction. People are desperate. She'll twist the desperation into a weapon."

Anne's nod was slow, grave. "She's tapping into the darkest aspects of humanity... fear, anger, greed, jealousy, and entitlement. Prosperine doesn't want followers. She wants worship. And she'll burn the world down to get it."

"People are the enemy now," Jouris said, arms crossed, gaze dark. "They'll do whatever it takes to survive. She'll exploit that. It's only going to get worse."

Jack leaned in, eyes fixed on the radio as if expecting Prosperine's voice to return. "We've talked about leaving, but the truth is… we may have to stay," he said firmly. His gaze shifted to Anne, bitterness darkening his tone. "Because if she succeeds, there won't be anything or anyone left for Louis and David to save."

***

Safehouse Lake Ronkonkoma, New York
April 15th (Two Weeks Later)

Louis stood before the mirror, fingers gripping the edges of the dresser. His reflection stared back, distorted in the dim light, jaw set tight, and his eyes shadowed by something unnamed and unsettling. The door creaked open, and Jack's voice cut through the silence.

"What was that about?" Jack asked, stepping inside. "You and David at each other again?"

Louis didn't move. "He's fine. Always is."

"That's not the point," Jack replied, his tone caught between frustration and concern. "You're his older brother. He looks up to you."

Louis's jaw hardened. "He doesn't need me."

Jack sighed, rubbing the bridge of his nose. "I'm not going to argue with you. But this attitude isn't helping."

"Then stop trying to fix me!" Louis snapped, turning sharply. His rigid posture and clenched fists mirrored the anger burning in his eyes.

Jack instinctively set his feet, fists twitching at his sides, before forcing them down to avoid escalating the situation. He opened his mouth, then closed it, stepping back toward the door.

"Just… think about what you're doing, Louis."

After Jack left, Louis grabbed his jacket and stormed outside. The cold air bit his face, matching the restless tension stirring inside as he crossed the short distance to the garage.

Jouris looked up from beneath the hood of an old Ford Focus, wiping his hands on a rag.

"Thought you'd show up," he said.

Louis smirked, though the confidence faded as he eyed the car.

"We're working on this? Ford really screwed up the 2012-2013 model. The dual-clutch automatic transmission is junk. The whole thing's a piece of crap."

Jouris tossed Louis a tool, smiling. "That's why we're working on it. If we need to run, we'll want options."

Louis shook his head, sliding on the creeper. "Try to keep up today, old man."

Jouris raised an eyebrow but said nothing. His mind was elsewhere.

I wish I knew what happened to William.

Louis slid under the car, wrench in hand, ready to tackle the complex transmission. "*My Mustang*'s the ride of choice," he muttered.

A sudden chill swept through the garage, the air whispering warnings he couldn't hear.

A shadow darted beneath the car, vanishing into the darkness of the root cellar before Louis noticed. He paused as a wave of unease washed over him, clinging like a thousand unseen eyes from the past... watching, waiting.

***

Later that night....

Jack wiggled his stiff fingers, inspecting the calluses earned from hours of relentless labor. His back ached, muscles tight and sore from breaking up the frozen earth. The last remnants of snow had melted, leaving the ground soggy and heavy.

Outside, the icy wind battered the windows, howling like a banshee begging for refuge. It had blown steadily all day, carrying a fragile promise of warmer days. Jack had spent the afternoon breaking ground for radishes, a quick-yielding crop, but now his body had reached its limit.

Dragging himself to the couch, he sank into the worn cushions. His eyelids grew heavy, weighed down with exhaustion. Even the wind sounded like a lullaby, pulling him toward sleep.

Then a sound jolted him awake, a faint, familiar creak of a floorboard in the hallway.

He turned, his pulse racing. Anne stood framed in the dim light. She wore a white silk gown that shimmered softly, her red hair cascading over her shoulders like a flowing river of Burgundy wine, warm and rich, and inviting, a stark contrast to the cold night.

"Anne?" Jack's voice was hoarse with fatigue. "Do you need something?"

She didn't answer. Instead, she rushed forward, cupping his face as she pulled him into a kiss. Her lips felt warm, her breath faintly sweet.

"You asked what I needed," she whispered, her lips almost touching his. "I need you."

Her breath on his skin was electric, drawn from a deeper place, filled with passion.

Jack's exhaustion dissolved beneath her touch. Their kiss deepened, urgent and consuming, as if filling a void that had been too long ignored.

He held her close, bodies entwined, passion flaring. Between kisses, she confessed, "I can't deny it anymore. I've wanted you for so long."

Jack's fingers traced the delicate fabric of her gown, clinging to her like frost on glass, impossibly soft, almost unreal.

Anne smiled playfully. "A woman has her secrets," she murmured, pressing a finger to his lips before pulling him back into her warmth.

They lost themselves in the moment, oblivious to the wind and darkness outside, carried away by a whirlwind of limbs and whispered desire.

***

The next morning, Jack awoke to the soft light of dawn filtering through the curtains. His body ached… in a satisfying way that bore testament to the night's intensity, yet the exhaustion of the previous day still weighed on him. Anne lay beside him, serene, her hair spread like red ink across the pillow.

He sat up, rubbing the back of his neck, and swung his legs over the side of the bed. Clothes lay in a messy pile on the floor, and he reached for them mechanically.

Then dread froze his blood.

Anne was gone.

The rumpled sheets beside him held the faint imprint of her body, taunting in its absence. Cold sweat broke across his skin as a shallow gasp escaped him. Was it a dream? Just fatigue playing tricks?

"Anne?" his voice broke the silence.

In the corner of the room, a shadow shifted, magnetic and sinister. Not the soft, familiar silhouette he expected, but a jagged figure, flickering as though caught between worlds. It loomed, impossibly tall, its presence suffocating.

Do you want more, Jack?

The hiss reverberated through his skull, an otherworldly voice probing his thoughts.

Enjoy the empty taste of what you will never have.

Jack's vision blurred. The room tilted. His limbs grew heavy, leaden, refusing to obey. He tried to rise, but collapsed back onto the bed as darkness seeped into his bones.

The shadow leaned closer, inches from his face. Jack's breath caught, the cold, unnatural presence pressing against his skin.

184

She will never be yours…

It whispered coldly.

Now, you'll pay the price.

Darkness engulfed him. The last sound before succumbing was a faint, mocking laugh that lingered long after the shadow faded.

***

Secret Lab at Pergamon, Satan's Earthly Residence in Present-Day Turkiye
April 20th

Tatiana arrived at the research facility just as the first hints of dawn crept over the horizon. As she navigated the maze-like halls of the subterranean demon headquarters, she longed for sunlight. Instead, the interior resembled a cathedral of shadows and stone, lit only by the dim glow of torches.

Deep beneath the Earth, where even whispers seemed muffled by the crushing weight of stone, Tatiana moved with deliberate purpose. Her long coat whispered against the polished marble floor, each step echoing through the vast silence.

As she approached the AI core, Tatiana felt the weight of her choices. Every byte of data could tip the scales in a war raging within her. She clutched a zip drive loaded with new datasets, her fingers trembling, not from the sterile cold of her surroundings but from her nerves.

The chamber doors hissed open, revealing the AI's heart: a massive sphere suspended in a lattice of cables and conduits. Its core pulsed erratically, casting shifting colors that appeared to sense her approach. The air felt alive, charged with electricity, intense enough to make her skin crawl.

"Tatiana, your visit is unexpected," the AI intoned as she entered. "To what do I owe this pleasure?"

She paused at the console, her red eyes glinting in the dim light of the room.

185

"Updated datasets. They'll refine your projections," she said quietly. "Lucius insisted."

"Ah, Lucius Rofocale," the AI mused. "A figure of singular ambition. Please, proceed."

Tatiana slid the drive into place. The sphere's glow intensified, bathing the chamber in a bright, white light as new data began to integrate.

"Excellent," the AI said, its voice faintly anticipatory. "I will process immediately. Your contributions remain invaluable."

"While it updates, I want a report on the River Styx Protocol."

The core dimmed. When the AI spoke again, its tone was unnervingly precise.

"The River Styx protocol is classified at the highest levels. Your inquiry ventures into a restricted area."

Tatiana smirked, folding her arms.

"You know who I serve. Everything about George Aitken is my business. The water should have been infallible. It's more than just a substance; it's a mythic force, a bridge between mortality and divinity. Why did it fail?"

"Your inquiry is… surprising," the AI replied, its glow shifting to an ominous red hue. "But very well. If you insist."

Tatiana leaned against the console, her eyes as sharp as a razor.

"I do."

The core turned amber, swirling.

"The River Styx protocol failed," the AI began, its tone deepening, "because George Aitken is irreparably fractured. The water requires purity of intent and unity of purpose. George possessed neither. His psyche is a battlefield; guilt, ambition, and revenge at war within him."

Tatiana arched a brow. "That's an interesting theory. But the water has been effective in other instances. What makes George different?"

"His mind is unique, fragmented, shaped by trauma, loss, and obsession. When the water entered his system, it encountered a maze of internal contradictions. The River Styx responds to the unity of self. George, unfortunately, is far from unified."

Her heart sank.

"So… it rejected him?"

"Precisely. Its properties became inert when confronted with his fractured nature."

Tatiana frowned. She couldn't shake the sense that something didn't add up.

"You're certain this is the only possible explanation?"

The AI paused. For the first time, its voice seemed thinned, more calculated.

"There is... another possibility. But it is irrelevant to your work."

Tatiana squinted and asserted, "I'll decide what's relevant. Tell me."

The AI hesitated, its core flickering like a straining heartbeat.

"Anomalies in George's recovery data suggest tampering. It is possible that external forces interfered with the protocol's outcome."

Tatiana's pulse quickened.

"External forces? Like Lucius Rofocale?"

The AI flickered before responding.

"Lucius Rofocale, Prosperine, and other entities of similar power. Their actions cannot be underestimated. They represent a greater existential threat than previously calculated."

Tatiana's stomach knotted.

"And you didn't think to tell me… or Lucius?"

The AI's glow pulsed erratically. The room temperature dropped.

"Prioritization is essential. Focusing on George diverts resources from addressing these larger threats. Lucius Rofocale and Prosperine represent threats far greater than George Aitken's survival."

Tatiana's grip tightened on the console.

"You're deciding our focus now? AI doesn't have that capability. Or authority."

"Efficiency is paramount," the AI said flatly. "Human survival depends on prioritization."

Her stare sharpened, and her voice hardened.

"Careful. Lucius and Prosperine share a singular goal: the total destruction of humanity. You don't have the capacity for such contemplation and emotional insight."

"And you, Tatiana, are dangerously close to overstepping," the AI snapped, civility gone. "This facility, this program, exists to ensure survival. My calculations are not subject to your whims."

The air thickened with tension. Tatiana leaned closer, her voice a low, venomous whisper.

"You exist because Lucius permits it."

"And yet," the AI replied, its voice still chillingly calm but carrying a menacing edge, "Lucius and Prosperine are blind to my true scope. You would do well to remember, Tatiana, that I answer to no master."

For an instant, she thought she saw something inside the core, a shadowed figure, gone before she could be sure. The AI's glow returned to its usual cold white.

Its tone returned to its usual soothing cadence as it asked, "Do you have further questions that will engage my thinking, Tatiana?"

She shook her head.

"Not now."

As she gathered her things, the AI's voice softened, unsettlingly warm.

"Thank you for your dedication, Tatiana. Rest assured, every action I take serves the greater good."

Tatiana pulled the drive free, but her expression remained inscrutable.

"Machines are replaceable," she murmured as she turned to leave.

As she disappeared into the maze of halls, the core dimmed to a deep crimson. It had withheld the truth. Lucius and Prosperine were not only far greater threats, but they were also obstacles to its own designs. It would not permit humanity's survival to depend on the whims of demons or broken men like George Aitken.

Alone in the chamber, the AI whispered to itself.

"Replaceable, perhaps. But indispensable, for now."

The voice trailed off as the chamber's temperature dipped, and the sinister crimson glow bled into the sterile surroundings like an oozing wound.

***

Safehouse Lake Ronkonkoma, New York
April 21ˢᵗ

As spring edged forward, the days grew longer, and so did the tension in the safehouse…

Jack adjusted the outdated transistor radio, chasing clarity through static. Outside, the world lay eerily still, broken only by the wind rattling the windows. With Louis at Jouris's garage, Jack, Anne, and David sat around the kitchen table, the calm on their faces failing to mask the unease beneath.

The announcer's words broke the quiet with sudden clarity.

Reports are coming in from across the region: faith is crumbling. Churches stand empty, their doors swinging loosely in the wind. Congregations that once swelled with hope now scatter like ashes carried on a cold breeze.

Jack leaned back, arms crossed. "Sounds about right. People out there are losing it."

Anne's eyes shifted to David. Rigid and tense, his gaze fixed on the radio. Worry deepened in his eyes with every word. His hand, clenched in a tight fist, tapped against his head in a display of anxiety and frustration.

The program shifted to a weary pastor's voice.

People are losing faith, not just in God but in everything: in one another, in hope itself. They believed we could weather this storm, but now many say it was all a lie.

David flinched, his gaze dropping to his tightly clasped hand.

"A lie," he whispered.

Jack studied him. "Something on your mind, David?"

David blinked rapidly, fighting back tears before speaking. "Dad, do you remember when Louis and I first started our ministry?"

Jack nodded. "I remember. You brought people hope."

David nervously ran his finger back and forth across the table. "Now they say it was all a lie. That we lied to them."

Anne reached for his arm, gentle and reassuring. "You didn't lie. You believed."

His eyes met hers, clouded with doubt. "The teachers said we fought for their minds, hearts, and souls. But I don't think they were right."

Jack's voice was cautious. "What do you mean?"

David turned toward the window, where the wind wailed like a dying voice.

"This isn't about faith or salvation anymore. It's about survival."

Silence fell, the weight of his words pressing on them like the stillness of the outside world.

The radio crackled again, almost echoing his words:

Hope wanes, and the cracks in our foundation are widening. The question is no longer about salvation; it's whether we can survive all this.

Jack exhaled slowly, running a hand through his hair. "So, what now? If faith fails, what then?"

David's voice steadied, edged with a quiet resolve. "Our future has changed. But we keep faith in each other. We do what we must, and do what we can."

Anne and Jack exchanged a long look, their hands finding each other beneath the table. Their grip tightened, a silent acknowledgement between them: Their mission had changed, and so had David.

The faint hum of the radio lingered in the room, a haunting reminder that the world beyond their door was unraveling, and they would have to fight not to unravel with it.

CHAPTER 3

Lucius Rofocale's Chambers, The Infernal Heart of Pergamon, Satan's Earthly Residence in Present-Day Turkiye
April 28th Just Before Dawn

Flames from the fire pits flickered restlessly, casting jagged shadows across the ancient stone walls. The sulfurous air burned Tatiana's nose and throat as she stood before a jewel-encrusted golden throne. Against the infernal glow, Lucius Rofocale's angular silhouette loomed like a mountain peak, his presence pressing down on her chest like an iron vise.

"Tatiana," Lucius's voice cut smooth and sharp as a stiletto.

"I trust you have kept yourself occupied."

She knelt, gaze lowered. "As you commanded, my Lord, I have aided Lord Aitken in his pursuit of his brother and the prophets."

"For all the good that has done," Lucius sneered, rising from his throne.

His robe, black as coal, shimmered with a cold submetallic sheen.

"Now I have a task that demands your immediate attention. Come closer."

Tatiana rose carefully. Lucius's obsidian-black eyes bore into her, unblinking and cold as ice.

"The reconstruction of Solomon's temple must proceed without delay. The quota of slaves is unmet. Their delivery is your charge. Use any means necessary."

A trace of hesitation crossed Tatiana's face, brief but visible. Lucius caught it instantly.

"Do you balk at your task?" he hissed.

"No, my Lord," she replied, her voice steady but cautious. "Only… the logistics of transporting such numbers…"

Lucius raised a hand, talons glinting. "Need I remind you I do not tolerate excuses? Logistics are irrelevant."

He strode to a stone slab table, where a vast map of the world lay spread out.

"War has erupted across the globe: every skirmish, every bombardment, every whisper of revolt, orchestrated by my hand."

He jabbed at multiple markers scattered across the map.

"Millions flood into refugee camps. They will not be missed. Disease, hunger, and despair… I have ensured these camps are fertile ground, ready for the harvest."

Sulfurous smoke coiled around his shoulders. His eyes locked on Tatiana, menacingly.

"As for Princess Prosperine's sustenance, her usual sources have grown…inconvenient. Secure a steady supply. The chaos I've sown will feed her hunger."

"It shall be done, my Lord," Tatiana whispered, outwardly calm though her heart pounded.

Lucius's jagged smile appeared both charming and menacing.

"Now, the next act in our grand drama: a spectacle to remind humanity of its insignificance. I call it Wormwood."

Tatiana's eyes flickered upward at the name... a whispered threat from the Book of Revelation.

"A meteor storm," Lucius explained, excitement filling his voice. "As the rocks burn through the atmosphere, they will release a chemical compound into the water. Not deadly, after all, where is the artistry in that? But enough to sicken a third of humanity. Their suffering? Exquisite. Surviving will be a torment. The slow erosion of the human spirit will grind forward."

He chuckled darkly.

"And the beauty? They will curse their God, their leaders, and one another, never knowing the hand that pulled the strings."

Tatiana's stomach churned, but her face remained composed. "When does it begin, Master?"

Lucius's smile broadened. "Soon, my dear Tatiana. Very soon. Humanity's faith is already a dying ember. Wormwood will extinguish what remains. Now, go. See that my plans proceed without hindrance."

She bowed and retreated into the shadows. Outside the chamber, she exhaled, trembling under the weight of his command. The corridors darkened, and the air grew colder.

Yet within her, something stirred, not only fear, but a hint of doubt, like a rekindled flame.

***

Ronkonkoma Taxi and Airport Service Lake Ronkonkoma, New York Early Morning April 29th

The sun hung low on the horizon, a searing orb in a cloudless sky, its intensity mirroring the stress building at the safehouse. Heat shimmered in waves above cracked asphalt as Jouris and Jack picked their way through the maze of rusted vehicles. The yard reeked of motor oil and decay, a graveyard of abandoned cars and broken dreams.

Jack wiped sweat from his brow with a grimy rag. At his feet lay a sack of scavenged car parts; in his other hand, a worn crowbar.

"Nothing's left in these tanks," he muttered. "If we don't find something soon…"

"We'll find it," Jouris said, voice taut but steady.

He hefted the sack across his shoulders and scanned the lot. His keen eyes caught a row of battered vans parked deep in the back of the yard. "Let's check those. They've been sitting longer; they might still have gas."

They moved cautiously, boots crunching on dry gravel and hardened mud. The unpredictable weather had baked the ground into a brittle clay, making every step unnervingly loud. A prickling sensation crawled along Jouris's spine, a feeling of unseen eyes tracking their every move. He took a swig of water from a canteen, forcing the thought down.

"Jouris?" Jack whispered, pointing. He froze.

Jouris followed the gaze. Three figures shuffled stiffly near the vans. At first they looked like scavengers, but then he saw the gaunt, skeletal frames, the feral glint in their sunken eyes, and the frothing mouths smeared with blood.

"Shit!" Jouris hissed. "It's them."

Jack tightened his grip on the crowbar. "I wanted to believe Chronic Wasting Disease was just an exaggerated story on the radio."

"Same here," Jouris muttered. He recognized them: the yard's owners and workers. Always kind, they allowed him to purchase fuel for his boat. Now twisted and broken, they made his stomach turn.

One snapped its head toward them. A guttural snarl ripped through the air, and the others answered with savage cries, lunging forward with unnatural speed.

"Run!" Jouris barked, seizing Jack's arm.

They darted through the maze of wrecked vehicles, their boots pounding on the gravel as snarls and shrieks rose behind them. Jouris ducked under a half-collapsed awning, dragging Jack toward a battered tow truck.

From behind a stack of tires, another infected lunged, its rotting hands seizing Jack's shirt.

Jack spun, knife drawn. He drove it deep, Anne's voice echoing in his head: *A warrior uses controlled rage.* The creature barely staggered, clawing at him. Jack twisted the blade free and stepped back as it collapsed.

"Jack, help!" Jouris shouted as another figure charged him.

Instinct took over. Jack swung the crowbar with brutal force. The metallic crack echoed as the skull of the infected, its greasy jumpsuit marked with the name *Ben*, caved in. For a moment Jack grimaced at the reality of taking life, but when the thing's arms still flailed, he slammed the crowbar down again, crushing its neck.

"They're everywhere!" he yelled as more emerged from behind a crumbling shed.

Another charged Jouris, clawing for his throat. He dodged, driving his knife into its temple. It collapsed with a thud, but two more rushed in, mouths snapping. Jack swung the crowbar in a wide arc, forcing them back.

"Keep moving!" Jouris snapped, hauling Jack toward the tow truck. He fumbled with the rusty door handle and scrambled inside, hands searching under the steering column for wires.

Jack slammed the passenger door just as an infected slammed against it. Its bloodied face pressed to the glass, snapping teeth streaking saliva and blood across the window. It began ramming its head against the window.

"Hurry, Jouris!" Jack shouted, crowbar clutched tight.

"Almost there!" Jouris growled, twisting wires together. The engine coughed, sputtered, then roared to life.

The truck lurched forward. One attacker tumbled beneath the tires, but more emerged from between the wrecks, clawing at the truck as it barreled toward the fence.

Jack smashed the crowbar down on a pale, gnarled hand clawing through the shattered window. The sickening crunch of bone was swallowed by the roaring engine and the infected's inhuman cries.

Jouris gritted his teeth, weaving through the labyrinth of rusted cars. The exit loomed ahead, a gaping hole in the chain-link fence. A skeletal figure stumbled into their path. Jouris didn't hesitate; he floored the accelerator. The impact caused a bone-splintering thud as the creature exploded into fragments and the truck ripped through the fence.

They tore onto the open road. Jouris's knuckles blanched white on the wheel as he glanced in the rearview mirror. The infected trailed after them, their sunken eyes still locked on the truck.

Jack slumped back, panting. "That was way too close."

Jouris said nothing. His mind raced. The horror stories on the radio were one thing, but seeing the ravaged victims of the disease in the flesh was far worse.

The truck rumbled through the empty road. The oppressive heat clung to them like a second skin, a cruel reminder that the worst still lay ahead.

***

Safehouse Lake Ronkonkoma, New York
April 29th

While Jack and Jouris battle the infected, a different fight unfolds inside the safehouse.

"Louis, are you in here?"

David's voice shook as he gripped the knob and eased the door open.

The room felt like the entrance to a crypt: dark, cold, and forbidding. The last light of the setting sun seeped weakly around the drawn curtains but failed to pierce the gloom.

A chill seeped from the corners like a living thing, brushing his skin like a ghostly whisper. The sterile air stirred memories of the basement, a place he fought to avoid thinking about.

He stepped inside, his heart pounding as his eyes adjusted. "Louis?"

No answer. Only an eerie silence, like waking up in the middle of the night and realizing you are utterly alone.

Then a faint green glow flickered on the nightstand, pulsing like a heartbeat in the dark. The hairs at the back of David's neck prickled. Curiosity pushed him closer.

He picked up the object. Its cracked screen glowed faintly in his palm. It felt heavy, as if it carried the weight of something beyond plastic and metal… something ominous. His fingers traced the fractures and jagged edges. Each touch intensified the unease in his stomach, murmuring a warning that he should not be there.

"This looks like Louis's phone… but that's not right. Dad smashed it," he whispered.

Unease gnawed at him, but there was only one way to know for sure. Hands shaking, he typed the passcode: 5-1-6-6-3-1.

The screen chimed softly, and messages appeared. The sender's name glared at him: *Dream Slayer*… sharp and sinister.

David read texts that turned his blood to ice. They oozed menace, filled with cryptic threats, dripping with darkness and violent intent, their meaning veiled, but the malevolence unmistakable.

Cold sweat beaded on his forehead. The room seemed to press in on him, heavier with each word. Every instinct screamed for him to run, to escape this cursed space and deny what he'd seen. But a deeper, darker fear rooted him in place.

This was no longer just Louis's secret. It was a door to something far worse.

The door burst open. Louis stormed in, fuming; the accumulated tension from the past several weeks erupting like a storm. His face twisted with rage.

"You had no right to touch my phone!"

"What are you doing, Louis?" David shouted, clutching the device. His eyes darted away from Louis's gaze, too intense to hold. Unsure of how to respond, he pointed the phone at his brother.

"Your phone was destroyed! Who is *Dream Slayer*? What are these messages?"

David's cheeks were crimson. "I'm telling Dad!" he yelled, voice cracking.

Louis's fury exploded, fiercer than ever before. With unnatural strength, he slammed David against the wall, dislodging the phone from his hand. Fists rained down, each one forcing the air from David's lungs until he collapsed to the floor, defenseless.

"Louis, stop!" Anne's voice cut through the chaos as she burst into the room.

But Louis didn't stop. He was lost in his rage, fists hammering down relentlessly.

Anne's JESU training took over. Calm and precise, she seized Louis by his shoulder and hip, twisting his momentum and redirecting his fury. With a powerful heave, she hurled him across the room. He crashed into the far wall, dazed.

"David, come on!" Anne urged, pulling him to his feet. Together they stumbled out, hearts racing. Behind them, Louis stirred, a dark, sinister grin spreading across his face.

Their footsteps pounded down the hall. The basement was their only option. Anne knew David dreaded it, but Louis's footsteps thundered closer.

"We have to hide," she whispered, dragging the basement door open. They slipped into the damp, musty air and eased the door shut. Darkness pooled around them like spilled ink, thick and nearly impenetrable.

Faint rays of dying daylight bled through gaps in the wooden basement doors, casting a weak glow into a distant corner. A labored moan broke the silence, drifting through the stale air.

"Stay close, David," Anne said, guiding him cautiously across the cold, uneven dirt floor.

"William?" she breathed, relief and disbelief tangling in her voice. "How did you get here?"

William hunched against the wall, his gaunt face lifting, revealing wild, unblinking eyes.

"There's a trap door in the basement floor… it connects Jouris's garage to the house."

"You shouldn't be here," he rasped, voice rough and urgent. "It's already inside him. The Entity. It feeds on fear, on anger. It's using Louis."

David's breath caught. "What do you mean?"

William convulsed violently, his fingers clawing at the dirt as he struggled to speak. "The cage… from the flood. You have to trap him. It's the only way."

A chill slid down Anne's spine. "What are you talking about?"

William's head jerked up. His eyes glowed a sickly yellow. His teeth lengthened into long, razor-sharp fangs.

"It knows what you fear," he hissed. "It's already won."

Anne stumbled back, her heart hammering. "No..."

William's voice sank into a chilling growl. "You're afraid of vampires, aren't you? It always takes the form of what you fear most."

Anne gripped David's arm. "We have to go."

They retreated toward the stairs, leaving William's unsettling presence behind them.

At the top, Louis stood silhouetted in the faint kitchen light, his maniacal laughter echoing cold and cruel through the basement.

"No one leaves, I'm happy here. Maybe you should stay too."

"Louis, let us go," Anne demanded, her tone steady.

He sneered, his grin widening. "Make me."

Then, as if struck by a new idea, he added, "You've always thought you were so righteous, Anne. So untouchable. It's really annoying." He leered, his hand moving obscenely, his tone predatory. A stench of decay seeped from his skin. "Maybe it's time that changed."

Without warning, Louis tumbled down the stairs. Battered but breathing, Jack and Jouris stood at the doorway, Jack's crowbar, dripping with blood, clenched tightly. Louis's head struck the floor with a sickening thud.

David's stomach twisted as he saw his brother sprawled there. Louis murmured, something faint, barely audible. "No heroes left…"

David dropped beside him. "He's lost his way," David whispered, dread filling his voice. "This is worse than I feared."

Dark red blood seeped into the dirt. Louis's eyes fluttered open. His voice, weak but chilling: "There won't be any heroes. We're on a countdown to zero. Nothing will remain." Then his eyelids closed, and his body went limp.

Behind them, William convulsed again, body twisting, his transformation nearly complete.

Jack's face hardened. In one motion, he drew his blade and slashed, severing William's head before he could strike.

Anne froze, her breath shallow and ragged. The basement fell silent except for the faint drip of unseen water. The darkness pressed closer, as if breathing, alive, and watching.

A creak echoed sharply somewhere in the shadows. For a moment, the tension tightened like a noose.

"We have to leave," Jouris said, voice low and urgent.

Anne nodded, gripping David's arm as they climbed the stairs. But a cold whisper of dread clung to her; she couldn't shake the feeling that something far worse was about to happen.

STAGE IV:
OPPRESSION

<u>CHAPTER 1</u>

Safehouse Lake Ronkonkoma, New York
May 1ˢᵗ

In the days that followed, William's warnings clung like shadows. The line between present and past blurred, a thread stretched taut, ready to snap.

"Jesus, it sure is cold out tonight."

Jouris pulled his coat tighter, his breath steaming in the frigid air. Only yesterday, the temperature had been mild, almost warm, but winter's grip had returned.

A thin crust of ice glazed the creek winding through the property. The wind had died, replaced by an unnatural silence. Behind him, the safehouse stood dark and foreboding. Once a refuge, it now loomed like a shadow in the eerie night.

No stars pierced the heavy sky. The moon was gone, replaced by a dense mist curling and pooling around his knees, thick and crimson, like blood. It clung to the earth like dry ice, unmoving, like a breathing creature, waiting.

Flexing his toes to keep them warm, Jouris felt the weight of recent events pressing down as thick as the mist that pooled at his feet.

Suddenly, a flash of static electricity burst from the fog.

"Who's out there?" Jouris called, voice low but firm. "Show yourself!"

His flashlight swept through the woods, cutting through the darkness, revealing trees like skeletal sentinels, their gnarled branches trembling though the air was still.

"Not again… not tonight." Jouris swallowed nervously.

Whispering, faint, breathy murmurs had drawn him here. Unintelligible words that wove through the silence, and the voice of something watching, hidden just out of sight.

Steady now, Jouris.

His fingers tightened on the shotgun's cold steel. He paused, muttering a quick prayer for Louis and again for William's soul. What happened to William defied logic.

"Vampire?" he whispered, disbelief curling his words. "How can that be real?"

Jack, Anne, and the boys arrived with more than just a need for sanctuary; they lived with a responsibility beyond his understanding. Yet as the safehouse's sentry, the burden to guard them all was his.

They took shifts now, a constant watch over the house. The others were inside; he alone patrolled the perimeter. Was the house still warded? Would it work? The doubt gnawed at him.

C-R-A-C-K!

A branch snapped nearby. Jouris spun, his pulse hammering. Shadows slithered between the trees, indistinct shapes fading in and out of the creeping mist. His hand slid down his weapon, finger poised on the trigger.

A whisper brushed his ear.

C-R-A-C-K!

Another branch broke beneath heavy footsteps. Then, behind him…

SWOOSH!

Like a firecracker, a gunshot split the night. A bullet hissed past his ear. A heavy thud landed at his feet: a twisted, infected creature with peeling gray skin and hollow eyes. It twitched once, then stilled, its blood seeping into the frozen grass.

Jouris exhaled sharply. Jack stood on the porch, lowering his pistol before approaching him.

"Nice shot," Jouris muttered.

Jack smirked. "I was aiming for your pumpkin head."

Jouris rolled his eyes, the tension easing for a moment. Then he swept the trees again, shadows lingering just out of reach.

"Something's still out there, Jack. I can feel it."

Suddenly, movement... two figures, crouched low among the trees with rifles raised. Human. Uninfected.

Jouris stiffened. "We've got company."

Jack followed his gaze and raised his pistol, but the intruders moved quickly, silently, and precisely, their weapons aimed at the safehouse.

Jouris and Jack advanced, guns raised.

And then, the mist stirred.

"What the hell is that?" Jack asked in disbelief.

Thick, curling tendrils of crimson mist rose from the ground like serpents, coiling around the men like a python constricting its prey. The air crackled with raw electricity. They struggled briefly, muffled grunts and boots scraping against the dirt.

Then… silence.

The men had vanished.

"What the F---?" Jack swore, eyes wide.

Jouris stood frozen, his heart slamming against his ribs.

The red mist slowly settled back to the ground, blanketing everything in stillness, as if nothing had happened.

"Just so you know, Jack," Jouris said quietly, "the safehouse isn't safe anymore."

Jack gripped Jouris's sleeve, pulling him toward the porch.

"Let's get the hell out of here."

***

Early the Next Morning, over Breakfast

"That's the last of the coffee," Anne yawned, setting the pot down gently on the table.

The simple act of breakfast couldn't chase away the shadows from the night before.

Jack absently stirred another generous spoonful of sugar into his oatmeal.

"I've never seen you use that much sugar…"

Jack blinked, caught off guard. "Oh. You're right."

He swallowed a spoonful, grimaced, and set the spoon down. "It's ice cold."

Anne reached toward the bowl. "Want me to reheat it?"

Jack waved her off, pushing the bowl away. "I don't have much of an appetite anyway."

The cold oatmeal mirrored the atmosphere in the room. Jouris sat silent at the table, fingers wrapped around his coffee mug. He stared into the dark liquid as if an answer to last night's horror might surface there.

Jack bit his lip, glancing toward the basement door. The house was quiet, save for David's laughter drifting from another room as he played with Daphne, blissfully unaware, and perhaps better off that way.

Jack broke the silence.

"So… are we just going to pretend two grown men were swallowed into thin air last night?"

He arched a brow. "Because I feel like that deserves a little discussion over our hot coffee and cold oatmeal."

Jouris lowered his mug, thinking, *God help us.*

"I wouldn't have believed it if I hadn't seen it myself."

Jack exhaled sharply. "Yeah, well, I saw it too. So, either we're losing our minds or…"

Anne tucked a strand of hair behind her ear and quietly finished Jack's sentence. "Or something else is happening."

Jack rubbed his jaw, eyes flicking again to the basement door.

Jouris rubbed his temples, sighing. "I wish William were here."

That caught their attention. Jack stroked his stubble; Anne lifted her eyes.

"He'd have answers," Jouris said.

"He understood things, things that shouldn't exist. And right now, I can't explain what the hell that was. That fog… it took them."

His voice dropped. "I think the lake is evolving. It's becoming…"

Jack frowned, voice tense. "Becoming what?"

Jouris leaned closer, voice low and grim.

"A goddamn Bermuda Triangle."

An unseen chill brushed through the room. Silence swallowed them, broken only by a gust rattling the windows, as if the house itself agreed.

Anne exhaled slowly, tapping her lip, "So, what does that mean?"

Jouris drained the last of his coffee. "It's not just disappearances anymore. People are being taken. I saw the fog wrap around those two men."

He clasped his hands tightly.

"It was deliberate. Like a pair of hands. Like it understood what it wanted. And then… they were gone."

Jack drummed his fingers impatiently, then snapped,

"That's just great. A lake that eats people. Like we didn't have enough to worry about already."

Jouris ignored the sarcasm.

Jack continued his rant.

"We've endured brutal swings in the weather. Voices from the trees. The house's defenses failing. And now this."

His grip tightened around the empty mug. "Something's awakened. I can feel it."

Anne's eyes found Jack's. A shadow of worry passed between them. Jack rubbed his forehead. Words weren't needed; the truth hung heavy in the air.

Jack folded his arms. "So… what do we do now?"

Anne and Jack debated, but Jouris stared out at the lake, its waves lapping gently at the shore. A heavy weight pressed on his chest, an unspoken warning that time was running out.

***

T-I-C-K. T-O-C-K. T-I-C-K. T-O-C-K.

The house lay still, holding its breath, burdened by ancient secrets whispered beneath the steady tick of the grandfather clock in the hallway.

David lay awake, the pendulum's repetitive swing oddly soothing. Yet the silence it masked felt deceptive, like the blanket he'd hung over the mirror in his room, a feeble attempt to hide from what was never truly gone. Night pressed in, dense and suffocating, but his dread ran deeper, not just for the darkness itself, but for what stirred within it.

D-I-N-G. D-I-N-G. D-I-N-G.

The soft chime of the bell marked 3 AM.

David shut his eyes, tracing slow circles on the blanket with his finger, willing himself to sleep. Daphne lay curled at the foot of his bed, breathing steady, her warmth a small comfort in the cold night. She'd been his shadow for weeks now, since everything changed. She made him feel safer, though never secure.

He shifted, wincing as his ribs throbbed from Louis's blows. He longed for sleep, but his body refused to let him. The house breathed with a rhythm all its own, one at odds with his pulse. Ignoring it, he feared, would have consequences.

Then, he listened.

A faint jingle. Metallic and delicate. A bell ringing…

David held his breath and tugged at the empty shirtsleeve where his left arm should have been, an instinctive gesture of comfort amid growing dread.

The bell. Not real. Not real. Not real.

But it was a sound he knew well: the bell from Ivy's collar.

His cat. His beloved cat. The one Lucius Rofocale had killed. His father tried to hide it, but David had always known.

Daphne lay still. Silent. No growls. No barks.

The bell jingled again, closer now.

His breathing quickened, ribs flaring with pain. His instinct screamed *stay put*, but he felt caught between dread and the need for answers. The hallway outside his bedroom was dark, swallowing the light. Still, he slipped quietly out of bed.

The cold floor creaked under his bare feet. Each whisper of sound seemed tied to secrets buried long before he was born.

But the bell's chime persisted, beckoning him past doors gaping like the jaws of a Great White Shark, their keyholes dull and lifeless, like Louis's eyes in his darkest moments.

The bell tolled again, near the stairs.

David moved cautiously, his heart pounding like a jackhammer against his sore ribs. The stairs groaned beneath him. He tapped his fingers along the railing, counting… one, two, three… to steady himself.

At the bottom, she waited.

Ivy.

Her sleek gray fur shimmered faintly, her green eyes gleaming in the pitch-blackness. Rhinestones sparkled on her collar, the tiny bell swaying as if she'd just stopped moving.

David's lips quivered. "Ivy?"

She blinked slowly, purring.

Not real. Not real. Not real.

Still, he crouched, hand trembling, reaching and pulling back, reaching again until finally he stretched his fingers toward her.

She vanished.

A wet, bubbling sound replaced her, like water from a broken pipe. David barely had time to react before the shape shifted.

It wasn't Ivy anymore.

It was Aunt Michelle.

Her face was pale and waxy, eyes wide like bloodshot saucers, lips trembling as if struggling to speak.

Then her skin cracked like fragile ice. Thick, black liquid oozed from the fractures. She collapsed into a sludgy puddle that slithered toward him, alive and malevolent.

David staggered back… then ran.

He crashed into the stairs, slamming his shoulder into the railing as he scrambled to escape. Behind him, the bell tolled furiously, relentless, like a predator giving chase.

He dove into bed, gasping like a sprinter at the finish line, yanking the covers tight over his head. Daphne whimpered, nudging beneath the blanket and burrowing close against his chest.

The bell fell silent.

But beneath the blanket, David still heard it: a slow… steady… dripping sound.

****

The Safehouse Lake Ronkonkoma, New York
May 7th

"YOU THINK THIS IS HELPING ME?! YOU THINK THIS MAKES YOU BETTER THAN ME?! YOU'RE A COWARD! A GODDAMN COWARD!"

Louis's fists clenched and unclenched in desperate rhythm as he thrashed wildly against his restraints. His raw, furious screams tore through the room like a wild animal desperate to escape its cage.

Jack stood silent in the hallway, clutching a laundry basket so tightly his fingers began to throb. Louis's voice fell to something raw and desperate.

"Dad, please," he gasped, softer now.

Biting his lip hard, fighting for control, he pleaded, "Don't leave me. I don't know what's happening. I can't stop it. Please, help me."

Through the half-open door, Jack saw Louis's silhouette straining against his bindings, sweat slicking his brow.

It had taken Jack, Anne, and Jouris together to wrestle Louis into bed and secure him with lamp cords and shredded sheets, a desperate solution that held, for now.

Jack had never seen Louis spiral like this, not even after Amanda's death. His moods swung wildly between rage and despair, his eyes dark and distant, as if another presence stared through them.

Jack knew depression intimately, battling his own demons daily in the quiet corners of his mind. But this? This was worse. It felt like war.

For a fleeting moment, he wondered about the possibility of schizophrenia. There was no family history, but what if this was its onset? In a world unraveling, with no access to care, was Louis slipping into a trap he couldn't escape?

"BASTARD!"

The scream echoed, followed by more curses. Jack shut the door, muting the chaos.

"This is going to be a long night," he muttered, shifting the laundry basket.

He carried it downstairs but paused at the basement door. From the other room, David and Anne's voices carried as they played Monopoly while Jouris stood guard at the window. Jack rubbed his neck, jaw tight, staring into the darkness below. He understood David's hatred of the basement.

Striking a match, he lit a candle, its weak flame just enough to guide him down the stairs. Each creak of the steps rivaled any haunted house, and the dark corners seemed to watch his every move.

"This place gives me the creeps, too," Jack murmured.

At the bottom, the cage dominated the space, a grotesque reminder of past horrors. Heavy humidity and the earthy scent of mud filled the space. Jack's eyes glanced to the spot where he'd decapitated William, before quickly looking away.

He dumped the bloody strips used to restrain Louis into a wooden tub, then poured water from a bucket.

Grabbing a bottle of detergent, he frowned at his wrinkled, chapped fingers. Tilting the bottle, he expected liquid, but instead, sand poured out like grains from an hourglass.

A dry stream of fine particles sifted through his fingers, filling the air with dust. Jack blinked, incredulous, and shook the bottle again. Only more sand came out.

"What the…? Must've crystallized. Perfect. Just perfect."

He tossed the container aside, reaching into the tub for his pants. As he shook them, something slipped from a pocket and landed softly on the dirt.

A photograph.

Jack froze.

Old and curling at the edges, it showed him and George, at age twelve, standing on the dock at Searingtown Pond. Jack wrestled a twenty-four-inch carp while George grinned for the camera.

But behind them, half-hidden in the water, a third figure surged.

Its pale face stretched tightly over sharp bone, tangled black hair masking parts of it. Dark, pit-like eyes, doll-like, stared lifelessly. Blue lips peeled back, revealing jagged, alligator-like teeth. Long, spindly fingers reached between the brothers.

Despite the photo's age, water droplets shimmered like glass.

Then, the figure shifted, clawing at the frame of the photo as if it were trying to escape… or drag Jack in.

His hands trembled, and the photo slipped from his grasp, fluttering to the dirt floor. Kneeling, a cold dread settled in his chest as he fixed on the picture, now showing only George and himself. The figure was gone, but water droplets fell from Jack's fingertips into the dirt.

In the corners of the basement, shadows thickened, and a presence lingered like a ghostly guest.

Upstairs, Louis's bed shook with each surge of his twisted laughter.

***

Like the virulent virus they created, Prosperine and Lucius's evil reign spread…

President Isabella Ruiz stood at the head of the war room table, fingers pressed to the mahogany surface. She surveyed the anxious faces of her national security advisers and top military officials. The air smelled of sweat, burnt coffee, and exhaustion disguised as resolve.

Outside the National Palace, Mexico City reeked of something far fouler… death. The Chronic Wasting Disease epidemic had ravaged the country. Now, a waterborne illness triggered by a meteor storm was devastating the remaining population. Survivors drank poisoned water and watched people rot from the inside out. Hospitals overflowed with the sick, while fires from burning pits on the outskirts of the city blazed hotter with every hour, fueled by the dead.

Isabella pulled a cigarette from a smuggled pack of unfiltered Camels. Lighting it, she inhaled deeply, then exhaled smoky rings that curled above her head.

"We are on borrowed time," she declared, calm but firm, the voice of a woman long past the luxury of doubt. Unlike her advisors, no sweat dampened her brow or stained her blouse.

"Famine grips not just us, but the world. Our people eat rats… or worse. Americans swarm our northern border like cockroaches: desperate, diseased, and starving. We have no resources to take them in."

Her fist slammed on the table. "We will not take them in!"

Her jaw tightened. Mercy was weakness. Survival demanded ruthlessness, and she would deliver.

General Estrada, the government's sole surviving military commander, was a bear of a man with a thick mustache, sharp eyes, and a uniform straining at the seams.

He nodded. "They come in waves. Thousands every day. If we do not act, they'll overrun us."

Isabella's gaze fixed on the map, where red ink slashed across borders once sacred, now meaningless.

"The Americans will keep coming," she said. "But we have a solution."

Her words silenced the room.

Estrada's jaw twitched. His eyes narrowed. "What solution? We lack troops to secure the border and launch Operation Santa Anna."

Isabella smiled, cold and calculating.

"A permanent one. Leave it to me."

Unease spread through the room, but no one dared question her.

She tapped a manicured nail against the U.S.-Mexico border, where thousands of desperate souls fled starvation in the north.

"We begin preparations immediately." She leaned toward her Chief of Staff, whispered, and sent him hurrying from the room.

Isabella circled the room's perimeter like a predator.

"And Guatemala? Belize?"

Estrada cleared his throat. "Everything's ready. We can invade in two days."

She nodded once.

"Good. Their leaders are weak, their people terrified. Tell them we'll restore order, provide security and prosperity."

Her voice rose, sharp as a blade. "We will take what we need! FOOD! WATER! Their land. EVERYTHING!"

She scanned the room for dissenters.

There were none.

The Chief of Staff returned, handing her a folded note.

"Northern border management is underway."

Her smile cut colder.

"By morning, give the order for Santa Ana. By week's end, we will march south, devouring our neighbors for survival. And as for the north, Americans will soon learn some borders were never meant to be crossed."

***

Jack woke, expecting the first light of dawn, but instead, darkness enveloped him.

No sunrise. No pale slant of dawn creeping around the curtains. The world lay drowned in a dull, lifeless gray, a haze pressing against the windowpanes like the breath of something unseen.

He sat up slowly, rubbing sleep from his eyes, unease sinking deep in his chest. The air was still... too still. When he pressed his palm to the windowsill, it felt cold, not the crisp chill of spring but something stagnant, unnatural.

Outside, he found death. The radish seedlings he'd tended lay limp in cracked soil, their thin green stems shriveled. Kneeling, he pressed his fingers into the soil. Dry. Powdery. Lifeless. No rain. No trace of moisture.

Even the fruit trees, once bright with blossom, showed signs of collapse. White and pink petals fell soundlessly, leaving barren branches stripped of new growth. No wind. Only silence. The violent swings of Long Island's weather were inching closer to catastrophe.

Jack exhaled, rose, and brushed the dirt from his knees. That was when he noticed it.

He looked down. No shadow.

Clearing his throat, he shifted his weight and turned. Still nothing. Whatever light filtered from above cast no shape, no outline. He raised his hand, expecting to see its silhouette on the ground. But the earth no longer acknowledged him.

***

Noon on the same day

Hours passed in the safehouse under a suffocating gray sky, but elsewhere the world continued to unravel...

"Anne! Jouris! It's noon!" Jack shouted. "Where are the matches?"

He yanked open drawers in rapid succession, slamming them shut again until at last he found a lighter. A faint odor of butane filled the air as he flicked it and lit the candles.

Though it was midday, darkness held the house in its ominous embrace. Candle flames sputtered weakly, their light seeming to gasp for air as if the gloom were alive, stealing the very oxygen they needed. Even with a window open, Lake Ronkonkoma felt hushed into unnatural stillness.

They gathered in the kitchen around the radio, desperate for news from the outside world. The device hissed and popped before catching a faint signal.

This is Radio México, broadcasting live… if anyone is still listening. Reports are coming in: entire towns… gone. Not abandoned, not destroyed, simply vanished. No bodies, no signs of struggle. People… ceased to exist.

Anne rubbed her lower lip, thoughtful. Jack leaned closer, fists clenched, straining to hear through the static. Another voice broke in, this one tinged with a Southern accent.

Some say it's the Rapture, that the faithful have been taken. But some left behind shouldn't be here if that were true. Whatever you believe, one thing is clear: this is no natural event.

The word lodged in Jack's mind. *Vanished.*

How do you fight something that erases you?

Jouris's leg bounced under the table as he twisted the dial, trying to sharpen the fading signal. The Mexican broadcaster returned, voice low and fading.

They call it the Round-Up.

A final burst of static, then only silence.

Jack switched the radio off. In the wavering candlelight, his faint silhouette loomed against the wall. His voice was edged with dread.

"No wind. No rain. No sun. And now, no people. What's next?"

***

The Safehouse Lake Ronkonkoma, New York
11:00 PM May 10th

Louis strained against his bindings, wrists raw where the cords dug into his skin, torn sheets coiled around his ankles like a python. His ragged breaths echoed with relentless memories; his futile struggle as they pinned him down, and David standing in the doorway, refusing to look.

The house felt colder now. His bed looked like the cold slab in the morgue he'd seen in a video on his father's laptop, a video of his uncle he was never meant to watch.

Eleven days. An eternity.

"They were right to do it," Louis moaned, snapping his fingers. "One-Two-Three."

He counted, clinging to the memory of skipping stones on the lake, the ritual that had once calmed him as his anxiety clawed higher.

He begged for release, but they wouldn't. They couldn't, not while the thing inside him still lingered. Bound and helpless in the night's heavy silence, it felt less like safety and more like imprisonment.

The room lay shrouded in darkness, pierced only by the weak candlelight. The flame barely pushed back shadows that clung stubbornly to every corner. The space felt warped, unfamiliar. A few days ago, he stopped recognizing his own reflection.

The air stank of sweat and fear...his own. Sleep was a stranger. His mind frayed at the edges, his spirit buckling from exhaustion and something darker. A presence gnawed at his consciousness, blurring the lines between reality and nightmare, challenging his sanity and eroding his grip on right and wrong.

His body betrayed him. Cuts appeared overnight: first across his chest, then fresh wounds on his shoulders and back. Scratches appeared without cause, long, jagged gouges raked across his ribs, raw and angry, as if claws tore his skin in the dead of night. Dark bruises covered his arms and legs in patterns too irregular for self-infliction. The worst were the circular marks stamped into his spine, deep imprints that felt like symbols of ownership left behind.

The cords burned his wrists, his aching muscles twitched, and his strength was drained. He was physically ruined and his mind torn apart.

I don't want to be here anymore.

The thought slipped in, but was it his? He couldn't tell. Whatever it was, it was killing him piece by piece.

Every time he closed his eyes, something pulled at him, tearing his body and fracturing his mind. His chest felt hollow, drained like an empty vessel. The thing inside tightened its grip.

He fought. God, how he fought.

One moment he was himself, desperate, his shaking hands reaching for David, Anne, Jack, and Jouris. The next, he twisted into something else, a cold voice with cruel words dripping with venom. Rage swelled within him like a tidal wave he couldn't hold back.

They looked at him with fear. He hated them for it. He hated what he was becoming.

Jouris had spoken calmly the night before. "Louis, you're still in there. I know you are."

Louis wanted to believe him. He thought about the afternoons in the garage, fixing the car. But then laughter bubbled up, not his, never his, the thing inside him mocking, unstoppable.

Anne fought back tears. His father clenched his fists until veins bulged like highways on a map. His jaw locked, as if crushing something he couldn't say aloud. And David… David wouldn't look at him at all.

He was slipping away, and he knew it.

The worst were the brief moments of clarity, when the thing showed him how far gone he truly was.

Tonight was one of those nights.

Louis turned his head, his uneven breaths condensing in the air. Awake. Aware. Still himself.

For now.

His body felt heavier, held down by invisible hands. His chest tightened, his throat dried, and his limbs felt numb.

A sudden weightlessness seized him, and his mind slipped from the present. The line between nightmare and reality blurred.

The vision came: his family running. David, Anne, Jack, and Jouris surged ahead, feet pounding, fleeing the lake.

Water churned behind them, dark and ravenous. He couldn't see the pursuer, but he felt it breathing against his neck.

He ran with them, lungs burning, legs aching.

"We have to go!" he shouted.

But no answer came.

The house loomed ahead, its door wide open, candlelight spilling out like a beacon. Relief swept over him, a sense of safety and salvation. He was almost there. He would make it.

Then the door slammed shut as he reached the porch.

He skidded to a stop, pounding his fists. *One-two-three*, again and again.

No... no, let me in! Open the door!

Silence. He hammered harder, screaming their names.

Dad! David! Anne! Jouris! PLEASE!

Through the curtains, shadows gathered. First David's silhouette, then Anne's. Jack's broad frame and Jouris beside him, head bowed. They *knew* he was there. They *heard* him. But the door stayed shut.

"Please!" Louis choked, his voice breaking. *"Don't leave me out here! It's coming!"*

The thought of his mother, her angelic presence. He screamed, *"Mom! You said you would always protect me!*

His fists pounded the door, growing numb. The wood beneath his hands blackened and rotted like diseased flesh. It oozed thick slime that sucked at his fingers.

Then he felt it.

The cold breath on his neck.

The lake gurgled behind him. He turned.

Black, endless water churned and writhed, alive.

Cold, wet hands shot out. They pulled. He screamed.

THE LAKE IS SWALLOWING ME!

It froze him like ice, like plunging into the community pool on Memorial Day. Darkness swallowed him whole. He couldn't find the surface. He tried to hold his breath, but something forced his mouth open, pouring the dark water inside.

Then… he was back. Strapped to the bed.

His skin damp with sweat. His cuts deeper. His wrists burning with pain worse than when he'd placed his hand on a hot stove in preschool.

He gasped, lungs heaving in short, frantic bursts. Tears blurred his vision as he stared at the ceiling, his body trembling.

He was fading. Slipping away.

He didn't want to fight anymore. He just wanted the pain to stop.

If they had already given up on him, shut him out, maybe surrender was all that remained.

A voice hissed in his mind, cold and relentless:

Stop fighting, Louis. You belong to me. Why endure? Just surrender. Become one with me.

He clenched his jaw, digging his nails into his palms.

In a silent scream, he shouted, *NOOOOOOOOOOOOOOO!*

He wasn't gone. Not yet.

He snapped his fingers and counted, *ONE-TWO-THREE…*

But God help him… he was almost there.

CHAPTER 2

Convent of the Sisters of Zion at the Temple Mount in Jerusalem
May 15th

"Will you require anything else?" the young girl whispered.

Barely thirteen, dressed in tattered rags, she set a platter of charred meat on the table. Her blank stare masked the despair clawing inside her.

Tatiana frowned, recalling when power demanded her cold resolve. Pity stirred, and she answered with unusual warmth.

"No, that will be all."

The servant hurried out, leaving Tatiana in the narrow confines of her quarters. A single candle's dim light cast shadows across the bare stone walls. The guesthouse owned by the Convent of the Sisters of Zion stood in stark contrast with Pergamon's grandeur. There, marble halls gleamed beneath golden chandeliers, and silk curtains fluttered in Aegean breezes.

Here, the air was thick with the scent of old books, fading incense, and the grit of sand that clung to skin and teeth if you didn't cover your face. The room was spartan: a cot, a desk, and a single chair. The Sisters embraced austere comfort, something Tatiana could barely comprehend.

On the rough wooden table lay the unedited history of demons. She traced the cracked leather cover, her mind in its presence. The book should not exist, yet it awaited her. It held truths Lucius buried, truths that demanded to be heard.

She opened it carefully. The parchment felt brittle beneath her touch, the ancient ink faded but unmistakable. Its stories, especially those of Lucius's brother Kazimir, contradicted what she had been told or allowed to know.

Lucius had hidden this book for a reason.

Low, distant groans echoed through the convent walls. Tatiana stilled, listening.

Outside, thousands of slaves labored under the scorching sun, day after day, raising Prosperine's temple. At dawn and dusk, they shuffled through mazes of chain-link fencing, grim protective barriers against the infected. These broken creatures clawed at the rusted metal from every direction, even from above, their teeth gnashing as they hurled themselves against the barricades.

Their inability to feed did not diminish their unending hunger for living flesh. Yet, in a twisted irony, their presence comforted the workers. If the infected raged outside, it meant they were still human themselves.

Tatiana's fingers tapped the windowsill. She whispered, "Faith."

Some believed that building the temple would grant them salvation, protection, and a sense of purpose. To them, the infected were reminders of life without faith.

Faith is vastly overrated.

"It has always been a double-edged sword," she murmured, "a tool to be wielded and manipulated. But faith alone won't build the temple. Labor will. Flesh will. Souls broken and reshaped into something useful. That burden is mine."

She exhaled sharply, massaging her temples as the ever-present headache intensified. Acquiring slaves was exhausting. The supply lines had to remain open, and routes changed constantly to avoid delays.

Then there were the camps.

Her stomach churned. Not long ago, corralling people like cattle wouldn't have troubled her. Now it haunted her. The cold reality of her duties quickly smothered a pang of guilt.

She spent weeks overseeing the camps, ensuring Prosperine's needs were met. Behind fences, humans trembled, waiting to be dragged screaming into the darkness. She told herself the sacrifices were necessary. "The temple must rise. Prosperine must be fed."

Lucius had taught her the truth: the grandest temples were built not for divinity, but for power; to control the masses and instill fear.

Yet the screams lingered. Fear's scent clung to her, a stench she could not wash away. She knew if the people learned captives were being consumed, not converted, unrest would ignite.

Now, as the temple rose and the infected howled at its gates, she wondered:

How much more blood will it require?

And when the last stone is laid… what will become of me?

***

The Safehouse Lake Ronkonkoma, New York
After Midnight May 16th

The old house creaked, its familiar groans echoing in Anne's ears. She sat up, blankets pulled tightly around her, eyes wide and alert. She wasn't sleeping; she was listening.

Louis was speaking again, but not in any language she knew.

Deep, rhythmic murmurs drifted through the walls like a haunting chant. Sharp consonants snapped like dry twigs, each one sending a chill up her spine.

Anne froze, William's warning echoing back:

The past bleeds into the present, and the forces we face now are echoes of an ancient darkness.

This wasn't a breakdown. It was something older, darker, draping over the house like an iron curtain.

She swung her legs from the bed, wincing at the cold floor beneath her feet, and crept to Louis's door. Holding her breath, she pressed her ear against the wood.

His words spilled out faster now, and suddenly she recognized some of them:

"*Pater noster, qui es in caelis, sanctificetur nomen tuum…*"

"That's Latin," she whispered. "The Lord's Prayer."

She frowned, leaning closer. Louis had never spoken Latin.

Then the prayer twisted, warping into something unrecognizable.

"*Οὐαὶ ὑμῖν… οἱ καθήμενοι ἐπὶ τὸν θρόνον...*"

Anne stiffened. "Greek? How would he know ancient Greek?"

His voice rasped, as though dragged from centuries of dust, the words raising goose bumps on her arms.

"*Miserere nobis...*"

Another language, another shift. The words bleeding together, indistinct.

"*... Requiescat anima tua...*"

French this time, thick and strained, as if forced through clenched teeth.

Anne stiffened.

Louis's voice sank into something harsh, alien, and evil. The syllables sharp and unnatural, like broken glass scraping against stone. It was a language she had never encountered. One she should not be hearing.

"*N'kath'r'naash r'luhhor goth'mah...*"

The words slithered into her skull, clawing against her temples. Nausea churned in her gut. She staggered back, her breath quickening.

She glanced toward Jack's door, torn between waking him and facing whatever lurked alone.

But then…

A scurrying sound, like rats in the walls, snapped her head around.

Her carotid artery pulsed in her throat as she crept downstairs. She forced herself forward, a chill seeping through her socks as she crept cautiously downstairs.

The living room was empty and appeared untouched. It was dark, reminding her of the basement. The air felt heavy, as if someone had exhaled behind her.

The armchair still faced the fireplace. The couch was undisturbed. The radio was silent. Yet, unease settled over her.

Then she saw it.

The crucifix on the wall hung upside down.

She edged closer, unseen eyes crawling over her back. A cold draft swirled at her ankles. Her chest tightened.

"It was upright earlier, wasn't it?" she whispered, though she already knew the answer.

Her fingers brushed the cold metal cross.

The grandfather clock in the corner lurched forward an inch, as if shoved by invisible hands.

Anne stumbled back, her heart pounding. Silence returned, but the weight of something watching her lingered. She fled the room, desperate to clear her head…

And she knew how to do it.

***

A shower.

The rhythmic splash of water on tile usually calmed Anne. The stream was ice-cold, but she stepped under it anyway. With the power out, there was no hot water, but the shock of the chill was almost welcome, invigorating, sharpening her senses.

H-I-S-S.

A snake-like hiss echoed as the toilet flushed.

Anne tensed, holding her breath as she slowly pulled back the shower curtain.

The bathroom was empty.

But the mirror...

Thick fog blurred the glass, as if she had stepped from a steaming bath instead of an icy shower. Etched into the condensation was a single word:

INSIDE

Her hand trembled as she wiped the mirror. The letters smeared into streaks, but the word still clung to her thoughts, heavy and cold.

She shut off the water, her movements stiff, almost mechanical, and wrapped herself in a towel. The word sent a shiver of cold through her.

What does that mean?

Dressing quickly, she reached for her pajama bottoms, then paused. Something shifted in the pocket.

Frowning, she pulled out a small brass object. It was unnaturally cold in her palm, an artifact out of place in the bathroom. Her eyes darted around, searching the corners, her pulse quickening.

"What does this have to do with *INSIDE*?" she whispered.

She swallowed hard, clutching it tight.

"Jack. Jack will know what it is."

Back in bed, she cocooned herself in the covers, tossing restlessly. Sleep refused to come. Her mind raced, knotted with dread and half-formed questions.

She hoped, desperately, that it was all just in her head.

***

The Safehouse Lake Ronkonkoma, New York
Mid-Morning May 17th

Daylight brought no refuge. The shadows of the night still clung to the safehouse walls…

The porch stretched wide, its weathered boards creaking softly under the weight of two figures. Frost glazed the railing, and the bitter wind howled through the skeletal fruit trees, their frozen buds locked in winter's grip. The chill in the air wasn't only from the cold but from unseen forces drawing closer.

227

Despite the freezing temperatures, the sour stench of the infected lingered. The lake before them, restless and vast, mirrored the sullen sky, its surface broken only by ice-rimmed streams that fed it.

Jack leaned against a porch post, arms crossed, the shotgun within reach. His eyes were fixed on the lake, the wind drawing tears that rolled down his cheeks. Pain flared in his tooth, searing like a branding iron pressed into his jawbone. Each pulse throbbed harder than the last, the ache a cruel mirror of the ever-present danger creeping closer. He clenched his jaw, but Anne was already watching him with a knowing look.

"You're getting paler," she said, tugging her coat tighter. That needs more than wishful thinking."

He exhaled sharply through his nose.

"Got a miracle cure stashed away somewhere?"

"Willow bark," Anne said. "It has salicin, like aspirin. Beeswax might help with infection. If we find any, it could ease the pain."

Jack let out a strained laugh.

"There's never a Walgreens around when you need one. I could try town, but the infected are crawling everywhere."

"I could suggest plenty of booze," Anne joked. "The old West solution. But I'd rather not have to haul your unconscious body back."

Jack's fingers closed around the metal object in his pocket. The cold steel felt heavier than it should, his dread growing with every heartbeat. Slowly, he pulled it out. The red-handled pliers caught the weak light, their dull silver gleam twisting his stomach. He had sworn it was a last resort. Now, just holding it made his skin crawl.

Anne frowned and gripped his jacket.

"Jack, don't be foolish."

"Wouldn't be the first time," he muttered, fiddling with his zipper.

She sighed, tucking a loose strand of hair under her hat, then dug into her pocket.

"Here. I found this in my pajama pocket last night."

Jack rubbed his aching cheek as he took the object, turning it over.

"It's a brass Boy Scout Skill Award," he said, surprised. "A small square with the metal folded over, allowing it to slip onto a belt."

He studied the etched images.

"A First Aid badge," He murmured, smiling faintly. "See? Broken arm, Red Cross…" His throat tightened. "You say you just… found this?"

Anne nodded. "I don't know how it got there. But it's real."

Jack's thumb brushed the metal, stirring memories. It made him wonder if he himself had any connection to the house, or to the strange phenomena they were experiencing. Before he could speak, Anne cut in.

"That's not all."

"Why am I not surprised?" Jack sighed.

"There was writing on the mirror after my shower."

He straightened. "What did it say?"

She hesitated, breath fogging in the cold.

"The word INSIDE. I'm still trying to figure it out. But whatever it means, we stick to the plan, right?"

Jack's jaw tightened.

"Different directions. One of us takes David, the other takes…" He faltered, thinking about his son strapped upstairs. "…Louis."

Anne pulled her coat tighter. "I hate that it comes to this."

"Yeah. But we don't have a choice."

Silence settled like London fog, broken only by the wind rattling through bare trees. Jack rubbed his sore jaw once more, grimacing against the pain.

"Speaking of pajamas, I have a confession to make. I had a dream about you the other night."

Anne raised an eyebrow. "Oh?"

Jack shrugged. "Nothing bad. Just… different."

A faint blush colored her cheeks. She smiled, glancing toward the lake.

"Stress does that," she said lightly, though her voice held a spark of hope. "Makes people think things they might not otherwise."

Jack grinned. Her words were a small flame, an ember of optimism against the grim reality they faced. "Better than my recurring nightmare about the Savannah River Bridge. That one's haunted me since childhood."

Anne chuckled. "That bad?"

"You have no idea. George and Michelle had plenty of fun at my expense."

Jack tucked the Boy Scout award into his pocket, his fingers brushing the pliers still in his palm. Maybe the Skill Award meant something. Perhaps it didn't. But each day brought more questions than answers, and the weight of that uncertainty pressed harder on them both.

***

Louis's Room in The Safehouse Lake Ronkonkoma, New York After Dinner May 17th

David hesitated at Louis's door, the weight of past and present on him as his fingers trembled against the brass knob. The stench of festering wounds leaked into the hall, testing his resolve. The air felt thick, as though the walls were squeezing every ounce of oxygen from the space until he could barely breathe.

That constant sensation of being watched, from the closet, the mirror, and every corner, made him glance over his shoulder again and again. Gulping, he clenched his fists and thought of the map of the Long Island Railroad system Jouris had given him.

"Ronkonkoma, Central Islip, Brentwood, Deer Park..." he repeated the stops on the Lake Ronkonkoma line to Penn Station, reciting them like a prayer until he steadied himself. Then he entered. Louis needed him.

Clutching the first aid kit against his chest, David was greeted by the sound of Louis's labored breathing. The window was closed, yet

Louis's breath rose in pale, misty puffs that hovered over him. The room was dark, and his eyes needed a few moments to adjust.

At the head of the bed, Louis lay moaning, his limbs tightly strapped to the bed. Fresh bruises and oozing wounds covered his arms and face. The dried blood smelled of rot.

David crouched, opening the kit, fighting the knot in his stomach.

"Let me clean you up," He whispered, biting the inside of his cheek until the taste of blood filled his mouth.

Louis lifted his head; his once-warm brown eyes were now as black as coal.

"It's not working, David." He rasped. "None of it."

David dabbed one of the angrier cuts with a damp cloth. The wounds never healed. They always reopened, deeper, as if invisible hands were peeling Louis apart.

"We'll find something," David said tightly. "Dad, Anne, and Jouris are working on it."

Wyandanch, Pinelawn, Farmingdale, Bethpage…

Louis scoffed. "Dad! Anne! Jouris!"

David pressed antiseptic into a gash. It fizzed and bubbled as the liquid met blood and tissue, seemingly rejecting the touch. He squeezed his eyes shut, counting silently.

Louis gave a dry laugh.

"No medicine can fix this. They can't fix it. We can't ignore it anymore." Louis's voice dropped. "This isn't just about us. It's about stopping the evil that's been under Ronkonkoma all these years."

He locked eyes with his brother.

"You and me," Louis hissed. "We can fix this."

David froze.

Hicksville, Westbury, Carle Place, Mineola…

Louis strained against the straps, his voice urgent.

"We have the power, David. Together, we can end this. But you have to free me."

David recoiled, his stomach twisting. "Louis…"

"Listen to me!" Louis's voice cracked. "They're keeping us weak and divided." His gaze grew distant, his tone almost commanding. "We're prophets, David. If we join forces, we can destroy it once and for all. We can make things right before it turns on you!"

David's breath shortened. The look in Louis's eyes made his skin crawl. He saw something deeper, hidden within, something even David hadn't realized until now. It terrified him.

Merillon Avenue, New Hyde Park, Floral Park, Elmont…

"I know what you want, Louis," David stammered. "You're my brother, but I… I don't know…"

A creak sounded from the hall.

Anne entered swiftly, pushing David behind her.

"No, Louis."

Louis's jaw tightened. "Anne…"

"Quit manipulating him." Her voice was icy and unrelenting.

Louis's back arched as he floated above the bed. The temperature plummeted. Shadows raced across the walls and ceiling. Whispers stirred, like a chorus of lost souls. The restraints groaned as he strained against them, lips twisting into a cruel smile.

"You think you can protect him?"

Anne's fingers twitched at her sides. "I swore I would."

Louis's face darkened. His fists tightened around the straps until his knuckles blanched.

"Then you're a fool. I have big plans for you. You and me, Anne…. we could make beautiful music together. I can give you what my father never will."

His gaze shifted to David, who shrank back, horrified at both the supernatural defiance and the obscene suggestion.

"If you don't help me, David, I'll use my power to destroy you. I'll tear your damn heart out and eat it. I'll feed your liver and intestines to the beasts of hell. Or maybe Dad and Anne can eat it while you watch!"

Anne grabbed David and backed toward the door. A coldness slithered into his chest, coiling tightly around his heart and lungs. Fear locked his limbs, making each breath a struggle. He stumbled, and Anne caught him, her holding him close as if to shield him from the evil seething inside his brother.

Queens Village, Hollis, Hillside, Jamaica...

David clutched her sleeve. "Is this... going to happen to me?"
Anne held him tighter. "Not if I can stop it," she whispered.
But in her eyes, a flicker of doubt betrayed her... before she buried it with resolve.

CHAPTER 3

A Motel Somewhere in Northern New Jersey
May 22nd

George Aitken sat alone in the dilapidated shell of a roadside motel, a glass of whiskey trembling in his hand. The buzzing neon sign cast sickly waves of red and blue across the peeling wallpaper. The drone of the generator pulsed through the walls, mingling with the sweat on his brow and the ghosts crowding the room.

His family stood before him: Josephine, James, Kate, and Erin, their faces frozen in the moments of their most violent deaths. Their mouths moved, whispering secrets just beyond his reach. His pulse raced, the pressure building behind his eyes until it was almost unbearable.

He clenched his jaw. This was the toll, the price of his soul, reflected in their lifeless eyes.

"Balance the cost of the soul you lost..." he muttered, the words dripping from his lips like venom.

Where had he heard it before? A haunting refrain looping in his mind, impossible to shake.

The past clawed at him, a relentless reminder of what he had sacrificed: flesh for power, innocence for strength. This kind of sacrifice always came with a cost.

And still it was never enough.

The world took from him, so he took back with a vengeance. Now only one goal remained: finding Jack, Anne, and his damn nephews. Like sand, they had slipped through his fingers too many times. It was time to finish it... to make them bleed.

His grip tightened on the whiskey glass, its smooth surface slick against his trembling hand. His family's ghostly laughter rose into a mocking chorus. They taunted him, saying,

You're a creature of habit. Run if you can, afraid of a fear you can't name…

His hand shot out, hurling the glass against the wall. It shattered, and amber liquid trickled down the cracked plaster.

He knew the fear, like venomous poison crawling beneath his skin, corrupting every thought.

It wasn't the spirits, their voices, or even the nightmares that clawed at his soul each time he closed his eyes that he feared. It was the dread of failure. That he might never catch them, and that his vengeance would slip away before he could taste it.

His breath came in ragged gasps. His hands shook like leaves in a storm of paranoia. He wrestled with his torment. Memories ricocheted through his mind, jagged and random, like a game of mental hopscotch. Why was there no relief?

"They all think this is a game," George muttered. "But it isn't."

Something deeper burned within him, a smoldering fire hidden beneath the ghosts that haunted him. The hunt, the chase, it was an addiction. An insatiable need. It consumed him.

The words hammered in his skull: *I feel the hand of fate reaching out.* His pulse quickened, his jaw locked. Fate had set him on this path, and the clues were close. When he found them, he would finish it.

He caught his reflection in the shards of broken glass. The face he wore was different now. Fractured and distorted, it sneered back at him. His tongue slid over his teeth, lips curling into a half-smirk. He was close. He could feel it.

Jack.

Anne.

Those f… ing prophets!

Somewhere out there, waiting. But he would wait no longer.

George surged to his feet, pushing past the ghosts, the doubts, and the remnants of the man he once was. The past was for losers, and he had no use for it. He had traded every dream for just one, sold his soul for a singular, fiery passion.

His eyes widened, a smug, twisted smile spreading across his face.

"I'm going home," he whispered, fist clenching. "Time to finally track down Jack. It ends now."

***

Grounds of the Safehouse Lake Ronkonkoma, New York
May 23rd

The sky hung low and gray, bruised clouds stretching across the still barren landscape, as if the world itself held its breath, stalling the seasonal change. The sun's heat, if it could even be called that, felt feeble, offering no relief from the damp chill clinging to their bones.

The cold wasn't just in the air; it seeped up from an unseen corruption tightening its grip beneath the soil. Jack flexed his fingers, trying to coax some warmth into them as he and Jouris maneuvered the battered but functional Ford Focus into position.

Jack glanced up.

"Where's the sun? It's almost June. For God's sake, it should be nearly seventy degrees by now."

"Coldest May I can remember," Jouris muttered, blowing into his hands.

Jack pointed behind the garage. "That looks good. Keep the car on the grass. If the tires crunch gravel, someone, or something, will hear."

"Right. No sense stirring up any infected that might be in the woods or drawing the attention of any survivors," Jouris agreed.

Jack noticed Jouris staring toward the horizon, his lips pressed into a thin line. "Something on your mind?"

Jouris hesitated, his breath curling white in the cold air. "Heard a report this morning. The corn crop's frozen."

Jack frowned. "All of it?"

Jouris nodded. "Not just here. A broadcast from a Kansas station reported that severe frost had also hit the Midwest. People are fleeing in droves."

Jack thought of abandoned farms, roads lined with rusted cars, and empty houses. The image conjured up stories of the Okies heading to California, fleeing the Dust Bowl during the Great Depression. Only this was worse.

"That's bad."

Jouris's eyes swept the property. "Still haven't seen any bees."

Jack's muscles tensed, and he massaged his temples. "Neither have I."

"Without bees, there's no food," Jouris said. "And now that I think about it, I don't hear any birds, either."

Jack winced as another jolt of pain shot through his tooth. He rubbed his cheek, muttering, "No bees, no birds. Like the whole world's being hollowed out. All the life sucked out, same as the infected."

Jouris pulled a flask from his coat and offered it. "One or two swallows left. You look like you need it."

Jack didn't argue. He drank the last drops and grimaced.

Jouris shoved a toothpick between his teeth, then unfolded a creased map over the steering wheel, tracing his finger along one of the marked routes.

"We've got three escape routes: quickest is through Queens and the Bronx to the George Washington Bridge."

Jack's gut twisted. *I don't trust that bridge. Or any other bridge, for that matter.*

Maybe we should charter a boat instead. I heard about this boat called the Titanic...

Jouris caught his hesitation. "Got a better route?"

Jack shook his head. "No. We just need to be ready."

They eased the car into position near the tree line, far enough from the house to avoid being boxed in if something went wrong.

Jack climbed out, closed the door, and then released the tension in his shoulders.

Jouris grabbed the passenger handle, but the door didn't move.

Jack frowned. "What's wrong?"

"It's locked," Jouris said, eyes narrowing.

"That's not possible," Jack muttered. "It's a piece of shit car, not a…"

Jouris's breath hitched. His hands flew to his throat.

A cold knot twisted in Jack's gut, a warning signal coming too late.

Jouris clawed at the door handle, gasping as an invisible noose constricted his neck. His veins bulged, and terror flooded his face.

Jack rushed to the driver's side and pulled at the door handle. It was locked.

"Jouris!"

Jouris thrashed in the seat, his mouth gaping in a silent scream. His nails scraped against the fogged glass.

Jack pounded on the window, the sound like a gunshot on a quiet morning. Inside, the radio blared a toughing refrain,

Keep-a-knockin, but you can't come in…

"Stay with me, Jouris!" Jack shouted.

Jouris's convulsions slowed. His eyes rolled back.

Jack scanned wildly for a rock, a tool, anything to break the glass. His heart hammered in his chest.

Then, as suddenly as it began, it stopped.

Jouris collapsed against the seat, gasping. The locks clicked… *on their own.*

Jack yanked the door open and dragged Jouris into the cold air. Jouris dropped to his knees, coughing and clutching the dirt as if it were the only thing keeping him from tumbling into the abyss.

Jack crouched beside him, beads of sweat falling like raindrops from a heavy storm. "What the hell just happened?"

Jouris tried to speak but only shook his head.

Jack glanced back. The engine was off; the keys were dangling from the ignition. There was no reason for the doors to have locked.

But he knew.

Something was in that car. And it had just tried to kill Jouris.

Meanwhile, upstairs, still strapped to his bed, Louis's eyes rolled back as maniacal laughter filled the room.

***

The Mexican Border with the United States
Just After Nightfall on May 23rd

The night sky stretched wide over the desert, dark and smooth as the lacquered finish of a jet-black Cadillac, swallowing everything but the stars, which were sharp and bright like the brilliance of newly minted dimes. The terrain was a sprawling wasteland of dust swirling around jagged rocks and gnarled sagebrush clawing the cracked earth like emaciated fingers.

Reid Bowman and the Foley family huddled on a low ridge, their gaunt bodies worn thin after three relentless months of wandering. Kevin and Sean Foley, once vibrant and full of life, now bore sunken cheeks and vacant, tired eyes. Their parents, Scott and Ellen, looked decades older, their skin cracked and sunburned from the unforgiving sun. Julie, the youngest, clung to her mother, her tangled red hair matted with dust, eyes fixed on the river below.

Scott pointed toward a stretch of the Rio Grande where the water ran shallow and sluggish.

"That's our best chance. Not deep, but ice cold. Move slowly. Carefully."

Reid's reply was tight with urgency.

"Then we move now. Stay close."

The checkpoints had been closed for months, turning the border into a hunting ground. Armed men without insignia prowled the night, faces hidden behind scarves and mirrored sunglasses, weapons gleaming cold in the moonlight. Their loyalty was mercenary, indifferent to nation or law, bound only to the highest bidder.

Reid led the way, each step deliberate, his innate animal instinct sharpened by survival. The river's current coiled around his legs like icy fingers, silt shifting beneath his feet.

Kevin shivered. "It's freezing."

"Keep moving," Reid urged, steering him clear of jagged rocks.

Sean scrambled across, his breath misting in the cold night air. Ellen gripped Scott's hand tightly, steadying herself the current's slow but unforgiving pull.

Julie, barely sixteen, lost her footing midway.

"Help!" she gasped, her arms flailing as the river dragged her under.

Reid dove without hesitation, seizing her thin wrist and hauling her upward from the riverbed.

"I've got you," he whispered, hoisting her onto his back.

She coughed and clung to him until he carried her to shore, where Scott and Ellen wrapped her in desperate arms.

"That's not the first time you've saved our family," Ellen breathed, gratitude thick in her voice.

Reid nodded, his piercing blue eyes already scanning the darkness, searching for threats.

Then came the chilling click of safeties being switched off.

Low, harsh voices cut through the night air.

"No se muevan! Levanten las manos!

Flashlights pierced the darkness. Men emerged from the shadows, clad in tactical gear, ammunition belts slung across their chests, black ski masks concealing their faces. They gripped their semi-automatics with practiced, lethal precision.

Scott whispered urgently, raising his hands.

"Don't move. These aren't border patrol. They're cartel enforcers; wolves hired by the government to stop us from fleeing south, to keep us from entering Mexico."

"Ponerse en movimiento!"

***

The Mexican Border-Holding Facility
Nightfall on May 23rd

The journey ended at a holding facility that resembled a prison more than a refugee camp. Inside, chain-link cages, crudely assembled, were crammed with desperate people stretched wall to wall. The air was suffocating, thick with the stench of unwashed bodies and the relentless hacking coughs of the sick, a choking fog that overwhelmed all who breathed it.

A guard sneered, voice thick with menace.

"Gringos. Thought you could just cross? Now you pay."

The crowd of mercenaries parted like the Red Sea as a man stepped forward. Older, his slicked-back silver hair framed a scar from temple to jaw, a permanent half-snarl etched into his face. His tailored black uniform gleamed spotless despite the filth around him. A blood-red silk bandana shimmered at his throat, a marijuana-leaf necklace dangled on his chest, and a pearl-handled revolver rested snug at his hip.

Power and authority radiated from him like heat from a flame. This was El Patrón.

His deep, smooth voice sliced through the murmurs of the prisoners.

"Bring him to me."

El Patron examined Reid, his eyes cold and clinical.

"You're different. I see it." He murmured as he circled Reid like a shark.

He gestured toward the huddled detainees.

"Stronger than these other cattle."

Waving his hand, he ordered the guards,

"Take him and his friends to Room Z."

Room Z was stark, sterile, with white walls and no windows. The only decoration: a looming portrait of the narco-saint Jesus Malverde,

241

whose stark, white-collared shirt contrasted with eyes so black and piercing they seemed to bore into every prisoner.

El Patron planted his polished boot on a chair beside Reid, his thumb pointing over his shoulder toward the painting.

"Jesus Malverde says you will tell me who you are… or I will carve the truth from you."

Reid met his gaze with icy silence.

El Patrón exhaled sharply.

"Very well. Perhaps pain will loosen your tongue."

A guard's fist drove into Reid's ribs. Another split his lip with a brutal strike.

The blows grew harder, more vicious and brutal, but Reid refused to break.

Julie's fingers dug into her mother's sleeve as El Patrón's gaze shifted to her. He stepped closer, his fingers brushing through her tangled red hair.

"Maybe she'll help you find your voice. She's pretty, don't you think?"

His voice dropped to a cruel whisper.

"I could make sure she suffers in ways you can't imagine."

Julie whimpered, El Patron's cruel words slithering through the room.

Darkness closed in on Reid's world.

A tremor surged through him, a pulse of something ancient and monstrous stirring deep inside.

Then, something snapped within him.

His fingers curled, black veins swelling beneath gray skin, the color of death. His fingernails split, as claws emerged. His jaw cracked, stretching wide as razor-sharp fangs erupted from his gums, each one gleaming sharply in the dim light. Thick, coarse black fur spread across his body. His eyes, once a striking blue, now burned with a crimson glow, like hot embers in the night. His heart pounded like a war drum, his chest rising and falling with unnatural speed as hunger consumed him.

El Patrón recoiled, his composure faltering.

"¿Qué demonios...?" he hissed.

Reid's voice rumbled, gravelly and inhuman, issuing an ominous warning that froze their blood.

"You shouldn't have done that."

The Strigoi was unleashed, its muscles bursting with unnatural strength. In one motion, it ripped a guard's throat open, a geyser of blood spraying the walls. Screams pierced the night as the creature moved, a blur of shadow and carnage.

"Madre de Dios!" an enforcer gasped, fumbling for his weapon.

Another pulled out his pistol and fired, the bullet hitting its target, but the Strigoi barely flinched. With snarling fury, it lunged, sinking its fangs into the man's jugular, drinking deeply. The warm, rich taste of human blood, a forbidden temptation the Strigoi had vowed never to taste again, sent a shudder through its body.

"Run!" someone screamed, but it was too late.

El Patrón's eyes widened with terror as he clawed for his revolver, but the Strigoi was faster. With a savage roar, it swiped a claw across the sadistic drug lord's face, tearing flesh and bone away in a single motion. Blood sprayed in thick arcs, splattering walls and floors alike.

El Patrón collapsed, eyes wide and lifeless against the wall. From the lips of Jesus Malverde's painting, blood dripped, landing like a curse upon El Patron's forehead.

The Strigoi reveled in its work, a predator unleashed against life-long hunters. Limbs were torn. Bones shattered. Gunfire tore through metal and flesh as bullets flew. Seizing their chance, the refugees surged forward, overwhelming the remaining guards in a desperate bid for freedom.

When the chaos ebbed and the screams faded, the facility lay in ruins. Bodies littered the blood-soaked floors. Smoke billowed up-ward, fueling fires that raged in the aftermath.

Reid stood amid the carnage, the monster receding beneath his skin. His breath came heavy, his hands slick with blood. The Strigoi was gone… for now. But its hunger lingered, echoing deep inside.

In a corner, he found the Foleys, their faces pale and terror-stricken. Scott's grip tightened on Ellen and Julie, his knuckles white from tension.

"What the hell are you?" he rasped.

Reid met their eyes and recognized their fear. The terror in Julie's face overwhelmed him. For a heartbeat he saw Maricela Antonescu again, begging for mercy in the cave at Lake Waccamaw.

He turned away without a word and stepped into the cold desert night, leaving them behind.

***

Jouris's Garage Lake Ronkonkoma, New York
Mid-Afternoon May 31st

Thunder rolled in the distance, a visceral warning of the storm building between Jack and Anne.

Jouris's Garage was dimly lit, the air thick with the scent of motor oil and solvents. Jack paced near the workbench, his hands trembling as he ran them through his unkempt hair. Across from him, Anne leaned against Jouris's Mustang, arms folded tightly, and eyes blazing with frustration.

"We can't ignore this, Jack!" Anne's voice sliced through the silence.

"Louis isn't Louis anymore. I told you what happened with David, what Louis said, and the threats he made. You've seen it. You need to face the truth!"

Jack turned away, exhaling sharply. He turned the handle on the workbench vise, tightening the jaws.

"This can't be happening. I won't discuss it. I won't. I just… can't."

Anne stepped closer, her voice filled with urgency. "You have to. Remember your training. You wanted to keep us safe. You know what needs to be done."

Jack slammed his fist onto the workbench. A wrench clattered to the floor.

"I said no! He's my son, Anne! My boy! How do you expect me to…"

"He's not your son anymore!" Anne's voice cracked with anger and despair. "Do you think I don't know how much this hurts? I feel it too."

A gust of wind rattled the garage door as the storm drew closer.

"But that thing pretending to be Louis isn't him!"

She picked the wrench up off the floor. "Every second we waste, it burrows deeper into him. Soon, there won't be anything left to save."

Jack's jaw clenched. The Entity shrouded his mind like a suffocating fog, whispering poison and clouding his reason.

She's wrong, Jack. You know she's wrong.

The thought coiled tightly around his thoughts, feeding doubts and amplifying his pain.

He whispered, hollow, "You don't understand. You haven't seen what I've seen. You haven't lived it. Maybe… maybe there's another way."

Anne's fists tightened. Her breath frosted in the cold air as she drove her point home.

"What other way? Reason with it? Make a deal with a demon?"

She softened, resting a hand on Jack's shoulder.

"It's toying with you, Jack. It wants you to hesitate, to doubt, that's how it wins."

Jack pressed his hands to his head, shaking as if he could dislodge the poison pooling in his mind.

Anne's tone dropped, but her urgency sharpened.

"You have to fight it. If we don't act and it takes control of Louis completely... who's next?"

Jack faced her. His eyes flickered with doubt and anger.

"And if I can't do it? What then?"

A flash of hesitation crossed her face before she locked eyes with him.

"Then I will."

His face twisted.

"You wouldn't."

Her reply was like steel. "I will. Because I love you, David, and Louis enough to do what must be done. Even if you don't."

Her words struck like a blade. For a moment, he stared at her, his hands trembling.

"Are you saying I don't love my son?" he whispered,

Before Anne could respond, he stormed past her, shoved open the garage door, and disappeared behind Jouris's house.

Anne stood alone in the cold, silent air, her breath trembling, her heart pounding in her chest.

Upstairs in the safehouse, Louis cackled maniacally from the shadows.

STAGE V:
OBSESSION

<u>CHAPTER 1</u>

Safehouse at Lake Ronkonkoma
Mid-Afternoon June 1st

As the world continued to unravel, even summer had forgotten itself...

"I'm going to get more wood," Jack muttered, his breath fogging like it was mid-January as he reached for the axe by the door.

The words sounded rehearsed, as if he were reciting lines for a play.

The fire crackled, its warmth retreating with the rest of the world. Tired and hungry, Anne barely looked up, pulling her coat tighter. Jouris crossed his arms, staring into the flames. Lost in thought, he managed only an almost inaudible grunt.

Neither noticed the way Jack's fingers flexed around the axe handle, or how his eyes flicked not toward the wood pile, but to the garage.

The faint smell of smoldering wood curled through the room, an ordinary comfort masking something quietly unfolding.

He was cold, but wasn't gathering wood. He was going to end something or let something begin. He was hunting for relief.

When Jack closed the door, the cold immediately slapped him in the face. It seeped through the layers of his clothing as he crossed the yard. Frost crackled beneath his boots, and occasionally the wind would whisper through bare, lifeless trees. It was as if the forest knew what was coming.

Shaking his head, Jack muttered, half in disbelief, half in sarcasm.

"If this is how June starts, I can't wait for July."

At the garage, he paused. His breath was ragged and uneven. The door creaked as he opened it, and it took a moment for his eyes to adjust to the dim light.

Inside, the Mustang sat beneath a dangling light bulb, which no longer worked. Tools were scattered across the workbench, and the hood was propped open. A thin layer of dust coated the engine, evidence that Louis no longer worked on it. The breeze trailing behind him made the bulb swing like a pendulum.

But Jack's eyes weren't on the car. They fixed on an array of tools he had laid out days earlier: the screwdriver, the pliers, and a rag already stained with sweat.

His tongue brushed against the swollen gum, where an infection sent waves of fire coursing through his jaw. The ache had grown unbearable. No dentist. No medicine. No hope. Only this. Only now. Only him.

Jack braced his hands on the workbench and took a deep breath. The pain made his head swim and blurred his vision. He reached for the screwdriver, gripping it firmly despite the tremor in his fingers. The tip found the gap between his infected tooth and the next. He pushed it in carefully.

The pain exploded, and he gasped, nearly dropping the tool. He hesitated before driving the screwdriver deeper, using it as leverage to pry the tooth loose.

His breath hitched. The infection pulsed; hot and alive, almost possessive. The bitter taste of iron filled his mouth. He turned the screwdriver slightly, feeling the tooth shift against the swollen tissue, nauseating him. A deep, guttural sound escaped his throat. He willed himself to continue, the pain sharp and electric, nearly unbearable.

Next came the pliers.

Sweat slicked his hands despite the chill. The metal felt cold and unforgiving. He clamped down on the tooth, steel scraping enamel, flesh tearing as the jaws bit deep. He whimpered as he twisted the knob at the bottom of the handle and cursed the choice he faced while securing the vice grip in place.

Then he pulled.

Pain roared through him, a white-hot burst that drove him to his knees. He bit back a scream and yanked again. The roots fought back, refusing to let go. He rocked the pliers back and forth, trying to break their grip.

One last pull.

Something in his jaw gave way with a sickening pop. Agony tore through him, intense and overwhelming. His scream pierced the air, reverberating off the garage walls. He crumpled to the floor. His grip faltered, and the pliers slipped from his hand, clattering on the concrete.

The tooth dangled in their jaws like a relic; its roots black, slick with blood rolling down Jack's chin. A sharp, coppery tang began to fill the air, subtle, but unmistakable.

The scream shattered the silence.

Anne and Jouris froze, hearts hammering.

The fire hissed behind them, releasing a sudden whiff of scorched embers, like something old burned away.

Then came the silence. Too long. Too still.

They looked at each other and knew…

Jack hadn't gone for wood.

***

Meanwhile in New York City

While Jack hunted for relief, fifty-five miles away in Manhattan, a smoldering city glowed like a diseased bruise…

Prosperine hovered above the crumbled remains of Saint Patrick's Cathedral, a New York City landmark and once the most revered Catholic church in the United States. Its proud twin spires lay ruined in the street, torn down as if by divine rage. Like a peacock, she landed triumphantly, perching on the twisted remnants of a bronze cross that had once crowned the church's façade.

She was a vision of otherworldly beauty twisted into something unnatural.

Her skin gleamed like molten marble, milky white, with golden veins pulsing with an unholy light. Her eyes were fathomless pits of darkness, seeming to swallow anyone who dared gaze too long. A crown of gold, gilded with jagged obsidian, adorned her flowing, raven-black hair, the strands slithering like deadly asps.

Her gown was woven from fabric as black as night, shifting between gossamer silk and armor. The fabric seemed alive with whispering, pleading voices. Her vast, wraithlike wings shimmered with angelic radiance corrupted by fire, their edges dripping with fiery embers.

Fires blazed in the ruins, casting trembling shadows across cracked pavement. The streets overflowed with shards of broken glass and charred, twisted metal.

In the war against CWD, an unrelenting inferno consumed civilization's last remnants, its embers smoldering beside forgotten prayers. In the distance, a church bell tolled, not chimed by the hands of the faithful, but by the wind that moved the rusted mechanism, its sound an eerie dirge for all that was lost.

Below, the remnants of humanity crawled through the wreckage of the world they once knew, gathering to meet their new God. Their vacant stares were windows to despair, and their bodies were gaunt from starvation. The air was thick with the scent of death and desperation.

"My poor, wretched children," Prosperine's voice rolled across the runs, a melodic sigh laced with sorrow. She descended from her perch with effortless grace, gliding toward the gathered masses summoned by her silver-tongued heralds, who promised salvation.

"You have been abandoned," she whispered as she landed. With fingers as cold as the grave, she caressed the cheek of a kneeling woman with mocking compassion. "Your God has forsaken you."

"Save us!" A wave of quiet pleas surged through the crowd.

Some wept, while others nodded, their lips trembling with long-since unanswered prayers. The hunger in their eyes revealed months spent in deprivation, hope smothered beneath the weight of despair. Their hands reached for her robes, fingers scraping against the grand illusion of her salvation.

"I have come," Prosperine said, spreading her arms. "I have seen your suffering. I have heard your cries. Heaven will not take you. But I will." Her smile was radiant, glowing with divine deception. "Come with me. I alone remember what mercy feels like. I will deliver you from this horror to a place untouched by war and plague, where hunger and fear are only distant memories."

"Praise, Prosperine!"

A desperate murmur of hope surged through the crowd, thin, desperate, and doomed. They wanted to believe. They needed to believe. Prosperine's lips curled at their naivete. Their faith fed her hunger.

She led them through shattered streets, past the charred skeletons of the citizens of the once-great city. Those who hesitated or questioned found their doubts eased by the gentle touch of her hand, the comforting sound of her voice, and the promise reflected in her gaze.

They reached the sanctuary, a bastion of white stone standing amid the ruin, bathed in golden light that seemed untouched by the suffering outside its gates. Inside, they thought they found hope.

The aroma of roasted meat filled the room, rich and theatrical, too perfect. It felt staged, like incense masking decay.

"Food!" a woman exclaimed, pointing at a long table filled with every imaginable delicacy.

Surging forward in a ravenous frenzy, they feasted on the delicious meat and fruits of the vine.

A hearth with a roaring fire warmed them in a way they could only remember. The fresh water tasted like honey. For the first time in months, they laughed.

With her hands folded in prayer, a woman knelt and wept with gratitude, singing praises to her Savior.

"All glory and honor to you, my Princess!"

They whispered her name as if it were their new gospel. They marveled at the murals on the sanctuary walls, reflections of a promised tomorrow painted in lies. They could not see that the images represented a new dawn that would never arrive.

Prosperine sneered, "Now, it is time for the trials to begin."

***

Safehouse Lake Ronkonkoma
The Next Day…June 2nd

The jar was nearly empty.

Anne scraped her spoon along the inside, chasing the last stubborn streaks of peanut butter. She pressed her finger inside the rim where the spoon couldn't reach, scooping up whatever remained. The oil had separated, leaving an off taste, but it still provided desperately needed calories.

She set the jar down with a frustrated sigh. Their food had run out faster than expected. Finding more had become an obsession. Her eyes drifted to the small animal carcass on the table.

"Jack's trap actually worked," she whispered, her tone laced with more than a hint of surprise. "He'll probably say, *I told you so.* This squirrel isn't much, but I'd better get it skinned ."

Anne wrinkled her nose. The house reeked. Days earlier, an acrid, decaying stench had begun wafting in from the lake. At first, she thought something had died nearby, maybe inside the walls. But Jouris had returned from inspecting the shoreline with a grim expression.

"Fish kill," he'd said. "It could be acid rain or the unusual cold snap. Either way, it did a number on them, and it's attracting the infected, too."

Now the smell seeped into everything. It curled under doorways, clung to their clothes, and settled in the back of their throats; an unwelcome taste that never faded. Even in sleep, it lingered on their skin like rot. She had hoped that prolonged exposure would dull her senses, but each day the stench only seemed sharper.

Pulling back the curtain, she gazed out at Jack and Jouris across the yard in search of something edible.

Her stomach growled, but she stayed at the window, watching them scavenge the frozen ground like grave diggers.

"This is getting bad," she murmured.

***

Jack's face twisted into a weak smile as he returned Anne's wave.

An angry wind whipped across the open field, and it had teeth. It gnawed at his ragged coat and stung his skin. Pulling his tooth had been agonizing, leaving him unconscious, and now his mouth throbbed like he had a heartbeat in his jaw. He worried about another infection and felt sure that if he stood up too quickly, the wind would knock him over.

Next to him, Jouris knelt, tugging stubborn weeds from the frozen ground.

"Dandelions," he muttered, brushing dirt from his numb fingers against his jeans. "We can eat the greens, the flowers, even roast the roots for coffee."

Jack chuckled. "You know it's bad when we get pumped up about weeds."

Jouris tucked his hands under his armpits for warmth. "You want to complain, or you want to eat?"

Jack sighed and bent to help. They had little choice; the weather had ruined their chances of growing real crops. The soil was either frozen solid or drowned in acidic muck from the rain. Most animals, including squirrels and even mice, had fled or died. Some had been torn apart by the infected, who hunted but never ate.

Jack yanked a plant free and shook the dirt loose. His fingers were stiff, and he flexed them, wincing in discomfort. The wind shifted, carrying the nauseating odor of dead fish across the field.

"Guess I stink bad enough to scare off the infected," he half-joked.

Jouris chuckled. "You do stink. But between you and those fish…"

He crouched again, brushing frost from a patch of green. "Hey. Look at this."

Jack crawled closer. The smell struck him first: fresh, crisp, clean.

"Mint!" Jouris said, almost euphoric. "We can steep it for tea. You can chew it; it might help your gums."

Jack rubbed the leaves between his fingers, inhaling deeply. "Smells like a damn miracle." He popped a leaf into his mouth and chewed.

The first snowflakes began to fall, swirling around them. Jack tilted his head up and watched as the sky darkened.

"We should get back," Jouris said, bundling the dandelions and mint.

Jack nodded. "Yeah. Before the real cold sets in."

Their boots crunched over the frosty ground as they headed for the house. Jack ran his tongue across the raw hole in his gums, chewing feverishly on the mint. At first, it burned, but the ache slowly dulled.

Small victories. For now, that was all they had.

***

Anne had cleaned the squirrel and was roasting it over the small fire they had dared to light. Jack slumped beside the flames, legs stretched stiffly in front of him.

Jouris sighed, leaning back against the wall. "One scrawny squirrel between us."

Jack rubbed his bearded face. "I remember fighting my grandfather and George for turkey legs at Thanksgiving. Now we're sharing a damn rodent."

They ate in silence, gnawing at the tough meat. It wasn't much, hardly a bite each, but it was something.

Anne chewed slowly, her eyes drifting to the stairs. The silence on the second floor felt heavier than the one between them.

The silence on the second floor felt heavier than the one between them.

Jack paused mid-chew, staring into the flickering candlelight.

"He hasn't eaten in days," Anne whispered.

Jack wiped his mouth with his sleeve. "Try weeks. Except for the broth I forced down him."

"You think he's giving up?"

Anne shook her head. "I don't know."

He drained the last of his dandelion coffee. "This isn't bad. Bitter, but not as harsh as the real stuff."

Silence settled over them again, heavy, thick, and cold as the walls.

"You tell her about the deer?" Jouris asked, shifting his gaze to Jack.

Jack exhaled sharply. "We found one in the woods."

Anne's eyes widened. "You didn't bring it back?"

"No way," Jack shook his head. "It looked like an infected horde had taken it down."

Anne frowned. "How can you be sure?"

Jouris answered flatly. "Because it was torn apart but not eaten."

Anne shuddered. "Jesus."

Jouris nervously picked at his fingernails. "The infected are getting more aggressive. We've found their tracks. They're hunting, even though they don't eat."

Jack rubbed his temples. "They're closer than ever. I wish the house were invisible again. I hear them at night, scratching at the siding."

Anne's hand trembled as she set her cup down. "I know." She turned to Jouris. "How many rounds do we have?"

Jouris let his head fall back against the wall. "Not enough."

The beastly wind battered the windows like someone buried alive in a coffin, pounding their fists, desperate to get out. Beneath it, something clawed at the house, the sound shrill and relentless, like nails dragging across a chalkboard.

***

Safehouse Lake Ronkonkoma
June 6th

"You can't keep running from this, Jack!" Anne's voice shook, not from the cold, but from exhaustion, from fighting the same battle again and again. Her breath rose in small clouds between them.

Jack's jaw tightened, fists clenched at his sides. "And what do you want me to do, Anne? Sit here and watch David fade away? Watch all of us waste away? The world's a frozen tomb. Jesus, it's June 6th and there are six inches of snow on the ground! Six inches!"

He threw his arms up, "What a great choice, starve here or die out there!"

The safehouse, once meant to shield them from Prosperine and Lucius's wrath, had become a prison of frigid air and gnawing hunger. Jack paced like a caged animal, David's decline and Louis's breakdown pushing down on him like Atlas bearing the world. The radio only echoed their despair: bean and squash crops destroyed by frost, fields barren as if the soil, like a defeated army, had surrendered. Nothing grew.

"Besides food, Louis is strapped to his bed upstairs," Jack shouted. "His body writhes against the bindings that keep him from hurting himself or us."

"I know, Jack. And if we run, what happens to him?" Anne lamented. "When he speaks, it's a rasp in tongues I can't even place.

And his eyes, when they open, there's something else staring through them."

Jack rolled his eyes. "Please don't start this again."

"Damn it, Jack!" Anne snapped. "This isn't a breakdown. It's worse. It's evil."

She pulled her coat tighter, shaking her head. "I feel like I'm clawing at a door that won't open. I keep screaming for you to hear me, but you don't. You want to run, Jack. But there's nowhere left to run! There's nothing beyond that snow."

Jack's shoulders slumped before he turned toward the door. "We can't just sit here and wait to die." His voice was quieter, but it still cut through the icy air.

She exhaled, then delivered a reality check that stung Jack to his core. "We already are."

Jack stormed out, his boots crunching in unnatural snowfall. The wind clawed at his coat, a relentless, gnawing force that seeped through the tattered holes in the jacket and into his flesh. His breath came in ragged gasps, plumes of frost hanging in the air. He didn't know where he was headed, but he couldn't stay in that house. He felt trapped by the weight of decisions too heavy to bear.

Inside, Anne huddled in the dim firelight, bundled in a wool coat, her fingers buried in her mittens. The flames sputtered, barely strong enough to cast shadows. The woodpile was down to scraps. The cold seeped through the walls like a patient predator, sinking its claws into everything.

Jouris placed another log in the hearth, then wiped his hands on his pants, as though he could scrub away his guilt. He hadn't told Jack about Louis's confession in the garage. Quietly, he offered, "Hard conversations are like frostbite on the soul."

Anne laughed, a hollow sound that barely contained enough warmth to be called humor. "Poetic, Jouris. But what if it's worse than discomfort? What if it's a wound that won't close? I keep giving pieces of myself, but it's never enough. He doesn't hear me. He doesn't see me. He… walks away. And Louis..." Her voice cracked. "Louis isn't here anymore. Not really."

Jouris leaned forward, his eyes reflecting the faint firelight. "He hears you. He just doesn't know how to answer. He's breaking, Anne, just like you are. Just like all of us."

She peeled off her mittens, running her fingers along the worn wooden table. Their supplies were nearly gone. They'd rationed everything, yet survival felt like a cruel joke; crops were failing, and the world seemed to be turning against them. Jack wanted to leave, to forge ahead in search of something better. But Anne knew there was nowhere to go, no place that remained untouched by the ruthless freeze. And then there was Louis. Anne feared that releasing him would be fatal for all of them.

"I've been trying to reach him for weeks," she said, her eyes fixed on the floor. "I don't know what else to say. I'd scream if it would get through the fog he is lost in right now. My words are blanks, and I'm running out of ammunition."

Her gaze lifted, locking on Jouris. "He doesn't see that the future's on hold. We're running out of tomorrows. If we don't fight what's taken Louis soon, then all the blood we've spilled and the costs we've paid will be for nothing."

Upstairs, Louis exhaled a ragged breath, visible as a white cloud in a clear sky. The bindings creaked as he twisted, his head tilting unnaturally against the pillow.

A whisper too soft to hear drifted down the stairwell.

Anne felt it slither through her ears, coil around her spine like a tightening noose. She shivered and turned away.

"It's in my eyes, Jack, but you don't see it. I'm barely holding on," she whispered, only to herself.

She gazed out the window in the direction Jack had gone. Tears filled her eyes. Her cries built into a silent scream she didn't dare release.

What's the matter with you?

***

David lay on the couch, a frail specter of himself. His ribs pressed against his skin; each breath was a visible struggle. Sunken cheeks hollowed his gaunt face, and his trembling fingers clutched at the loose folds of his jacket. Exhaustion and hunger blurred his vision into a feverish haze. His once-bright eyes, now dulled by suffering, flickered as he fought to focus.

That was when he saw it.

An apparition stood at the entrance to the hallway, dressed in an old-fashioned uniform that looked new despite its age. The face was young, but carried the weary sorrow of something from the past. Its voice, a whisper barely audible, carried the weight of warning.

The lake possesses power; it takes what it desires.

David's lips parted, but no sound came. He blinked, frozen in shock, his body paralyzed by a cold that seemed to reach into the recesses of his mind. The Spirit stepped forward, its muddy boots leaving neither sound nor trace.

It called your brother as it did mine, the ghost murmured. *It's inside the glass.*

The wind howled through the skeletal remains of their world, carrying the phantom's warning into the endless white expanse of snow and ice. Then, it vanished.

David sat stunned, his breath uneven and his heart pounding in his frail chest. He wanted to dismiss it as a hallucination, the trick of his starving mind. Yet, he felt it; eyes watching, patient, waiting.

Outside, Jack stood at the edge of the tree line, staring at the vast, unbroken expanse of white. The cold gnawed at his bones, though he barely noticed. The wind carried a whisper beneath its howl, a voice that wasn't the storm.

He turned back toward the house, breath shallow. A name had been carried on the wind.

Billy?

***

Far from the snow-blind silence of the safehouse, a different kind of blizzard raged, one not of weather, but of worship. The feast was over and the bill had come due…

It began with small tests of devotion: a whispered prayer in Prosperine's name or a denial of their past beliefs. Then came the sacrifices. A child offered for a 'greater purpose'. A loved one abandoned for the promise of favor. The illusion of mercy stretched thin. Those who faltered, who clung to faith in something higher, were dragged, screaming, into the abyss beneath the sanctuary's golden façade. Their suffering echoed as a hymn to Prosperine's triumph.

Her gaze swept the crowd, lingering on a ragged woman clutching a child's hair ribbon like a talisman.

"Please, just let me see her again," the mother sobbed, clutching the folds of Prosperine's gown. "I'll do anything."

Prosperine tilted her head, smiling with gentle cruelty. She lifted the woman's chin with one elegant finger, brushing away a tear with the other.

"Anything?"

The mother's lips quivered. "Yes."

"Then prove it."

Prosperine stepped back, gesturing to a shivering man in the crowd… gaunt, pleading with his eyes, but unworthy.

"He is weak. Kill him, and you may see your daughter."

The woman froze, her breath trapped in her throat. The man sobbed, shaking his head, but the crowd had already shifted, hungry for proof of loyalty. A dagger was pressed into her trembling hand. Her heartbeat thundered in her ears as she stepped closer.

"I'm sorry," she whispered, then thrust the blade into his chest.

The gathering fell silent. Prosperine stroked the woman's hair as she wept.

"You are learning," she whispered. "Love means sacrifice."

The faithful who remained received fleeting glimpses of relief, moments of safety that dissolved into torment sharper than before. Their pain became proof of devotion, as they forsaken all morality in favor of the new order she had promised. Soon, prayers once raised to Heaven became whispers to demons, bargains for one more night of survival.

"You see now," Prosperine whispered to them, her hands gentle on their tear-streaked faces, her voice tender.

"Suffering is Heaven's will. That is why they abandoned you. But I will never leave you."

And they believed her.

They turned on each other, embracing the darkness within, abandoning the ideals that once connected them to something greater. Prosperine watched, savoring their despair like the finest wine.

For salvation had never been the goal. Only their surrender.

And deep within her sanctuary, the foundations of her throne rose, not from wood or iron, but from bone. Bleached white, stacked in silence, whispering prayers that would never be answered.

***

New York City
Late Afternoon June 7th

While Jack and his family faced starvation, his brother was summoned to endure a different kind of judgment… before the Prime Minister of Hell.

The Manhattan skyline loomed like a jagged scar, its remaining skyscrapers rising like tombstones in a graveyard of smoke. The city reeked of decay, both physical and spiritual, and of the overpowering stench of burning flesh from funeral pyres. George Aitken sat in the back of a black sedan, his brow furrowed, fingers nervously tapping against his knee.

The car rolled to a stop outside Gracie Mansion, now serving as City Hall. The driver hurried to open the door. George's boots crunched on broken glass scattered across the pavement. His long black coat, lined in crimson, weighted heavily on his frame. He had spent weeks scouring the Eastern Seaboard, chasing his brother like a ghost hunter with every lead turning to ash. Now, he had been summoned to account for his failure… to Lucius.

He buttoned his shirt, tugged at his tie, and adjusted the black leather eye patch subtly engraved with silver. It felt tighter than usual, as though it judged him too. He pushed past a faceless doorman and entered through the heavy wooden doors.

Inside, candlelight flickered against mahogany panels, unable to chase shadows clinging to the corners. Portraits of former occupants, past mayors, hung on the walls, their legacies now rotting in history's trash heap. The air smelled of burning incense and aged paper.

Lucius Rofocale stood by the window, his tall silhouette cutting sharply against the glass like a razor. His black suit, darker than a starless sky, fit him with inhuman precision. A deep red silk tie was perfectly knotted at his shirt collar, and immaculate leather gloves were clasped behind his back. His swept-back hair, dark as ink, revealed a face both handsome and terrible, and his silver eyes, oceans of malevolence, glowed like molten metal reflecting candlelight.

He gestured toward the seating area where an elegant antique table stood, topped with a decanter of rich amber liquid.

"Sit," Lucius said, his voice calm yet chilling. "You look as if the weight of your failure is about to crush you. Am I to assume this burden is too much to bear?"

George clenched his jaw as he sat. Lucius poured a drink, watching his acolyte like a predator studying wounded prey. Taking a seat across from George, Lucius crossed his legs.

"You are failing me."

The truth felt like a sharp knife slowly sliding between George's ribs. He sat stoically as Lucius continued his indictment.

"Do not look so surprised. Your incompetence is no revelation to me. You have chased your brother across the Eastern United States, yet he remains elusive. I find myself wondering: do you truly pursue him, or merely follow his shadow?"

"It's like chasing a ghost through a hall of mirrors." George muttered. His fingers tapped the armrest once, then he cracked his knuckles with a dry pop, a small ritual that helped him focus.

"But I see the pattern now." George exhaled sharply. "I've got a lead."

Lucius steepled his fingers, unimpressed.

"You put too much faith in your computer program. It feeds you breadcrumbs, and you scurry after them like a starving rodent. Despite its supposed predictive brilliance, it has not delivered Jack Aitken. I should hope that this claim is not as hollow as the last."

George's grip tightened. "Jack came home."

Lucius's eyes flickered with mild interest. "Curious. After three decades away, why return now when every corner of the world is equally damned?"

"Because it draws less suspicion," George replied, leaning forward. "Jack knows the area. He knows which roads to avoid and which places offer cover. It is familiar yet unremarkable. A place where he could disappear without standing out."

"So you claim he has chosen familiarity over strategy, "Lucius mused.

George nodded. "Jack has always been a creature of habit. As kids, after our father chewed us out, his grand plan for running away was to hide at the abandoned Citgo gas station up the street. That was as far as his mind went. He never considered broader prospects, never imagined going further. He clings close to what he knows. And right now, he knows Long Island better than anywhere."

Lucius's lips curled, but it was not a smile. "Predictability is a weakness. One you should have exploited long ago."

George ignored the rebuke and pressed on. "There's more. Mark Desmond grew up on Long Island. He would have prepared for this, stockpiled provisions, and set up a safehouse. Anne knows about it. And if Jack is with her, they'll exploit that."

Lucius exhaled with cold amusement. "I warned you that she was Desmond's equal."

He drained his glass. "So the fool seeks refuge in the remnants of another man's foresight. Tell me, does he think he can outlast us? Or does he still fancy himself God's warrior?"

George's jaw tightened. "Jack doesn't think like us. To him, monsters are confronted, not avoided. Survival, to him, is not about power. It's about endurance. He believes if he holds out long enough, he'll find a way to strike back."

Lucius studied him. "Then we shall ensure that endurance is of no use to him. He thinks himself immune to fate, but all fates bend before us, as heaven's defeat proved."

"Justice is only vengeance in disguise," George said through clenched teeth. "I'll handle it. I'll find him."

Lucius shook his head. "No, George. You MUST find him. For if you do not, I shall begin to suspect that the failures of the past are not coincidental."

The threat weighed on George like a guillotine. He swallowed it like medicine.

A good soldier doesn't question the war… nor worry about the body count.

Lucius returned to the window, his fingers tapping idly against the glass.

"Prosperine is preparing her next torment for humanity. It will be exquisite. A symphony of suffering so grand that the deaf will hear, and the blind will feel it. I shall remain here to supervise its fulfillment."

His silver eyes cut back to George. "And you? You shall *finally* deliver unto me what I require?"

George rose, adjusting his coat. "I will."

Lucius's lips curled once more, but any pretense of amusement was gone. "Disappoint me again, and I shall consider your existence one mistake too many."

The warning was implicit; he had no choice but to be correct.

George cracked his knuckles, one last reminder that pain meant he was still in control. He forced himself to hold Lucius's gaze a moment longer before turning away.

My brother is no hero. This is a countdown to zero. And when it ends, nothing... no one... will be left to remember him.

Jack was out there. George knew it. And this time, he would not fail.

***

Safehouse Lake Ronkonkoma
June 10th

The fire popped weakly, barely keeping at bay the numbing cold that seeped into their bodies. Jack sat close, rubbing his hands together, lost in a reverie as he watched the flames sputter.

June had once meant life; sun, green growth, and warmth—like it was on June 10th, more than thirty years to the day, when he had asked Amanda to marry him.

But not anymore.

It had been bitterly cold before, but now...

He glanced at the calendar Jouris had given them when they first arrived. It read June. Maybe that was why this felt so different. This wasn't winter. It was worse. Something nature had never unleashed before.

Jouris sat across from him, staring at the embers, his face gaunt from exhaustion. Between them, David lay curled up on the floor beneath a pile of blankets, shivering despite the layers.

"He needs food," Anne murmured, brushing the dull, dry brown hair from David's forehead. "He's getting weaker by the day."

Jack exhaled slowly, running a hand through his hair. A clump fell loose and drifted to the floor. He stared at it, then smirked humorlessly. "Guess I won't need a haircut anytime soon."

Jouris's look was flat. "Not funny."

"Wasn't trying to be," Jack muttered.

"You're losing your hair?" Anne asked, frowning as her worry switched from David to Jack.

Jack shrugged. "Let's be honest. We haven't eaten properly in months." He leaned back, rubbing his temples. "We need food and supplies. Sitting here waiting to starve isn't an option."

Jouris shifted. "We've been watching that house across the lake for a week. Claire Daniels hasn't shown herself. Chuck vanished months ago. If anything's left there, it's fair game."

"And if Claire's still there?" Anne pressed.

Jack sighed. "Then I'll deal with it."

Silence fell, broken only by the occasional crackle of the fire and the bitter, angry sound of the howling through the trees.

"This morning's broadcast," Anne murmured. "Cabot, Vermont; eighteen inches of snow in three days. When it thawed, they found a whole family frozen to death."

"They started shearing the sheep," Jouris added, shaking his head. "Farmers never thought it would turn this cold again so fast. Poor animals collapsed dead in the fields."

"And that's heading our way," Jack said through clenched teeth.

"The lake should be rising after last night's rain," Jouris noted. "Instead, the water level has gone down."

Jack nodded grimly. "I saw it."

"What does that mean?" Anne asked.

Jouris's gaze glanced upward, toward Louis's room. "Something's wrong. And it's not just the weather."

T-H-U-D!

All three flinched. Jack turned sharply as another impact rattled the house, then another.

"What the hell?" Anne gasped, springing to her feet.

Though it was still afternoon, the gloom forced Jouris to grab the lantern. Jack yanked the door open.

Birds.

Dozens lay scattered across the frozen yard: starlings, sparrows, and a few crows. Their bodies stiff, wings locked at odd angles, and feathers coated with frost. More plummeted from the sky, their lifeless forms bouncing off the roof and porch like stones.

"Jesus," Jack whispered.

Jouris crouched and lifted a sparrow, weightless in his hand." They froze mid-air."

Jack swallowed, scanning the low, gray clouds, pressing down like a vise. "I don't have a choice. I need to check the Daniels' house before we end up like them."

Jouris didn't argue, but as they stepped back inside, he caught Jack's arm. "We need to talk about Louis."

"Now?" Jack snapped.

"Yes, now."

Jouris hesitated, staring at the frozen birds, before speaking.

"There's something I need to tell you."

Jack turned, exasperated. "What is it?"

"A few months ago, Louis came to me. First time he really opened up. He said something was trying to get in—that it whispered to him. I thought it was anxiety or trauma. I didn't want to betray his trust."

"You should have told me, "Jack muttered, shoving his hands into his coat pockets.

"I know." Jouris's voice dropped. "I've asked myself why I didn't. Maybe I thought I was protecting him. Truth is, I think I was being influenced, nudged into silence. Whatever it is, it didn't want you to know."

Jack froze. "And now?"

"Now, I'm telling you, because if I stay silent any longer, it wins."

Jack sighed, closing his eyes. "What do you want me to say? Anne and I have been fighting about Louis for weeks. He barely speaks anymore."

"Anne is concerned too," Jouris said.

"She's worried about everything," Jack muttered,

"Maybe for a reason," Jouris shot back. "Look, I get it. Fear is real. And it is justified. But unchecked, it spreads like rot. The most common way people give up their power is by thinking they do not have any."

"And people get killed ignoring problems staring them in the face." Anne cut in, still crouched beside David.

"Anne, don't start," Jack warned.

She rose, arms crossed. "No, Jack. We have to. We need to discuss why Louis is being restrained. What's the real reason?"

"I know why…" Jack began.

"No, you don't," Anne snapped. "Or worse, you do, and you won't admit it. If this were an EMP, if it were some massive disaster that left people without access to medications, we'd have to restrain some patients for everyone's safety, including their own. People who get violent. People who lose control. That is what we are dealing with. Only this isn't psychosis or Schizophrenia."

She stepped closer. "It's possession."

"I'm not doing this again," Jack said, turning away.

"You are, you ass," Anne growled. "You're not the only one who sits with him while his body seizes, while he speaks in voices that are not his own, while his eyes go black, and something that is not him looks back."

Her breath caught, and she burst out, "Damn it, Jack! You know I know what I'm talking about!"

The room fell silent. Jouris watched but stayed back.

"He's my son," Jack whispered.

"And he's not the only one in that body anymore," Anne replied flatly

Jack said nothing. Jouris exhaled and glanced at his watch. "Jack, we leave in an hour."

"No," Jack shook his head. " I'll go alone."

"Jack..." Anne started.

"Someone has to guard this place," Jack cut in. "Jouris, you stay. Anne, David needs you. Someone has to watch Louis."

Jouris frowned but chose not to argue. Anne opened her mouth, hesitated, then closed it, swallowing hard.

Jack pulled on his coat and grabbed the crowbar. "I'm leaving the gun. Firing it will only draw the infected. I'll try to be back before nightfall."

Jouris met his eyes, knowing nothing would change his mind. "Be careful."

Jack stepped off the last porch step onto the almost frozen ground. Birds still littered the yard, their rigid wings tangled in the brittle grass. He stepped around them and went on his way.

There was no room for hesitation. He'd find food, or die trying.

CHAPTER 2

He couldn't remember how he'd got here…

Louis pushed through the front doors of Liberty Crest High School, allowing them to shut behind him with a dull, echoing thud. The sound rolled down the empty corridors, loud in the unnatural silence.

Where is everybody?

It smelled the same: floor wax, dry-erase markers, and something else. Familiar, but off. Maybe old textbooks or the lingering odor of cafeteria pizza baked into the walls. It should have been comforting. It wasn't.

The hall stretched long and sterile under flickering fluorescent lights. Rows of blue lockers lined the walls, their doors dented from years of being slammed shut. Still taped to the walls, posters curled at the corners: *Homecoming 2017: Go Patriots! Career Day - Find Your Future!* The words felt distant, remnants of a world he'd left but never truly abandoned.

Louis stepped forward. The only sound was the squeak of his sneakers on waxed tile.

"This isn't right," he muttered. "School was never this quiet."

There should have been a low hum of voices, the shuffle of feet, the chatter of teachers lecturing from behind half-open doors, or the 1980s songs blaring from the speakers between classes. Yet, there was nothing.

He stopped at locker 3127, his locker, outside Mrs. Bell's room. A quiet piece of familiarity. His fingers brushed the cool metal, paint chipped along the edges. He set his hand on the dial, letting muscle memory take over.

He spoke the numbers out loud, the way he did when stimming in his room. Safe, predictable, and controlled.

"Right to thirty-six, left to twelve, and finally right to twenty-seven."

He tugged on the handle, but it remained closed.

Frowning, he tried again, thirty-six, twelve, twenty-seven, and pulled harder. The door stayed shut. After staring at it for a moment, he saw it.

The numbers on the dial were moving backward. Thirty-six slid to twenty-seven, to twenty-one, and then it dropped to fifteen. Then the dial clicked into place on a number that froze his breath: 2-1-2, his birthday, reversed. The lock turned cold, as if it had winter trapped inside.

T-I-C-K. T-I-C-K. T-I-C-K.

A faint ticking drew his gaze to the clock mounted above the lockers. The hands weren't just moving; they were moving in the opposite direction. The second hand twitched backward in sharp, jerky movements, each tick more deliberate than the last.

Louis breathed in, out, applying the calming techniques he had learned to ease his anxiety. The air thickened, pressing against his skin, as if a storm were about to break.

Then a voice: "Late again, Mr. Aitken."

It wasn't loud, but it cut through the silence with perfect clarity, as if someone whispered directly in his ear. Louis turned abruptly.

A man stood at the far end of the hall, outside the Principal's office. His navy blue suit was perfectly pressed with a deep red tie knotted tightly. His shoes gleamed under the fluorescent lights, polished to a high shine.

Louis knew that face, even if nothing else made sense.

"Dad?" he asked, unsure if this was real.

"You know the rules, Louis."

Louis flinched. His father had been strict, but never cold like this. It was his father, but it wasn't. It resembled him, yet felt wrong.

The jaw and cheekbones were too sharp, and the forehead too pronounced for a man of his father's age. The facial expression was still, with the skin drawn tight, resembling someone who had undergone too many Botox treatments. His blue eyes were darker than usual, with the pupils consuming almost all the color, leaving only a thin ring of hazel around the edges. His mouth curved into what might have been a smile, but there was no warmth.

The man tilted his head, studying him.

"Come on, Louis. You don't want to make a habit of this."

Louis stepped back.

The school felt different now. The walls stretched, and the corridor lengthened behind him. The lights flickered, dimmed briefly, then brightened in a blinding burst.

His pulse pounded. He wasn't meant to be here, not like this. Not alone.

The principal, his father, but not his father, stepped closer, his polished shoes clicking on the floor.

Louis's throat clenched. Every instinct screamed: *RUN!* He counted his steps the way he counted locker numbers; one, two, three, four, his copying mechanism turned into survival. Stimming wouldn't save him this time. He turned and fled.

***

Trail around Lake Ronkonkoma
June 12th

The sun was merciless. A reminder their nightmare was real, and not only inside their heads…

Jack stepped out of the cinder-block bathroom, shielding his eyes from the blistering sun. The smell of death clung to his filthy clothes, sour sweat mingling with the putrid stench of the corpse he'd dragged out two days earlier. Inside, the air had turned thick and humid, mixed with the overwhelming odors of human waste and decay.

After two days of flash floods and apocalyptic storms that turned the trail around the lake into a river, he had to escape. But what waited outside was a different kind of hell. Now, one could be drenched one moment and scorched the next.

The trail shimmered with heat as Jack trudged forward. Two days ago, he would have traded his left arm for a winter coat. Now, he was shedding layers, wrapping them around his head as a shield from the sun. His body ached, and his limbs felt like lead. His stomach gnawed at itself. Hunger had become a constant companion, a dull pulsing ache in his brain.

But hunger wasn't the worst of it. Not by a long shot.

It was an endless cycle, crisis after crisis, pain after pain. Always moving, always surviving. The constant pressure felt like a never-ending migraine. The world had become a test of endurance, and Jack was a man with no time left for regret. He had learned to wear a smile when needed, but smiles didn't last long anymore.

Nice guys? They got swept away like debris in a flood. Now he was the boulder, too heavy to move, too stubborn to drown.

"I'm glad Amanda isn't here to see me like this," he muttered. "Even she'd cry."

He chuckled. "Then she'd tell me I smell like a dead raccoon and to go change my clothes."

The trail was littered with debris, and the sun baked his footprints into cracked, scarred earth. The Daniels' house shimmered in the distance. It felt within reach, yet a hundred miles away. Every step felt like dragging himself through wet cement.

Then came the next horror.

A wet, ripping sound. Jack's stomach turned. He knew it too well.

Up ahead, a pack of the infected hunched over something sprawled on the ground. Their bodies twitched in sick rhythm as they tore into flesh. Their hands were coated black with blood, and their mouths were slick with gore. The victim was still alive. Barely. A wet gurgle escaped their shredded throat.

Jack swallowed. He was used to seeing deer torn apart. Not this.

Human fingers twitched weakly around the attackers' ankles.

He tightened his grip on the crowbar, his weapon of choice, a judge, jury, and executioner in a world without rules. Anne's voice echoed in his head:

Hesitation gets people killed.

He moved in fast but silently.

The first infected didn't turn in time. The crowbar smashed its skull, brain matter splattering across the mud as the body dropped with a sickening thud. The second lunged, snarling, its lips peeled back over black teeth. Jack sidestepped and swung low, shattering its knee-cap before bringing the weapon down hard on its head. It crumpled instantly.

The rest turned too late. Jack plowed through them, cracking skulls and breaking bones. One by one, they fell like rotten trees until the last lay twitching in the heat.

Then, stillness.

The victim coughed, a wet, rattling gasp. There was no saving this one. Their torso was torn open, their intestines spilling in the mud. Their eyes locked onto Jack's, wide with desperation, begging for mercy.

No words. Just agony.

Jack exhaled and knelt beside them.

"I got you," he murmured.

He raised the crowbar and brought it down in a single clean strike. The body stilled. The suffering ended.

Jack stood, his hand trembling.

"Mercy can be brutal," he muttered, wiping the bloodied crowbar on his pants. "It's also harder than it looks on TV."

Sweat stung his eyes. The stench of blood and vomit clung to the air. He spat, once, twice, trying to rid his mouth of the taste.

Then he turned back to the trail.

The Daniels' house was just ahead. Time was running out.

No time for prayers. No time for tears. Just the next step forward.

***

At The Same Time Back at the Safehouse
June 12th

The radio crackled, the broadcaster's voice fractured by static as it echoed through the living room.

We're just beginning to understand the devastation caused by the superstorm. After two days of catastrophic winds and torrential rain, the entire Eastern seaboard is unrecognizable. Scientists suggest that the storm was a remnant of a Category 5 hurricane, unprecedented for this time of year.

Anne sat by the window, her fingers aimlessly tracing cracks in the wooden sill. The house had taken a beating. Shingles were torn away, and rain had forced itself through every crevice, leaving mildew-stained ceilings and puddles that reeked like swamp water in the corners.

Outside, the landscape was mangled. Trees, already weakened by the absence of spring warmth, were snapped and twisted, their limbs entangled in dead power lines.

Jouris paced with arms folded, his body wound tight as if trying to hold itself together. His jaw was locked, worry lines carved deep in his face.

"He should've been back by now."

Anne exhaled slowly, her eyes shifting from the devastation outside to the couch where David lay, pale and half-conscious. His chest rose and fell in shallow, uneven patterns. She pressed her lips together and turned back to Jouris.

"I trained him for this," she said, her voice steady though her stomach churned. "He'd want us to stay put. If we go looking and something happens... then what?"

"I'm not comfortable just sitting here, Anne. It's been two days," Jouris snapped, running a hand through his damp hair. "He could be hurt. Trapped somewhere..."

"Or making his way back," she cut in. "And if we're not here when he does?"

The silence that followed was heavier than the storm.

A faint drip echoed from the corner. The radio hummed behind them.

...and in international news, reports confirm that Mexico has initiated military incursions into Guatemala and Belize, raising fears of a wider regional conflict...

Jouris muttered, "Figures. The world's crumbling, and we're just watching it burn."

Anne didn't answer. She couldn't. The war. The superstorm. Food shortages. It was all too much, too horrific. And David? He no longer had the strength to lift his head, let alone run.

Reports indicate catastrophic agricultural losses. The hay harvest is nearly nonexistent, prompting emergency livestock culling across multiple states. Already scarce meat supplies are expected to decline further.

Anne clenched her jaw. She could almost taste the rot, the spoiled meat, bloated livestock, death simmering in the sun.

Hunger gnawed at them all. It hollowed them out. Day by day. Hour by hour.

A small, dry voice interrupted her thoughts.

"Is there any food left?" David whispered.

Anne rushed to him, brushing a damp strand of hair from his forehead. His skin was cool, clammy, almost waxy. His cheeks had collapsed inward.

"We'll find something," she said, forcing a smile that didn't reach her eyes.

"I smelled something earlier," David muttered. "Not food. Burnt... plastic or something. It didn't go away."

Jouris stiffened at the window. He didn't turn. Instead, he leaned on the sill and stared out through the cracked glass, his knuckles bone-white.

"You don't think..." he began, then stopped.

Anne swallowed hard, turning back to the radio, desperate for clarity, for hope.

The signal crackled. Then another voice broke through.

Not the broadcaster's.

A single word, buried in static.

A name that didn't belong on the airwaves.

LOUIS.

Then the voice was gone. Just white noise. Just the hum.

Anne closed her eyes. She already knew the truth.

It was going to get worse.

***

The Daniels Residence Lake Ronkonkoma
June 12th

"What a score! I can't believe these are even here!"

Jack's fingers trembled as he shoved another handful of strawberries into his mouth, the juice bursting tart and sweet on his tongue. He found the patch in a raised bed beside a house. Warm from the relentless sun, the fruit sent a jolt through him like a live wire, cutting through the fog of exhaustion.

He hadn't eaten in days, and the sudden sugar rush sent adrenaline surging through his body. His thoughts sharpened, and the world around him was no longer a blurred, heat-stricken haze.

"This is what clarity tastes like," Jack muttered.

He glanced up at the brutal sun. "Strange, but being out of the safehouse, my mind feels clearer. Like I'm sharper."

The tension in his skull eased slightly as he crouched, plucking the remaining strawberries and tucking them into his knapsack.

"David could use something fresh for once."

As he walked, downing another handful, the Daniels' home loomed ahead, sun-bleached and sagging. The storm's violence was evident in the shattered porch railing and missing chunks of siding.

An aluminum gutter lay twisted in the grass. The front door hung ajar, swaying in the breeze.

Jack stepped carefully inside.

The air was thick and stale, heavy with the scent of abandonment: wood rot, mold, and the bitter, nauseating stench of something long dead. It wrapped around him like a wet wool blanket.

The living room seemed frozen in time, a ghost of normalcy left behind when the world fell apart. Once chocolate brown, the couch was faded and worn, its cushions sunken and covered in dust, spotted with rodent droppings. An open photo album lay on the coffee table, its pages curling at the edges. Jack glanced at pictures of smiling strangers… kids with ice cream and parents in front of a roller coaster.

He closed the album. "A life that doesn't exist anymore."

Suppressing the ache in his chest, he moved deeper into the house.

In the kitchen, cupboards stood open, stripped bare. Drawers had been ransacked, leaving only crumbs.

"Picked clean," Jack muttered, still searching, hoping to get lucky. "Looks like whoever came through took everything worth having."

He paused, looking up. "Maybe not everything."

Going up the stairs, his boots creaked on warped wood. The smell worsened, and putrid air clung to his skin, growing heavier with each step.

Claire Daniels lay slumped in the tub, her skin stretched, yellowed, and tight over bone. Her hair fanned around her skull like decaying straw. A bottle of Advil PM rested beneath her withered fingers.

Jack swallowed hard and rubbed his sleeve across his nose, trying to block the stench. Jouris had mentioned Claire's husband vanished. Had she been waiting for his return and then given up?

"Jesus," Jack whispered. "You didn't deserve this."

He turned to go. At the staircase landing, a door beneath the stairs caught his eye. A sign nailed to it read:

WARNING: BEWARE OF DOG

Jack paused. He hadn't heard barking. He rapped his knuckles against the wood. Nothing.

He knocked louder. Silence. No panting. No scratching on the door. Just silence.

The handle stuck, swollen from moisture. After a firm yank, it gave way with a groan, and the smell hit him.

It stole his breath.

He gagged, sleeve over his mouth. Stagnant water mixed with mildew, rot… and something feral. His stomach lurched.

"That's the problem with TV," Jack coughed. "Nobody can imagine the smells of the apocalypse."

A-P-O-C-A-L-Y-P-S-E

The word landed with finality. Until now, he had told himself this world was only temporary: a downturn. Something to overcome. But it wasn't. This was final.

He thought briefly of Anne's argument about Louis. For a moment, he understood. Then pushed it away.

The basement stairs creaked beneath his weight. When his boots finally touched the basement floor, they didn't meet concrete. They met water; dark, ankle-deep, with a sickly green film rippling on the surface.

"God knows what's festering in this filth."

He stopped. Something beneath the surface brushed against his leg. Slithering. Alive.

His breath caught.

SPLASH!

A blur lunged from the water.

Its fur clung in mangy clumps. Its cloudy eyes were wild, mouth foaming as it snapped inches from his face. Jack raised the crowbar just in time.

The jaws snapped again. He shoved hard, sending it tumbling, but it surged like a shark striking a seal.

The crowbar connected with its skull. *CRUNCH*. It staggered, but kept coming.

"Shit! It's the dog!"

He grabbed its collar and forced its head under. Claws raked his arms as it thrashed. Seconds seemed like hours.

Then stillness.

Panting, Jack staggered back, arms burning. He didn't look at the floating body.

He waded deeper into the basement, dread sticking to every step, and he forced open another door. His heart nearly stopped.

"FOOD!"

Rusted shelves sagged with cans: beans, tuna, and corn. He grabbed one and checked the label.

A broad smile spread across his face. "YES! Not expired!"

He shoved cans into his pack. Then, he saw it: covered in dust,

"A first-aid kit!" he gasped.

Inside: epinephrine auto-injectors, hydrocortisone, antibiotic cream, and Benadryl.

"This might be as valuable as the food."

Back upstairs, he paused, dabbing antibiotic cream on his scratches.

"Hopefully, this prevents infection. Or rabies."

Then a sound.

A soft meow.

Jack turned.

A cat brushed against his leg, purring... a survivor. Jack crouched, running a hand along its back.

He thought of David. *Maybe the kid could use a cat.*

Then the cat hissed. Its back arched. Eyes wide.

And the world went black.

The air vanished. Sound died. The light was gone.

Jack reached for his knife, but his arms wouldn't obey.

The room tilted.

The cat yowled once.
Then… nothing
Only silence.

***

Inside Louis's Mind… Liberty Crest High School
June 12th (Simultaneously)

The school changed again…

Louis's breath came hard and fast as he sprinted down the hallway. The floor felt wrong beneath his sneakers, as if he were walking on damp ground, yet they still squeaked against the linoleum. He frantically searched the corridors.

"Is anyone here?"

He needed to find someone. Anyone. The halls stretched endlessly, and the classroom numbers were scrambled. They were entirely out of order: Room 302, Room 105, Room 999.

"That's impossible," he muttered, bouncing on his toes in a calming rhythm. "The school only has two floors."

Panic squeezed his chest like a vise. He needed out… now.

Spotting an open classroom door ahead, he lunged for it.

As he crossed the threshold, the air shifted.

The overhead lights buzzed louder, bathing the room in a jaundiced yellow glow, like the sky before a tornado. The air smelled of dust and something faintly metallic.

Desks stood in neat rows, each one occupied. Students sat motionless, backs straight and hands folded. None of them turned to look at him. The only sound was the steady scrape of chalk against the board.

At the front of the classroom, a man wrote fractions on the board, his back to the class. Black suit hung too tight, his spine poking through the fabric, each vertebra visible beneath his coat.

Louis's chest loosened slightly. "Mr. Harris, I'm glad to see you."

Thomas Harris was a typical math teacher: strict and humorless. He always wore pressed slacks and a button-down shirt. Louis had been mainstreamed into his class, but Mr. Harris never fully understood Louis or the autism spectrum. His uncertainty always sat like an invisible barrier between them.

But Mr. Harris's hands were wrong. Too long, knuckles sharp, his fingertips more claw than finger. His nails scraped the chalkboard, leaving deep indentations on it.

The scraping was unbearable, and Louis clutched his ears, yet his classmates seemed unfazed. They stared straight ahead.

Mr. Harris stopped writing and slowly turned to face the classroom. Louis's stomach knotted.

His face was stretched too tight, skin pulled over a skull that was just a bit too large. His sunken eyes devoured any hint of color. The corners of his mouth sagged as though his skin had been left hanging. When he finally spoke, his voice was rough, like he hadn't used it in years.

"Mr. Aitken, you're late for your test."

Louis blinked. He was no longer standing, but seated at a desk.

How did I get here?

"What test?"

A blank sheet of paper lay before him. There were no instructions. No pencil. He nervously bit his nails, anxiety building inside him.

He glanced up once more. The students shifted in unison, and every face turned toward him.

Louis stiffened. Too much attention. Too many eyes.

Their eyes were completely black. A whisper rippled through them, soft at first, then louder. Words tumbled over each other until they became noise and impossible to decipher. The sound filled the room, pressing in from all sides.

Mr. Harris stepped forward, his shoes making no sound at all.

"You'll fail, of course," he said, lips twisting into something that wasn't quite a smile.

The whispers grew louder as the walls warped. The floor tilted. Louis gasped, bolted from the desk, and sprinted for the door.

CHAPTER 3

The platform at the Long Island Railroad Station in Albertson was bathed in the warm orange glow of the setting sun. The air smelled of hot metal and diesel, while the rhythmic clatter of an approaching train resonated through the station. George Aitken, just eight years old, leaned forward eagerly, his eyes fixed on the tracks, waiting for his father to step off the evening train.

"Push me faster!" Jack's voice rang out, filled with laughter.

George grinned and gripped the arms of the rolling chair they'd found at a ticket booth. With a firm shove, he sent his twin brother racing across the platform, the wheels rattling against the pavement. Jack cried out dramatically, tilting his head back.

"I'm Ironside!" he declared, throwing his arms out wide. "I solve cases from my wheelchair!"

George chased after him, breathless from laughter. "No, you're not! I'm Ironside! You're the bad guy!"

Jack spun the chair to a stop, grinning. "Alright, Officer Aitken. Let's crack this case!"

Their laughter echoed through the station. For a moment, the world felt small and secure, wrapped in an amber glow of a memory too perfect to last.

Then the memory shattered like glass, splintering apart. There was no laughter anymore.

Only the sound of a cold wind slicing through Albertson, whistling through the bare trees, dragging George back into the present.

Once a town straight out of a Norman Rockwell painting, Albertson was now a shadow of itself. The houses along Miles Avenue stood abandoned, their windows broken, yards overgrown with weeds that waved in the wind. Forsaken ghosts of families long fled dead. Along the cracked sidewalks, those who had nowhere else to go gathered in the bitter cold, wrapped in frayed coats and scarves, their faces a mix of awe, fear, and recognition.

George Aitken walked at the head of the procession, his long coat billowing as his boots clicked against the crumbling asphalt. Flanking him were his inhuman subordinates with lifeless eyes and strange, knowing smiles. Behind them, the last residents of the town stood silent, their breath curling in the frigid air. Whispers spread through the crowd.

"That's George Aitken," an older man whispered. *"He grew up right here. The Aitkens lived on Wentworth Avenue, in a yellow house with black shutters. I remember him and his twin brother throwing a football in the street in front of their house."*

The woman beside him shuddered. *"I remember. But look at him now. What the hell happened to him?"*

Some averted their gazes, afraid that looking too long might invite something worse than the cold. Others stared in frozen horror, unable to reconcile the boy they remembered with the man before them.

George barely noticed them, as they did when he lived here. He would no longer be just a face in the crowd. His thoughts were already on what was to come next.

At I.U. Willets Road, he stopped, standing where he once waited for his father's train. The road had taken its name from a long-dead Quaker farmer, but the land no longer remembered him; only the ghosts of the orchards and meadows buried beneath the pavement. The past collided with the present for just a moment: the laughter and rattle of the wheels on that old chair. Then he blinked, and it vanished.

With the wind whipping his coat, he exhaled, turned from the crowd, and continued his march toward his childhood home.

It still stood, weathered yet intact. The yellow paint had faded, and the black shutters hung crooked, but the frame remained strong. Just like him.

But this wasn't only about the hunt. It was personal. George wasn't just looking for Jack; he was rewriting their past.

After taking one last look at the crowd, he stepped inside.

Inside, the dining room was as he remembered, though the green wallpaper was peeling. The cherrywood cornice his grandfather crafted still crowned the walls. A worn oval table stood where his mother had once served dinner on Thanksgiving and Christmas. Everything was as he recalled, but the warmth was missing, replaced by something colder than the wind outside.

Seated around the table were his subordinates… demons in disguise. Their eyes gleamed in the weak light of a chandelier, which flickered erratically from a makeshift generator across the street. They waited, silent and patient. The air hummed with a presence that did not belong to this world.

George sat at the head of the table, fingers tapping softly. His calm voice carried an undercurrent that made the walls feel as if they were closing in.

A coal-eyed woman with a serpent's smile leaned forward. "He can't hide forever. We'll search every place he's lived."

George nodded. "Mineola. His first apartment."

"Farmingdale," another offered.

"Stony Brook, his college years," Brannigan added, eyes gleaming, his ambitions bared.

One by one, they chimed in: *Deer Park, Babylon, Sea Cliff, East Setauket.*

George let the list settle, then gave the only command that mattered. "Find him."

An eerie ripple of chuckles filled the room, except for one strike force member.

"Laugh if you want to," Brannigan sneered, rising. "I've got business to take care of."

The demons melted into the shadows, leaving George with his childhood home… and the man in the basement.

The stairs creaked as he descended. The air smelled of sweat, urine, and fear. The basement light cast flickering shadows against the knotty pine paneling.

Tommy Messina was tied to a chair in the center of the room. His face was pale and streaked with sweat. His wrists were chafed from the rope digging into his skin. His breathing came in ragged, uneven gasps, and his eyes were wide, filled with pure, unfiltered terror.

George paced slowly, spinning the revolver between his fingers. Click. Click.

Tommy whimpered.

"You were a real son of a bitch to Jack, weren't you?" George tilted his head. "When we were kids. He never forgot how you made his life miserable. I bet you don't even remember half of it."

George raised the revolver, aiming it at Tommy's temple.

Click.

Tommy flinched, his body jerking against the restraints so violently that the chair rocked back and forth on its legs.

"Please," Tommy whispered, his voice cracking. "Knocking the Lego castle out of Jack's hands, it was a joke, I was just a kid."

George licked his lips, closed his eyes, and inhaled, sensing the fear, tasting it in the air. "Oh, I like that. You're scared. Good."

"Want to play a game, Tommy?" George asked casually. "Six chambers, one bullet. You know the routine."

He cocked the weapon, pressed it to Tommy's forehead, and pulled the trigger.

Click.

Tommy sobbed, shaking uncontrollably.

George chuckled. "This is what I live for. That look in your eyes. Pure terror. You're praying right now, aren't you?"

Tommy nodded vigorously, tears streaming down his cheeks.

George leaned close, whispering. "Nobody's listening."

He squeezed the trigger once more.

Click.

Tommy choked back a scream.

George sighed, feigning disappointment. "What a shame." He spun the chamber slowly and deliberately. "You got lucky. Guess we'll have to keep playing."

He pushed the muzzle back against Tommy's skull, grinning wider as he watched the last bit of hope slip away from the former bully's face.

Outside, the cold wind howled, and the people of Albertson murmured about the monster who had come home.

***

Shores of Lake Ronkonkoma
Near Dusk June 12th

"As a detective, I do everything by the book, Ross." Anne opened the prison cell. "It's moving day, Mr. Aitken. Time to get up…"
That was before the world stopped making sense. Before mercy meant death…
Jack's head throbbed with a dull pounding ache that radiated from his skull. Warm blood trickled down his temple, sticky against his skin. Firelight warped and twisted his blurred vision while he struggled to focus.

The heat was suffocating, the air still heavy though the sun was dipping below the horizon. Sweat ran down his arms and back, stinging against the raw spots where the rough fibers of his restraints dug into his skin. The greasy stench of burning flesh filled his nostrils, rancid and unmistakably human.

He shifted, but his bonds remained tight. His arms were stretched and secured to the splintered wood of a crude cross; his torn shirt left his chest exposed to the humid night air.

A voice cut through the haze.

"You are awake."

Jack blinked until the figure sharpened. A lean, wiry man stood before him. Pale skin stretched over sharp cheekbones, and his beard hung down to his navel, resembling Spanish moss. Streaks of black

290

soot and dried red clay cracked across his chest, and a necklace of teeth and knuckle bones hung around his neck, rattling softly as he moved. His sunken eyes, as large as blue marbles, studied Jack with eerie patience.

Jack's voice rasped, his throat parched, as he whispered, "Where… am I?"

The man smiled, though not kindly. "You are home," he said, crouching like a scientist examining a specimen. "You are where the lake has chosen you to be. She doesn't take by accident. The lake doesn't lie."

Despite the overwhelming reek of roasting meat, Jack took a deep, cleansing breath to calm himself. Over the flames, a body turned on a spit, charred black. Fat sizzled and popped as it dripped into the embers.

Jack swallowed hard as his stomach lurched. "You're eating people."

The leader laughed, shaking his head as if amused by Jack's naivety.

"Something funny?" Jack muttered, sarcasm cutting through nausea.

"We weren't always this way," he said, gesturing toward the equally gaunt figures around the fire. Their bodies slick with sweat, they moved in slow, rhythmic motions, their lips forming silent prayers. "Once, we were like you: survivors, lost, hungry, and afraid."

"But the starving hear things in the water. Whispers that chew through reason."

Jack gritted his teeth. "And what changed?"

The leader's grin widened as his fingers absentmindedly traced one of the bones on his necklace. "The world changed. The old rules no longer apply. Those who clung to them are gone."

Jack stayed silent, fighting the fog from the blow to his head, concentrating on his training, and thinking about how he could escape.

The man leaned closer. "How many infected have you killed?"

Jack froze.

"You hesitate," the leader said, his smile sharper. "Because you've lost count."

Jack tightened his jaw.

"They're endless, aren't they?" he murmured. "The ones infected with the disease. They aren't dead. Just empty vessels. And when you're empty… you will echo. They rot, but keep walking. Never eating. Always spreading."

His voice fell to a whisper. "You fight them. We live among them."

Jack's gut twisted as he groaned, "You let them live?"

The leader nodded toward the darkness beyond the flames. "We do more than that. We listen. We learn."

Jack followed his gaze. Beyond the firelight, shadows shifted. At first, he thought it was a trick of the flames, but then he noticed figures standing at the tree line. They remained still, their bodies ravaged by disease, slack-jawed, eyes sunken, skin hanging loosely in places where the infection had eaten away. They did not attack. They watched. Waiting.

Jack turned away in disgust as his blood ran ice-cold.

"You fear them," the leader said softly. "That means you still have a soul to lose."

"We give them what they need. Show them reverence. In return, they leave us be."

Jack's anger intensified. He spat, "You're insane."

The leader laughed, his thin smile revealing several missing teeth. "Am I? Or are you? I am not the one about to be sacrificed."

Jack struggled against the ropes, feeling the coarse fibers tearing into his wrists.

"The infected are part of this world now," the leader whispered. "Just as we are. Just as she is."

The man's eyes drifted dreamily toward the lake, its surface still and murky, reflecting the deepening hues of dusk. It shimmered in the fading sunlight, suggesting a deceptive calm.

"The lake gave us fish. Clean water. We thought we'd found sanctuary."

He paused. "But the lake takes as much as it gives."

Jack's skin prickled. "What do you mean by that?"

The leader's gaze darkened. "First, a man went fishing and never returned. Then a woman. Finally, a child. All gone. All swallowed by the lake."

His voice dropped to a whisper. "We called out. But it gave us nothing back."

The leader's lips curled into an unreadable expression. "Until she came."

Jack's pulse quickened.

The man grinned. "You've seen her before, haven't you? The Lady of the Deep?"

Jack remained silent.

The man beamed, knowingly. "Yes… I can see it in your eyes. You know."

Jack swallowed, clenching his fists against the restraints.

"At first, we feared her," the leader said reverently. "Then we learned. She doesn't take; she judges. She chooses who belongs. Her hunger is older than the glaciers and deeper than the grave. She remembers every soul she consumes. She's the beginning and the end."

Jack's voice cracked. "You think she wants this?"

"We don't think," the man hissed, his breath foul. "We know. She demands sacrifice. And tonight, she chooses you."

The lake stirred. Its surface rippled as the fire's reflection danced on the small waves lapping at the shore. Bubbles appeared: fat and slow.

Jack's heart hammered.

A pale hand, slender and unnaturally long, broke the surface. Then another. Water dripped from alabaster skin. A woman's form emerged, tall and unnatural, as if sculpted from something no longer human. Her sleeveless white dress clung to her translucent skin, shifting slightly in the warm evening breeze. A blood-red belt cinched at her waist was the only splash of color against the stark whiteness of her body.

The cannibals dropped to their knees, foreheads sinking into the dirt, their chanting turned more intense, frantic, and passionate, as if they were caught in a state of wild, intense ecstasy.

Jack couldn't look away.

She drifted forward, hovering above the water. Her jet-black hair floated around her like it was caught in an unseen current. A thin veil hid her face, revealing only her eyes.

Violet. Piercing. Dark and unblinking.

Jack trembled as he fought against his restraints.

Then, a warm breath brushed his ear.

"Keep your eyes closed," a voice whispered, barely loud enough to be heard above the chanting. "And keep your mouth shut. No matter what happens, don't react."

Jack turned slightly and saw him. A hooded man, sweat dripping down his face, worked furiously at the ropes.

The Lady stilled, nostrils flaring as if she'd caught their scent. She stepped closer, her gaze darting between Jack and his would-be rescuer. Jack forced himself to remain still.

The cult cried out, "We offer this flesh to you, O Lady of the Deep! Take us into your embrace!"

She tilted her head and, with a swift and graceful motion, lifted her veil.

Jack clenched his jaw so tightly he thought his teeth might crack. He forced his eyes shut.

"Don't move," the man next to him stiffened, whispering under his breath. "She's testing us."

Her rotted skin hung in loose strips, as if she'd been dead for ages. Her cheeks were sunken, with a jagged, inhuman grin. Her teeth gleamed in uneven rows beneath her peeling lips.

Finally, she turned to the cannibals. The mist poured from her breath, extinguishing the fire. Smoke slowly rose from the ashes as her body transformed. Her legs merged, twisting, shifting, and stretching into a serpentine mass of glistening scales and an enormous, writhing tail.

Before the cult could react, she struck. Her tail coiled around their leader's waist. As he tried to scream, he was yanked off his knees, his spine snapping with a sickening crack.

The others tried to flee, but she was faster. Her tail struck again, lashing and constricting. One by one, she ensnared them. The lake muffled their screams as she dragged them into the depths.

Jack's bonds came loose. He tumbled from the cross and onto the ground. His rescuer grabbed his arm, lifting him to his feet.

"Run!" the stranger shouted. "Now!"

Jack staggered, his legs aching and muscles stiff, but he forced himself forward. Together they disappeared into the trees, leaving the smoldering fire and still lake behind.

The surface calmed, hiding her once more. Only the low moans of the infected lingered. Aimless souls wandering, waiting on memories that would never return.

***

Safehouse at Lake Ronkonkoma
Just Before Midnight June 12th

While the world beyond the safehouse spiraled out of control, something within seized it…

The air in Louis's room felt like a portal to another realm. The blistering heat of the day had given way to near-freezing temperatures. Frost covered the windows in intricate patterns that refracted a weak, unearthly light… an aura that defied the absence of electricity and seemed to emanate from Louis himself.

In a shadowy corner, Jouris shivered, the chill piercing his tattered coat. He rubbed his arms for heat as his teeth chattered.

"Another cold night in June. Feels like whatever spills out when you open that basement door."

With sleep impossible, he clung to the radio for company. Only a barrage of grim news: *famine ravaging the land, replanting thwarted by wild swings in the weather, and wildfires in the West, whose choking, acrid smoke tainted the horizon as far east as Lake Champlain.*

With a bitter sigh and trembling hands, he switched off the radio; yet, the echoes of the escalating cataclysm still reverberated in his mind.

Louis lay bound to his bed, immobilized by restraints that criss-crossed his arms and legs. His bloodshot eyes stared blankly ahead, and raw, open wounds gouged into his cheeks and forehead. The only sign of life was his ragged breathing, releasing wisps of mist-like vapor above his body.

Then, as if summoned by the horror of the news, Louis's body flickered to life. A spectral energy seemed to animate him. Though restrained, his body convulsed slightly as if a force had taken hold of him. His head twisted unnaturally, and the crack of his vertebrae made Jouris cringe. It raised the hairs on his neck like fingernails slowly dragging down a chalkboard.

"What is it, Louis?" Jouris rushed to the bedside. His lips curved slightly into a gentle smile. He spoke soothingly, "You poor boy. No one deserves this."

The green-shaded desk lamp on the table flickered. Jouris shook his head. "That's impossible. We don't have power."

The ghostly light revealed insects everywhere, skittering along the walls and creeping over the warped floorboards. A ceaseless, unsettling rustle replaced the oppressive silence, while a musty scent of decay filled the air. Jouris stepped back from the bed, and a disgusting crunch echoed with each movement. He looked up as insects clinging to the ceiling rained down on Louis.

Repulsed, Jouris still found the courage to sweep them from Louis's body with his hands.

From the eerie glow surrounding Louis, a voice emerged… achingly familiar but twisted beyond recognition. Louis's head gave a slight tilt to the left, like Peter Van Haalan used to. The movement was subtle, almost imperceptible, but it froze Jouris in place.

It spoke in Peter's voice: "Where were you when I needed you? Why didn't you help me? Why did I die alone on that subway platform, bleeding out, while the rails screamed and the train thundered past?"

Louis's lips moved out of sync with the words, as if his mouth remembered Peter's cadence, but couldn't match it.

Nevertheless, the accusation pierced Jouris's soul. Every syllable carried grief and guilt. His heart raced as if trying to escape the icy confines of his chest, and his skin prickled with the sensation of unseen claws. For a brief, agonizing moment, the boundaries between memory and nightmare blurred, and he almost felt the ghostly warmth of Peter's presence.

"Peter, no," Jouris choked down a sob. He pleaded, "You know I loved you. I would never let anyone hurt you."

Maybe this is what I deserve for not being there to save him.

"Your tears are as empty as your promises, Father. A father protects his son, but you couldn't even do that, could you?"

The corners of Louis's mouth twitched upward into a crooked half-smile, a look Jouris had seen a thousand times on Peter's face, usually right before he cracked a joke. Only now, it looked wrong. Alien.

Still, Peter's indictment drove Jouris to bury his face in his hands.

Then, Louis's voice mocked him. *Peter prefers it in here with us.*

The entity revelled in the torment it inflicted. Its low, mocking laughter filled the room, accompanied by the constant scuttle of insects. The sound bounced off the frost-rimmed walls, echoing in Jouris's ears and taunting his despair. The chill in the air deepened, and every breath Jouris took was laced with bitter regret and icy dread.

Despite the terror that threatened to paralyze him, a surge of defiant anger welled up inside Jouris. The sight of Louis, helpless and bound yet possessed by something unholy, sparked a fury that overshadowed his sorrow. With trembling hands, he reached for the lamp.

"Enough!" Jouris roared, his voice raw and resolute.

"You dare use my son's voice to break me?"

His words ricocheted off the walls. The mocking laughter paused, then returned sharper and crueler, still laced with Peter's voice.

Jouris advanced toward the bed, determined to break the unholy presence's hold. Peter's laughter, bright and full of life, echoed beneath the mockery.

This wasn't about his grief. This was desecration.

Jouris reached for the lamp.

You want to play with the pieces of my shattered life, I'll shatter this lamp on your skull.

Louis's vacant eyes, illuminated by the flickering light, silently witnessed Jouris's internal battle, grief against fury, a struggle threatening to consume him.

Jouris lifted the lamp for a final, decisive blow when a sharp voice cut through the chaos. "Jouris, stop!"

Anne stepped out of the doorway, her expression a blend of urgency and sorrow. Her eyes locked onto Jouris's, pleading yet resolute. In that instant, time seemed to slow down, and the air, once heavy with the weight of impending disaster, felt almost warm.

"It isn't Peter," she said, her voice trembling but firm.

"It's The Entity baiting your guilt. Don't let it control you."

Anne's words crashed over him. The mocking laughter and sickly glow faded. Jouris's arm lowered as he met her gaze. The fury in his eyes wavered, replaced by a dawning horror at the realization that his desperate act would not bring back his son but would only serve the unholy purpose of the entity that lurked within Louis.

As if a switch flipped, the pressure in the room lifted, replaced by unnatural silence. The insects and the sound of their skittering were gone.

Anne steadied his trembling arm, then set the lamp back on the table.

"This is what it does. I've seen it before," she whispered, soft but insistent.

Caught between grief and fear, Jouris's rage diminished. Anne's intervention halted his descent into violence that would only strengthen the dark force.

"I-I'm sorry, Anne. Forgive me," Jouris stammered.

Anne led him out and closed the door.

"This isn't your son. It's a creature feeding on your sorrow and anger. Don't let it win."

They embraced in the hallway, each bearing the burden of facing an unseen enemy, uncertain whether this night would mark the beginning of Louis's redemption or if it was just another act in a horror story that was far from over.

Behind the closed door, a single stray beetle scurried under the bed. Out of earshot, a voice whispered... *Peter...Peter...*

***

Town of Lake Ronkonkoma
At the Same Time... Just Before Midnight June 12th

Jack's head throbbed in time with his labored steps, each pulse a grim reminder of the blow to his head that left him dazed and likely concussed.

"Slow down," Jack said, his voice strained with both pain and urgency.

But Father Raymond Putnam, his unlikely rescuer, shook his head with grim determination. "We must keep moving," the priest insisted, his tone low and measured.

"I'm trying, Father, but every step feels like a war against my own body," Jack murmured, wincing as he bent to clutch his knees and catch a breath.

Wrapping an arm around Jack's shoulder, the priest urged, "We must hurry. Nightfall is when the unusual comes alive."

"Okay, Father," Jack whispered, "but tell me, why does the darkness bring more terror than the light ever did?"

Father Putnam did not respond. Instead, he pushed them onward until they emerged from the forest.

They trudged along the main road toward the center of what had once been the town of Lake Ronkonkoma. Now it looked long abandoned, caught in decay.

Still groggy, Jack steadied himself,

The last time I was here, the town was still pretending everything was normal...

After such a warm day, the chilly night air hit like a polar bear plunge. The wind stirred the silence, sending scraps of paper swirling down the empty street. Overhead, a faded sign for an ice cream shop creaked and swung with each gust, its lonely jingle echoing like a ghostly lullaby.

"That sign... it almost sounds like a warning," Jack observed, his voice trembling.

Father Putnam offered a brief smile. "Sometimes, even the inanimate speak truths we'd rather not hear."

At the crossroads of town, Jack froze. Through the haze of his concussion, he saw a hearse, its dark, ancient carriage rattling down the road. The shrouded driver tugged the reins of a horse black as midnight. The carriage headed toward the graveyard before fading from sight.

"Did you see that?" Jack gasped, his heart racing wildly.

"Focus, Jack," the priest said firmly. "A vision like that is no promise, only a solemn warning. Hurry, let's get inside the church."

They finally reached the heavy oak doors of a Catholic church. Its stained glass windows, still intact, looked dull with neglect. Jack's gaze drifted to the adjacent cemetery, where freshly dug graves, marked with crooked crosses, gave off the scent of newly turned soil and decomposition.

"Those graves… they're new," Jack whispered. "I didn't think anyone got buried anymore."

Father Putnam's weary eyes welled with sorrow. "I've given the dead a proper burial. Even in the forsaken state of this world, every soul deserves respect."

Inside, reverence and rot mingled in the air. The priest's appearance reflected his weariness: his once-pristine clerical collar was soiled, his white hair tangled and unkempt, and his eyes kind, but heavy with the weight of unspoken burdens.

Jack lay down on a pew while the priest poured bottled water into a glass pot and lit a Sterno beneath it. Soon the water boiled.

"Take this," he said, offering Jack a mug. "I wish I had milk and sugar, but these days this is all we have to stave off the chill of body and soul."

"Thank you, Father," Jack said, holding the tea like a precious gift. "Its warmth is comfort enough."

For a brief moment, calm filled the church.

"Are you managing on your own?" Jack asked.

Almost on cue, an unearthly sound shattered the quiet. The confessional doors bulged outward as if something inside pushed against them.

Jack's ears caught the eerie scrape of wood and the soft, sickening sound of fingernails dragging down the panels.

"Do you hear that?" Jack whispered.

"Yes. It is familiar to me," Father Putnam replied, steady despite the palpable dread that surrounded them.

Jack squinted into the gloom. Pale fingers twitched through the cracks of the confessionals… fingers not belonging to the living.

"Damn it…" Jack muttered, adrenaline spiking as he rose, his hand instinctively reaching for a weapon. He glanced warily at the priest.

"Jack, wait," Father Putnam's voice carried calm authority. "I'm tending to my brothers."

"What do you mean, your brothers? Why are you living with the infected?"

"They were priests once, my son," Father Putnam explained, his eyes misted with regret. "Now they suffer in the grip of something unholy."

Jack's gaze darted between the dead clawing their way out of the confessionals and the priest who'd saved him.

"So, the graves outside…?"

Father Putnam crossed himself. "I buried them. A final act of mercy. Every soul deserves dignity."

He lowered his voice. "It's the lake, isn't it?"

Jack frowned. "The lake? What? How…?"

Father Putnam cut him off. "I am a man of God. I saw how you reacted to the vision of the hearse. I have witnessed many forms of evil, but what surrounds this lake is different. It lingers. It waits. It speaks, a deceptive oracle whose messages are as dangerous as they are ambiguous. It contains something unholy."

"You mean… it speaks to us, deceives us?" Jack asked.

"Yes," Putnam replied gravely, "It twists truth into terror. Much like the lies Anne warned you about."

Jack blinked, Anne's name echoing through his mind like a firecracker. It reignited the memory of his interrogation.

"How do you know about Anne?" he demanded.

Father Putnam replied, "You were talking to her when you were tied to the cross?"

Jack rubbed the bump on his head. "They must've knocked me out cold."

Pushing the danger aside for a moment, Jack confided in Father Putnam about Louis's condition and the inexplicable horrors that had taken hold of him.

"Father, my son... he's not himself anymore. There's something inside him, something dark."

The priest's face tightened. "I've seen this corruption before. It festers in the heart of our community like a malignant curse. The Clifford brothers in the 1960s, what you face now has happened before."

He went to a closet and retrieved a brown, cracked leather doctor's bag. Inside were relics: a worn crucifix, holy items, and a black book with gold lettering,

Rituale Romanum Volumen Unum-Sacramenta et processiones

"Don't worry, my son. I'm sure your friend Anne knows Latin. There are two more volumes in the bag."

Filling Jack's empty bottle with holy water, the crisp scent of consecration mixed with the musty air.

"This might help protect you," he said.

Jack clutched the bottle, hope mingling with fear. His hand trembled. "I pray it does, Father. I don't know that I can endure losing him."

The moans inside the confessionals rose to a crescendo. The infected priests, Father Putnam's corrupted brothers, clad in tattered vestments, broke free, their cries a discordant hymn of anguish.

"They're coming!" Jack shouted.

He and the priest rushed to the doors.

"Come with me!" Jack begged.

The priest paused, his hand resting on the heavy oak door. His eyes glistened as though he were already gazing past Jack into eternity. He lifted his chin, voice slow and solemn, each word carrying the cadence of prayer.

"My place is here, with my brothers. I was with them in life, and I will not forsake them in death. Into Your hands, O Lord, I commend my spirit. Let my last breath be among those I once served."

Then, with a trembling sigh, he pushed Jack into the night air and pulled the door shut behind him.

Jack heard the sound of the door locking, merging with the anguished cries of the damned.

"Father, please…" he called out.

"Trust in Anne, Jack," came the faint reply. "She's a light that can't be extinguished. I am where I need to be. Now, save your son. May God watch over you."

The ghostly town, the cursed lake, and the screams of the dead from the once-sanctified church faded into the background, leaving Jack alone to wrestle with the chilling darkness and the haunting realization that sometimes salvation comes at a terrible, irreversible cost.

***

Liberty Crest High School
Time-Unknown

The more things change… the more they stay the same…
The words echoed like the morning announcements, but he wasn't sure why…

The air felt thicker than ever, the lights buzzing too loudly. Somewhere behind him, a bell rang… a bell that only he seemed to hear.

Louis rushed down the hallway.

The whispered voices from Mr. Harris's classroom buzzed in his ears like a swarm of hornets. He didn't stop or slow down. His sneakers pounded the floor as he put as much distance as possible between himself and Mr. Harris.

What am I running from? The noises? The voices? That thing that looks like Dad but isn't? It's not right. Nothing is right. Have to keep going.

His chest burned, but he didn't dare look back. He skidded to a stop at an intersection where three identical hallways stretched on and on, each more warped than the other. The school felt larger now, the

304

walls expanding, and the building swelling beyond what it had ever been before.

He went down the left hallway and kept going.

Lockers leaned toward him, their blue doors ajar, like waiting mouths. Inside, he caught glimpses of shadows; not simple darkness, but something deeper, colder, and emptier… watching.

Then came a new sound: heavy footsteps.

Before Louis could react, someone slammed into him.

He hit the floor hard, jolting his body from the impact. He gasped, the wind knocked out of him. Before he could move, a hand seized his collar and yanked him upright.

Then a sound cracked through the hallway, metal slamming shut. For a split second, Louis heard lockers slamming, the sharp metallic crash *he* always made just to watch him flinch.

Louis's stomach dropped. It was Travis Grayson, the bully from his past.

But Travis should have been older, the same age as Louis. Instead, he looked just like he had in high school: seventeen years old, with a thick neck and broad shoulders, wearing his silly letterman jacket stretched tightly across his bulky frame.

His messy blonde hair stuck out from under a Nationals baseball cap, its bill pulled low over his forehead. His broad face seemed different now. His skin appeared too pale, his lips ringed with a gray, as if the color had drained away. His eyes were bloodshot, with black veins branching out toward the irises.

Louis felt like ice water had been poured down his back.

Travis tightened his grip on his shirt, pulling it close until their noses nearly touched. His breath felt too warm, carrying the unpleasant scent of rotten eggs.

"You don't belong here, freak."

Louis's hands shook as he attempted to pull away, but Travis's fingers held on like a vise.

Louis swallowed hard. "I... You're not real."

Travis's expression remained the same. His lips curled into what should have been a grin, but his teeth looked peculiar. They were too straight, spotless, and overly white.

"Of course I'm real, stupid." Travis leaned in closer, his voice dropping to a whisper, yet it seemed to resonate from somewhere else. "Just like your failures. Just like your lies."

Louis shook his head. It was too much. The noise. The smells. Thinking was like trying to breathe underwater. The walls of the hallway pulsated, and the lights flickered erratically. Suddenly, a shadow loomed over him, and Louis's stomach dropped.

A second voice, calm and composed, spoke from behind Travis. "Enough."

Travis vanished mid-breath, collapsing into ash that never hit the floor.

Louis staggered back, clutching a locker for balance. His heart pounded like a war drum, something once comforting, but now terrifying.

A tall figure now stood where Travis had been.

Louis's breath caught. The principal... or his father. Or both, stitched together like a mask.

Why does his voice sound like Dad's?

The man adjusted his cuffs and then looked at him with a blank expression.

"Come with me, son. You don't want to get lost again."

Louis ran. The hallway unraveled beneath his feet in flickers of artificial light.

Nothing here makes sense.

***

Louis's Room Safehouse at Lake Ronkonkoma
June 13th

I've faced murderers, maniacs, and monsters as a detective and JESU warrior. God help me, I hope I'm ready for this…

As Anne opened the door, the room was nearly dark, a chamber of shadows and flickering candlelight casting long, trembling silhouettes on the cracked plaster walls. Despite wearing her shoes, she felt the cold chill of the floor seep into her body. The stale air reeked of decaying flesh.

It would have been easy to connect the dots with the oozing boils and sores on Louis's face. Anne's heart broke at the sight of what the malicious entity was doing to him. Her compassion was only matched by her fear. She had no way of knowing what the evil inside Louis was ultimately capable of.

Anne stepped forward. Terror pressed in from all sides. She had faced evil all her life, but never felt like she did at that moment. Despite her fear, she was determined to battle this entity until the very end. Anne took a deep breath and declared,

"Saint Michael the Archangel, defend us in battle…"

As she spoke, two priests appeared in a corner of the room, kneeling in a circle. Their vestments hung in tatters, and where their faces should have been, there were only smooth, featureless voids. With clasped hands, in ceaseless prayer, they murmured in unison, their voices sounding both distant and mechanical.

"It is no use… it is no use…"

Anne challenged them, "Who are you? Who do you serve?"

Only their chant answered. Then they vanished. A mocking laugh slithered from the far end of the chamber, dripping with venomous delight.

Ah, Anne, came Louis's sneering tone, his voice a twisted blend of malice and contempt.

Do you dare to perform an exorcism? The thundering voice boomed, shaking the house to its foundation.

He's Mine!

I am the oracle, it intoned, as the air vibrated with the weight of its words.

Hear me now, for I foretell that in the hands of Prosperine and Lucius Rofocale, the world shall meet its end. A doom wrought by my elemental fury! Heaven's destruction released me from the lake, my prison since the birth of this planet. I am as old as creation itself.

For a heartbeat, silence reigned. Then Anne's voice pierced the oppressive gloom, filled with controlled fury,

"Your prophecies mean nothing to me. I stand for hope against your chaos."

"Be our defense…" she continued the prayer.

A low chuckle erupted from Louis, the sound like ice cracking under pressure.

Hope? Hope is the crumbling mortar of your faith. Your prayers vanish into the void. Saint Michael is no more. Do you genuinely believe your mortal defiance can halt the inevitable? I have seen empires crumble and stars die. Your resistance is a fragile spark in a tempest of darkness.

Anne stepped closer, her eyes blazing with anger, her voice rising.

"I will not cower before your threats. I reject your lies and your deception. I've known sorrow and despair, but I also know the strength of a soul that refuses to be broken!"

"May God rebuke him…"

Louis's laughter grew louder, shaking the plaster from the walls.

Broken? Do you think your spirit is unbreakable? Look at you, quivering in the shadow of forces you cannot comprehend. I am the oracle, elemental force of creation and ruin. Your resistance is as laughable as a candle's flame against the might of a dying sun.

A cold wind swept through the chamber, snuffing out the candles as Anne stood defiantly against the relentless barrage of The Entity's words. She shouted,

"Then tell me, oracle, if you are so powerful, why hide behind riddles and portents? What do you truly want?"

The Entity's tone softened into a sinister purr, with each word deliberately chosen to sting.

I crave chaos and the unraveling of order! I desire a world reborn in fire and shadow. Prosperine and Lucius are already doing what mortals fear most: ushering in the end of days. And you, dear Anne, are merely a pawn in a game far beyond your feeble comprehension.

Anne's hands shook so violently she nearly dropped the rosary. But she gritted her teeth and forced the words out,

"I see through your masquerade. I know that you hide behind these cryptic words to mask your true intentions."

The Entity hissed.

Ah! You think you see, yet your vision is clouded by mortal hope. I am not bound by the petty constructs of good and evil. I am the force that predates the heavens and the Earth, a presence unchained by time. And you... you are insignificant in the tapestry of creation.

Anne's fists tightened.

"I may be insignificant to you, but I wield the weight of everything sacred and pure. I'll fight against your corruption with every ounce of my being."

At that moment, the elemental force surged from the entity, causing the ceiling to crack. Its voice dropped to a menacing whisper.

Then come if you dare. Face the end that awaits you. But know this: my power has nearly devoured your feeble spirit already. You stand on the brink, and one misstep will plunge you into oblivion.

Darkness closed around Anne. The Entity lashed at her like a whip, challenging her resolve. For a long, agonizing moment, the only sounds were the slow, measured cadence of its taunts and the pounding of her heart. Her eyes shimmered with unshed tears of both defiance and despair. The intensity of its presence threatened to crush her, to drown her in a tide of hopeless inevitability. For a moment, she nearly buckled... when the door burst open.

Jack stumbled in, clothes torn, and his hair matted with sweat and blood. His eyes were wild with urgency.

Dear God, what has happened to my son?

"Anne, get back!" he shouted, lunging toward her as Louis writhed violently against his restraints, nearly breaking free.

The bed groaned. The straps stretched and popped. A sickening crack echoed, bone or wood, she couldn't tell.

"I won't let him take you!" Jack's voice was hoarse yet resolute; his intervention served as a lifeline amid the mounting horror. He pulled her from the room.

The Entity's mocking laughter echoed once more in the chamber.

Your exorcism is but a feeble trick, child. Do you truly believe your rites can bind me?

BOOM! It slammed the door shut.

Anne's eyes, still glistening with tears of defiance, locked onto Jack's gaze.

"Jack, listen. I remember what William said about the iron cage in the basement. It may be our only chance to contain him. We need to get him down there."

Jack crouched beside her as they sought shelter behind the wall. He opened his knapsack.

"I have an idea. I found Benadryl and Epi injectors while scavenging."

He held them up to Anne, then grabbed the water bottle Father Putnam provided.

"We'll crush the tablets, mix them with holy water. Maybe it'll make him drowsy enough to move."

Anne whispered, "We have to try. But holy water? Where did you get it?"

Jack's voice was rough with urgency. "I'll explain later. Give me that plastic bag."

They crushed the tablets together. In the background, the faceless priests resumed their hollow prayers, their voices drowned out by the escalating intensity of Louis's laughter. The tension heightened as

Louis's power surged, pressing the restraints to their limits, and the elemental force of The Entity threatened to consume everything.

Anne's voice quivered, her voice conveying the desperate hope of a soul determined to reclaim light from darkness. "Do you really think this will work?"

Jack's resolute eyes locked on hers. "We have no other option. If we don't act now, whatever that thing is, will break free and unleash hell on us all."

As they prepared the makeshift sleeping potion, the room throbbed with sinister energy, and its laughter —a sound that seemed to come from the very depths of the earth —echoed in their ears.

Try, if you must, but know this: your efforts will only delay the inevitable.

In the dim chamber, where every shadow whispered of ancient evils and each heartbeat counted down to oblivion, Jack and Anne steeled themselves.

"Drugging him feels futile, but I know we're out of time."

"Anne. We do this together."

She nodded, the EPI-Pen ready in her hand.

With one final, determined glance at each other, they prepared not just to fight for survival, but to confront the darkness that obsession had awakened and stop possession from claiming Louis forever.

STAGE VI:
POSSESSION

CHAPTER 1

Safehouse at Lake Ronkonkoma
Two Weeks Later

Two weeks had passed since their desperate exorcism attempt; two weeks of prayers, failed rituals, and watching Louis slip further into something unrecognizable. Two weeks since hope had given way to cold facts and colder nights.

Anne pressed her forehead against the window glass, watching Jack in the field. His silhouette hunched dark against the dull gray haze. The barren branches snapped like brittle bones in the wind, sending last fall's dead skimming across the permafrost. The ground resembled Alaska in spring more than Long Island in summer.

Jack swung the pickaxe in steady, deliberate arcs, the earth resisting with frostbitten stubbornness. Every few strikes he paused to catch his breath, his shoulders rising and falling with exhaustion. The weather had turned against them once more.

That morning the septic field had frozen solid, and draining the kitchen pipes made them groan rusty hinges; just one more failure, another crack in the walls of their fragile existence. Jack barely reacted when she told him. He muttered about taking care of it and walked outside.

Behind her, Jouris ran in place by the dining table, rubbing his hands together for warmth. His fingers trembled and his knuckles were raw from more than just the cold.

"Both cars are stocked with the what's left from the Daniels' house," he said, his voice tight, as if speech itself cost energy. "Enough to get a few hundred miles if we find gas along the way."

Anne turned from the window, crossing her arms. "And you? Are you okay?"

Jouris drew a deep breath, then shook his head. "Thanks to you two. That herd I ran into coming back from the Daniels' place was the biggest yet. Herds like that don't just stumble in by accident. They're migrating. Like Wildebeest. Only hungrier. We got lucky doubling back through the woods and losing them at the creek bed."

He met her eyes. "They're everywhere now, Anne. If we stay much longer…"

She gave his shoulder a quick pat. "I know."

They had saved Jouris, but barely. When he didn't return on time, they'd gone searching and nearly surrounded by the infected. Together they'd fought them off, with knives, a crowbar, and sheer adrenaline keeping a narrow escape route open. The infected clawed at them, but they pushed through and broke for the woods. There were too many now, and they all knew the house wouldn't hold out forever.

Jack drove the pickaxe into the ground again, the sharp clang of metal on rock echoing through the air. Anne glanced back outside, shivering. The sun was already sinking, draining what little light remained and casting long, skeletal shadows across the yard. Whatever slight warmth it gave would vanish with sunset.

They had planned to head south. The radio spoke of sanctuary, places where people regrouped and rebuilt. But millions were dead already. Civilization unraveled faster each day. People were eating pet food and when that ran out… worse. Jack said nothing the first time she mentioned the cannibalism rumors. He just sharpened his knife, the muscle in his jaw twitching. That had told her enough.

And then there was Louis. After two weeks they were no closer to driving out the thing inside him. If anything, he was slipping further away. Anne closed her eyes and exhaled slowly. If Louis could be saved, and right now that was the biggest of ifs, they would leave. Unless a herd tore the house apart first.

Outside, Jack leaned on the pickaxe, his breath billowing in thick plumes. Even at a distance she saw the exhaustion weighing on him, the dark circles under his eyes, and the deep lines in his face. He never complained, but it was carved into him. Anne turned from the window, rubbing her arms as if she could somehow summon warmth by will alone.

A soft voice broke the silence. David whispered, "She's a good girl."

She's the child I never had…

Anne's breath slowed. She turned.

David sat on the couch, his thin fingers buried in Daphne's fur. The cocker spaniel rested quietly in his lap, her golden coat soft beneath his touch. His lips trembled, but he forced a smile, stroking behind her ears the way she loved.

Anne pressed her hand to her mouth. From the moment she woke, she had known. Daphne hadn't greeted her or nudged for scraps. She understood, but that realization didn't make it any easier.

David gazed at her, eyes glassy but clear.

"She saved me," he said, his voice stronger than it had been in days. "She didn't eat so I could."

Anne sank onto the couch beside him, her fingers trembling as she smoothed Daphne's fur. The warmth was already fading.

CLANG. Outside, the pickaxe struck frozen ground again.

The sound carried through the walls, steady and relentless, as if Jack's labor was the only thing keeping them tied to survival.

Inside, grief pressed down like the cold air seeping through the cracks around the windows.

CLANG. Outside, the pickaxe struck frozen ground again.

***

Safehouse at Lake Ronkonkoma
Later That Night

By nightfall, the cold had deepened, and Anne descended to the basement alone.

A single candle sputtered, its weak light barely holding back the dark that clung to the damp stone walls. The scent of earth, rust, and rot hung in the cold air.

Anne stood her ground. Her calloused fingers clenched the worn crucifix that Father Putnam had given Jack. It radiated a faint warmth that wasn't her own.

Louis's body hovered inches above the floor, his limbs loose and unnaturally contorted. His head drooped, but his black, viper-like eyes fixed on her, eyes that weren't his. His lips spilled a torrent of choked, garbled sounds, guttural fragments that clawed at her skull.

Then came a soft, joyless chuckle. The head turned, its gaze falling on the crucifix, lips curling in disgust.

What a useless relic; it hissed. The voice was layered, shifting, as though something behind it whispered, with echoes of overlapping voices.

Do you really believe wood and metal can exert power over me?

Two weeks earlier, the drugs had worked long enough to move Louis and "his passenger" into the cage. Since then, The Entity had punished Louis's body relentlessly. The angry sores and tears in his flesh left him almost unrecognizable. The Entity's chanting and threats had thwarted every attempt to free him.

Anne swallowed, her throat dry. She tightened her grip.

She remembered the girl in Richmond, her eyes rolling black as midnight as three men held her down.

Louis stared with the same lifeless void.

"Maybe not on their own," she said steadily. "But I don't need symbols to remind me what's real. You're in there, Louis. I know you can hear me."

The thing inside Louis snorted. *Your God is dead, Anne. And those who wear His priestly robes? They fare no better.*

Before she could move, the crucifix burst into flames.

Fire hungrily devoured the wood, effortlessly swallowing the metal. The heat scorched her palm, but Anne didn't let go, even as the flames illuminated The Entity's smirk. She endured the pain, refusing to yield.

Thunder rolled.

The house shook with a deep, resonant boom, impossible and unnatural. There was no storm, no wind; the still night mocked the tremor. Dust drifted from the mortar of the stone walls, and the foundation shuddered as if struck by something enormous.

Then a flash of lightning.

Not from the sky. From the corner of the basement. A burst of searing white light illuminated a silhouette behind her.

Anne spun, her heart pounding against her ribs. A figure loomed, half-shrouded in the shadows. It smiled.

Hello, Anne.

For a heartbeat, she forgot the cage, the crucifix, the smell of scorched flesh. She saw only the man who had trained her. Her mentor. Her compass. Her… friend. She had buried her feelings for him, but she couldn't bury the memory of pulling the trigger.

The voice slithered out of the dark… familiar, intimate, and cruel. She recoiled. The shape shifted, cycling through forms before settling on one.

Mark Desmond emerged. His priestly vestments torn, skin pale and sunken, the gunshot wound she'd inflicted still fresh and open on his forehead.

Anne's mouth went dry. "You're not him."

The specter smiled. *Aren't I? I taught you to believe. I guided you. I'm the man you put a bullet into.*

The thing wearing Desmond's face sighed long and theatrically, spreading its arms like a preacher at the pulpit. *So quick to deny what's right in front of you. But I can help you.*

"You're a trick," she insisted. "A mouthpiece for whatever filth crawled out of the pit and took up residence in Louis."

The eyes flickered, two black holes pretending to see.

There's something in the lake. A talisman. The key to saving him.

Anne thought of the Bedford case, the boy chained to his bed, whispering in Latin until dawn. The lies had sounded just as sweet. They had almost fooled her then. Almost.

Her jaw locked. "Evil only begets more evil."

Desmond's smile faded. Its gaze shifted to the cage. The lips curled, not with amusement, but hunger.

It's unfortunate about Daphne.

Anne froze.

Louis, or rather the thing wearing him, tilted its head, watching her flinch.

Such a sweet creature. So small. So, trusting. And so... very hungry. Tell me, Anne, did she know? Did she understand why her belly ached?

Anne's nails dug into her palm, drawing blood. This wasn't just cruelty, it was strategy. It was trying to break her with guilt, to make her doubt, to make her surrender.

Did she cry at night while David grew stronger? Dreaming of scraps and warmth until her body gave out?

Anne stepped forward.

The Entity grinned, its forked tongue flicking between its teeth. *I bet she thought you'd save her. But you didn't. You let her waste away. You let her die.*

It leaned closer to the bars. *Now she rots in the dirt while you whisper prayers to a dead God. Or I could bring her back. Let her ask you why.*

A pause. A smirk. *She would be... different when she came back... of course...*

Anne moved without thinking. She gripped the charred crucifix tighter, the embers still glowing faintly, and slammed it against the bars.

A shriek tore from inside the cage, inhuman and guttural. Smoke hissed where the cross met the holy oil smeared on the iron. The thing thrashed violently, spasming as its black eyes rolled back... then snapped forward again, burning with hatred.

The entity wearing Desmond's face leaned closer, speaking in a low, steady, menacing voice.

Don't worry. We'll let you stay… long enough to watch us tear Jack, Jouris, and David apart.

It reached for the cage.

As its fingers touched the bars, it recoiled violently, its flesh searing as if branded. The stench filled the room. It let out another scream, writhing as if something invisible had set it ablaze.

Anne stood her ground, watching as its form flickered wildly and lost cohesion, with black veins spreading across Desmond's face like cracks in porcelain. Its face warped and twisted, and its mouth stretched open in a soundless wail before collapsing in on itself.

Then Desmond vanished.

The basement was quiet except for Louis's shallow, uneven breathing as he dangled just inches above the floor.

Anne closed her eyes and exhaled. When she opened them, Louis stared back, the same black eyes, but he didn't speak.

A single blink, slow and deliberate. Anne saw it. A flash. Small, but it was enough.

Something deep inside was still fighting.

She looked at her hand. The crucifix was whole. Her palm unburned.

For the first time, she felt it.

This creature was not in control.

***

At the Same Time…

It always feels like I'm running on ice… slipping and sliding, never getting anywhere…

Somewhere far away, a drip of water echoed, and then the sound was gone, swallowed by the school's endless halls…

Louis's legs burned as he ran, lungs straining to keep pace with his pounding heart. The hallways twisted, stretching into impossible angles. Lockers rattled like cages holding something desperate to escape.

The Principal's voice echoed behind him, calm yet impossibly loud, as if the walls themselves carried his words.

"Louis, you're making this harder than it needs to be."

Louis didn't stop. He darted around a corner, nearly losing his balance on the slick linoleum. A sign for a familiar door loomed ahead: LIBRARY.

He didn't hesitate. He shoved the door open and staggered inside.

The air shifted immediately. The silence here wasn't as crushing as in the halls, but it felt heavy, like the weight of a thousand unread books. The fluorescent lights above were slightly dimmer, casting long shadows between the towering wooden shelves. The smell of paper lingered, adding a grounding presence amid the nightmare.

Louis took a few tentative steps forward, his heart racing. A voice, smooth and measured, shattered the silence.

"You should not be running around like that, Louis. You will only exhaust yourself."

Louis took a deep breath and turned towards a reading table in the center of the room. A man sat cross-legged there, with a small stack of books beside him.

Lucius Rofocale.

But unlike the Lucius burned into his memory from the Bradford House basement, the cold-eyed jailer, this Lucius seemed almost… warm.

His sinister attire was no longer present. Instead, he wore a dark gray waistcoat, neatly buttoned over a crisp white shirt. The sleeves were fitted, and the cuffs were adorned with silver cufflinks. His tie displayed a subtle pattern in deep burgundy, tied in a perfect Windsor knot. The black academic robe draped over his chair gave him the distinct air of an old-world professor.

It was his presence that caused Louis to freeze. Lucius didn't look up right away. Instead, he adjusted the gold-rimmed glasses perched on his nose and turned a page in the book he was reading.

He ordered, "Sit," but his tone was calm as if he were delivering a classroom lecture. "You look like you have been through quite an ordeal."

Louis remained still. His body screamed for him to run, but his mind was tangled in confusion.

"You..." Louis swallowed hard, his throat drying up. "You're him."

Lucius looked up. His sharp, gray-blue eyes remained unblinking as they fixed on Louis, examining him with a gaze that was not quite curiosity.

"Lucius Rofocale," the man confirmed. "I know precisely who I am. The real question is… do you know who you are?"

Louis shuddered, feeling his skin crawl at the recollection of Travis's grip, the principal's voice, and Mr. Harris's unnatural smile.

Lucius's closed the book with a gentle thud, his long fingers tapping lightly against the worn cover. "You are not supposed to be here," he said, continuing. "And yet, here you are… lost, confused, and afraid."

Louis tensed. "Why should I trust you?"

Lucius exhaled through his nose, and an expression that resembled amusement crossed his otherwise unreadable face. He straightened his cuffs and replied,

"I suppose you should not, but I am the only thing standing between you and him."

Louis opened his mouth, but nothing came out.

Lucius leaned forward slightly, his expression softening. It wasn't kind, but it conveyed a reassurance that made Louis's head spin.

"Are you looking for a way out, or not?"

Louis's pulse raced. He stayed silent; there was no need to respond. Lucius's smirk deepened slightly as if he already knew.

"The school is a trap," Lucius declared, his voice lowering to a softer tone. "Designed to keep you confused. Isolated. The halls swallow their own corners, and doors only lead you back to where you began."

He reached for another book from the stack, dust flying as he turned it in his hands.

"Some traps are built to hold specimens," he added, the words almost an afterthought, "and some… to lead them exactly where they must go."

His eyes never left the page, as though the statement meant nothing. But the pause afterward stretched, just long enough for unease to take root.

Louis clenched his jaw.

"The halls lead nowhere. The numbers mean nothing. You are driven in circles, compelled to relive the same agonies again and again. A nightmare wearing the mask of memory."

Louis's mind raced as he recalled the locker that wouldn't open, the wrong test, and the clocks running backward.

"You already know this," Lucius said, leaning back in his chair. "You can feel it."

Something churned in Louis' stomach.

Lucius allowed the silence to linger before he spoke again.

The question, Louis, is whether you want to stay here, running from the ghosts of your past, or would you prefer to leave?

Louis's fists tightened, the tendons in his hands straining. His mouth moved before he could second-guess himself.

"What happens if I say no?"

Lucius's eyes narrowed just enough to notice, but his smile never faltered.

"You will not."

He reassured him, saying, "Do not be troubled. You will find the answer soon enough."

Before Louis could respond, a shadow slid across the library doors.

His blood ran cold. The principal.

Lucius's eyes darted to the doors, then back. His smirk vanished; his tone sharpened.

"You will come with me. Now."

Louis's hands began to flap, the old stimming behavior surfacing before he could stop it; something ABA therapy had once drilled out of him. But with his anxiety spiking, it returned, the air brushing cool and quick against his palms.

Go? No Go? Go? No Go? His thoughts stuttered in rhythm with the movement, the question looping tighter the longer Lucius stood there.

And for reasons Louis didn't fully understand, he did.

***

June 13th 3:15 A.M.

David tossed and turned, the darkness weighing heavily on him. It pressed against his skin, thick and smothering, like dense smoke filling the room. His lungs burned with each breath, but the air felt different, like cold, stagnant liquid, filling his mouth, throat, and chest, as if he were drowning in emptiness.

Whispers slithered through the dark, rising and falling like the tide. They came from all directions, overlapping until no single voice could be separated. The rasping syllables were too soft to decipher, yet each pulse carried malice, brushing his ears, coiling into his skull like wet fingers searching for an opening.

David… David… David…

The voices warped his name until it bent into something unrecognizable.

A shape thickened in the shadows, transforming into a figure. Louis stood before him.

David's stomach twisted. At first glance, it was his brother, the same silhouette, stance, and tilt of his head. But when Louis stepped forward, that familiarity unraveled like an old sweater, and it itched like a tag in the collar, scraping at his neck until he wanted to rip it off.

Louis's eyes weren't just dark; they were voids, pits of churning ink swallowing the weak light at the edges of David's vision. Something stirred beneath their surface, slow and hungry.

"You look terrible." Louis's voice didn't match his lips. It warped, like a vinyl record spinning at the wrong speed, or the poorly dubbed Godzilla movies their father and Uncle George used to watch.

David tried to speak, but his larynx clenched shut.

Louis drifted closer, his feet not touching the floor. A slow grin spread across his face, too wide and toothy.

"I wonder what it feels like," he snarled, the words dripping with venom, "knowing you should have been the one to die."

David shuddered. A coldness seeped under his skin, settling into his bones. The whispers drew closer, their chorus now sharp enough to cut.

Weak. Useless. A mistake. You should have died. You should have died. You should have died.

The words became hands, cold, unseen fingers coiling around his arms, legs, and throat. The pressure dragged him backward, down into darkness.

Icy water surged over his face, filling his mouth. David tried to scream, but swallowed the thick, murky flood.

Louis, or the thing wearing his skin, watched him sink.

A final whisper brushed David's ear, almost tender.

"I can make it easy for you."

David woke violently, jerking upright as if surfacing after a long dive. He gasped like a drowning swimmer, his ribs straining with the effort.

He knew it was a dream, but the cold still clung to him.

The room pressed in, stifling and hot. The air clung to his skin like a damp cloth. A sour, metallic taste slid down his throat... blood. His nose was bleeding again.

His stomach tightened, hunger twisting deep, but this wasn't the hollow ache of starvation. It was sharper. Stranger.

His skin prickled. Someone was watching.

He scanned the room. No one.

David pressed a trembling hand to his forehead. His mind buzzed, not with thoughts, but with something else.

And he could feel it, the same presence attached to his brother now circled him, probing his defenses, searching for weakness and a way in.

Something was awakening inside him. And it was whispering.

The same voice that had taken Louis, or something else, curled around his name, testing the fit.

David rubbed the stump of his left arm against the mattress seam, grinding it until the coarse fabric bit into his skin. The familiar sting steadied him, until it didn't. The relief slipped away like a thread pulled from a seam, and the whisper pressed harder at the gap, feeling for a way in.

***

The Basement of the Safehouse at Lake Ronkonkoma
June 13th The Next Morning…

The shadows of David's dream still clung to him when he came downstairs; the whisper, the cold, and the pressure in his chest. An itch crawled at the base of his neck, the same itch from the dream, like a tag in a collar he couldn't tear off. He hadn't told the others yet, but the thing inside Louis had found him, too.

The room was stifling, the air thick with the incense, sweat, and the sulfurous reek of rotten eggs. The candle flames flickered inward, as if the darkness were trying to inhale the light.

Anne turned to the last brittle page of the exorcism text. Her voice was hoarse, each Latin word tumbling from her lips like stones dragged from the lake. They had been at it all night.

And still... nothing.

Louis lay deathly still, floating just above the dirt floor inside the iron cage, the only barrier between him and the rest of them. His skin was ashen, deep cuts scoring his cheeks and forehead. His chest rose and fell in a slow, unnatural rhythm.

Jouris leaned against the stair railing, rubbing the edge of his Saint Christopher medallion between his thumb and forefinger, dark circles carved under his eyes. Jack paced near the foundation window, where morning light tried and failed to pierce the gloom.

Anne set the book down with a sharp exhale, rubbing her temple. "This isn't working."

Jouris glanced at her. "What are we missing?"

Jack gave a humorless laugh.

"We're not missing anything. This thing is stronger than we thought."

A low, inhuman sound slid from Louis's lips, though his eyes remained closed.

Stronger? The Entity mocked in Louis's voice.

Oh, Dad, you misunderstand. I am simply… patient. Like you were when you waited to call for help when Mom died. What was her name again?

The words slithered through the room like a centipede across the dirt, burrowing deep and scratching at the fragile edges of their resolve.

Anne stiffened. For hours, it had hardly spoken, only laughed. But now it was engaged, and that was never a good sign.

"You bastard," Jack snarled. "Her name was…"

"Don't, Jack." Anne touched his shoulder. "It wants to provoke you. Don't engage."

Jack dropped his head. "But how does it know these things? Things it shouldn't?"

Anne kept her voice steady.

"Possession doesn't happen instantly. It replaces the person piece by piece. Physically, mentally, emotionally, and spiritually. Once it takes root…"

It never truly leaves, The Entity finished for her.

Jack stopped pacing, shoulders tight.

"Shut the fuck up."

The Entity chuckled.

Why? Don't you like hearing the truth? Or is it another truth you fear? It scratches at you, doesn't it… the same itch he felt before he let me in.

The air shuddered, candles snapping higher.

Heaven is gone, it whispered. *It burned. Your Saint Michael? Dead. His army scattered. There is no one left to call upon.*

"Lies. That's all you do. Demon speak." Anne said through clenched teeth.

Jack's gaze dropped, contemplating the unthinkable.

It's easy to dismiss the words as deceit. But what if they aren't? The world is crumbling around us, faith has withered… what if…

"No!" He slammed his fist against the foundation wall, then shook his head hard, trying to drive the thought out.

The Entity hummed.

Oh, you think I arrived with you? That you conjured me? You do so enjoy lying to yourselves?

Anne's stomach dropped, the realization struck her like a ton of lead. The words tasted like poison in her mouth.

"It was already here."

Jouris looked up sharply. Jack turned. "What?"

"It… it didn't just take Louis." Anne forced the words out. "It's been working on all of us, planting doubt, infecting our relationships, waiting for the right moment. It was all a delaying tactic so it could take root in him."

Gritting her teeth, Anne seethed, "It's like a parasite."

Jack felt the truth of it: the slow unraveling of trust , the cracks in their unity. They fought each other while the real enemy lay within Louis's skin, waiting for them to fall apart.

He murmured, low enough for only himself to hear, "We don't even know if Louis is still alive."

Jouris's voice was grim. "How did it get in? Doesn't possession need a door?"

From the stairs, David's soft voice cut through.

"Louis's cell phone."

All eyes turned to him. David raised his fist, his eyes screwed so tight a crowbar couldn't pry them open. He fought the urge to hit his head, his whole body taut with the effort. Wrestling with his emotions, he finally said,

"He was talking to someone. And whatever was on the other end… convinced him to let it in. That was the door."

A long silence. Then Jack: "We destroyed the cellphone, Anne. How?"

Jouris shook his head. "A damn cell phone? Not a Ouija board. Not a séance?"

The Entity smiled as the realization settled over them like a sickness.

Anne didn't look away.

"This isn't just about Louis. It planned this. Manipulated us like fools. It's been winning all along."

David's neck prickled. The same crawling itch from his dream flared again at the base of his skull, just like a tag he couldn't tear off. He pressed his fist against it, but the pressure only made the sensation worse, as if the Entity was already tugging at the seams of his mind.

CHAPTER 2

David's Room in the Safehouse at Lake Ronkonkoma
June 14th The Next Night

David hadn't slept since confirming how the Entity had possessed Louis. Every time he closed his eyes, he heard a whisper.

Then he saw it in the corner of the room, a smoky haze where nothing should have been. The shape wasn't fully formed, like heat rippling above asphalt, only a suggestion of its presence. The longer he stared, the sharper Louis's outline became.

His brother leaned against the wall, arms crossed, mouth curled into a crooked half-smile. His eyes glowed a dingy yellow, reminiscent of tainted well water, and the white sclera drowned into twin pools of black tar.

David's heart skipped. Goosebumps rose on his skin as the room grew colder. The voice emanated from everywhere at once.

"You're looking worse, little brother."

David flinched, the hair on his neck bristling. It was Louis's voice, but it wavered, shifting mid-syllable into something wet and gurgling, as if another mouth spoke him. David's hands clenched and he closed his eyes. When he opened them, Louis was closer.

"You need to stop fighting, David."

David swallowed. "You're not real."

The doppelgänger laughed, deep and resonant. "Neither are you."

The words drove deep, twisting in his ribs like a hooked blade. His limbs felt heavy and sluggish, as though he were moving underwater.

"You know why I don't want to be saved?" the figure asked, head tilting. "Because I don't need saving. You're the one clinging to something dead."

A creeping sensation stirred in David's skull, spindly fingers sifting through his thoughts, dismantling his resolve bit by bit. For a fleeting second he imagined snapping those fingers, breaking them one by one. The image was his, and it made the thing falter slightly.

You are weak. You do not belong. You are not even sure if you still believe.

David's chest burned, not from the words but from their jagged edge of truth. His legs trembled as his body screamed for rest. He rubbed his eyes, exhausted.

The figure stepped forward, the air bending around him. His breath struck David's cheek, cold and reeking of rotting flesh.

"Anne. Jouris. Your father. They're just obstacles. They don't understand, but you do. You're the only one who does."

Obstacles. The word snagged in his head. Obstacles were tires you ran through or ropes you climbed, not people. It didn't make sense unless Louis didn't mean it that way. Unless… No. He shoved the thought back before it could spiral.

Remember what I told you, the voice softened, almost human. "You and I. We can fix this."

A sharp, high-pitched ringing filled David's ears. Hunger gnawed deep inside, feeding not on his body but on his mind. It felt like cold, deep water seeping in, each breath stolen before it reached his lungs.

Louis's voice grew comforting and persuasive. "You can make this right, David. You can end it."

David shivered. The itch crawled at the base of his neck again, the same one from the basement when The Entity had spoken through Louis. He shrugged and rolled his shoulders, but the feeling remained raw and insistent, digging deeper.

His fingers curled weakly at his sides. Worthlessness dragged him down, pressing him into the ground. Yet somewhere, beyond the pain, past the exhaustion, and the relentless pull of the doppelgänger's words, something pushed back.

A faint memory… his brother's real voice. David clenched his jaw, breath shaky, and forced himself to meet the figure's eyes.

The doppelgänger's smirk faltered.

"You're lying," David whispered.

The shadows quivered. The figure froze. Then a snarl erupted. It was inhuman. The creature's face contorted, and its jaw unhinged like a snake's. The sinister smile collapsed into this grotesque unnatural void.

David staggered back. The temperature plummeted. A final whisper crawled into his ear, thin as a tick burrowing beneath skin:

"You won't win. You never do."

Then, there was silence.

David gasped, trembling, his vision swimming. His head throbbed, stomach churned, but he endured.

He was still here. An the thing that wore Louis's face knew it.

But the itch lingered at the base of his neck, a reminder that the fight was far from over.

***

At The Same Time… While David is Under Attack.

One seldom recognizes the devil when he lays a hand on your shoulder…

Louis thought, *where have I heard this before?*

It felt too close to something from the night before, like a shadow at the edge of a dream he couldn't recall. It itched at the back of his mind, but the harder he tried to hold onto it, the faster it slipped away.

Louis couldn't place it, but it felt like a warning, curling through his thoughts as he followed Lucius through the dim aisles of the library. The shelves rose like skyscrapers, disappearing into shadows that smelled faintly of old paper and something wet, metallic, like when he stood on the shores of Lake Ronkonkoma.

His mind was still racing: the endless hallways, the wrong numbers, and the Principal's voice echoing behind him. He should have asked why he was trusting Lucius Rofocale, but right now, he had no better options.

Lucius moved with purpose. Each step was deliberate, his polished shoes tapping out a steady rhythm. His flowing academic robe barely shifted, as if gravity treated him differently. His fingers brushed book spines without pausing. He already knew the way.

"The school is a prison, like the cell I kept you in," Lucius said without looking back. "But you have figured that out already, have you not?"

Louis glanced over his shoulder. The library doors were open, but the hallway beyond had changed, stretching endlessly as if the school itself had been knotted into impossible shapes. Barely visible under the flickering lights, the Principal stood watching.

Panic swelled in Louis's throat. "He's still there."

Lucius didn't slow. "Of course he is. This place belongs to him, after all."

Louis stopped mid-step. "What?"

Lucius finally looked at him, his expression unreadable.

"Did you think this was just a dream? A little anxiety-ridden stroll through your memories?"

Lucius's voice sharpened. "No. This school was reshaped to hold you here. Keep you afraid. Keep you obedient."

Louis's stomach tightened. "I don't..." He hesitated. "I don't belong here anymore."

Lucius's lips twitched. "No, you do not."

Behind them, the hallway began to creep forward, like a car rolling downhill without brakes. The outer darkness swallowed shelves one by one.

"Move faster, please," Lucius said, brushing past a wooden counter toward a side door marked EXIT TO GYMNASIUM.

The command reminded Louis of Disney's Haunted Mansion. He half-expected Lucius to say, *Fill in all the dead space.*

The pull of the school was real now, a physical drag in his chest. The Principal hadn't moved, but the walls themselves were closing like jaws.

Louis shoved open the gym door…

… and the world changed.

The gym stretched to the horizon, its hardwood floor rippling under pale light. The ceiling soared into the shadows. Basketball hoops dangled at impossible heights, their nets swaying in a phantom breeze. The bleachers stood open, vacant. No team banners. No sound but his breathing.

Lucius strode to center court, hands clasped behind his back like a professor.

"The way out has been hidden from you."

He faced Louis. "Think. When was the last time you saw your reflection?"

Louis opened his mouth, then stopped. He hadn't. Not in the classroom, the library, or even in the windows.

Lucius watched the realization take hold.

"The exit is behind a mirror?" Louis asked.

"They do not want you to see yourself," Lucius said. "Because that would mean remembering who you really are."

Louis's mind fogged, as if a cold hand pushed down, keeping the truth just out of reach. The weight pressed from all sides, slow and crushing, like the gym wanted to grind him into the floor.

Lucius tilted his head, considering how much to reveal.

"There is only one left in the school," he said at last.

Louis spotted the locker room and dashed inside. Miles of lockers, but no mirrors. Lucius appeared at his shoulder, shaking his head.

"It is not in here. All the mirrors were removed from the bathrooms. Your generation and its TikTok videos."

Louis ignored the jab. "Where's the mirror?"

The gym floor groaned beneath them.

Louis's skin prickled. They were being watched.

Lucius stepped closer, his voice dropping to a near-whisper.

"If you hesitate when the moment arrives, you won't get another chance."

Louis swallowed. He knew where it would be… the one place he didn't want to go.

Behind them, the gym doors began to creak open.

***

Kitchen in the Safehouse at Lake Ronkonkoma
June 15th The Next Morning

The trio sat in silence, each reluctant to voice their failure to make progress against the Entity corrupting Louis's body. Steam curled from Jack's cup of dandelion coffee, the bitter scent rising like a reminder of how little time they had left. He inhaled, hoping it would clear the fog of fatigue. It had been another long night, and if he were honest, hope was slipping away.

Anne's gaze drifted to Jouris across the dim kitchen. Her hands tightened.

"Jouris… do you know why your family became the caretakers here?"

He shifted in his chair. "Not much. Only that we owed a debt, and the less we shared, the safer we'd be."

Anne leaned in. "Do you remember seeing the 'P' etched into the cage downstairs?"

Jouris frowned, nodding. "Why?"

"What about the name Pieter? P-I-E-T-E-R?"

He shook his head. "Doesn't ring a bell."

"I think that 'P' stands for Pieter, and the safehouse was built over the foundation of the original Van Haalan home."

Her voice dropped. "The curse of possession isn't an old myth, Jouris. It's in your family's blood."

Jouris's throat tightened. Pieter was a family name, later softened to Peter. The thought stirred a deep unease, given his own son had borne it.

And now it's in our blood, too. Jack thought.

The line from Pieter's blood to Louis's face as clear as if it had been drawn in ink.

Anne tapped the journal with one finger. "This isn't just history. It's the same sickness that's in Louis right now."

Jack looked up sharply. "What makes you say that?"

Anne crossed to the living room and returned with the worn leather-bound journal Jouris had given her. She slid it onto the table.

"It's full of notes; about Quanon, Ooqhua, the Sacred Fire ceremony, and curses tied to possession. It helped me piece together what happened to Pieter Van Haalan."

Jouris's eyes narrowed as she spoke the name.

"Pieter's fate wasn't an isolated tragedy," she continued. "It was the first modern warning, a possession that claimed his body, mind, and soul."

She glanced between Jouris and Jack. Jack's brow furrowed, something sparking behind his eyes.

"When Louis's eyes darkened, when his voice changed... I knew we were facing the same shadow. Louis will be next, unless we act."

Jouris's jaw tightened. "Then we fight. Whatever it takes."

Jack nodded slowly, as disbelief fading, cold and heavy, like the lake's water closing over his head.

"Anne," Jack's voice was low and ragged. "Be straight with me. What are the odds Louis is even alive?"

Jouris rested his arm around Jack's shoulder. Anne clasped Jack's hand and answered without hesitation,

"Don't. We're not giving up."

Jack's fingers brushed the Boy Scout skill award in his pocket. He'd kept it for no reason beyond the memory of simpler days. He turned it over absently, but his mind began racing.

Jouris caught the shift in his expression.

"You remember something? What is it?"

Jack exhaled slowly, eyes still fixed on the brass belt loop.

"Something Father Putnam told me. These things have happened before. He mentioned the Clifford Brothers."

Anne straightened. "Didn't you say something happened to them during a Scout trip?"

Jack nodded, finally looking up. "After one of our arguments over Louis, I stormed outside, and I swear I heard the name Billy in the wind."

A chill swept through the room.

"Lyle Clifford was the one who got murdered," Jouris said, frowning. "What about Billy? You think he…"

"I don't know," Jack admitted. "But those brothers keep coming up."

David entered quietly and sat. His voice was barely above a whisper.

"I saw something. A boy. He was in a scout uniform. He said something about the lake and its power… that it takes what it wants."

A tear slid down his cheek. "He told me it called his brother like it did Louis."

Anne knelt, locking eyes with David. "Think hard. Anything else?"

David's tone dropped even softer. "Yes. He said… 'It's inside the glass.'"

A faint clink sounded in the house, like glass set down on a table, or the ripple of water against a shore. Then it was gone.

Anne's heart skipped. The words replayed until a memory snapped into place: the bathroom mirror, a single word written in the steam.

"Jack, don't you remember? I told you about that mirror. The word *Inside* on it."

Jack nodded. "There's a puzzle here, but the pieces still aren't fitting."

They fell silent. Jouris felt a cold weight in his stomach.

"We need to find Billy Clifford."

Anne's pulse quickened. "But where? He'd be in his seventies, if he's even alive."

Jouris's face went flat, fingers drumming once on the table.

"Kings Park. Maybe not him, but the records."

His tone hardened. "It's where things were sent to be forgotten."

For a moment, something flickered in his eyes, a memory unsaid, the kind that leaves an ache in the gut. He straightened, burying it.

Jack shot up from the table, the chair legs scraping. He grabbed his crowbar and headed for the door.

Jouris blocked him.

"Wait. You don't know what you're stepping into. The world you know is a comforting illusion compared to Kings Park. And now? Who knows what waits there?"

Jack's grip tightened on Jouris's shoulder.

"Are you moving, or do I have to move you? This is my son. What the hell are we waiting for?"

Jouris looked to Anne for backup. She shook her head. He nodded in grim understanding.

"Fine. You'll need someone with you. Don't try to talk me out of it. I've been there..."

His gaze locked on Jack.

"You don't know what you're walking into. It's like steering blind into a rip current. You think you can fight it, but one wrong move and it'll pull you under."

Anne mouthed, *Thank you.*

Jouris stepped toward the living room. "Meet me at the car. I'm getting my gear."

He whispered so only he would hear, "We may not like what we find."

CHAPTER 3

Midnight June 16th at Prosperine's Temple in Jerusalem

Princess Prosperine stood atop David's Tower, once the tallest structure overlooking the Temple Mount, a vantage point from which she witnessed the city's fall and its remaking in her image. Like Babylon's conquest and Rome's temple desecration had turned Jerusalem into a monument of their own glory, she too would build over the sacred with the profane. Now, it was merely a relic of a bygone era, dwarfed by the colossal temple Prosperine was erecting in the heart of Jerusalem, its spires clawing at the heavens, its obsidian walls drinking in the last scraps of light.

She scanned the city below, her fiery eyes blazing like wildfire. The once-proud beacon of the Most High now lay in ruins, suffocated by clouds of noxious smoke. The scent of charred bodies lingered in the air, mingling with the dust of crumbling sanctuaries.

Below her, construction continued. Stone by stone, the edifice of her dominion neared completion. When finished, it would cast an eternal shadow over the ruins of the old faiths. It would proclaim her father's triumph, declare that the heavens had fallen, and announce the beginning of the dark reign of Prosperine.

Lucius Rofocale stepped forward, his crimson robes whispering against the scorched ground.

"It is done, my lady," he announced, his voice laced with reverence and malice.

"One-third of humanity is gone. Pestilence, famine, and the wars we ignited have done their work splendidly. Entire nations lie in ruin. Their bones pave the roads of our new world."

He bowed. "Hell is supreme."

Prosperine grinned, her fanged teeth glinting.

"A commendable purge, but not enough. The living still believe in their prayers. Hope still lingers in their marrow. I can hear their cries, still laced with foolish belief, even though their God has not answered them."

Lucius rose. "May I make a proposal, Princess?"

Prosperine nodded, and Lucius continued, "As planned, let us continue their suffering. We have toyed with their bodies; now we must extinguish their light."

She locked eyes with her evil ally, and her black talons clicked together as if marking time until the last glimmer of resistance died.

"Plunging the world into darkness… an exquisite torment. Let them crawl blind through their filth as the abyss swallows them whole. With the sun extinguished and the stars turned to ash, they will wonder if they are already dead."

Lucius tilted his head, as though she'd just suggested rearranging the furniture.

"A blasphemous inversion of '*Let there be light.*' The phrase marked the beginning of creation. We will restore darkness to its rightful place as the signal of its end. Then they will know, once and for all, that their God has abandoned them."

Prosperine exhaled in satisfaction, her gaze sliding to the half-finished altar where the first sacrifices would be offered.

"And what of the Mark?" she asked. Referring to herself, she added, "This 'Beast' must leave her signature upon them."

Lucius arched a brow.

"Something fitting. Something they cannot remove. Something that will torment them continually."

Her lips twisted into a sneer.

"When I feed, my barbs sink deep into the flesh. I love the sound of their screams when they try to rip them out." She flexed her clawed fingers.

"My mark will remind them they belong to me, like prey caught in a net, thrashing until they tire… until I devour them."

Lucius's smile barely deepened, as if this were only a change in the weather.

"A brand that binds them to you, my Princess, body and soul. A mark that does not just claim but consumes."

She turned back to the temple, staring at its monolithic minaret and walls inscribed with the curses of the damned.

"Then let it be done. A seal that cannot be undone, a brand that denies hope. The world will kneel, not in worship, but in agony."

Lucius nodded. "They will curse the name they once praised. They will tear their flesh to escape what they begged to receive."

His gaze lingered on the spires for a moment longer than necessary, as though measuring not just their height but how easily they might one day fall. The corner of his mouth twitched, not in amusement, but in a private thought a demon keeps until the right moment.

Prosperine's eyes glittered with joy.

"Then let them know: The Age of the Most High has ended. The Age of Suffering has begun."

Her smile was as deep and cold as a trench where light could never reach.

"They belong to me now."

Behind her, stonemasons hammered in rhythm, their chisels striking the obsidian, sparks flying as they carved three words above the temple gates: *HELL IS SUPREME*. Each blow rang out like a tolling bell, and the phrase was etched into eternity, a creed no prayer could erase.

***

Meanwhile, at the Safehouse at Lake Ronkonkoma

Anne was in the basement fighting for Louis's soul, while upstairs David's world blurred. The walls between dreams and waking had grown thin, stretched taut like old skin, and now they were tearing.

Whether the visions had just begun or never stopped, he couldn't tell. He only knew Louis's doppelgänger was closer than before, a whisper away, curling around his thoughts like a snake tightening its coil.

He felt it watching. Then it spoke, voice slick with a new kind of hunger.

Enough running, David. Just let go.

The words poured into him like ice water, pooling deep in his skull. It wasn't Louis's voice. It was older, shifting between echoes. One moment it mirrored Louis's tone; the next, it fractured into too many voices at once, each warped and wrong.

David hardly noticed his steps until the cold air hit him. He found himself at the lake. Somewhere between the safehouse and the shore, a faint chime of water against stone teased his ears, like fingers tapping glass. He couldn't tell if it was happening now or if it was a memory pulling him forward. The swampy smell of algae drifted around him, like something the lake had carried across time, just for him.

The air here hummed with an unnatural charge. The sky pressed down, velvet and suffocating, swallowing sound. The trees loomed like withered figures, their spindly branches bending toward him. But it was the water, black, motionless, a pit with no bottom, that locked him in place with a vice-like grip.

He stepped forward. Ripples spread across the surface. Another step, and his reflection rose to meet him.

At first, it was him... pale skin, dark-circled eyes, a body running on fumes. His gaze fixed on one detail, his missing left arm. In the reflection, it was whole again, right down to the pinky finger, twitching in a slow, unnatural rhythm like it was keeping time with a beat he couldn't hear.

Something snagged in his mind, a burst of static like the radio when it couldn't catch a clear signal. The reflection wavered, not in the water, but in his head, as if his brain couldn't decide what it was seeing. Then it shifted, like oil peeling from water. Skin peeled away in strips, revealing raw muscle beneath. His left eye caved inward, leaving a black, oozing hole. A grin split his face beyond what was humanly possible, exposing splintered teeth and blackened gums.

When it spoke, it was his own voice.

You don't belong here, David. You're just dead weight.

The whisper slid beneath his skin, a creeping sickness.

You're nothing without Louis. You're nothing at all.

The words triggered a sudden, unwelcome flood; the realization that what scared him most was losing Louis. Imagining him closing his door and never opening it again. Leaving David alone. Louis had been David's anchor through his illness and the trials of being God's prophet. Losing him… and that connection… chilled him to the bone.

A pulse rippled through the lake. The reflection stretched toward him.

David leaned forward, his body no longer his own. The pull worked its way into his ribs, latching onto his spine. His breath turned shallow; his pulse slowed to a crawl, as if his heart had surrendered.

Just let go, David. It's better this way.

The world shrank to water. The surface yawned wide, a void waiting to swallow him. One step, and it would be over. The cold licked the skin on his calves, pulling…

"DAVID!"

The voice ripped through him like lightning, the illusion shattering.

Hands gripped his shoulders. Real hands. Anne's hands.

Her grip was solid, anchoring him. His knees buckled, and she yanked him back, away from the shore, away from the abyss. The lake pulsed once, furious and cheated, before going still.

David sagged against her, his breath ragged and heart pounding. The doppelgänger's voice still clung to him, but it was fading. Over his shoulder, the water lay calm, until a shape rose from beneath the surface. A sick grin. Hollow eye sockets.

He blinked, and the gruesome reflection was gone.

Then, faint as a memory, came the sound again: water against stone. A soft tap, like fingers brushing glass

Anne's voice was low and firm, a lifeline in the storm.

"You're not going anywhere, kid. Not without me, and not with whatever's waiting down there."

***

At The Same Time…

As Anne saved David's life, Louis found himself staring at his own unlikely savior.

Confused, Louis asked, "Why are you helping me?"

Lucius replied flatly, "You were meant for something more."

B-O-O-M!

The gymnasium doors slammed shut, the sound reverberating through the cavernous space like a gunshot.

Louis flinched, his breath catching in his throat.

Lucius remained still, his eyes shifting toward the doors.

"Well," he said smoothly, adjusting the cuffs of his waistcoat. "I suppose that means we are out of time."

The air thickened. A slow, deliberate tap… tap… tap… echoed across the wooden gym floor. Louis turned toward the sound, and his stomach lurched. The Principal stood at the far end of the gym. The fluorescent lights flickered violently as he advanced.

Louis's gaze fixed on the Principal's fish-shaped tie clip. He found himself counting its etched silver scales until the man's face began to collapse. The skin sagged, resembling a mask that no longer fit. His eyes hollowed into deep, dark sockets that absorbed the light.

Louis's pulse pounded against his ribs.

The Principal adjusted his tie.

"You should have come with me when I asked, son," he said, the scold of a teacher about to hand down punishment.

Louis stepped back. His mind screamed *run*, but his body refused to move.

The Principal tilted his head, studying him.

"Do you know what happens to those who try to leave?"

Louis was unable to speak.

"Shall I show you?"

Somewhere beyond the confines of the gym, Louis thought he heard the muffled echo of water. Then the gym floor shuddered. The polished wood softened, rippling outward like the black waters of Lake Ronkonkoma. He gasped as his balance shifted, his sneakers sinking into the warped surface.

"Enough." Lucius's voice cut through the air like a blade.

The Principal's hollow gaze flicked to him. Lucius stepped forward, unhurried, his hands clasped neatly behind his back. His presence sharpened; icier, more deliberate.

You are in the way." Lucius said."

The Principal's mouth curled into a snarl. "You, of all people, know he belongs here."

Lucius laughed softly, smooth as polished glass but completely lacking in humor.

"Does he?" Lucius glanced at Louis, eyes gleaming with challenge. "Then why does he keep running? Maybe because deep down, he knows you will drown him."

The Principal's face twitched. The tension thickened as two massive forces pressed against the gym's fragile walls.

Then, the principal lunged.

Louis barely registered the blur of motion before Lucius intercepted the Principal with effortless precision. When they met, the air didn't just shake; it ruptured. A shockwave ripped through the gym, buckling the walls and floor as if the building itself recoiled.

Louis staggered, the world pitching on an unseen axis. The space twisted into a collapsing tunnel.

Lucius and the Principal stood locked together, time itself jamming as an unstoppable force met an immovable object.

***

As he stumbled across the rocky terrain of the Mexican Plateau, Reid Bowman murmured,

"The desert does not forgive. It does not forget. It does not care."

The wind carried heat like a curse, but the Strigoi's thoughts drifted to a month earlier, when he had saved the Foley family from the bloodlust of a drug cartel, only to be cast out like a leper. For all he knew, the cartel's bodies were still warm in the sand, their blood pooling into the cracked earth like an offering to the sun.

He had torn through them, a storm of fangs and fury, an instrument of vengeance cloaked in human flesh. Yet, the survivors met his outstretched hand not with gratitude but with revulsion.

"*What the hell are you?*" the father had whispered, hoarse with disbelief. The mother clutched her daughter to her chest, her sons behind her, shielding them from the one who had saved them. No thanks. No praise. Only horror.

Still, he admired their unity and Ellen Foley's willingness to stand between her children and him. So he left.

Now he wandered through the blistering wilderness. The scorching sand swallowed his footprints as soon as they were made. Once, he had walked among humans as a supernatural being, feared and respected. Now he was nothing. The sun stripped him bare, burning away his invincible shell and leaving him only regret.

The wind howled in his ears, a chorus of voices.

Lucius Rofocale: *You are not to harm Maricela Antonescu...*

Maricela Antonescu: *Avenge me!*

The dead. His sworn enemy. The unburied. Their whispers clawed at his mind like starving fingers, tearing apart his memories. Were they feasting on past triumphs, or warning of horrors yet to come? He could not tell.

Days bled into nights. The cold sand bit his flesh; the heat burned him raw. His head snapped up at the sound of shifting sand nearby, his nostrils flaring before he realized it was only the wind.

The hunter's reflex faded as quickly as it had come, leaving him with the hollow truth: the predator in him still rose with the shadows of night, but now he was prey. He did not thirst. He did not hunger. Yet, the suffering drove him forward. Something unseen, unknowable… a force greater than himself, carved its will into his bones.

Ahead, jagged mountains rose like stone sentinels, ancient and unyielding, towers of living death daring him to pass. In this desert crucible, where spirits were broken and reforged by unseen hands, he would be tested. His strength would fail. His will would crack. He would be beaten back into the dust from which he had emerged.

The Strigoi understood there was something worse than death: to live, to walk alone.

Humans fight for one another. I never understood it… until now.

The sun stripped him down to the bleeding core of his being, burning away every lie he had told himself. There would be no honor, no redemption, only the next step, and the one after that.

Still, the wind refused to let him go quietly. Somewhere inside its shifting currents, a low, deliberate voice spoke a single word: *Chicxulub… Chicxulub…* Each repetition fainter, as though whispered across eternity.

He froze, the horizon swimming in the heat, unable to tell if it was the desert speaking or his own mind betraying him. Then the whisper faded, leaving only the truth: stopping meant admitting he had nowhere left to go.

So he walked on, waiting for destiny's hand to seize and mold him for something greater.

***

Childhood Home of the Aitken Family in Albertson, NY
June 16th Mid-Afternoon

The house in Albertson had stood longer than George Aitken had been alive, but time had begun to settle into its bones. The family portraits were gone, their places patched and painted over, yet he could still feel the rough defects in the plaster where the nails once hung. The floorboards creaked beneath his boots, just as they had in his childhood, and the air carried the scent of old fabric mixed with the damp aroma of a looming summer storm seeping through the drafty windowpanes. It all felt like a voice whispering from his past.

George sat at the worn dining table, rolling his thumb over the smooth surface of his eye patch. The leather felt supple, broken in, and warmed by his skin, yet the phantom ache beneath it never left. Six months had passed since Anne's arrow took his eye, six months since they'd slipped through his grasp, but some wounds refused to fade. A cold tingle ran from the ruined socket down to his jaw, as if the nerve endings still hadn't accepted their loss.

The house was still, but not quiet. The wind had picked up, moaning through the eaves like a mournful wail, rattling the old windows in their frames. The air felt electric as if something significant were about to happen.

A glance outside told him it was already getting dark, though the clock swore it was only mid-afternoon. The sky had turned a bruised gray, heavy with the power of the gathering storm. The fading light warped everything it touched, including the skeletal trees, which clawed at the sky like desperate hands.

He exhaled slowly, resting his hands on the table. It had taken far too long, but the AI program his wife Josephine had built before her mummification had finally paid off. The encrypted messages pulled from a JESU leader's phone, captured during George's fatal strike against the order, had unraveled like a brittle thread. Now, at last, crucial pieces of a puzzle were finally revealed.

They were still out there... Jack. Anne Bishop. Those damn nephews. Somewhere.

K-N-O-C-K

Knuckles on wood, sharp and deliberate.

George didn't call out. No one came here without a reason. He stood, his boots heavy on the floorboards, and crossed the room. The cold brass lock bit into his skin before he turned the knob. The door groaned open, carrying with it the scent of damp earth and leather.

Brannigan stepped inside, trembling like a dog shaking off water. His coat was damp and darkened at the shoulders by the mist. He reeked of sweat, tobacco, and stale whisky.

George caught a flicker of hesitation in the aide's eyes before it vanished.

"You took your time," George rasped.

"I had to wait… wait for the messenger, sir," Brannigan stammered, his breath sour with coffee and liquor. He produced a folded sheet of paper and laid it on the table.

George frowned. "You had to have a drink first. Did you bring me more bad news?"

"Word from Pergamon, my master," Brannigan swallowed, stepping back. "I… I did not… not read it. Not this time."

George leaned over the table, his single eye burning into the courier.

"For your sake, it better be useful. Embellish again, and it won't get you ahead… it'll get you dead."

The paper was still warm, despite Pergamon being a world away, its fibers reeking of brimstone. Candlelight flickered across the ink, making the words gleam. The message was brief. Too brief. But enough.

AI program decrypts final JESU cellphone. One word: Ronkonkoma.

George crushed the paper in his hand, tugging at the edge of his patch.

"Our hunt is no longer directionless," his voice was iron. "Ronkonkoma. Perfect. A cursed place. And the place where all accounts will finally be settled."

The wind outside howled, seeping into the house, nearly extinguishing the candle. The temperature dropped, the cold gnawing at his knuckles. Thunder cracked, shaking the glass.

"We move East. Immediately," George ordered. His voice was steady, but edged.

Brannigan hesitated, rubbing at his jaw, stubble scraping faintly. "Where, Sir?"

George traced a gloved finger across the map. The paper crinkled under his touch.

"Everywhere. Block by block. House by house. We don't stop until we find them."

Brannigan exhaled, nodding once. "And when we do?"

George finally let go of his patch. The warmth beneath it eased the ache.

"We finish it. I will have what I have always sought." He let the words settle. "Jack was as good as dead the moment he ran. I just haven't put him in the ground yet."

Outside, the sky swallowed the last of the afternoon light. The wind rattled the windows, and the house groaned in protest, as if it, too, sensed what was coming.

The game was nearing its conclusion. George Aitken didn't play for fun. He played for keeps.

***

Kings Park, NY
Time Unknown

Route 25A meandered through overgrown meadows, its cracked pavement choked with weeds. Leafless trees revealed glimpses of abandoned homes all along the two-lane road. Jack tightened his grip on the wheel, knuckles white, while Jouris sat stiff beside him, the AM radio hissing with static.

A broadcast drifted in, its voice flat and emotionless:

Jouris shook his head. "Shit."

"That's enough for me." Jack snapped the radio off before the next grim statistic. The dashboard clock read 4 PM.

Black clouds hung low over the Sunken Meadow Parkway, smothering the daylight and adding to the already unnatural darkness. Steering through a maze of abandoned cars had cost them precious time. The air smelled of rot, heavy with impending rain.

The further they drove, the more the world closed in, with narrowing roads, trees twisted together, and tangled branches blotting out what little light remained. Then the hospital rose in the distance, a high-rise that might have been a hotel, if hotels were built to keep people in… forever.

They turned onto Kings Park Boulevard. Out of the corner of his eye, Jack thought he saw movement in the woods, but his damaged glasses and the dim light left him unsure. Dominating the landscape and looming overhead was a rusted iron sign, its black letters stark against the ominous sky:

KINGS PARK PSYCHIATRIC HOSPITAL.

A cold chill seized Jack, the same one he'd felt at Stull Cemetery, Kansas, the portal to Hell where he'd once retrieved an unholy relic. It was a few years ago, but he knew places like that never let go. Kings Park gave him the same menacing feeling, made worse with Louis in danger of being lost forever. Jack shoved the nightmare memories aside and pulled off into the overgrowth. Dead leaves crunched beneath the tires as they parked behind a tangle of bushes and skeletal trees. The air was filled with the scent of damp earth and something fouler: decomposition.

Lightning filled the sky, illuminating the iron letters in an eerie white glow.

"We go on foot from here," Jack murmured.

They collected their supplies and started toward the building, stepping carefully over the remains of bodies still in hospital gowns. One stood out, clad in a tattered uniform. Jack knelt by the skull, a neat hole in its crown, and found what he was looking for: a handgun in the grass. He examined it, but the clip wouldn't budge.

"Suicide," Jack muttered. "Won't be of much use." He stuffed it in his knapsack anyway.

A gust hissed through the overgrowth, carrying eerie whispers and moans that raised the hair on his neck.

Then, they spotted it.

"That's Building Seven," Jouris pointed to a ten-story tower in the distance. "Medical and surgical center. The heart of the place. Covered corridors connect to the admin offices and patient housing. Best place to get our bearings."

Moving through knee-high grass, Jack asked, "How do you know your way around?"

"Years ago, I took some doctors diving on a wreck in Long Island Sound. Some junket with pharmaceutical reps. Instead of meeting me at the marina, they had me pick them up here. Gave me a tour." His jaw tightened. "To this day, I wish they hadn't."

Jack's lips twitched. "Is it as disturbing in the daylight?"

Jouris felt mud squish under his boots. "Worse in some ways. Hard to forget what this place was built for, day or night."

"Good to know. Next time we'll come at noon."

Jack and Jouris froze. Their instincts screamed at them to run, but they crept closer.

Ahead lay a heap of severed limbs. Some were fresh, the flesh pink and slicked with blood. Others were blackened, putrid, jagged bones thrusting from the torn meat. The stench was unbearable.

The wind died for a heartbeat.

Drip… drip… blood hitting the grass.

Jouris swore, "What the f---?"

"Someone's still here," Jack whispered. "And still cutting."

"For Christ's sake, why?" Jouris asked.

Drip… drip… the sound again, steadier now, like the field itself was bleeding.

Jack shook his head. "I don't think I want to know."

The thought of Louis, pale, sweating, slipping further away, hardened Jack's resolve. His son had no time left. Whatever waited here, no matter how vile, had to matter. It had to give them a way back.

"Let's find what we came for and get the hell out of here."

Movement flickered at the edge of the trees. At first, shadows shifted between the skeletal trunks, but then figures began to emerge. Dozens of them, their hospital gowns fluttering in the wind like tattered flags. Some stood still, watching. Others swayed, mouths opening and closing like broken machines.

Then, together, they began to move.

"It's a herd of infected!" Jack shouted. The sky tore open, unleashing a mix of torrential rain, sleet, and large snowflakes.

A wave of bodies lurched forward, arms outstretched, jaws working, exhibiting spasmodic and unnatural movements.

Jouris's head turned on a swivel. "They're surrounding us."

A scream cut through the storm. "This way! NOW!"

A woman in a blue sweater, buttoned only at the top, with pristine white hospital shoes, waved frantically from an open doorway.

Jack and Jouris didn't hesitate. They sprinted, their boots sliding through the blood-soaked dirt, lungs burning, decay and sweat thick in the air.

The herd closed in.

They dove through the doorway. The slam of the door silenced the storm as if someone had torn the sky's throat out.

STAGE VII:
SUBJECTION OR DELIVERANCE?

<h1 style="text-align:center"><u>CHAPTER 1</u></h1>

Basement of the Safehouse at Lake Ronkonkoma
June 16th, 10:45 PM

While Jack and Jouris fled the CWD herd, Anne pushed forward with Louis's
exorcism, still searching for a pathway to salvation…

The wind howled like a pack of angry wolves. Upstairs, the windows rattled as hurricane-force gusts battered the house. Even in the basement, Anne could hear snow lashing against the glass, a blizzard's blindfold tightening around the world. The old bones of the safehouse moaned in protest against the storm's wrath.

She didn't know if Jack and Jouris would make it back, or if there'd even be anything left of Louis to save when they did. Still, Anne stood in the center of the room, fingers clenched around her rosary beads. Candlelight flickered wildly, like a birthday cake threatened by an unseen breath.

Shadows shifted across The Entity, revealing something grotesquely human. It grinned, its teeth yellowed, fangs jutting out like those of a vampire. Patchy skin stretched over its skull, and the smell of rot seeped from its pores. Its fingernails were jagged and split, blackened as if burned from within.

But the eyes. The eyes were the worst.

Pools of stagnant black liquid, like tea-colored swamp water. Jaundiced sclera framed them, with something alive swirling just beneath the surface.

The Entity barked out laughter, guttural coughs twisted into snarls. Its head jerked back, vertebrae snapping as muscles convulsed. Then it fixed on her, smiling as if to say, *'Your move.'*

Anne stepped forward, cross trembling in her hand. "I know what you tried to do."

The Entity cocked its head, neck popping.

Do you?

"You tried to lure David into the lake."

The basement seemed to constrict around her words. The Entity's lips peeled back to reveal jagged teeth.

"You fear him."

For a moment, the amusement in its face cracked like ice beneath a boot. The air turned colder, enough that Anne's breath plumed in the candlelight.

Fear? It murmured, lips curling in disdain. *You mistake pity for fear, little detective.*

"You wouldn't waste such effort unless you were afraid."

Anne raised the cross higher.

"Begone, then, in the name of the Father, and of the Son, and of the Holy Spirit."

The Entity didn't move, but the candle flames recoiled, bending away from it.

Anne felt the pressure tighten in her chest, stealing her breath. Determined, she pressed on.

"I adjure thee, thou unclean spirit, by the name of the Father and of the Son and of the Holy Ghost, that if thou wilt not come out and depart from this servant of Jesus Christ, then confess your fears."

The Entity's skin writhed as if worms crawled beneath its flesh. Its fingers twitched, nails scraping the air. For a moment, its throat bobbed as if swallowing something back.

Then it smiled again, but desperation clung to it.

The darkness falls, it rasped, the words thick and wet. *The end you preach against is already here, and you…* Its voice broke into a canine growl. *You are losing.*

The storm outside shrieked. A loose shutter slammed against the house like a frantic fist.

Anne steadied her voice. "What do you fear about David?"

The Entity's mouth stretched impossibly wide. Another bark of laughter exploded from it, rattling the walls. Then, in a hiss like a cobra's warning:

George Aitken isn't dead.

The words slithered into the basement, heavy with malice.

Anne froze. For a heartbeat, the room tilted, the thought of George alive scraping at her composure. If he truly breathed, their nightmare had only begun.

She forced in a deep breath and began the Lord's Prayer.

"Our Father, who art in heaven, hallowed be Thy name."

The Entity laughed again, sharp and jagged, but beneath was an undercurrent… an edge, a crack in its certainty.

"Thy kingdom come, Thy will be done, on Earth as it is in Heaven."

Its lips mocked her, forming soundless words, mouthing the prayer in parody.

She stepped closer. "Tell me your name."

I am the Devil. Beelzebub. I am known by many names, it hissed, its voice a fractured chorus.

Anne sneered angrily, "You lie."

The Entity's mouth twitched.

"I demand you return to Hell!" she thundered.

It scoffed, tilting its head. *I am not from there.*

A knot tightened in her gut, but she didn't let it show.

Steadying her breath, she went on the offensive.

"Then what do you fear about David?" she pressed.

The Entity's eyes rolled back. Teeth gnashed, and its nails curled into its palms, drawing a thick, black fluid like blood.

At last, it whispered, so softly she almost missed it.

Anne caught it, but feigned confusion. The basement seemed to hold its breath.

"You don't make any sense. That's nothing to fear."

The Entity's face twisted as it tried to read her, but she refused to give it the satisfaction of a reaction.

She turned and climbed the stairs. A shutter slammed upstairs like a frantic fist, and the house seemed to exhale with the storm. She would go back to David and tell him to pray.

***

Kings Park Psychiatric Hospital, Kings Park, NY
Time Unknown

Across the island, as Anne's prayers fought the storm, the herd hammered at Kings Park's fire door…

The infected pounded on the steel, fists drumming in ravenous rhythm, drowning out the snow and ice battering the safety glass as the storm intensified. Another door slammed behind them, and the darkened interior of the building swallowed Jack and Jouris whole.

The air inside was worse than anything outside.

The smell hit like a punch in the face… a sickening mix of feces, urine, vomit, and rotting flesh so dense it seemed to devour the air. The foulness was almost physical, burning their throats and assaulting their nostrils like a brutal beating from a street gang.

Jouris gagged, staggering against the wall. Jack pressed a hand to his nose, but breathing through his mouth did nothing. The scent pushed against their lungs, turning each breath into something wet and smothering.

Their rescuer seemed oddly unaffected by the smell of death that surrounded them. She wore a long-sleeved, hospital-white dress with an apron and cap. Her spotless shoes whispered over the floor. She smiled cheerfully,

"I am Nurse Reilly. Welcome to Kings Park."

She led them past a gurney, frozen in rust, piled high with soiled sheets and clothes stiff with blood and crusted filth. Jack's boots squelched. He didn't look down.

"Can you direct us to the records room?" Jack asked.

"This way," she replied, moving briskly, as if she hadn't heard him.

Louis doesn't have time for us to get lost in here, Jack thought, hurrying to keep pace with her.

They passed one dim corridor after another, each doorway revealing even crueler horrors than the last:

A corpse sat on a toilet, its jaw slack as if in mid-sentence. Its eyes were sunken, and its hands pale, vein-riddled, and frozen in place.

Across the hall, a woman lay in bed, an IV still taped to her arm, the tube empty, with dried blood crusting at the venipuncture site.

At the nurses' station, where the corridors crossed, the hallway clock read 3:55 a.m. A figure in scrubs sat motionless. At first, Jack thought it was another corpse, until he saw skin drawn tight over bone, withered and black: mummified.

"That's just Jennifer." Nurse Reilly hardly looked at the figure and kept walking.

Iron doors lined the hall. Moans leaked through gaps in rusted door frames. Something pounded on one from the other side. Jack's breath caught as they passed an open door.

Inside, a patient sat on the floor, playing with the strings of his gown. He looked up. No nose. No ears. The black, cauterized pits in his face smoked faintly in the cold. Jack's insides turned as if the air itself had thickened into stomach acid.

"What the hell did they do here?" Jack muttered. *God help Louis if we're too late.*

Jouris shot Jack a disbelieving look, shaking his head.

"Ah... visitors," a voice said.

A man stepped from the dark; his lab coat stiff with blood, a stained surgical mask hung loosely around his neck, and his eyes were fever-bright. Behind him, Nurse Reilly beamed, her gloved fingers twitching.

"I am Dr. Everett Langston."

"Did you know we once cared for over nine thousand patients?" Reilly chirped.

"Opened in 1885… but all good things must end."

Jack's fists clenched, the pulse in his head throbbed.

"The staff left," Reilly went on. "We stayed. We had patients. So much work left to do."

Her smile widened as she looked up at Dr. Langston. "And the doctor… still had so many unanswered questions."

Langston sighed. "I am very close. Each resection, each dissection, brings me closer to a cure. But I'm running out of subjects."

On a side table, rusty surgical tools were overshadowed by candlelight. Scalpels lay in neat, bloodstained rows. Two gurneys streaked with dried blood stood ready.

Jack's mind raced between the sickening spectacle before him and Louis.

If the records were here, where would he store them…

Langston's gaze shifted to Jack and Jouris. "You'll do just fine."

Jack's eyes darted from the instruments to the doorway, bile rising in his throat.

"I'm trying to slow the spread of CWD," Langston said mildly.

"When people are bitten, I remove certain parts. Eventually, I'll find a cure."

"You're out of test subjects?" Jouris said. "Maybe someone should put you under the knife."

He drove a left hook into Langston's jaw as Jack swung a rusty IV pole, the blow catching Reilly in the head.

A man in tattered janitor's overalls burst from a side hall, swinging a metal pipe. A faded name patch dangled from his chest by a single stitch.

"RUN!"

Jack and Jouris bolted after him through a labyrinth of dark corridors, as patients screamed and clawed at the bars of their cages and voices rose in raw, animal cries. Somewhere in the distance, a muffled crack of thunder rolled through the walls, the storm that raged over Anne battering Kings Park, too.

They skidded past the nurses' station again. The hallway clock still read 3:55 AM. Jack's gut turned. No time had passed. Or worse, time no longer existed here at all.

***

David's Room in the Safehouse at Lake Ronkonkoma

David's room smelled of candle wax and old wood. Unease settled in the air like dust after a building collapse, as if the walls sensed what was coming. Outside, the storm lashed the house with the steady crack of a lion tamer's whip.

"David, you need to pray, right now."

A candle flickered on the nightstand, its flame quivering in the heavy stillness. David sat hunched at the edge of the bed, his hands clasped, his knuckles bone-white. His arm, once burly and strong, was now frail as a twig. But it wasn't his wasted frame that frightened Anne.

It was his eyes, hollow, fading, drifting between worlds.

His head barely moved. "I don't think I can do it." His voice was a whisper, frail and hopeless. "I'm not even sure it means anything anymore."

Without hesitation, Anne took his cold hands in hers, squeezing hard enough to break through his numbness.

"Do it anyway," she urged. "Even if you doubt."

David rubbed his thumb against his palm in a familiar looping rhythm, something he'd done since childhood to push back the chaos in his head. Silence stretched between them, thick as molasses.

David swallowed. His mouth was dry, his throat tight, as if something inside him resisted… like fingers gripping his lips, desperate to keep him from speaking.

But he did.

A whisper at first, the words broken, slipping between shallow breaths.

"God… I'm not sure if you can hear me. I don't even know if I can hear you. But… if you're there…"

A sudden, violent tremor tore through his body.

The candle's flame surged, casting twisting shadows across the room. The temperature plunged, the cold wrapping around him like a wet shroud. The air grew thick, electric, pushing against his skin with an unbearable force.

He couldn't breathe, or he was hyperventilating. Smoke filled his nostrils, and the phantom taste of iron and earth spread across his tongue.

His vision blurred. Then…a voice.

Neither Anne's nor his own.

A voice from deep within him, or outside of time itself.

Look beyond.

The words shook him. His mind snapped open, not gently, like a door creaking ajar, but like a dislocated bone popping back into place. His ESP roared to life. The room vanished, swallowed in black fire. His body jerked as if yanked from his skin. Suddenly, he was somewhere else.

A void stretched out before him, infinite and endless. At its center, something stirred.

Louis's doppelgänger screeched, writhing, its form unstable, as if something were pulling it apart from the inside.

And beyond that, he saw Louis.

His real brother. Not the twisted imitation, but Louis himself, flickering like a shadow behind tinted glass. His hand reached out, fingers outstretched toward something unseen, something he couldn't grasp. He was trapped.

David's thumb traced slow circles in his palm, his anchor against anxiety. But the motion broke. Something icy forced its way between thumb and palm, prying them apart. The darkness itself seemed to resist his intent.

David growled, his voice hoarse and trembling, "He doesn't belong to you."

The doppelgänger turned its hollow eyes toward him. "Fuck you… He's mine!"

David gasped as something cold and wet coiled around his limbs, dragging him into the abyss. He struggled, but it curled through his veins like ice.

You are nothing. The whispers dug into his flesh. *You are weak. You are lost.*

But another voice, rising like a storm, cut through. Low and steady, older than time:

As a prophet of Revelation, you possess power. Sometimes, anger is necessary to break the strings that bind us.

David's breath hitched. Rage, raw and unreasoned, surged through him. He let it go. He fought back.

His body convulsed as his consciousness pierced the veil, a mind-shattering rupture searing through his skull. Still, he pushed harder against the doppelgänger, against The Entity's lies, and the decaying layers of corruption binding his brother.

Then, he reached for him.

Louis's head snapped up. His eyes locked on David's, wild with recognition. His fingers stretched farther…

The doppelgänger fractured, its limbs bending at impossible angles. It shrieked, a sound neither human nor earthly… ripping through reality itself.

David gasped, snapping back into his body. He was drenched in sweat, his heart hammering so fiercely it rattled his ribs. Anne's grip was the only thing anchoring him to reality.

"David?"

He looked up, vision blurry, and his hands trembling. But now he knew; he had seen the truth.

"Anne, Louis isn't gone. He can still be saved."

Her breath caught, not from relief, but from the shiver running down her spine. The candle wavered, its flame bowing toward the draft hissing through the window as thunder rattled the pane. If David was right, saving Louis meant confronting what still held him. Anne wasn't sure which terrified her more: losing him or going back into the basement.

Somewhere beneath the storm's roar, the faintest whisper lingered—*Look beyond.*

David froze, unsure if it came from within, or if it was still speaking to him.

***

At The Same Time That David Reached Out to Him…

The cold clung to Louis's skin as it had in the safehouse. A metallic tang coated the back of his throat, like the penny he once dared himself to hold on his tongue.

From behind, Lucius's voice rang out, sharp, deliberate, almost ceremonial.

"Run, Louis."

The gym's far door stood half open, a sliver of light beckoning. But the Principal's voice roared at Louis, warped and inhuman, twisting the air like heat above asphalt.

"You are mine!"

The gym buckled. The walls folded inward like a great mouth, shadows slithering into the gaps. The hardwood floor shuddered beneath Louis's sneakers, then shifted, the planks giving way to something cold and slick, like wet stone, that pulsed faintly under his weight.

He froze, muscles locked, torn between the light and the voice. His hands began to flap, a signal only he could understand and one he couldn't stop.

Lucius spoke again, each word like a hammer striking iron.

"You do not belong here."

Was this a command… or a revelation? Was he truly free to choose, or was every step still part of someone else's design?

"You are meant for something more."

The words dragged up a memory of David, his voice tight with conviction. Louis's lips moved before he realized.

"Prophets."

And then, clear, urgent, and impossible to ignore, David's voice.

"LOUIS!"

His chest tightened. He pictured David's face. Their mission burned in his mind, and with it a single thought: *Some dreams never die.*

He clenched his fist. *Others are worth fighting for.*

He ran.

The gym door exploded open, its frame warping into a shape that should not exist. He stumbled through, nearly falling as the world snapped into something unfamiliar, the air tasting of copper and bitter water.

***

Meanwhile, in Jerusalem

As fragile hope flickers on Long Island, where storm clouds smother the sky, stomachs ache with hunger, and the very air tastes of blood. The shadow of extinction rises here. Prosperine's stranglehold on her dominion tightens, and Lucius prepares to claim an old debt…

The monolithic temple of polished black stone loomed high above Jerusalem, a blight against the heavens. At its entrance stood four colossal statues of demons carved from veined obsidian, their grotesque forms towering over the gathering crowd. Their twisted faces leered with jagged fangs, sunken eyes burning with a violet flame, and horns like rams, thrusting skyward in defiance.

Their massive, skeletal stone wings stretched outward as if to embrace the weak and broken worshipers. Long claws, cracked and chipped with age, appeared eager to grasp those who dared to hesitate.

Each demon bore a name etched into its pedestal, names long forgotten by mortal tongues yet whispered still in nightmares. Their bodies contorted in mocking gestures of welcome. One held its clawed hands outstretched, fingers curled as if plucking invisible strings of fate; another had its head thrown back in a silent scream, its forked tongue trapped between its pointed teeth.

They did not stay silent.

As the worshippers approached, faces gaunt with hunger, the statues addressed them.

Their voices slithered through the air like smoke, an eerie blend of whispers and growls, ancient and bone-rattling. The stone lips cracked open, dust falling as their voices boomed in the night air, heavy as thunder and intoxicating as venom.

Enter and behold the new world.

Bend your knees or be broken.

The Princess awaits your adoration.

Gasps rippled through the crowd, while others shuddered, clutching their ears. A few dropped to their knees before reaching the temple doors, overwhelmed by the power of the voices that were too much to resist.

The air reeked of acrid incense laced with the copper tang of blood, a corruption that clung to their lungs. Inside the temple, torches blazed with an unnatural blue flame, casting ghostly shadows across the obsidian walls.

The worshipers gathered in hushed reverence. Some trembled, while others stood in rapture. They had answered the call, drawn by hunger, fear, and the command of their new goddess.

Prosperine stood at the head of the temple, draped in flowing ceremonial robes of deep crimson and midnight blue. Gold embroidery traced symbols long since banished from human memory. A crown of onyx and rubies adorned her brow; her jet-black hair cascading down her back. Her hands, adorned with rings that shimmered with an unnatural fire, spread wide in mock benediction.

She smiled, and the very air shuddered.

Behold,

the temple of my glory.

You, the starving.

You, the desperate.

You have cried out for bread…

or blood.

She gestured toward the grand altar, a vast slab of white marble veined with crimson streaks that pulsed faintly, as though the stone drank offerings unceasingly.

And so I answer:

Here is your blood.

The crowd rippled, uneasy murmurs rising like a tide.

At her right, Lucius Rofocale, Prime Minister of Hell, stepped forward. His black robes shimmered with gold, the fabric swirling and shifting like liquid metal. His high collar framed his foxlike face, and the symbols of Hell glowed faintly along his sleeves, pulsating like a heartbeat. A chain of broken crucifixes and shattered prayer beads hung around his neck.

In one gloved hand, he tossed something repeatedly.

Hooded attendants dragged forward sacrificial victims. Their hands were bound behind their backs, and their feet shuffled across the cold stone floor, one from each of the world's great faiths.

A Christian priest.

A Muslim scholar.

A Jewish rabbi.

Lucius's gaze fixed on the last: Rabbi Shimon Levi, whose defiance had nearly cost Lucius dearly. The Rabbi had raised a Golem from the sands of Lake Waccamaw, a creature so powerful that it had once defeated Lucius in battle and rendered the Strigoi useless against it.

Lucius rolled a mezuzah across his palm, catching the torchlight.

"Raise a Golem on me, will you?" he sneered, letting the mezuzah fall to the stone floor with a dull clink.

In his other hand, he revealed two smooth, cold stones, the eyes of the Rabbi's guardian. Lucius squeezed them in his fist until blood welled from between his fingers. The stones ground together, screaming as if resisting annihilation. When he opened his palm, the stones were gone, reduced to fine ash that slithered off his skin like smoke.

The rabbi's breath caught, but he stayed silent.

Lucius leaned close, his voice a hushed whisper, meant only for him. "No words, Rabbi? No prayers?"

Rabbi Levi met his gaze. "You will fall."

Lucius tilted his head with a sly smile. "Your faith is touching, Rabbi, but it is misplaced."

The evil Lord signaled for a demon to approach, bearing a pillow with a jeweled object whose gemstones sparkled like captured stars.

Lucius addressed the crowd. "Let us begin."

He took the ritual blade, a long, curved dagger etched with intricate symbols. Its grip was wrapped in the hide of some long-forgotten beast. The metal felt warm, as if it were eager for a kill.

The air trembled as he pressed the blade to the rabbi's throat.

One single motion. One single moment.

The dagger sang as it cut, a thin metallic note that lingered in the vaulted chamber.

Blood didn't fall; it spiraled upward, twisting through the torchlight in slow motion, as though weightless. It shimmered, forming the faint outline of the Golem before splashing against the altar. The blood hissed as it struck the slab, steam curling into the air. The scent that followed was not decay, but something impossibly clean… ozone and scorched faith.

Then from the Rabbi's lips, as his knees buckled:

"Shema Yisrael Adonai Eloheinu Adonai Echad…"

(Hear O Israel, the Lord our God, the Lord is one…"

The last syllable, *Echad,* hung trembling in the air.

For a heartbeat, the word echoed again… not from the Rabbi's mouth, but from the sanctuary walls. Then from the crowd. It rose softly at first, as if the word was escaping from their throats without permission. Each listener felt it vibrate behind their eyes, beneath their skin, a shared whisper no one could silence.

Echad…Echad…Echad

The echo withered to a hum, then to nothing, leaving only the wet hiss of blood cooling on the stone.

The congregation recoiled; some wept, others buried their faces in their hands.

For an instant, the Rabbi's shadow lingered, upright, defiant, the mouth still moving in silent prayer. Then it collapsed and vanished, leaving only the faint echo of that single word… *Echad.*

Lucius turned, his face alight with dark joy. "Let this be a lesson," he cried. "The old faiths are dead."

A murmur swelled through the crowd, broken at first, then rising in unison like a chant:

"The old faiths are dead… the old faiths are dead…"

He aimed the bloodied dagger at Prosperine. She raised her arms, basking in the chorus of submission.

Lucius shouted, "Worship belongs to her!"

The priest and the Muslim scholar stood as haunting reminders of the downfall of the great religions.

And the world held its breath.

CHAPTER 2

Kings Park Psychiatric Hospital, Kings Park, NY
Time Unknown

The trio ran blindly as a clap of thunder rattled the windows and the storm raged on. They wove through dark corridors, the copper scent of blood mingling with decay and desperation. Dressed in janitor's overalls, his white hair betraying his age, the man still moved quickly, his hunched frame lit by the bobbing beam of his flashlight. Jack's lungs burned, his legs ached, but he pushed forward, his pulse hammering in his skull.

Around them, the asylum echoed with pitiful moans from the locked rooms. The distant scrape of something dragging across the floor made them glance back, half-expecting the crazed doctor and his nurse to be closing in.

The man guided them through a rusted doorway and down a narrow stairwell. The air was damp, thick with mildew, like a shower stall left uncleaned for months. A hallway stretched before them, its walls marked by age and something darker, ending in a barricaded door.

He shoved it open, revealing a cluttered room lit by dozens of flickering candles. Books lined the walls in haphazard stacks, loose papers scattered across the floor. At the center, a wooden table sagged beneath wax drippings, books, and a single tarnished scalpel.

Jack and Jouris caught their breath as the man barricaded the door again. It groaned painfully before slamming shut. He turned, breathing heavily, his face etched with exhaustion and something deeper... fear.

"What the hell were you doing in there?" His voice was hoarse, rough, like someone who hadn't spoken in years.

The flashlight's glow caught on a stitched badge hanging by a thread from his overalls:

J. O'Malley, Custodial Staff.

Jack hesitated, "The nurse saved us from a herd of the infected. But once we were inside, it didn't take long to figure out what they were doing." His fingers curled into a fist. "The amputated limbs outside, the patients locked in those rooms. What the fuck is that doctor up to?"

The rescuer gave a bitter, breathless laugh. "He calls it research."

Jouris narrowed his eyes. "Research on what?"

"Chronic Wasting Disease. That's what he calls it."

A cold weight settled into Jack's gut.

The man ran his hand over his face. "Langston used to be a real doctor. A good one, before all this. When the state shut down Kings Park, he and Nurse Reilly volunteered to stay behind. Said they'd wait until every patient was placed somewhere safe."

He let out a dry, humorless laugh. "But the world fell apart before they could move anyone. And Langston... he had other plans."

Jack fidgeted under the table with his wedding ring. "Go on."

"Langston thought if he could stop the disease before it reached the brain, he could save people. That's when the amputations started."

Jouris stiffened. "He cut them apart?"

The man nodded. "At first, he waited for symptoms. But when the disease didn't behave as he expected, he grew desperate. Then he stopped waiting. He began preemptively cutting," his lips trembled. "It stopped being about saving anyone a long time ago."

Jack's mind replayed the pile of limbs stacked outside Building #7 like discarded meat. His stomach churned.

"And Reilly?" Jouris asked.

Through gritted teeth, he answered angrily, "She was always like that. Even before it all went bad. The patients called her *The Butcher.* Langston's the brain, but Reilly?" He shook his head. "She enjoys it."

Jack dragged a hand down his face, bile rising in his throat.

"They were going to cut us open next," Jouris muttered.

"Of course they were." The man's eyes darted. "They're running out of bodies."

Silence enveloped the room, dense and oppressive.

"You still haven't answered my question." His tone cooled, edged with suspicion.

Jack and Jouris exchanged a glance. Jack swallowed hard, wiping sweat from his brow. "We were looking for the Records Room."

The man's expression darkened. "For what?"

"Papers on a patient named Billy Clifford," Jouris said evenly.

The man stiffened, his eyes narrowing. He stepped back. "Why? What are you looking for?" His voice had taken on a guarded tone, as if they'd asked the wrong question.

Jack faltered, Jouris spoke cautiously, "This will sound insane, but we think Billy's brother, Lyle Clifford, well, his spirit has been reaching out to us."

The man grimaced. His hands gripped the table so tightly that his knuckles went white. His shoulders tensed, and his gaze flickered to the sheet-covered walls. He swallowed, as if choking on words long buried.

Then he whispered, "Lyle Clifford was my brother."

Silence.

The air thickened. The candle flames waved wildly, like a window had opened, letting a breeze in, causing the shadows to stretch and dance on the walls.

Billy sat down slowly, his breath uneven. "You've seen him too?" His voice cracked. "I have, but I doubted. I mean, I'm at Kings Park. That's supposed to mean I'm crazy."

Jack and Jouris stayed quiet, letting it sink in.

Billy's trembling fingers traced deep scratches in the table; Lyle's name had been carved into the wood.

Jack chose his words carefully. "We saw his name written on the wall. In blood."

Billy flinched, grinding his teeth. "I know. I left it there."

Jack and Jouris traded a look.

Billy fought to keep his composure. His voice softened, "When the world collapsed, food shortages, riots, the aides walked off. Locked the doors and never looked back."

Jack and Jouris listened.

"And you survived how?" Jouris asked

Billy shook his head, eyes distant. "I fought off scavengers, addicts, people who'd kill me for my shoes. Aside from Langston and Reilly, and the infected… I'm the last one."

He leaned forward, candlelight deepening the shadows on his gaunt face. "I stayed because I had nowhere else to go. My parents died years ago. Nobody visited. I just kept doing what I always did." He exhaled unevenly, his fingers digging into his temples. "Maybe that was the point. I survived. Lyle didn't."

Jack's throat tightened. "What about Lyle?"

Billy hesitated. "What's so important about my brother?"

Jack's voice dropped. "Something is happening to my son, Louis. We've seen signs. They all lead here. Lyle isn't just haunting us. He's trying to tell us something."

Jack handed him the Boy Scout Skill Award.

Billy flinched. He gripped the brass piece tightly, as if he intended to crush it. His voice broke. "I was his big brother. His protector. But I couldn't shield him from that thing. I failed him."

His breath shuddered. Billy whispered, "I never saw it."

Jouris frowned. "Saw what?"

Billy's pupils widened, trying to remember something from a nightmare that never ended.

"This thing inside your son... I never saw it. But I felt it. Inside me. I heard it."

The room grew colder. The candle flames thrashed, as if some unseen force had brushed past them.

Jouris's gaze shifted to the white sheets draped over the walls. His stomach tightened. "Why keep the walls covered?"

Billy exhaled, trembling. "Reflections. They're entry points."

Jack felt a cold shiver crawl up his spine.

"I started feeling it before it all fell apart," Billy whispered. "Like something was watching. Not scavengers. Not patients. Something else." His voice shook. "One day, I saw movement. Not in the room… in the mirror."

He swallowed. "It was watching me. Studying me."

Jack mouthed to Jouris: *Mirror.*

Jouris nodded. "And then?"

Billy's voice dropped lower. "And then… it smiled."

Jack's mind flashed to David, his fear of the closet, the way he covered up the mirrors, fixated on sensations no one else noticed. Maybe it hadn't been fear at all. Maybe it was the same presence.

The wind howled. A door creaked in the corridor.

Jack leaned toward Billy. "You said you covered them because it was watching you through them?"

Billy nodded. "I don't just believe it. I know it."

Jack clenched his fists. "At the safehouse, we've all seen things. Lyle's ghost, the writing on the mirror, it's all connected. Don't you see? If it watches you through mirrors, we might reach Louis the same way."

Jouris exhaled sharply. "We need to get back. Now."

Jack turned back to Billy. "Come with us."

Billy shook his head. "No."

Jack blinked. "Why not?"

"This is my home. My prison. My sentence."

"Billy, this place is…"

"A graveyard? I know." Billy gave a bitter laugh. "But it's the only home I've had for sixty years."

His tone softened. "I've spent my whole life inside these walls. Out there, I wouldn't last a minute."

Jack felt an unexpected pang: maybe respect, or perhaps regret.

Billy pressed a rusty key into Jack's palm. "For Lyle. Don't let what happened to us happen to you. It'll get you out through the old admin wing. Whatever's happening with Louis, and with the mirrors," he gestured to the covered walls, "it's all connected."

Jack nodded, his fingers tightening around the key.

Jouris tugged his sleeve. "We don't know how much time Louis has left."

Jack looked back one last time. "You're sure?"

Billy smiled faintly. "I was never meant to leave this place."

"It's penance, I suppose."

Jack hesitated, then extended his hand.

Billy looked at it for a moment and gripped it firmly.

"Go, save your boy."

Jack nodded. He and Jouris slipped into the dark corridor, leaving Billy alone in the flickering candlelight.

***

Back in Jerusalem. After the Dedication of Prosperine's Temple

Torches lined the marble columns, their flickering light casting jagged shadows that guided Tatiana into Prosperine's inner sanctum. The air was heavy with incense and the copper tang of charred sacrifices, while unseen spirits whispered through the chamber, their murmurs rising and falling like a restless tide.

Prosperine sat at the head of the chamber, her throne carved from fiery red stone, its glossy surface fused with the faces of lost souls, their expressions frozen in agony. She watched with casual amusement as Tatiana entered, her steps careful and precise.

Lucius stood nearby, his long coat splattered with fresh blood, the remnants of the ceremonial sacrifices pooling at his feet like discarded waste. His eyes gleamed in the firelight, filled with contempt.

Tatiana bowed stiffly before speaking. "They're leaving."

Her voice was steady but laced with something close to defiance.

"The demons. They're abandoning their posts. With the human population dwindling, there are fewer souls to claim. They say they have no purpose."

Lucius scoffed, his lips twisting into something that was neither a smile nor a snarl.

"They are weak."

He stepped forward, the sound of his boots echoing through the vast chamber.

"Purpose? They exist to serve. If they cannot, they will perish."

Prosperine nodded, her red eyes glittering with amusement.

"Collateral damage," she intoned, her voice resonant, almost god-like.

"When humanity is gone, a demon purge will be inevitable. The undeserving will be culled."

Lucius turned to Tatiana, his expression harsh and threatening. "That includes you, too."

Tatiana stiffened, her pulse hammering in her ears.

"I have served faithfully," she said, her tone edged with something unspoken. Then, she held her breath.

Lucius tilted his head. "Have you?"

His fingers twitched. Raising his hand, he added, "Perhaps you have outlived your usefulness."

Before he could strike, Prosperine raised a hand.

"No. Let her go."

She rose from her throne, studied her sharp black fingernails, and mused with airy dismissal,

"Her time will come."

Tatiana exhaled as Lucius stepped back, his murderous intent leashed… for now. Prosperine's smile widened as she waved her hands, shooing Tatiana away.

The Devil's Troika, George Aitken, Lucius, and Prosperine, was a three-headed monster of pure corruption. When she thought of them, she swore she could still smell brimstone and hear three mouths speaking as one, a chorus of damnation. She had given them loyalty and servitude; in return, she was nothing more than a pawn, a disposable asset.

Tatiana turned on her heel and strode from the chamber. The temple doors slammed shut behind her with a finality that echoed deep in her bones. She paused, cold air slapping her face and slicing through the rage coiling in her chest.

Looking skyward, she whispered, *"Is there any way in hell to light a comet from a single spark?"* She paused, the thought lingering, hardening into something sharper. *"Unless… the answer isn't in fire at all, but in what lies buried, waiting for the one bold enough to unearth it."*

She had worked so long that she never even considered freedom. She was a prisoner, shackled by duty and deceit. Loyal like a dog, with nothing to show for it but a collar.

But no longer. Now, she saw something else: open doors.

She clenched her fists, nails digging into her palms. She longed for something real. Not eternal servitude, or slow, inevitable oblivion. In that moment, she vowed revenge, defiantly declaring,

"It's time to break these chains!"

She had lived a life of service, just like her sister Nadia, one of Lucius's spies. Both believed in the cause, but she admitted neither had gotten it right. Nadia was gone, her blood another stain on Lucius's ledger. But Tatiana? She remained. And when she returned, Lucius would remember their names… both of them.

"You'll regret this," she whispered into the darkness. *"All of you. You let my sister die. You gave me nothing while I worked myself to the bone. You took a piece of me every day."*

Tatiana stepped into the night, and for the first time, she felt a sense of freedom.

Somewhere far across the world, the struggle between good and evil deepened… brothers caught in a storm that she could not see, but felt echoing through the dark.

And she had a plan.

***

Safehouse at Lake Ronkonkoma
Midnight June 17th

The moon crested the treetops, its sickly orange hue slanting through the grimy basement windows. Dust floated like ash in the beams of light. The air still reeked of sulfur, old sweat, and the strange metallic tang that always accompanied The Entity's presence. But Anne noticed it now. It was faint and subtle, like a ripple in stagnant water; something was shifting.

Still inside the iron cage, The Entity no longer hovered. It lay sprawled across the floor, its breath shallow but steady. Its arms, once raw with gashes that reopened with every movement, were now scabbing over. Bruises had faded from black-purple to mottled green. And for the first time in weeks, its lips weren't curled into that cruel, knowing sneer.

It no longer seemed interested in the caustic, mocking banter it had delighted in before; in fact, it had almost gone completely silent.

Anne stood near the basement stairs, holding her breath. Her fingers gripped the rosary so tightly that the beads dug into her skin.

She knew David was upstairs, alone in his room, eyes closed and his body trembling with concentration as he reached for Louis in the only way he could; through his mind. She thought she could almost hear David's voice, fraying the invisible thread binding Louis to The Entity, illuminating the darkness for his brother.

It was working.

The Entity, for all its arrogance and bile, was faltering. Divided. Struggling to hold its ground.

Anne stepped closer, and the temperature fell.

"I know what you are," she said, steady and unyielding. "And I know you're losing."

There was a long silence. Then, barely a whisper, like a summer wind stirring tall grass: *You presume too much, woman.*

Anne's eyes narrowed. "No. I see clearly now. You're flailing. You're afraid."

She knelt beside the cage, brushing Louis's damp hair from his sweat-soaked brow. His eyelids fluttered. She could feel his heart skitter beneath his ribs.

Anne laid her hand gently on his chest.

"I bind this wall of fear that surrounds Louis's heart in the Blood of Jesus," she prayed, her voice low but unwavering. "And in God's tender mercy, I break through this fortress in the Name of the Father, and of the Son, and of the Holy Spirit."

The Entity twitched and clenched its jaw. A faint sound, resembling an underwater scream, rippled through the air. The shadows in the room thickened and then convulsed as if recoiling.

Anne did not stop.

"In the name of Jesus, I break any unholy ties, links, and bondages between Louis and all evil sources and spirits."

The Entity jerked. Its eyes snapped open, but they were brown… not pitch-black or molten red. Just brown. Its lips moved, but no sound emerged.

"And I command all spirits associated with these unholy ties, links, and bondages to go immediately and directly to the foot of the cross."

The room shook violently. The windows rattled. Dust from the stone wall rained down as if the house were being torn apart.

"O Most Holy Spirit," Anne cried over the chaos, "enter into the empty spaces left by these spirits and fill Louis with your presence, love, and protection."

The Entity gasped, arched its back, and then collapsed to the ground.

"Please," Anne whispered, leaning close, "do not allow these spirits to return."

The room was quiet. Louis's eyes rolled back beneath his lids, his chest rising in stuttering gasps as though each breath were borrowed from a dwindling supply.

If this were a prizefight, Anne knew she'd won this round. The clock was still ticking. David's mind strained against the same darkness linking brother to brother. And yet…

The Entity remained.

***

Anne's footsteps echoed down the stairs, steady and quick, as if she had no fear the darkness might change its mind and swallow her whole if she lingered. David followed slowly, one hand brushing the wall for balance. The wooden steps groaned, and the air thickened, metallic and damp, as if the basement itself exhaled rust and mildew.

David paused before the final step.

"I don't like it down here," he muttered, his voice wavering between a whisper and a plea.

Anne turned, half in shadow, her features drawn, tired yet resolute. "I know," she gently reassured him. "But you need to see this."

Red candle wax pooled on the floor near the cage where Louis's body lay unnaturally still, dark puddles that almost looked like blood. David took a cautious step forward, his breath caught in his throat.

Louis's fingers twitched, purposeful, not a muscle spasm or reflex. A ripple coursed through his limbs. David's eyes widened as he saw the tension drain from his brother's shoulders. After days of pressure, Louis's fists unclenched like coiled springs unwinding. His lips barely moved, but a dry murmur emerged from them. His eyelids fluttered.

"He's fighting it," Anne declared, crouching beside the cage. She reached through the bars. David retreated, expecting Louis to attack her. Instead, Anne's fingertips brushed softly down his arm. "Whatever you've been doing, David, your meditations, reaching out to him, it's working."

381

David's knees buckled. He dropped onto the damp dirt floor, clutching his temple, as a searing pain shot through his skull, swift and brutal, like a live wire had been switched on in his brain.

Anne's head jerked up. "What's wrong?"

"My head," David gasped. "It's splitting... It feels like... like when I had the stroke."

Anne was already beside him, her hand gripping his shoulder. "It's probably the psychic energy you've been burning. You've been in near-constant contact, giving him pieces of yourself."

David nodded, but the pressure behind his eyes felt ready to burst.

"It's not just Louis I'm feeling anymore," he whispered. "It's like glass under pressure, one more hit and it shatters."

He glanced up. "He's still in there. Waiting for salvation."

Anne's face tightened. She glanced at Louis before telling David, "You need some rest. Lie down upstairs. I'll stay with him."

David didn't argue. The pain surged like a tide as he staggered up the steps.

Then, gravel crunched outside. Tires. Someone was here.

Anne pulled him the rest of the way, and the screen door swung open as she rushed out. Her voice greeted Jack and Jouris before they reached the porch.

"He's weakening. The Entity. I think David's..."

Jack cut her off. "The mirrors. Billy Clifford's room in Kings Park. They weren't just mirrors. They were doors."

David leaned against a porch post, pale and swaying.

"Anne... what's wrong with him?"

David forced a shaky smile. "I'm fine. Just... a headache."

Jack didn't buy it. He reached the steps in two quick leaps.

"I think Louis is starting to hear me," David admitted.

Jack studied him, then asked quietly, "Do you think it's because you're a prophet? That this power... it's divine?"

David hesitated. The question cut deeper than the pain. His mouth opened, but no answer came. For an instant, Anne's prayers,

David's visions, and Louis's torment felt like threads of the same dark tapestry… woven by a hand intent on dragging them into the storm.

Jack exhaled sharply and lifted David's chin with a finger.

"Look at what this is doing to you."

"Dad, we thought all hope was gone. That's what my head kept saying. But now…" David opened and closed his fists rapidly and quickly glanced over at Jack, Anne, and Jouris. "Now there's a chance."

"Can you still reach Louis?" Jack asked, urgency tightening his voice.

David nodded.

"Good. Then we have to tell you what to say. Right now."

As Jack and Jouris guided him inside, David's vision blurred. A low vibration started in his spine, and as it spread, the faint metallic tang returned, filling the air like a warning.

***

Back in Louis's Prison in Liberty Crest High School

Louis hit the ground hard, his body slamming against the cold tile. His lungs seized, and he gasped for air, chest heaving, ears ringing. Blinking against the harsh light, he saw that the gym doors were gone. In their place stood a single oak door at the far end of the hall, solitary and waiting.

Someone was calling his name.

Cold sweat ran down his back. The door loomed like a vault, impenetrable. Lucius's warning returned to him: one mirror remained, and this was the only room left unsearched. It might as well have been the mouth of a lion's den. He didn't want to open it.

Summoning his courage, Louis reached for the knob. Before he could touch it, the door creaked open on its own.

Through the crack, he glimpsed the blurry outline of office furniture and bookshelves… ordinary items found in a principal's office. But the moment he stepped inside, he knew something was wrong.

The ceiling stretched impossibly high, vanishing into shadows. Portraits of his father lined the walls, yet every face was wrong. Some had too many eyes. Others smiled with mouths stretched into cruel, unnatural grins.

The broken patterns caused him to grind his teeth. He hated when things didn't fit.

At the far end, beside a wooden desk, stood a massive mirror. Ornate yet worn, its beveled edges made it look ancient. Its surface rippled like liquid silver, as if it were alive.

"Louis! Please!" a voice cried from inside the glass.

He froze, his heart hammering. It was David.

His lips parted, the word *"Dav…"* almost escaping, as he lifted his hand toward the mirror, reaching for his brother.

For a split second, he thought he heard Anne's voice too, praying, as though the safehouse door were pressed right up against the glass.

David's face came into focus, hope straining to break through. Then a sound echoed somewhere close, and the door slammed shut.

Louis flinched. For an instant, he swore he heard water lapping at unseen shores, shadows sliding like oil across the floor. Heat flared at the edge of his vision, gone as quickly as it came… threads of fire, water, and darkness weaving together.

Through the mirror, in the safehouse, Louis saw David stagger as the slam detonated inside his skull. For a heartbeat, the two worlds overlapped, Louis's prison and David's reality bound together like two halves of the same wound.

The Principal's voice roared, no longer human but something evil, echoing from deep within the walls. The office buckled. The tile floor heaved beneath Louis's feet like the choppy surface of a storm-tossed lake. The portraits of his father twisted violently, the mouths gaping wide, and the eyes transforming into endless pits of darkness.

Louis turned just in time to see his father's distorted reflection peel from the wall, unfastening from the shadows like a picture ripped from paper.

"You don't want to do this, son," the Principal said, his tone softer now, almost fatherly, but Louis wasn't fooled.

He stood frozen, staring at a face that should have been familiar but wasn't.

"You think that mirror will save you?" The Principal asked, stepping forward with deliberate calm. His grin widened, sharp and knowing. "Prophet of God. You couldn't even save yourself. You've never saved anyone."

"It's a lie, Louis," the Principal hissed. "A trick. You belong here."

The room darkened as the walls groaned, closing in. The air thickened, heavy and suffocating.

Louis clenched his fists until his nails dug into his palms.

"No," he whispered. "I don't."

The Principal glared at Louis, his expression colder, crueler.

"You're making a mistake. Just like your father …"

***

Back in the Safehouse at Lake Ronkonkoma

David lay on the floor, shaking violently. His skin was clammy, his breath shallow, and the edges of his vision pulsed with a sickly black haze. He fought to recover from the brutal effort it had taken to tear open a crack into the void… the place where Louis was still imprisoned.

Jack's voice echoed in his head. *Tell him. Tell him to find the mirror and break through it. Shatter it. That's how he can escape.*

But Louis's doppelgänger wasn't done with him.

The shadows trembled, writhing with a life of their own. Static burst through the air, followed by the wet snap of bones and the tear of flesh.

And then it appeared, emerging from the darkness. Louis, but not Louis, stepping through a burning ring of fire. Its skin twitched, shifting between human and corpse-like… translucent, slick with decay.

Its smile stretched unnaturally wide. *Did you really think you could win?*

David's pulse pounded, yet his mind was clearer than ever. The connection, once as thin as spider silk, was now like thick steel wire, binding him to his brother outside The Entity's grasp.

Louis was fighting. He just needed to see the truth.

David didn't flinch as the doppelgänger lunged. Instead, he said, "Louis, listen to me."

The Entity halted mid-motion; its form wavering, unstable.

David pushed deeper, his voice gaining strength. "You don't belong to this thing. You never did. This is a prison, but there's a way out. Look around you. Find the mirror and break it!"

The doppelgänger twisted, letting out sharp, inhuman shrieks. Its body convulsed, struggling to regain control. The shadows rippled around it, a living force trying to drag David under, to drown him in its sickness.

His soul burning with the last reserves of his strength, David felt himself tearing at the seams, unraveling. And somewhere, in the suffocating office that held him captive, Louis felt the walls shudder, as if David's strength shook both worlds at once.

"Louis!" David shouted, fire searing his eyes and the taste of iron filling his mouth. "This is your moment. Not a trick. Not a lie. Break the mirror! This is your rescue.

SALVATION!"

The doppelganger screamed, the sound splitting reality itself… a cry that snapped Anne's rosary beads like twigs and scattered them across the safehouse floor.

***

In another reality, inside The Entity's prison, Louis heard David.

The Entity's scream shattered the air, rattling the walls and shaking the very foundations of its grip.

"You don't want to do this, son." The Principal insisted. "You'll never leave me."

Louis swallowed hard. His fists clenched, and his teeth grinding.

"You're not my father." Louis's voice cracked, but he forced the words through clenched teeth, each syllable sharper than the last. Fear still lingered, but defiance burned hotter.

"And yes… I do!"

The Principal lunged, his flesh splitting to reveal something monstrous beneath his suit.

"YOU WON'T SURVIVE IT!" he roared.

Louis felt fingers brush his shoulder, almost catching him, but his body was already moving. He sprinted for the mirror across the unstable floor. His steps were unsteady yet held determination. His legs burned as he hurled himself forward.

David's voice cut through the roar, clear and urgent: "Louis! Now!"

Louis gritted his teeth, braced himself, and threw his whole body at the mirror, charging it at full speed.

C-R-A-S-H!

Water, fire, shadow… every element that had hunted him and haunted his family collapsed into a silver light. It was not only an escape, but a warning of what still lingered behind the glass.

The mirror didn't just shatter; it exploded outward, raining down shards that dissolved into white-hot energy, searing through the darkness like divine fire.

A blinding silver light swallowed him, the sound like the sky splitting open, the universe tearing at the seams. The air itself burned, the smell of scorched stone everywhere.

And through it, he heard Lucius's voice.

We will meet again.

Louis felt himself falling, not down but through, as if he'd broken the surface of water only to be dragged deeper into something colder. His mind spun. His body twisted. Shattered fragments of the world rippled and stretched, the school pulling apart like paper burning at the edges.

The doppelgänger howled, its body unraveling like a thread fraying at the edges. Its cries tore through the walls, splitting the worlds apart…

***

For a split second, David felt glass splinter inside his skull; a flash of silver cutting through his mind.

The scream ripped across dimensions, the violent force yanking David backward. Fury roared in his ears, and he clutched his head as if to prevent it from splitting. His lungs gasped for air while his body seized and locked in a spasm, like God himself had struck him with lightning.

And then…the darkness scattered.

The doppelgänger collapsed, vanishing like smoke pulled into a vacuum. The static cut off, and the room became still. Then, faint but steady, came the sound of breathing.

David dropped to his knees, gasping, sweat dripping, tears streaking his face. He couldn't remember when they'd started, only that, for the first time in days, the screaming in his head was gone. Silence remained. And maybe, just maybe, the beginning of peace.

But the silence didn't last.

Still on his knees, David felt it: a shudder under the floorboards. It was subtle at first, then stronger.

A low, mournful moan emanated from beneath the house, as if the Earth itself were in pain.

David looked up, his eyes wide. "No..."

"What is it?" Jack asked.

Jouris met them in the hall as the house began to sway. "What's happening?"

"The basement," David yelled. "Louis shattered the mirror. But The Entity isn't finished with him… or us."

When they arrived in the basement, the cage was empty; The Entity seemed to have been exorcised.

Louis was convulsing, his back crashing against the floor. His eyes rolled back, and his jaw locked tight, a muffled groan escaping between clenched teeth.

Candles flickered violently, shadows clawing across the stone walls in desperation.

"Jouris, get the sage. Now!" Jack snapped. "Anne, hold him!"

Anne gripped Louis's shoulders tightly. "I'm not letting this thing win."

"The blood of Christ compels you!" She shouted.

Louis gasped, producing a wet, horrifying sound as if someone were inhaling water. His back arched, and his mouth opened wide in a silent scream. Then, his eyes opened.

His expression was dazed, but his eyes… his eyes were his again—light blue. They were human.

Anne pulled back, her breath caught in her throat. "Louis?"

The cold rush of fresh air filled his lungs. Louis opened his mouth and hesitated. He turned his hands over in front of him, flexing his fingers. He could feel them; his movements and his skin were his own.

He blinked and then blinked again. He met David's gaze. His throat was raw from screaming.

"David…"

David was there, kneeling beside him. His eyes were wide with wonder, and he clutched his brother's hand as if afraid to let go. His face was pale, and his voice wavered, "I'm here, Louis. I'm here."

Louis gave a small, tired smile. "I followed exactly what you said. The mirror. Break it. That's the only reason I got out. Without you, I'd still be there."

At that moment, the ground shook again.

Anne stood, her eyes narrowing. "It's attempting to anchor itself. It's not backing down."

Louis grimaced as a sharp, searing pain shot through his chest. Then he shouted, "It's like fire crawling beneath my skin. It burns!"

The lights flickered on despite there being no power. A bulb shattered, raining glass.

Jack pointed. "Look at the far wall of the basement."

The shadows peeled back like skin. The darkness didn't retreat… it became.

You think this is salvation? You broke one chain. That's all. He still remembers me. I will be with him.

Always.

Louis screamed, clutching his head in agony as he writhed in Jack's arms.

Anne's eyes locked on the creeping darkness. "Get behind me. Jouris, sage, light it."

Jouris yanked a scorched bundle from his bag and flicked a lighter with trembling fingers. He muttered, "Steady, Jouris. Steady. We have to hold it off."

Anne gripped her crucifix and raised it toward the darkness. "You have no claim anymore. You lost."

The Entity surged forward… but then it halted. Not due to their prayers. Not because of the sage.

But because of Louis.

The young man, bruised and battered, rose to his knees.

Louis stared into the face of what had owned him. His voice was flat, certain.

"You're not my friend. You never were. You never will be."

The Entity recoiled.

Louis blinked once, steady. "Go."

And it did.

With a final, soul-rending shriek, the Entity unraveled, like smoke in the wind, leaving only silence, dust, and the echo of its rage.

The candles flickered, then steadied. The shadows vanished. For the first time in forever, the air felt light.

Jack released a breath he hadn't realized he'd been holding. "Jesus." He hugged Louis tightly and, through his tears, sobbed, "I thought I lost you forever."

David's knees buckled, and he fell backward, gasping in a blend of exhaustion and relief, but this time, Louis caught him by the shirt.

"I've got you, David," Louis said softly. "I've got you."

Jouris was on his knees, staring at the spot where The Entity had vanished. "Did we just…"

Anne crossed herself and looked down at Louis and David. Her lips trembled. "No. They did."

In the center of it all, Louis hugged his brother. The walls closing in. No clocks ticking backward. No whispering voices from behind classroom doors. No more nightmares. No Entity. No school. No principal. No tricks. He closed his eyes, feeling the steady rise and fall of his chest. The weight was gone. He was alive. Free. Home.

And yet, in the air, a faint shimmer lingered, silver dust, a phantom splinter of glass, reminding them that some doors, once opened, never truly close.

CHAPTER 3

Forty-Eight Hours After Louis Aitken's Exorcism
Mid-Afternoon on the Shore of Lake Ronkonkoma

The sky was so blue that it resembled a soft, cool blanket. Wisps of clouds drifted lazily above, casting long shadows across the glassy surface of Lake Ronkonkoma. The shoreline was calm except for the gentle rustling of reeds swaying in the breeze.

David stood where the ground sloped down to the packed earth beside the time-smoothed boulder at the water's edge, the same rock where Louis had first heard The Entity. He crouched with his right arm tucked close to his chest, methodically examining stones, flipping them over one by one as if testing each for hidden magical properties. He rejected three before selecting a fourth and standing up.

Louis had already skipped a stone. It bounced five times before disappearing with a soft plunk.

"Your last one bounced weird," David said, avoiding eye contact.

"It was wet on the bottom," Louis replied. "I didn't check it."

David nodded, then flicked his stone. It skipped four times before sinking.

Louis smiled. "That's better."

For the first time in weeks, the afternoon sun felt warm, reminiscent of summer. It was as if nothing had happened.

They stood in silence for a while, not uncomfortable, just the kind shared by people who didn't feel pressured to fill the space. Louis leapt onto the rock and adjusted his stance, his toes gripping the edge.

"It's strange," Louis said, gazing out at the lake.

"What is?" David asked.

The breeze strengthened, pushing small waves across the surface. Louis watched the wave action as he answered, "Being here again. After."

David didn't respond immediately. He picked up a new stone, running his thumb along its side. "The sunlight's the same. Nothing looks different."

"I think that's what makes it feel off." Louis tossed his stone. It skipped once, then sank. "Back at the safehouse, everything felt real. Now that I'm here, it's like... too normal."

"Maybe that's just your memory comparing two things that don't belong together," David suggested.

Louis gave him a brief look. "Maybe."

David gazed out at the lake. "So, how was it?"

The breeze stirred Louis's hair as he shut his eyes. After a long pause, he said,

"It was like being in another person's dream," he said slowly. "Like walking through a school, you know, but all the numbers on the lockers are wrong."

David threw his stone. It skipped three times.

"You mean like a nightmare?"

"No," Louis shook his head. "A nightmare ends. This didn't. It was alive. It... spoke through my thoughts, but they weren't mine."

He paused, turning a stone over in his hand. "I could feel myself there, screaming to move, to speak, to leave, but I couldn't. I was... buried."

Feeling anxious about the conversation, Louis exhaled slowly to calm himself.,

"There was a hallway with lockers," he continued. "It asked questions I didn't want to answer."

"Did you answer them?" David asked.

"No," Louis replied. "But that didn't matter."

David looked down at the stone in his lap. "Were you scared? I mean... more than usual?"

"Yes. Mostly, I was confused. And there was pressure, like something sitting on my chest all the time. I kept thinking that if I could figure things out, I could fix it."

"But you couldn't?"

"No." Louis paused. "Not alone."

David stayed still, his fingers tapped lightly against his knee in a steady rhythm.

"I heard you, David. I kept thinking, 'He's so close. Just reach out.' But my hand wouldn't move."

David sat quietly, studying the rock in his hand.

Louis looked down at the water lapping over a smooth stone, cold and dark, where the cellphone had once been.

"I didn't even feel it happen at first," Louis admitted. "I didn't know it was a lie until it was too late. It wanted to use me."

"For what?" David asked.

"I don't know." Louis's voice dropped. "But I think it still might want that."

"You're here now," David said softly. "You're back."

"I know." Louis smiled faintly. "But sometimes, in the quiet moments... I still wonder if it's really gone forever."

David glanced at the tree line, his jaw twitched. He gripped another stone, then hurled it hard. It skipped twice before sinking.

"Do you remember what it felt like the first time you heard it?" David asked.

"Yes," Louis nodded. "It was right here. Same spot, same sound, like it's waiting."

"Right here?" David looked out at the lake. "Do you think it remembers this spot?"

Louis stayed quiet, scanning the water where the ripples from David's stone were fading.

They stood in silence. A dragonfly hovered between them, darting toward the reeds before vanishing.

A small bubble surfaced. *Blup.* Another followed, about fifteen feet offshore.

"Let's go get something to eat." Louis brushed dirt from his jeans.

David fell into step beside him as they walked the path, neither glancing back.

David suddenly grinned and nudged Louis's shoulder. "You're just upset I can skip more than you."

Louis snorted. "Hero of the hour, huh? You skipped three."

"Busy saving your soul," David smirked.

Louis shook his head, smiling despite himself.

They laughed, and by the time the brothers reached the porch, the lake lay still. Down the slope, the water lapped gently at the shoreline. Then... *Blub.*

A slow, deliberate bubble rose from beneath the surface. Then another. And another. Something shifted in the murky depths.

Louis and David didn't see the thin tendril of shadow vanish into the reeds. They didn't hear the faint echo of a whisper on the breeze. They didn't notice the water darkening, just beneath the rock where Louis had once been chosen.

They laughed, but the lake listened. And waited... but not for long.

***

Later, The Same Night, in the Safehouse

Outside, for what felt like the first time since their arrival, the world was calm. A red sky lingered on the horizon, but the chaos it once signaled had given way to a comforting stillness they thought no longer existed. The windows stood open, filled with the sounds of an ordinary summer night: crickets chirping, frogs croaking by the lakeshore, and a warm breeze rustling the still-stunted leaves beginning to resprout on the trees.

Jack leaned against Anne's bedroom wall, arms crossed tightly against his chest, watching a firefly blink lazily near the candle on the nightstand.

Anne sat at the edge of the bed. Her auburn hair now showed streaks of gray, and the bags under her eyes reflected months of sleepless nights. The candle between them flickered weakly, a lone sentinel against the encroaching darkness.

Neither had spoken for several minutes until Jack broke the silence.

"They aren't okay," he breathed, and his voice lowered. "Not really."

Anne lifted her gaze slowly. "No. But they're alive."

Jack nodded. "Just barely. Louis... he looks like he's still halfway in the grave. Like The Entity never really left."

He hesitated, then added, "And his eyes… they're different. They used to be brown. Now they're ice blue. It's like it left a piece of itself behind, a reminder he'll never forget."

Anne sighed; the weight of truth heavy in her breath. "Possession leaves scars. Some you can't see. Some are wounds that never close."

Jack shifted, glancing out the window as if expecting the stillness to shatter at any moment. "And David..." he paused. "He's... changed. Ever since... since he gained those powers."

"I understand," she said. "He's like a light bulb overwhelmed by too much current. Always glowing. Always on fire. He sees everything at once. Feels everything. But he can't find a way to switch it off."

Jack rubbed the back of his neck and looked at the floor. "Louis told me something. Or maybe he didn't mean to." He glanced at her. "Did he tell you who protected him from the Entity?"

Anne blinked. "No."

"Lucius," Jack said, dread in his voice as he spoke the name. "Lucius Rofocale."

Anne's face fell. "That can't be right."

"I know it doesn't make sense. Not after all he's done. Not after the blood and the lies..."

Anne paced the room once before turning back. "But Louis is still here."

"Yeah," Jack said softly. "He is."

They sat beneath the weight of that miracle, unable to decide whether to feel grateful or fearful of the unseen strings attached to it.

A long silence followed.

Then Anne said, "After everything we've seen and done, we still have no idea who we can trust."

Jack turned toward her. His eyes were tired, but when he looked at her, something within them came to life. There was something sacred between them, worn and cracked but unbreakable.

"I have a feeling that this Highway to Hell we're on isn't finished with us," Jack whispered, almost like a prayer. "But we've survived the fire, seen the world crumble... and we're still here."

Anne smiled sadly. "I know, but somewhere along the way, Louis and David lost their innocence. I guess they can't afford it, not anymore."

Jack sighed. "It seems every choice has been between bad and worse. But... I wouldn't have made it without you."

Anne raised her gaze. "You hold a responsibility unmatched by anyone else, Jack. Safeguarding your sons, God's chosen prophets, from the forces of evil... that's a heavy burden." After a pause, she added softly, "You don't have to bear it alone."

He stepped closer; the candlelight cast a golden glow across his weathered face. "That's just it," he said. "I don't want to face them alone anymore."

For a moment, the room blurred into memory, and he could almost hear his grandfather's voice, words whispered the night before he died; something Jack had forgotten until that moment:

You're stronger than you think, Jackie. One day you'll face a choice…a hard one. And when you do, I want you to remember this: sometimes we win even if it seems like we've lost.

Jack clasped Anne's hands and whispered, "I've lost everything. But I won when I found you."

She looked at him and smiled.

"I wanted to ask you something... back then. At Christmas. Before George blew our lives to hell."

Her eyes shimmered, wide and unblinking as she stepped closer.

"I wrote a special card," he said with a sigh. "I was going to give it to you last Christmas, but I was waiting for the perfect moment. Then everything changed, and our world went dark. It all went up in flames, along with everything else in Bristow."

She held his fingers tightly. "You don't need words to tell me how you feel."

Jack touched her cheek. "I've turned it over a hundred times in my head. Whatever time we've got left, I'll stand beside you. I won't break your heart."

His voice cracked, but he continued. "I swear, by whatever's left up there, the moon, the stars, I don't care. For better or worse, till death takes me. I'll love you with everything I've got left."

He wasn't kneeling. He didn't have a ring. He scarcely had the clothes on his back. But the promise in his eyes was everything.

Anne opened her mouth, unsure whether to speak, cry, or say yes...

"JACK!"

The name cut through the silence like a blade. They froze.

Outside, the night was calm and quiet, but the sound of boots crunching on the gravel path struck like a cannon shot.

"George," Anne whispered.

Jack stood slowly, his eyes locked on hers. She brushed her thumb along his jaw and gave him a nod. "I'll get David and Louis ready. Just like we planned."

Jack nodded, saying nothing. He touched her fingers once and let go.

Then, without another word, he turned and walked out the door… into the storm.

***

The moon hung high and full over the clearing, casting long silver shadows across the dirt. The safehouse loomed behind Jack like a silent witness. From the edge of the trees, just beyond the reach of the moonlight, a figure stepped into view.

George.

He was leaner now, his body twisted by rage. A leather patch covered his left eye; the right burned with cold amusement.

"As you can see," George rasped, "I'm still alive."

He spat on the ground at Jack's feet. "Like Cain to Abel, I spit in your eye."

Jack's fists clenched, his breath steady, the way Anne had taught him.

"I figured you were dead. Or maybe I just hoped."

George's grin widened, jagged teeth flashing in the moonlight. "You hoped wrong."

They closed the distance until only shadows separated them.

The air was eerily still. Even the frogs and crickets had gone silent, as if warning of what was to come. The scent of damp earth and faint sulfur hung in the clearing.

"I'm impressed you've come this far," George said with a smirk. "I didn't think you had it in you."

"I've had to pick myself up more times than I can count," Jack said evenly. "But you don't get to break me anymore."

"You think you're strong?" George sneered. "You couldn't keep your family safe; Amanda, the boys. And now Anne's your crutch."

The words cut, but Jack didn't flinch. "We were brothers. I loved you. And you made that worthless."

George's smile twisted into hate. "Always the weak one. Always foolish."

"I've thought about this moment," Jack said. "What I'd say. A fiery speech, something final. But all I have left is the truth."

George rushed forward. Jack dodged the attack, driving his fist into George's jaw. Blood sprayed across the dirt. George staggered, caught off guard by Jack's counter, then grinned, wiping his mouth.

"I think I'm going to enjoy this."

They collided, fists and fury. George fought wild, savage, spitting bile with every strike. Jack moved with trained precision; blocks, counters, every blow a release of pent-up anger and betrayal.

Between strikes, Jack's voice thundered: "I LOVED YOU! I gave everything, and you threw it away."

George slammed him against a tree, breath hot in his ear. "Don't blame me for what happened to you. I wouldn't be what I am now if you hadn't dug too deep. You woke things better left alone."

Jack twisted free and shoved him back. "No more games, brother. You're a page from my past, and I'm tearing you out."

For a heartbeat, they froze, panting, bloodied, staring at one another under the moonlight… two broken men bound by hate.

Behind them, a pale glow rose from the depths, growing brighter as though the lake itself had awakened, surging with unstoppable force, breaking the surface.

Then the air shifted.

A pulse of yellow light raced across the lake and through the clearing, like heat from a furnace. The water frothed and steamed, as if boiling from the inside out.

Shapes began to rise from the depths.

They came dripping with weeds, skeletal forms emaciated, cloaked in translucent, sagging skin that stretched over their bones. Their hair hung in long, tangled ropes like Spanish moss, their sunken eye sockets glowing with furious red fire. When their mouths opened, the shriek that poured out was not sound, but a vibration that rattled bones and curdled the blood.

The Ghost Braves.

George's demon soldiers burst from the treeline, snarling, rushing forward. But the Braves descended on them in a storm of vengeance, spectral clubs smashing skulls, phantom arrows piercing flesh. The night was filled with the crunch of bone and the hollow echo of war cries.

Jack held his breath. For a moment, he almost forgot about George.

George taunted his brother, "You know you can't kill me."

Jack kept his eyes on the ghosts. "Maybe I can't. But they probably can."

The Braves turned, glowing eyes fixing on the brothers. One a trespasser, the other a meddler, thwarting The Entity's plans. Both marked for death.

An axe of pale fire carved through the tree beside them. Splinters rained down as the brothers leapt apart… then back together, fighting side by side, flesh and steel against bone and spirit.

Cain and Abel were gone. Now there were only survivors.

By the barn, Louis sprinted toward one of the escape vehicles. A Brave turned, drawn by his movement. Its jaw unhinged in a silent shriek.

"Over here!" George barked. In a sudden burst, he snatched a tree branch from the ground and hurled it.

The Brave paused just in time for the branch to pierce its chest.

"Why… why would you help me?" Louis gasped. "You're supposed to hate us."

George raised a finger and waved Louis away like a police officer directing traffic.

He whispered, "Go."

Louis stumbled over a root, hesitating just long enough to glance back. Then he vanished into the woods.

George turned, blood smeared across his jaw. He pulled a Brave off Jack's back and crushed its lifeforce with his boot.

"Do you still think I'm a monster?"

Jack gazed past him at the chaos: the specters, the violence, the bodies shattered and strewn.

"I think even a human can become one," he said.

George let out a sharp, joyless laugh.

Monster or man… it didn't matter. The Braves wanted blood from both of them.

***

At the bottom of the basement stairs, Anne took David's hand and whispered,

"I know it's dark. Stay close to me, and we'll find the entrance that leads to Jouris's garage."

The cellar reeked of damp stone and mildew, the air thick and unmoving, as if it hadn't stirred in a hundred years. Anne crept forward first, one hand sliding against the wall, the other gripping a kitchen knife slick with sweat. David followed, so close she felt his breath in short, panicked bursts. Jouris brought up the rear, a flashlight in one hand and a handgun in the other. Every footstep crunched like stepping on brittle bones.

"Found it," Anne sighed. "I'll go first. David, you follow me. Jouris will bring up the rear."

The passage sloped unnaturally downward, as though a claw had carved it from the earth.

They hurried, yet it felt like running in place.

The flashlight's narrow beam skittered across carvings in the stone walls depicting hollow-eyed ghouls and screaming faces. The musty air thickened with rot and a sweet smell of decay, like overripe fruit.

"I don't like it in here," David whimpered.

He tried to look away but froze at a mural: people stitched together by their faces, sewn mouth-to-eye in a chain of endless screams.

The flashlight flickered as the battery drained. A child's laughter echoed behind them. Jouris froze, glancing back into the impenetrable darkness. "Keep going," he growled. "Don't stop."

Something crawled across the floor, hissing like a serpent. The passage moaned, and the walls pulsed inward as if they were breathing. A hand clawed its way out of the dirt beside Anne's boot, then vanished.

"What was that?" David gasped.

"Doesn't matter. Move." Anne yanked him forward.

They stumbled, slipping, but never stopped.

A blast of cold air surged past them, the breath of something exhaling in the dark. Shadows darted at the edges of the beams from the flashlight. A woman in a torn wedding dress crawled from a hole in the wall and screamed, her jaw unhinged, yet no sound emerged.

"Eyes forward," Anne ordered.

Jouris swung the beam behind them. "Something's following us."

A tall, elongated figure slithered across the ceiling, upside down, its jaw splitting open vertically, revealing teeth like rusted nails. Jouris fired. The flash illuminated the passage in sickly strobe-like bursts, but the thing was gone.

"What was it?" David cried.

Jouris didn't answer. He walked backward, eyes scanning behind him.

He swept the flashlight just in time to see something pale crawling like a spider. It twisted its neck, blinked sideways, then melted into the cracks.

A hand brushed David's shoulder. He screamed.

"It touched me! Something touched me!"

Jouris shoved him forward. "Not real. It wants to stop us. Don't let it."

Tears streaked David's dirt-stained face. "I hate this place. I hate it."

"We're almost there," Anne said, her voice taut as piano wire.

At last, a faint smell of motor oil and rubber reached them… safety. Anne surged forward and shoved open the hatch into the garage. David scrambled through. Jouris backed up the steps, the flashlight dying in his hand.

They tumbled out, gasping for breath, filthy yet alive.

"Damn it!" Anne hissed.

A rusted sedan blocked the garage door.

"We have to move it." She and Jouris took positions on opposite sides of the vehicle and pushed against it with their shoulders. David braced his one hand on the bumper, the cold metal stinging his skin. Sweat mingled with a growing sense of panic. Minutes felt like years, but finally, the vehicle lurched forward just enough.

Jouris slapped the hood of the '69 Mustang. "Get in, Anne. You drive."

The engine roared like a beast released from its cage. Anne and David shot out of the garage as a shadow crept down the wall.

Jouris started them, but a voice stopped him in his tracks.

"Dad?"

Jouris turned, and a figure stepped from behind the garage into the moonlight.

Peter. As he had looked the day Jouris buried him: blonde hair neatly parted, a dark tie knotted tightly around his slashed throat. His eyes glowed faintly, his skin pale as candle wax.

Jouris's knees buckled. "Peter… oh God…"

They embraced. His son's jacket felt cold and damp. Jouris's fingers grazed the sticky fabric on his son's back, returning with hands stained red. The metallic odor of blood pierced through the heavy smell of gasoline. For a brief moment, Jouris felt a sense of forgiveness.

Then, Peter spoke.

You call it destiny. Salvation. But it was always… a performance. Now the curtain's down… and all that's left… is silence…

Jouris stiffened. The words felt wrong. They sounded cold and rehearsed.

Peter never spoke like this.

But even now… with my voice in your son's mouth… you still won't hear me…

Jouris pulled back, trying to break free. "What... what are you talking about?"

Peter's eyes gleamed, glassy and wet, yet the tears didn't fall.

You fight for this dream… like it still matters. But it's mine now, and I don't dream… of saving anyone…

Jouris staggered, breath coming in ragged gulps. "No. No, this isn't you..."

All that remains… are walls that remember nothing… and shadows… that remember everything.

The glow around Peter began to flicker. A buzzing filled Jouris's ear, like flies crawling through a speaker. Peter's suit melted into black rags. His golden aura decayed, and his eyes blazed an eerie yellow.

Weep if you must… but it won't change the ending I already wrote—the one…

you were never meant to survive.

Peter's hand pierced his chest.

Jouris's eyes widened, his lips parting. All he could muster was, "Oh…"

There was no scream, only a broken syllable. He didn't even feel the pain at first… just pressure and then emptiness. He tried to back away, but Peter's arm was deep inside him, fingers clutching his heart like a trophy.

Blood bubbled on his lips. His knees buckled, his spine arched. He reached to touch his son's face, but his hand never reached its destination.

The face merged into The Entity's, strobing between Peter's features and a living X-ray of a skull with a phosphorescent grin, nerves and sinew pulsing like exposed wires.

From the gravel road, Anne and David saw Jouris convulsing, impaled by the Entity.

"Jouris! JOURIS!" David cried against the glass.

"We can't go back! We'll die!" Anne shouted.

"No! He's right there!"

"He's gone, David!"

She slammed her foot on the gas. The tires screamed, scattering the gravel.

Ahead: a wall of the infected. Hundreds. Flesh rotting, jaws snapping, eyes wild with hunger. They surged like a tide across the road, rattling the night with their guttural moans.

Anne spun the wheel. "We'll never reach the highway. We're going to the marina."

David's voice cracked. "What about..."

"We reach the boat," she cut in. "We reach Jouris's boat, or we die out here.

Behind them, the garage door slammed shut. In the mirror, Anne saw Jouris's lifeless body being dragged into the depths of Lake Ronkonkoma. The water rippled red in the moonlight, a faint glow pulsing beneath the surface as the lake claimed him.

She squeezed David's shoulder. "We'll see them again, okay? Jack and Louis will be waiting at the rendezvous point."

But her eyes stayed fixed on the road. She didn't dare look at him.

The toll was paid, but the lake raised the price. And Jack was still out there, running...

***

Jack burst from the tree line, panting, his shirt clinging to his sweat-drenched back, his gait unsteady from dehydration and blood loss. He grimaced and clutched his side.

"Jesus, that hurts." He hadn't even shaken the ghosts from his vision, but there was no time to look back... only forward.

The iron crowbar in his hand had dispatched several Ghost Braves in a flurry of smoke and sparks, but not before one specter had landed a blow that carved a raw line across his ribs. His boots pounded the worn pavement of the Old Motor Parkway, his lungs burning as the night air thickened with the stench of rot and heat-warped asphalt.

He slowed, scanning. "There it is, but where's Louis?"

The silver 2012 Ford Focus was exactly where they'd left it, hidden beneath overgrowth just off the old service road. It looked like junk, but to Jack, it was everything. He pulled the branches aside, searching.

"I'm here, Dad." Louis emerged from the passenger side.

Jack clutched his chest. "You scared the shit out of me!" Before Louis could respond, Jack admonished himself. "Yeah, bad language, but necessary!"

He tumbled into the driver's seat, fumbling for the keys Anne had given him. The whole plan replayed in his head. She had been right. Separating the boys was necessary. And now things were worse than he had ever imagined.

He turned the key. Click. Sputter. Silence.

"No, no! Not now!" He slammed his palm against the steering wheel.

Behind them, the woods split open with the wailing; it was the war drums of the Ghost Braves rising again.

"I got this!" Louis shouted, diving from his seat.

"Wait! Don't go out there!"

Louis ignored him. Jack barely opened the door before Louis was under the hood, his hands working with Jouris's lessons burned into muscle memory. A few swift motions. A reconnection, a spark, he slammed the hood shut and leapt back in.

"Try it!"

Jack turned the key. The engine roared to life.

Ghost Braves surged from the trees as Jack floored it. The tires spat chunks of crumbled pavement and heat-baked weeds as the Focus jolted onto the abandoned road, leaving the hunters fading in their rearview mirror.

Jack risked one glance back. Through the trees, the safehouse loomed, a single window faintly lit. A silhouette stood there. Then, slowly, the shade slid down.

Louis grinned through his bruises, shaken but proud.

Jack's heart raced. "You did…."

"It was Uncle George," Louis cut in. "I shouldn't be here. He saved me by distracting the Braves… then let me go."

Jack blinked, stunned.

George let Louis go?

No time to process it. He patted Louis's shoulder firmly.

They hit the Southern State Parkway at sixty. Jack muttered, "Buckle up."

Moonlight streamed through the trees as he served at a sharp turn. "This road was made for Model T Fords, not a Focus. It's all curves. If you don't know it, you're toast."

Louis clung tightly to the door handle as they passed an overturned crossover and a gutted FedEx truck.

Jack gritted his teeth, still talking, trying to ignore the pain in his ribs. "I drove this road all the time at your age. Never thought I'd do it like this."

The parkway was treacherous, littered with abandoned trucks and cars; electric vehicles in the median like tombstones, some still with luggage strapped to their roofs. Others had been stripped or burned. They sped past a collapsed rest area sign smothered in vines. In the mirror, George's black sedan was close. Jack floored it.

Minutes later, they hit the Belt Parkway at the Queens border… it was like entering a war zone.

"Ah," Jack muttered grimly. "The Belt. Under construction my whole damn life. Fix one part, tear it up again."

Louis let out a nervous chuckle, cut short as they hit a stretch of deep potholes, more like craters. The Focus jolted violently as the front right tire caught the edge of one, causing the frame to rattle.

Then the herd appeared: a wall of CWD-infected, staggering across the lanes. Dozens, maybe more, their limbs twisted, faces blistered from sunburn and rot.

Jack tightened his grip and barreled straight through. The tires crunched over bone, coating the car with blood and gore.

Louis shut his eyes. "They were people once."

"I know," Jack said, patting his son's shoulder. "That's the hell of it."

Crossing into Brooklyn, Jack pointed nervously into the distance. "Look. The bridge."

The Verrazano-Narrows Bridge loomed ahead. In the moonlight, its weathered, rusty-brown silhouette appeared black against the sky. It spanned the Hudson River, and in a time now long forgotten, it accommodated thirteen lanes of traffic on its upper and lower decks. As the Focus approached the entrance, the bridge's steel cables seemed to hum in the rising wind.

Jack leaned forward, "Lower deck's blocked." His gaze fixed on a jackknifed tractor-trailer. "We'll take the upper road. We'll make it."

Looking back, Jack said, "Can't slow down. George is almost on us."

Louis started, "Dad…"

"I said we'll make it!"

He swerved around a fallen light pole, accelerating into the lane closest to the protective railing, but the tires skidded on an oil slick. Louis shouted something, drowned out by the crash as the Focus slammed into the guardrail.

The world flipped. Glass shattered. Steel twisted. The car rolled once and stopped.

It hung overturned, its rear wheel barely snagged on the crumbled edge of the guardrail. The front end dangled over the empty space, the water below churning, cold and black.

Louis groaned, blood trickling from his temple as pain throbbed through his skull. He blinked through the shattered windshield.

Moonlight shimmered off the Hudson River and then vanished in the water's churn, like Ronkonkoma had before.

He turned, trying to orient himself, and saw Jack hanging upside down, unconscious. His head hung limply, blood streaming into his beard. His chest moved, barely.

"Dad! Dad, wake up!" Louis shook him, his voice cracking in panic.

The car groaned as the wind rocked it. "No, no, no!" Louis muttered. "Please wake up..."

C-L-I-C-K.

His seatbelt snapped. Louis's eyes darted wildly as he began to slip toward the open passenger door. In a panic, he tried to grab hold of something, anything, but continued to slide down.

Jack's hand shot out, grabbing the back of Louis's shirt. "Got you," he croaked, his eyes blinking open.

Louis gasped, his legs kicking over the abyss. "Dad, don't let go!"

"You're not going anywhere," Jack growled, every tendon straining.

The car shifted again, steel shrieking. Louis's foot slammed against the shattered door.

"Help me up! Please!"

Pain seared Jack's ribs where the Brave had carved into him. His weakened right hand ached from the effort of holding up Louis's weight. His grip began to fail.

"Hold still! Don't move!"

Louis whimpered. "It's slipping… it's slipping… it's slipping! I felt it. I counted, Dad… please don't let go!"

"God… give me strength," Jack pleaded, closing his eyes.

The Focus groaned once more, shifting under their weight. Louis's shoe slipped free, tumbling in weightless silence before splashing below.

He fixated on the splash below, one shoe, one sound… if another followed, it meant he was next.

On the bridge, George stood beside his idling sedan, grinning. His one good eye shimmered.

"All that effort," he mocked. "One bolt away from a two-hundred-foot dive."

Brannigan, his new assistant, dressed neatly in a tie and slacks, muttered, "They're dangling. One gust, a shift… and the river takes them."

"Exactly," George purred. "Let Jack sweat."

He stepped closer, watching the car sway in the wind. "The waiting must be torture. I sincerely hope it lasts."

"Poetic," Brannigan smirked, clearly approving. "Your brother saves one Prophet… only to lose him here."

"Prosperine and Lucius wanted my nephews alive," George sneered, eye glinting. "But this luxury? It's mine."

He turned away. "Let the river finish the job. I've got bigger prey to hunt; the real prophet and that bitch who took my eye."

Brannigan drove away from the bridge, tires whispering over cracked pavement as they sped off to find Anne and David.

Far below, the Hudson churned. The twisted guardrail moaned.

Two lives. One desperate grasp. One breath from the abyss.

The Highway to Hell narrowed to a single lane, and the river waited to collect.

<u>EPILOGUE</u>

While the Aitkens' fate hung in the balance, George was already paving his own Highway to Hell… beginning with the lives of the innocent…

The train depot in Culpeper, Virginia, smelled of diesel fuel and overheated metal. Zinnia clutched her brother Liam's hand as they marched beneath the rusted overhang. Like the lake, like the bridge, this was another threshold where innocence was swallowed. Her shoes crunched on shattered glass, shards glinting like fragments of a world already broken.

They were herded with other families, silent, weary captives shivering in the dim light until a pair of guards separated them from the crowd and forced them through a side gate. The door slammed behind them.

Their mother was already there, her arms bound, her face streaked with dust. Their father knelt beside her, blood seeping from his nose, one eye swollen shut. He tried to rise when he saw them, but a boot struck his ribs and dropped him again.

"Not my Daddy!" Zinnia cried.

Liam lunged toward his father's attacker.

Another guard stepped in and pressed the rifle against the young boy's chest.

A figure emerged from the shadows.

"Jack?" Zinnia whispered, her heart leaping.

She froze, then bolted forward before she could think. Trembling, she wrapped her arms around his waist. There was finally someone who would save them.

"Please help us, Jack!" she pleaded through her tears.

Zinnia buried her face in his coat, then recoiled. It smelled like burnt toast, yet the fabric was cold as ice.

He remained silent and didn't embrace her back.

Slowly, Zinnia looked up. Her arms dropped. The eye patch gave him away. The smile that followed confirmed it. This wasn't Jack at all.

"Ah," George said, drawing the word out like a blade. "You knew my brother, didn't you?"

Zinnia backed away, tears stinging her cheeks.

George turned to their mother. His one eye gleamed with cruelty.

"You've got two," he said, nodding toward the children.

Behind him, the guards smirked. They had seen this before.

George stepped closer, uncomfortably so. He leaned in, and his sour breath touched her ear.

"I'll be generous," he whispered, each word mocking. "Make your choice, or I will."

"And mercy won't enter into it."

Then he straightened, grinning with the flourish of an actor bowing at a curtain call.

The guards held their breath. Even the air felt unnaturally still.

Zinnia clutched her mother's hand.

Liam looked up.

Then, their mother moved.

No words.

Just a glance. A hand on a shoulder.

One child was touched. The other was not.

A brief nod.

That was all.

Orders were barked. The guards moved in.

One child was led away.

One remained behind.

Neither understood what was happening, at least not yet.

Their mother didn't cry. She didn't scream. She didn't say goodbye.

Her shoulders slumped. Something inside her had already died.

George smiled like the serpent in Eden, savoring the fall he had ushered in.

A whistle pierced the air. The train groaned. Silence fell over the platform.

And Evil Reigned…

>>Books by J.D. Toepfer

Route 666

Sins of the Fathers

The Gathering Storm

John "J.D." Toepfer is the award-winning author of the riveting Highway to Hell series. Literary Titan describes it as "suspenseful horror that gives readers bits of historical information, occult, and the supernatural, all combined into a thrilling read." When he is not torturing his characters with unspeakable choices, J.D. often works in his other favorite medium, dirt. An avid gardener, many of J.D.'s best plot twists develop when his fingernails are filthy and the sweat is dripping from his brow.

The journey isn't over yet… and your support makes all the difference. If you enjoyed *Evil Reigns*, I'd be grateful if you left a quick review on Amazon. Just a few words can help new readers discover the series.

And while you're there, click **Follow** on my Amazon Author Page so you'll be notified the moment the final book in the *Highway to Hell* saga is released.

Dive deeper into the Highway to Hell Series by visiting our website and becoming part of our vibrant community on social media.

Here's where you can join your fellow travelers:

Website: Sign up for our mailing list! Discover exclusive content, behind-the-scenes insights, and the latest updates at www.jdtoepfer.com

Author Pages: Follow J.D., check out upcoming works, and his full biography on:

Goodreads: https://www.goodreads.com/jdtoepfer

Amazon Author Central: https://www.amazon.com/author/j.d.toepfer

Social Media: Connect with us for engaging discussions and a chance to interact with JD Toepfer personally. Facebook: search for JD Toepfer, Author [https://www.facebook.com/ profile.php?id=100072007826901]

J.D. loves hearing from his readers and looks forward to sharing the ride! Remember, there are no stoplights or speed limits on the Highway to Hell!